# LONDON CALLING

## Jalu Rises In The West

Bruno Nua

**Bruno Nua/Outside In**

**www.osi.xyz**

Proof-Editor: MICHAEL SWEENEY (EditCorrectWrite)
Cover Art: SUCHART PHUMKHED
Cover Layout: JOHN MARSHALL


**LONDON CALLING/ Bruno Nua.**
ISBN 978-1-9998785-0-4

O S I

U I N

T D

E

www.osi.xyz

Supporting

OUTSIDER INDIE AUTEURS

**Books by Bruno Nua**

The Jalu Series:

LONDON CALLING

Buddhist Philosophy:

BUDDHA'S FAVOURITE WORDS

for Pedro Almodóvar

(This was supposed to be a book about Meditation
and the Nature of Mind)

*If the doors of perception were cleansed*
*Everything would appear as it is ... Infinite.*

William Blake.

Part One

# VIRGINIA BLAKE

1

*London calling...* the voice on the telephone repeated. Gini hung up, as she had been doing for God-knows how many days. Gently. Silently. Hoping it would never ring again. Not knowing quite *why* she was hoping that. Quietly wishing – I suppose – she could just return to whatever she had been doing before. But she couldn't. The past was accelerating into the present, shattering the air as it arrived. So much hope and fear rising within her. Much worse than usual. And she had *no* idea why.

The next time the phone rang it was a few days later. Pedro was there. Washing the lunch dishes.

Even though it was the one thing Gini was simply dreading, she felt she just *had* to face it. With every step she took, closer and closer to the ringing phone, time continued to compress and churn. It folded back into itself: Gini relived her first weeks alone in that apartment after Benji died, and the day decades before that when Benji and she had moved there (the magnificence and splendour of *Gran Via* compared to the old flat in *Espoz y Mina*).

Each time her foot hit the floorboards, en route to the old black telephone, Space itself seemed to shimmer and fizz. Time stood absolutely still. Virginia, her mind now frozen, was transported through portal after portal. Key moments from her own past. Further and further back: the day she married Benjamin... before that, when she first arrived in Madrid from England... earlier still, the training camp in Kent... Cambridge... so many happy years in the Spanish Department of Trinity College Dublin...

Finally the receiver was in Gini's hand. Scooping her brittle grey hair to one side, she held the phone to her ear. Without the slightest trace of a foreign accent, Gini said *¿Aló? Buenas tardes. Habla Virginia Léon. Dígame.*

'*London calling*', came the dreadful reply.

*Si. Diga,* she responded, not wishing to commit herself either way to a conversation in either language. You see, Virginia Léon hadn't actually spoken English for quite some time. And she was feeling confused and disoriented anyway. The doctor had said she should be resting her mind at her stage and – to tell the truth – she *had* been rather overdoing it of late (to the point where she'd begun to wonder which experiences, voices and personal memories were real and which were just in her head).

'*London CALLING*', the man's voice on the telephone chimed. His tone was a mixture of forced joviality, sing-song cajoling and a singularly superior insistence. As if his two-word introduction was meant to be some kind of alarm clock intended to awaken Virginia from a very long slumber, he persisted as he'd done all the other times he called.

But that day she didn't hang up. She stayed on the line. Gini wanted to face the music and see where this (real or imaginary) was leading. She allowed the gentleman to repeat his opening gambit a few more times before it dawned on her that this was going to be the beginning and the end of the conversation unless she could say something 'meaningful' in response. She desperately wanted to progress things along. But *what* was the appropriate response supposed to be. If *he* was waiting for *her* to say 'the correct thing' in order for him to continue, then Gini was at a total loss as to what to say. She simply didn't have a clue.

Virginia instinctively knew somehow that this was the voice of Authority. But she also knew that 'authority' (and even the human mind itself) was not always trustworthy. She could feel herself becoming more and more tense and tongue-tied. If things went on like that, she may not be able to say anything at all. When Gini felt her brain seize up like that in recent years she knew profound and agonizing frustration was sure to follow. She'd resort to scanning all the neuro-databases in her brain. Whether looking for the names of people that should have been well known to her, or feverishly searching for the right words to put together in response to a simple question like '*Where did you go this afternoon?*' Virginia knew instinctively – from bitter experience – that the only way to enter into *any kind* of conversation with 'London calling' was to relax, deeply. With every exhalation, she had to recompose herself one breath at a time. Gini allowed the knot in her brain enough space to gradually loosen. Just enough for the subtle channels of the mind to become naturally open again. For an easy flow to start up once more.

Eventually, Gini's gentleman caller, ever-hopeful, repeated his familiar phrase one more time. By now, she perceived it as an ancient mantra intended to unlock the rusted vaults of her brain.

*London calling*, he offered in a last-gasp, coaxing tone.

From somewhere deep down inside her garbled but slightly more pacified psyche Virginia somehow managed to dredge up a long-forgotten phrase, to regurgitate as a plausible response:

*I'm listening*, Gini said.

That was it!

Also very brief and to the point. *Somehow* she just knew this was exactly the right thing to say. She didn't know how or why. But she just *knew* that '*I'm listening*' was precisely what she was supposed to say. Then things started to gather pace. They were like two babies taking their first clumsy steps towards each other...

*Identity code?* – he ventured quizzically.

With miraculous confidence, Gini replied: *Bravo Lima Alfa Kilo Echo, Zero One Three One Four Seven Niner.*

(*O Jesus, help me!* Virginia thought to herself) She didn't know if she was losing the plot altogether. Maybe she was channeling someone from a previous lifetime or something. But Gini was beginning to recognise the caller's prompts and simply *knew* what to say next. From that point on, she didn't hesitate or falter. She just didn't put a foot wrong. Outwardly, no doubt, they appeared to speak total jibberish to each other. But just between the two of them it all made perfect sense.

Overheard by a mystified Pedro in the kitchen doorway, Gini stood in her chic 19th Century Madrid apartment and gazed through the enormous dirty living room windows out into the late afternoon Gran Via below. A woman possessed. Feeling one-third her true age. She was young again. Her brain was coming alive with a fresh sparkle she thought would never return. And, above all, Gini felt capable of anything...

*I hope you enjoyed your long sleep,* he continued.

*Yes. Very much. But I'm wide awake now,* Virginia replied.

*'Control' speaking. Time to go to work.*

*I'm ready to play. Ready, willing and able,* she said.

Gini still didn't fully understand what the hell was going on. But she did feel she was responding according to a kind of pre-programmed *script*. Even though she couldn't say with any certainty her own phone number or what she had eaten yesterday for lunch, she really *did* know what she was saying to Control. Her mind was firmly drawn toward the distant past. And that made her feel extremely comfortable. Capable. No longer a useless, muddled, old bag.

*So,* Gini asked (wondering what they wanted her to do), *What are the rules?*

*All in good time, Virginia. All in good time,* Control said rather patronisingly (now that she was hooked). *Stay by the phone, same time tomorrow.* Then the line fell silent.

Having replaced the phone's receiver, her mind came hurtling back into the room. Pedro was still nearby, watching her, his jaw dropped in disbelief. As she continued to stare in his general direction, Virginia couldn't help but notice that his dishcloth had fallen to the floor and was resting on his feet. She also noticed tears forming in his eyes – although she couldn't imagine why. He couldn't possibly have known what the phone call meant. What little sense he could've gleaned from Gini's end of it anyway ... well, it would hardly have brought tears to your eyes.

If he'd simply looked confused, or intrigued even, then that would've been understandable. But the poor thing had all the appearance of someone for whom the penny had suddenly dropped that their loved one had finally gone ga-ga. Gini's newly-emerging ability to focus one-pointedly wandered slowly from his face to the brush-strokes on the painted door post beside him, to the chipped vase of jasmine blossoms on the sideboard, to the swirling *vajra knots* and snow lions on the Tibetan yaks-wool rug they had inherited from the previous owners of the apartment. Her gaze drifted, but it *was* truly focused wherever it landed. Perhaps for the first time in ages.

She saw every detail of the floral curtain fabric. But she didn't even try to remember where or when she'd bought it. Gini's heart neither leapt for joy nor crashed in grief when her eyes scrolled across the old photo of Benjamin and her on holidays somewhere snowy. Nor did she torture herself when, just momentarily, she couldn't recall for the life of her the name of the child sitting between them. Although Virginia observed she was in possession of a fully-functioning, old-fashioned record player, she had no recollection whatever how she'd acquired it. Nor did she really care. She was no longer grasping onto what she saw. She wasn't taking anything much on board. Nothing required further processing. She really was seeing things in the finest detail. But she simply chose to let them be... just as they appeared. Deeply rooted in the present moment now – quite carefree – it was a return to former dignity. Gini was feeling more like her old self than she had in years!

As soon as her eyes settled on the dirty sitting room windows, a mischievous little divil rose up in her. Suddenly finding herself full of energy, she barked instructions – quite tongue in cheek – at poor Pedro: *Hey Pééédro! Consuelo, Darling! When you get a minute, Princess love, would you please drag your gay arse out onto that window ledge and clean those windows for me, will you Dear? That's what I pay you for, isn't it Consuelo? Pedro love, do you hear me?*

*...Yes Gini. I hear you loud and queer. I mean CLEAR. I'll get to it tomorrow, Love ... Hopefully.* Pedro tried to join in the fun though his heart was breaking.

From the corner of her eye, Gini watched Pedro wipe the inexplicable tear from his cheek, turn slowly with a half smile, and walk back into the kitchen. The sadness gradually subsided in him. Another mini-crisis averted.

The episode was over. This truly momentous event, a mysteriously liberating occurrence, had come ... and gone. It had passed off without too much fuss or nonsense. The reality was this: Gini had received a phone call that in all honesty she'd thought would never actually come. And because she believed it would never happen, she'd entirely 'forgotten' the possibility of it *ever* happening. She'd buried deep down inside herself even the faintest whisper of the slightest chance of it happening one day in the future.

Without realising it, from that pivotal moment in her past onwards, Gini had suppressed so many other possibilities in life too. Benjamin was dead and in her grief she'd become frozen, blind to even the most ordinary possibilities of life. She no longer saw reality at all, in fact. Gini had been dreaming all these years. Projecting. A drowning woman clutching at imaginary straws. Gini had been falling deeper and deeper into dreamland without knowing. She'd become ever more petrified by her self-made, grief-stricken terrain. Gini's so-called *life* had been slowly driving her insane.

But *now*... Virginia felt alive again. The call had given her new purpose. She was breathing the present moment in with great gusto. Tentatively, she gradually began letting go of Benjamin's passing with every out breath. Even though he'd been dead for nearly a decade, she was only now starting to truly accept it. The realisation that she couldn't change that *fact* was strangely liberating for her. Benjamin was dead... Time had not healed. The world had moved on regardless... without her. It was now time for Gini to catch *up* with reality. And quickly.

She gently placed the stylus onto the well-worn surface of her favourite record. Today was a special day indeed. The perfect day to open all the windows and blast the cobwebs off this old city flat. But she didn't. She just sat there quietly. In her favourite comfy armchair. Totally relaxed. And simply listened.

She was transported to a concert hall in Paris. Sitting in the darkness... The Spanish Civil War a dim and distant memory, from a book. So too Trinity College and Cambridge. Her unused degrees in Spanish Literature and Liberation Theology. No longer a source of embarrassment to her. Rather, the stepping-stones required to get her to where she now found herself... As if her whole life had been preparing her for *this* precise moment. Right here. Right now... Present moment. Wonderful moment...

Bach's introduction for orchestra slowly reveals its trajectory, under the masterly direction of Benjamin Léon, the love of Virginia's life.

Grace and Glory gradually unfurl. Stretching and yawning, their skyward union gathers pace, to greet the entry of the choir:


*'Wachet auf', ruft uns die stimme!*
*'Wachet auf! AUF!!'*

*'Sleeper, wake up!', the voice calls out.*
*'Awake! Wake up!!'*

**2**

On a magical, golden afternoon in late September Virginia sat on a bench under an ancient oak.

From her vantage point near The Pavillion, she passed a long hour soaking up the last of the sun, leafing through a magazine. Occasionally, she glanced out over the young men playing cricket below. Gini was 18. It was 1968.

She was away from home and family for the first time in her life. The spirit of the age was so refreshing and potential liberation lay around every corner. Her life in England thus far had been so suffocating and stuffy. But Gini's darling parents – to her enormous surprise – had given in to her moody nagging and actually allowed her to take up a *four year* scholarship at Trinity College Dublin. She simply couldn't believe her luck. The scholarship – referred to lovingly as the *Schol* by those who pursued it – meant everything to Virginia. Life was surely going to take a dramatic turn for the better.

Having moved to Ireland, Gini was ready to explore whatever life had to offer. As she sat there on her bench, she could look at a flimsy dress on a model on a page and think '*I could wear that, if I wanted*'. As she looked at the boys in their cricket whites, she thought '*I could kiss any one of them, if I wanted'. She was a young woman, after all. She had her secret needs. Thanks to the Trinity scholarship, Virginia also had her own room overlooking the tennis courts in 'Botany Bay' - one of the college's quiet squares. But most of all, she had freedom.

Women had been allowed to study at Trinity since the beginning of the century. But Roman Catholics, of either sex, were not to be admitted until 1970. In 1592, Queen Elizabeth had established Trinity College with the express intention of educating and training the Protestant ruling class in Ireland. There was a mandatory oath of allegiance to the Crown for all staff and students. They even had to swear a declaration against Transubstantiation (the Roman Catholic belief that the bread and wine used at Communion actually *became* the body and blood of Jesus Christ).

Gini felt privileged to be there at all; she was a poor, though clever, ordinary English girl. She was also mindful of how lucky she'd been to attend Trinity in an age that allowed women to study there. However, she was totally dismayed that one group could – in her day and age – continue to exclude and oppress another. It made her ashamed of her race and her religion. But she was there for a good reason... Virginia was at Trinity College in order to 'find' and 'express' herself. She could have taken up the *Schol* at either of Trinity's two sister colleges in Oxford or Cambridge. But they were too close to home, and she wanted to spread her wings. So she decided to move to Dublin lock, stock and barrel. Apart from all the freedom that living in Dublin would afford Virginia, her intention was also to study her two greatest passions.

She was very keen on the Spanish language, and related political matters. So she chose Spanish Literature, with the hope of eventually honing in on the writers of the Spanish Civil War. Her other passion, which was only beginning to awaken in her, was very unfashionable for the times; Gini had discovered in the Christian Tradition a truly rare treasure. A strand of spiritual philosophy, as preached by Jesus and the Prophets, which actually favoured the poor and the marginalised above their rich overlords. It inspired Gini so much that she decided to read Theology and Biblical Studies as her second subject. She was hoping to focus eventually on the Theology of Justice. She had always been quite a serious child. In the event, Virginia had grown into an equally serious young woman. But she longed for romance too: Under the Cherry Blossoms, before a glass of peasant Tempranillo, followed by a steamy night of passion on her narrow single bed. Preferably – if one could be found – with a dark-haired, blue-eyed, erudite gypsy.

As the sun set for the day, casting long Autumnal shadows, Virginia strolled towards the Dining Hall alone. Parched leaves crunched underfoot. She knew practically nobody. So she chatted politely to the diners on either side of her about the weather and the news. As she glanced around the grand, oak-panelled room, and down the long tables that stretched out through the candlelight, she couldn't help but remark to herself what a surprisingly mixed bunch they were. One-quarter women. One-quarter middle class. A colourful band of foreigners too. Several Africans, Indians, Asians and Arabs. There was even a Royal Princess from Thailand. After dinner, another solitary stroll around Front Square. Back under the *Campanile* and right, towards her room in Botany Bay. There, the pure joy of translating Cervantes' *The Ingenious Gentleman Don Quixote of La Mancha* awaited her. For young Virginia Blake, life couldn't get much better.

As she climbed the stairs to the top floor, she could see a note pinned to her door. Wondering how it might feel to receive a love letter, or even a message from some future friend inviting her to their room for cocoa before bed, on arrival at the top landing she trembled to read the note's brief contents: *Urgent telegram from home. Please come to Bursar's Office, immediately.*

After finally discovering just where the Bursar's Office actually was, Gini knocked on the ancient, heavy door. A rather obese, elderly Englishman invited her to enter and sit down.

The news from home, he said, was not good and she should prepare herself for the worst. Both her parents were dead. A domestic gas explosion as they sat at the kitchen table enjoying breakfast. Since Gini was the only child, a now distant relative had sent the word and wanted to know if she intended returning for the funerals, a week from Sunday.

Understandably she was dazed and in shock. The dreamlike nature of what we call 'reality' was more apparent to her now than ever. Though she seemed to drift through the sequence of events that followed, her awareness and recall was (at least in those days) most vivid and detailed.

She took the mail boat on the Friday night after lectures. Rough crossing, horrendous train journey down. Slept in next-door's spare bedroom on the Saturday night, her own house resembling a bombsite. The gardens remained curiously floribund and lush, despite the obvious chaos of frightened neighbours and the many firemen running through.

On the Sunday, the neighbours prepared kippers and toast for breakfast. You could still smell the damp stench of the charred debris from Gini's house next door. She wondered what Mummy and Daddy had been having for breakfast before the explosion. The Church Service was a mixture of the tragic and the heroic. The vicar painted the middle-aged couple consumed by the flames as the saddest thing he had ever heard. And the attempts of the firemen to recover their near-cremated, poor bodies, locked in a final embrace of terror, was described as heroic but alas in vain.

At the graveside, Gini's tears fell like a torrent of injustice until she remembered it had just been a horrid, tragic accident and that nobody was to blame (not even the Gas Board apparently). Then and there, she knew in her heart and soul that *these things* really do happen. And there is nothing we can do but grieve and move on afterwards. Life was teaching her so many lessons. No substitute for direct, personal experience. The kind of truth most people can accept intellectually, but never fully embrace. There is a vast ocean of difference between the two truths: Death is real, it comes without warning, and THIS body will be a corpse.

It is all the difference between *knowing* and *truly realizing*. The cavernous gap that exists between the intellect and *consciousness* itself.

Another truth hit home that afternoon as they buried Virginia's parents. Vicar reminded the congregation that her Mum and Dad had been a very private, sweet couple. But, in truth, theirs had been a really great love story. He said he knew both of them very well. They had been completely devoted to each other, both as friends and as man and wife. He said their love was strong and enduring. They'd been looking forward to getting away for a romantic weekend, perhaps to Paris, provided the student riots hadn't gotten totally out of control. Gini knew only too well that her parents were incurable romantics. They were so in love with each other. Like old souls, or two doting swans, they had met and mated for life. She envied them. She also had flashbacks, as the vicar spoke, of coming home early from school to find them slow-dancing in the kitchen to some tune or other on the radio, or to a melody they were singing quietly into eachother's ears. She longed to have that for herself someday, when she grew up.

The rest of the day was spent in dull agony as Gini was forced to sit in yet another neighbour's parlour while people who hardly knew her queued up. Cups of tea in hand, and a slice of madeira cake on the side, they tried to console her. Some enquired politely what her intentions might be *vis-à-vis* her studies abroad and her soon-to-be-inherited shell of a house.

Eventually, Virginia allowed a cruel pot of rage to boil over within her. Driven to lash out and insult their frail, suburban sensitivities, she completely shocked them by standing to her full height and announcing to all assembled that her intention was to sell the house to the highest bidder, bank the lot till she had grown up enough to know her own mind. And, in the meantime, she would be finishing the degree she'd started in Dublin while probably living in sin with a young Irish Gypsy gentleman she had recently taken as a lover. The sadistic flare with which Gini spoke had, of course, come from a place of deep sadness for her own sake and without a jot of feeling for how it might affect anyone else. She observed the anger as it grew in her like a rampant flame. Although she'd been raised to know better, Gini had struck out anyway.

As the years rolled by, she moved from Dublin to Cambridge for post-grad in 1972, and from there to Spain. Virginia never actually had to face any of them again.

On the Monday, she took an early train to meet the ferry to Ireland, and was soon back in her room with Don Quixote only having missed a single day of lectures.

Since nobody really knew her yet at Trinity, she wasn't constantly being reminded by others of what had happened. The books and the lectures were a God-send. But the anger and the shock turned to deep resentment and self-pity as the months slowly passed. Thanks to something as inanely random as a faulty gas main, Virginia was now cast in the role of *orphan* as well as loner. The subtle psychological damage was undoubtedly causing her chipper English façade to crumble and crack. But she managed to narrowly avert the abyss by allowing herself to become distracted by the epic search for love. *After all*, she concluded, *who wants to be with an angry, self-loathing so-and-so?*

The bottom line was clear to her. She needed more than anything to move on. The worst had already happened. But she'd survived. By midnight Tuesday, Gini had left it all behind her and was fast asleep in her own little bed in Botany Bay.

As the days turned into months, she gradually found her feet and and tried to become incrementally more grounded. She was determined to keep moving forward. She became very forward indeed. There were new friends, and the occasional drunken fumble. But nothing too serious.

Virginia found that the more frivolous and free she was the stronger her main friendships became. So that's what she did. As her confidence grew, she even went through a phase where she played the androgynous Tom Boy in hot pursuit of the Thai Princess, of all people. By New Year's Eve, in the snow, outside Christ Church Cathedral, so liberated and shameless was Gini that she went as far as to kiss the royal hand. As the bells rang out the old year, Gini read her exotic beauty some poetry she had recently written in Spanish, and clumsily translated into Thai, just for her.

By Easter, the princess was called home to Bangkok – the City of Angels – and Virginia had slept with two men.

# 3

The next day, Virginia left her apartment on Gran Via to meet Pedro and his friend Maria in a favourite nearby café-bar for a light luncheon. As she strolled along in the sunshine, she wondered if tapas and salad followed by coffee would be enough. It *was* going to be a momentous day after all. *Be at your phone same time tomorrow*, Control had said. And the Englishwoman in Gini hated to disappoint or detain. She couldn't even allow herself to be a few minutes late for a rendezvous. Pedro and Maria must have wondered what on earth was going on. Gini had still refused to explain anything at all. She wanted to buy lunch. And she needed their support with something very important. That's all she said.

When she arrived into the side street, she could see Maria outside smoking and chatting on her phone in the shade. Maria motioned Gini to go ahead inside. She mouthed words to the effect that Pedro was waiting at the bar, and had already spied something yummy on the Menu of the Day. When Gini entered the familiar shabby-chic interior she saw Pedro, his back to her, perched at the counter.

As Virginia approached she noticed Pedro was watching her, with that familiar crooked grin, in the long mirror behind the bar. Their eyes met in the reflection and without turning around he greeted her with a blown kiss.

*What's going on, Darling?* He said, playing down the whole affair. Gini could see the back of Benji's head in Pedro's as she adjusted her gaze to look at him directly. Pedro was sitting on a high stool, his knees pressed up against the counter. His big feet had slipped out of their flip-flops and were now resting on the coolness of the gleaming brass pole running along the bottom. Gini noticed she was noticing more today than she had noticed in years.

*O Hi*, Virginia chirped, as if nothing amazing was about to occur.

Maria joined them, with a similar air of near pretence... No one was really communicating.

So then there were three.

Looking around the place, you could tell at a glance that mainly local people ate and drank there. Generations of them, for over a century. The décor was old-world comfy with a twist of fashion around the edges: the window-dressings, the choice of retro 70s light fittings, all the stainless steel behind the bar.

The toilets were to-die-for. Someone had spent a lot of time and energy turning what must have been a crumbling shambles into a proper modern loo. In the main dining room, on the roughly plastered, beige walls hung an impressive reproduction of El Greco's *Christ as Saviour.*

And a huge, framed poster for *Todo Sobre mi Madre.* Even though the choice of music could hardly be enjoyed – with the din of Latin diners – Virginia marked with a private swoon that it was Jordi Savall's rendition of a Mass by Morales.

A booth came available. The waiter gently tapped Gini's arm as he passed to invite her and her companions to move over if they preferred. Virginia couldn't recall the last time she had been touched by a man. Even inadvertently, she mused. Even in Spain, people so rarely touch nowadays. The waiter glanced again across the room at them. He raised a cheeky eyebrow. So, to smooth over the underlying awkwardness of not really talking, they all jumped at the chance to move. They were soon seated on the leatherette benches, scanning the menu. They chatted easily about what to share and whether they should venture as far as a bottle of wine instead of three glasses.

About three-quarters of an hour into eating the most sumptuous tapas of cured meats, roasted vegetables, tortilla and salads, once again Pedro's nerves started to get the better of him.

*OK Gin. Out with it! What did you want to tell me?* Pedro blurted. *And why the fuck have you invited Maria along? Be honest, Love. We all know you can't stand her.*

*Patience is a virtue, Princess,* Virginia cut across him, looking at the menu again, for something sweet to follow.

Dessert came. Then coffee.

Finally. Speech after long silence:

*Well, it's this... You both know I haven't been feeling well in recent years...?*

*O for God's sake! Mrs Léon! Cut to the chase, Baby,* Maria snapped. *None of us is getting any younger, you know? And YOU look like you might actually expire at any moment! (Mmm. Nice shoes).*

*Maria, please don't,* Pedro interjected, staring deep into Gini's pale, strong eyes for some reassurance.

*Don't worry, Sweetheart,* Virginia announced (taking command of the whole situation). *Moving on... I feel I want to share something extremely important and very private with you both... just in case my life takes a funny turn for the worst later this afternoon...*

*Hostia! Con-yO!! Gini... For fuck sake!!!* (Maria again) *Get a move on. The suspense is killing us... Your husband is dead. Pedro's queer. You don't like his tranny friend Maria. You're losing your fucking marbles pronto. And, O yeah, that's it, there was a 'mysterious' phone call yesterday afternoon sometime. What else could you possibly have to tell us?! Don't tell me. Yes! I know. You've found a used condom up your snatch but don't remember how or when it got there!* Maria laughed at her own insults so heartily she let rip a Trojan Horse of a fart. Silent but deadly. She sat back and watched for the moment of impact on the faces of the others.

This gave Virginia a chance to gather herself and start to say what she had come to say:

*The gentleman who phoned yesterday is going to call the flat again in less than an hour. Now, because I'm that little bit older and hard of hearing sometimes, and because I may not actually be able to take in everything he says to me, I want you two to listen in on the call and note every detail of whatever he says. It WILL be of vital importance. And I just don't want to mess things up. Got it?... Good!*

Pedro and Maria stared at each other in semi-disbelief.

**4**

Thirty-seven minutes later, all three of them were waiting by the phone in the sitting room. Pedro had temporarily moved a more modern phone to that point, to facilitate everyone being able to listen together on the speaker. Virginia insisted they both had pen and paper to write down the necessary. Of course, Pedro's English was good enough to catch every word the caller might say. But Maria's was not so great. She'd had a very rudimentary education. However, she understood more than she let on. And anyway, her main function was to listen in mainly as a support for Pedro. She was, after all, his best friend and would also serve as his confidante should he feel the need to discuss the matter with anyone afterwards. He had Gini's permission to dump on Maria, but no one else. The pair of them were beyond intrigued. Two further minutes passed sitting nervously. Virginia brushed her hair back into a tight bun, as if she was about to greet a guest at the door. The phone rang.

*London calling...I'm listening...Identity code? ...Bravo Lima Alfa Kilo Echo, Zero One Three One Four Seven Niner...I hope you enjoyed your long sleep...Yes. Very much. But I'm wide*

*awake now...'Control' speaking. Time to go to work...I'm ready
to play. Ready, willing and able. So, what are the rules?*

Maria and Pedro, their eyes transfixed by the phone,
were practically catatonic.

*Are you alone?* enquired Control.

*O yes Dear. Quite alone. Do go on, please. I'm a little
nervous. It HAS been such a long time and I thought...*

*Yes, you thought this day would never arrive,* interrupted
Control rather dismissively. *Most of them never get a call.
The world and its methods have changed so much. But you,
Virginia Blake, YOU are just what the doctor ordered in this
specific situation. You have certain – shall we say – 'skills' and
qualifications for the job. And as you have been in the field (as
it were) for so long, you have already completely blended into
the background ... to the point of near invisibility. Hiding in
plain sight. The perfect 'sleeper'. Do you follow?*

*O yes. I am reading you loud and clear, Dear. Plain sight, I
like that. But I am not really a sleeper. I never enrolled as a spy.
Just a humble functionary of the crown. Willing to do Her
Majesty's bidding, if ever the chance arose. That was the
agreement, wasn't it?*

Gini glanced over at her trusty eavesdroppers. Pedro
and Maria sat dumbfounded, their throats becoming dry.
Sweat gathered around Maria's Vetiver-scented neck. A
now-daily tear of sad frustration rolled down Pedro's
stubbled cheek. Virginia Blake-Léon was back! She felt alive
and fascinating again. *Why not go wherever this path was
leading?*

Control went into some detail about the intended
mission while Gini took it all in, wide-eyed, and the other
two scribbled copious notes.

On a certain day at a certain time – yet to be disclosed – Virginia would meet a certain person at the airport. He would be arriving on one flight and leaving on another. Gini would have to wait with him, like a long-lost relative, and chat. To make it appear as though they were really engaging with each other, they would chat about their mutual interests. These mutual interests were precisely why Ms Blake had been hand picked, trained, and now selected all these decades later by British Intelligence. Gini was the perfect woman for the job. Her transitory conversationalist would greatly appreciate chatting for an hour or so about The Spanish Civil War and Liberation Theology with someone who was also biologically pre-programmed for politeness and how not to ask awkward personal questions.

*That was the sum total of it,* Gini thought to herself: *Meet some guy off one flight. Chat to him. Put him on another. Ask no questions. Then go back to being a demented old bag, slowly losing one's grip on life until the day it inevitably slipped away altogether. How lovely! Just what every old lady wants in her dotage: espionage, delirium, then death!*

*... Very well then. Leave it to me,* Virginia addressed Control in agreement. *Once I am told where and when, I will be there to do the job, come hell or high water. You know you won't be disappointed. My whole life has been one long rehearsal for just such a chat with just such a man. I must have done it a million times already, in my sleep too... You'll be in touch, I take it? So what now? Do I just hang up or must you go through the politesse of saying your goodbyes first?*

*Don't get cocky Ms Blake. That was always your downfall. Your file says as much. Today has also proved a veritable mine of insightful information about you and your present life. For example, your choice of cornflour blue dress tells us you accept your age and your destiny. Your choice of food at lunch implies you still look after yourself, despite some mental deterioration... You have not completely lost your marbles yet, at least not the ones WE need.*

So you do acknowledge that YOU need ME, Gini bit back. *You do at least see that even an old bag like me has proven useful, if not indispensable, even at this late stage in the game? ... But I presume you still have some respect for Free Will in England? Presumably, I still have some say in the matter? A 'Sleeper', once awakened, still has the choice to roll over and go back to sleep, agreed?*

Agreed, atoned Control. *Apologies Ms Blake but time is of the essence here and we just need to know if we can depend on you as promised. Of course you know we've been observing you your whole life... As a matter of fact, we're looking at you right now. We don't even care that you lied to us by pretending to be alone. We just want to encourage you to play your part so that Britain can play her part in getting a V.I.P. from A to B. By the way, he asked for you specifically. He chose YOU – from a list WE gave him, admittedly – but he said 'That's my girl', 'She's the one for me'... Pleasant discourse for an hour or two... 'On Her Majesty's Secret Service'? What do you say, Virginia? Ready to play?*

Gini took a moment. And, looking deeply through Pedro's beautiful eyes, way down into his soul, she said to Control: *If you insist on taking the blatant liberty of watching who you are talking to on the phone, then I'm afraid my dear Control that I must ask for the same courtesy to be extended to me. I want to see YOU too, face to face. After all, we won't be collaborating on anything illegal. Will we? So there's no danger in us meeting in person. We will simply be organizing a chat, somewhere in a Madrid airport, between two lovers of Liberty and Equality....*

Control was a bit taken aback by Gini's odd tangent – given the covert nature of espionage and all that – but he consented to a chat over afternoon tea between her and someone high-up at the British Embassy, at a time of her own choosing – provided it fell between the hours of 3 and 5pm one day very soon (the day after tomorrow, if at all possible).

Becoming somewhat tired and bewildered now, Gini admitted she'd grown exhausted by the whole episode. So she agreed a time and day for tea. Control said she could bring along 'the other two' for moral support if she wished. But they would have to take tea with the secretaries while she got her final instructions face to face from the high-up... And of course, he reminded her, she'd have to go alone to the airport to do the actual job when the time came. There'd be a handful of operatives from several 'interested parties' dotted about the place observing the smooth transition. She wasn't to be concerned in the slightest.

He made his apologies for having to terminate the call so abruptly, and for not being available to meet her in person. In any case, he said, he wasn't even in Spain – not that his whereabouts was anything she need worry herself about either. HE was Control after all, not Gini. And it was his job to oversee and run the whole show from the shadows. That's why he was Control and Virginia was Virginia. She was invited, temporarily, to be Her Majesty's agent on the ground. But when it was over, it was over. She should be under no illusion.

Gini said: *So, 'London Calling', you're in that training camp in Kent then, are you?*

*Goodbye Virginia,* said an exasperated Control... *And Good Luck.*

*Yes. You too, Dear. The best of British to ya,* chimed Gini in a fake Cockney accent, fractionally after London Calling had already hung up.

Once a few beats had passed, having recomposed herself, Gini turned to a stupified Pedro and Maria. Now in a flat *Dublin* accent, she asked: *So...What does the Quare Pair make of all that then?*

5

Virginia's brain – like most of us – never quite stopped thinking and scheming. The past and the future always appeared to intrude. So much so that when she was a little girl she often thought her dream time was the only time she ever truly dwelt in the present moment at all.

Her dreams were usually brief and rarely memorable. Nothing out of the ordinary. You know the kind of thing: being chased, trying to find some place in an unknown town... flying. And when she was in her early teens she found she could experience a kind of lucid dream state. She 'knew' she was only dreaming and could even 'change channel' if needed.

It was around that time Gini began writing down what she could recall of her dreams the next morning, or during the night if she awoke. She had no interest whatsoever in the various theories that abounded regarding the actual meaning of dreams. In fact, she considered it all hokum. She just wanted to keep a record of the main themes, for no particular reason other than as a kind of mental discipline.

Later, when she had returned to Dublin after her parents' funeral, Gini made three particularly telling notes in her Dream Journal.

Her room at Trinity College had become so much 'home' for her that she mused it was probably only a matter of time before she'd have one lover a week in her bed. However her new-found sexual liberation, she noted, never manifested in her dreams. She had 'no sexy liaisons on the nocturnal plane'.

Virginia also noted with youthfully drole abandon, 'Dug up Mum and Dad last night to see if they were actually dead. Brought their bodies into the house to warm them up in their chairs either side of the fire. Daddy never stirred but Mummy came round ever so briefly only to explain that she was sorry for everything, that she loved me madly, and that Dad was calling her back and she'd have to fly'. Gini apparently felt no need to elaborate or comment further.

The third note-worthy thing in the journal at that time was a curious entry about a new recurring theme that read: 'Getting jelly or yoghurt so frequently for dessert in the Dining Hall these days (BOTH at Lunch AND at Commons in the evenings) that I have begun dreaming about mountains of it. Great jelly alps with yoghurt-covered peaks. The sound of a train running on smooth tracks below me as I doze... *je-lly yo-ghurt je-lly yo-ghurt...* my mind soothed by the mantra-like quality of their murmurings. Content to be going towards who or whatever lies ahead of me... I feel open'. 'Lately', she added, 'the images of jelly-yoghurt snow-mountains are accompanied by an abundance of rainbows'.

This jelly-yoghurt symphony of rainbows was to recur again and again, throughout Gini's life. She no longer considered it a dream but a portent of sorts. She found it so peaceful and loving that she opened her heart and mind to it completely, receiving whatever the rainbows had come to share with her.

In her twenties, the rainbows began speaking to her... speaking words of wisdom, 'Let it be'.

In her thirties and forties, the rainbows took more of a form. It was a man. His body was made of light. You could say he had a rainbow body. He spoke directly to Virginia about her life and the nature of everything. He didn't speak to her very regularly but he always manifested as Truth when she needed to hear the plain truth. He never revealed anything as mundane as his name or what he was supposed to be, or where he was from. Time was always so precious, neither one of them was willing to waste a second.

Their exchanges were never solemn or 'holy' in any way. In fact, an irreverent frisson often darted about in the rainbow-flooded air. Gini talked about Socialism, seduction and sex. Whatever was foremost in her consciousness at the time. And the man with the rainbow body, who she named Jelly Yoghurt, responded wisely and compassionately to her every situation. However, he was also capable of tough love if necessary. He was no saint. Just a guide who knew the terrain. The origin of this voice of reason always remained a mystery. Perhaps it was Gini's own conscience emerging. Or maybe it was some kind of Universal Consciousness waking up within her. Either way, if this new emergence was 'real' at all, it couldn't awaken fast enough for Gini. Her life was about to roller-coaster at an alarming pace.

Virginia's Junior Freshman year at Trinity had offered such highs and lows it could only have been described as her 'most significant year to date'. Michaelmas Term, notwithstanding her parents' deaths, had revealed to her so many new freedoms and insights. She had even dallied with cross-dressing and kissed the most beautiful girl in the world.

In the new year, Hilary Term had brought with it overwhelming, fully-fledged sexual passion. In her head she'd been with a series of men who resembled Gypsy Poet Kings. They had pursued, romanced and made passionate love to her. Every pore of her body longed for their tongues to revisit and consume her. In reality she had allowed a college porter she bumped into on the prowl in the corridor one night to go back to her room. He'd sucked her nipple, made her scream with his thick fingers. Then he entered her roughly, and shot his frenzied panic across her belly. They never even kissed. He smelled rank. Another gentleman caller, also dark and stocky, licked her behind then sucked her clitoris till she squirted. He shot on the rug. But her main crush developed after Easter, during Trinity Term.

Ms Blake had ravaged and lapped up every last drop of her academic studies. She excelled at most everything she took on. She was now fluent in Spanish, including a few dialects, both ancient and modern. She was well on track to mining the depths of the Medieval and Civil War periods in the coming academic year. Gini promised to make an extra special effort in her Senior Freshman year to engage more with her Religious Studies. She particularly wanted to parallel her Spanish curriculum by exploring the works of the Mystics such as Teresa of Avila and John of the Cross, and the new 'Liberation' Theology that was flowing out from Latin America.

However, between April and May 1969, when Gini was supposed to be concerned only with her exams, or preparing for them, she had a torrid love affair with an older student and several of his friends from outside college. There had been a kind of grooming of Virginia by John. Once she was hooked by him, there followed what can only be described as a bout of disturbing, suburban, bi-sexual orgies. The frenzied 'sessions' between the new couple and his friends usually culminated in an explosion of aggressive orgasm. There was hateful name-calling. Physical bullying. Sometimes even blood. It became a regular ritual. A desperate scenario, which amounted in truth to nothing less than gang rape.

Gini was always the only girl. There were never less than three men. Often more. Different ones.

Gini had started down this path willingly. There's no doubt about that. However, it HAS to be said, nobody who enjoys the energy of group sex ever enters into it actually wanting to be forced or raped... For God's sake, even sado-masochists have codes of behavior and 'safe words' for calling a halt to it.

But Gini rapidly grew to love John. She was intoxicated. He was dark and smouldering. Stocky, well-hung, and sweet as a lamb. Most of the friends he brought along were too, actually. The kind you could bring home to meet your mother, and she'd be none the wiser. The type who played Rugby twice a week, drank three times a week, loitered in public toilets four times a week, and had somehow, quite miraculously, managed to find each other in the mire of their crazy existence. They'd met in a dark, secret world but had emerged together into the light of day as a newly-formed, inter-dependent entity that they called The Team... Nowadays, with the internet and everything, that would be of little surprise; basically, they were bi-sexual men who were into one another as much as they enjoyed Gini. But back in the 60s such sexual expression was still so repressed and suppressed that when it finally forced its way to the surface, it could run riot completely. People got hurt. Badly.

But, for the time being, for the most part, Gini thought the group encounters were great. She adored John, and if he and his friends got a little too rough and insulting from time to time, what could she do anway?

Sometimes, Gini would lie back and simply observe the orgy in minute detail as it unfolded – which ones spent how long pleasuring her, and how long they all seemed to spend pleasuring one another. She adored watching them suck John and equally loved gasping out loud as they teamed up to kiss and lick her. But they continued to gang up on her at the end, and use their combined force against her. She swore 'never again'. But she always went back for more, like so many victim-addicts. The emerging truth of it was clear: she now loved John, and he was the gateway to satisfying her growing carnal obsessions. Gini had become addicted to sex as sport. She even kept all her other 'regular' partners, including the night porter and several new, dark, stocky men.

As time progressed, and Gini got in deeper and deeper, she saw most men she passed in the street as fresh meat; walking penises and tongues, bulky shoulders and thighs.

When May came and Gini should have been sitting her Biblical Studies in the Exam Hall she was being rogered in the quiet ladies loo in House number 7, Front Square. The subdued sound of her own panting. The constant running water of the dodgy cistern overhead. She was cutting it extremely fine. It was imperative to shatter the precious atmosphere and break through the lusty fog in her mind. So she pushed the off-duty busman out of the cubicle, fixed herself, grabbed her stuff and sprinted to the exam where she took her seat with only seconds to spare.

Gini had accumulated so much knowledge. Even in this field, she thought she knew it all: She knew she was allowed enter the exam hall up to ten-past the hour. She knew she would find sex in No.7 just before. She knew she would just make the exam on time. She knew the answers to all the questions on the paper. She appeared to know so much about so many things. She was just a thundering 'know-it-all' really. She even thought she knew pretty much everything there was to know about life... She was wrong.

Gini didn't know she was pregnant. Neither did she know she was riddled with syphilis. By the time Virginia realized what was actually going on inside her own body, her exams were finished and she'd just arrived in Paris for the Summer.

She felt she had chosen Paris because her parents never got to go. She imagined their spirits had accompanied her in order to vicariously experience the *Joie de Vivre*. But in her heart of hearts she understood they were not with her. She was utterly alone.

In reality, an arrogant nineteen-year-old English girl wandered the streets of an indifferent, alien cityscape.

Insurrection, rioting, and civil disobedience were rife. Barricades could crop up unexpectedly anywhere! Clichéd young lovers, actually wearing berets and striped t-shirts, sat smoking *Gitanes* at café terraces, gazing into each other's eyes.

The sound of Ray Charles' *Goin Down Slow* was everywhere in Paris that Summer. President Nixon recalled U.S. soldiers from Viet Nam. John Lennon and Yoko ruled the world, then crashed their car. The French government was overthrown by the people. A 22-year-old Cuban stowaway claimed asylum having survived a 9-hour flight to Spain, holding onto the inside of the front wheel housing. Shostakovich's 14th Symphony premiered in Russia; its devastating theme emanating from a poem about premature death by Garcia Lorca ...

When she should have been having the time of her life, a forlorn Virginia Blake wandered about the Marais, not a friend in the world, looking for a back-street abortionist. Perhaps mercifully, she miscarried up a lane near the Rue Charlot where a nice African lady found her and took care of everything. Her venereal disease was diagnosed at the hospital. And poor Gini spent the rest of the Summer taking the cure.

But Paris was swinging. There was no denying the vibrant energy of youth. By the end of July, Virginia was back having sex and never referred to the baby or the syphilis again.

6

Later that night, Pedro and Maria invited Virginia for dinner at *Mastropiero*, the old Argentinian pizza and pie restaurant on *La Calle Dos de Mayo*. It was near *Malasaña*. So not too far to walk. The stroll took about thirty minutes as they wound their way across *Chueca*. Through all the old narrow streets that used to be full of drug dealers and prostitutes. Past many of Madrid's gay bars. And finally over *Fuencarral* and up *Vicente Ferrer*. The pace was comfortable enough for Gini who chatted happily with both Pedro and Maria. *Mastropiero* was an old family favourite. They always used to refer to it as 'The Revolutionary Place'.

It was a small, peasant eatery with people seated on high chairs at old wooden ledges around the walls. Regulars dined late. They ate using their hands, and chatted raucously about whatever came into their heads. THE most superb dessert on the planet. Ricotta and chocolate cake with a good dollop of Argentinian 'dulce de leche' was always offered there, on the house.

They called it 'revolutionary' because it had old posters for otherwise forgotten South American rebellions. They were in various states of decay, peeling off the walls. It was on the corner of a tiny street known as '*Dos de Mayo*'. May 2 1808 was the noble day the citizens of Madrid unleashed the revolt that would eventually vanquish Napoleon, ending his tyrannic occupation of Spain. Even today, Mastropiero has many small hand-written and mass-produced calls for rebellion. They're stuck into every available gap between the posters, fuelling the anti-government, anti-Europe, post-recession fires that were raging all across Spain.

When they entered the busy restaurant, it was clear they were going to find it difficult to arrange themselves so they could talk face to face. The only option was to sit at one of the ledges, alongside each other, facing the ancient stone wall. This created a curiously anonymous, 'confessional' energy between them. They each seemed more ready to speak from the heart once they didn't have to watch the facial reactions of the others. Because they were so over-stimulated, and worn out by recent events, there was very little by way of small talk. Getting directly to the heart of the matter seemed the best way forward. They each ordered their favourite, high-carb dish from the menu and prayed they'd still have room for *dulce de leche*. A large jug of good, honest, down-to-earth *Tempranillo* arrived with three small peasant glasses. Virginia decided to open up first.

*O God. Where do I begin? I know you must have a few questions.* (Pedro and Maria were trying to suppress their desire to shout *WHAT!!?*)... *I must say, the atmosphere we've somehow managed to create here is like a meeting of Alcoholics Anonymous,* she giggled.

*My name is Virgina Blake, and I sometimes feel that nobody close to me really knows who I am... Dear Jesus, I hardly know myself some days. What you see before you now is Gini Léon: batty old lady, grief-stricken widow of the gorgeous Benjamin Léon. And, while that is all true, it is not the whole truth. The surface never tells the truth, does it? To know me – the real me – you have to go back in time. Back to another country. Another era.*

*Before I fell hopelessly head-over-heels in love with a well-known Spanish conductor named Benjamin Léon, I lived in England where I was doing my Masters degree and sang in a choir at St. John's College, Cambridge. Towards the end of my time there, I was approached by a representative of SIS (Secret Intelligence Service). I could never actually work out if SIS was part of MI6 or some other British Intelligence agency. I later discovered the code name they often used for SIS was 'Box 850'. That was the old Post Office Box number for MI6 during the Second World War.*

*But the point is, I was still very young; it was the early 70s sometime, so I was probably around twenty-three or four. I still knew nothing of the world really. For all I knew of the Intelligence world, the man who recruited me that day could've been anyone. He could've been a Russian spy who'd chosen me for my almost fanatical interest in Socialist Revolution. In any case, what I agreed to was not espionage per se, or anything of the sort. I didn't even hold out much hope of being asked to gather intelligence for them at any point in the future. They knew I'd met Benji in College and was about to move with him to Madrid. But there was no need for anyone new on the ground in Madrid to gather Intel. After all, they had the Embassy minions and their cohorts for that. No. What I had been approached for was precisely what occurred in your presence earlier today. I just became someone they knew they could rely on if they ever needed me to do some small service for the Crown. They also knew they could make the call at any time during my life – wherever I ended up living – and I would probably still feel like being of assistance. We were selected according to our strengths and interests, and they kept an eye on our lives and careers as the decades rolled by. Of course, there was always the possibility they would never call upon us. I have always been on file as a fluent Spanish speaker who was totally mad for Revolutionary Politics, Classical Music, and what has come to be known as Liberation Theology (Gustavo Gutiérrez, and the like). So, in all honesty, I NEVER in my wildest dreams imagined they'd have the need for someone with my peculiar background.*

*So that's that. Now they HAVE called. I didn't think they would, but they have. The jibberish and gobbledy-gook you overheard was what I was brainwashed to say at the training camp in Kent before we left England. I'm amazed I was able to dredge up any of it the way my head is these days, what with this wretched disease and everything.*

*So that's it really, Darlings. What you see before you now, perhaps just a silly old woman, was not always so. Even now, it's not that true... I'm only 62, for God's sake! If it weren't for this blasted brain-muddle thing, you probably wouldn't have been so shocked to discover I was a 'sleeper'.*

*When I was a young woman studying in Dublin, I was considered quite a catch you know. Intellectually, I was streets ahead of most people in my class. And physically, I really blossomed into something of a centre-fold. If we're going to be open with each other about things, you may as well know that I was also a bit of a sexual athlete. I'm sorry if you find that embarrassing, but there it is. I was a total 'goer'! It WAS the end of the Swinging 60s and the start of the Sexy 70s after all. Especially for women, it was a time of tremendous liberation. What freedoms we weren't afforded by right, we simply took for ourselves as a revolutionary act. Sex was a big part of that whole scene. I'm sorry, but without our generation having lots of sex, YOUR generation wouldn't even be here, Sweethearts. Yes, you with all your Gay Liberation and you with your Gender Realignment Surgery, you were born only because WE had lots and lots of sex. And you were born into a world that could grow to accept and support your life choices, largely because us lot made that world possible.*

*But it wasn't all orgies and afros either. There was some serious politics ushering in all that change too. But, mainly – I have to tell you – it was mainly sex. Lots of sex. And love – lots of love, real love, Darlings. Unfortunately, so popular was I that I developed a bit of an addiction to all the sexual attention I was getting at one point. It nearly ruined my entire life. It could have killed me too. But that story's for another day.*

*For now, in the noble spirit of a proper AA meeting, let's just say: Hello. My name is Virginia Blake. And I'm a sex addict turned British Intelligence 'sleeper' turned loving wife and mother turned senile old bag by 62 ... And now I've just turned International Woman of Mystery, who gets to serve On Her Majesty's Secret Service for a day.*

Having miraculously managed not to interject at all, Pedro and Maria glanced at each other then looked with fresh admiration at Gini. In unison, replying: *Hello Virginia!*

*Dulce de Leche* on cake arrived with strong coffee and, after a short period of chit-chat, Pedro piped up.

*OK. It's my turn. Listen up and don't interrupt me, alright?* The other two nodded in agreement with fake 'serious faces' followed by a wry grin.

*I was born the son of a famous conductor. But years later my mother told me he wasn't actually my father at all. I have never really gotten over the shock. Or forgiven my mother... if she is indeed my real mother...*

*Now Pedro,* Gini said. *You can't blame me for everything,* she muttered from behind a raised napkin.

*My therapist wondered if my homosexuality was in fact a tragic attempt to find my real father and make him love me. So, naturally... I changed therapists. The next one advised me to try rebirthing so I could at least begin to accept the body I HAD been born into, regardless of my parentage or sexuality. Well, we all know the hilarious results of that particular little escapade. Decades of sex, drugs and rock n roll later, here I stand before you. A man with a shattered ego...*

*But that's a good thing Sweetie,* whispered Maria.

*... A broken man with a rampant Daddy Complex. I swear, it's all I can do not to check my messages on silverdaddy.com as we speak. Here I stand... half a man. Even my fucking mother calls me 'Consuela'!* Pedro laughed a huge belly laugh and knocked back the last of the wine... *My name is Pedro Léon, and I'm a tortured writer and a functioning alcoholic. What a fucking cliché!*

Virginia and Maria chimed in, *Hello Pedro.*

Just then, Maria spied a small flyer on an adjacent wall. *I don't believe it,* she squealed. And, seeing the nearby diners standing up to leave, she went over to take a closer look.

The flyer said:

*THE REAL REVOLUTION!*

*A WAKEN THE MIND*

*OPEN THE HEART*

*An Online Talk*

*By*

*Jalu Yogi, Tibetan Buddhist Master*

*(Search 'Jalu Yogi' on YouTube)*


*'The REAL Revolution'. I love it... Priceless!* said Gini. *But who or what is a Jalu Yogi when it's at home?* Maria transformed momentarily into a different, previously unseen Maria. An altogether heartening, defrosted Maria. *Jalu Yogi is my Buddhist teacher. We met in Bangkok.*

*Jesus Christ, Maria,* cried Gini. *You're a Buddhist!? Why the hell are you so angry all the time then?*

7

Maria wanted to explain to Gini and Pedro that she'd become Buddhist precisely *because* she was so angry all the time, and not the other way round. So she told them about her life, who she really was.

A year or two before Maria met Pedro, she'd lived in Thailand. As a young boy she looked like *Mr Bean* and had always detested having been born male.

Her mother said Maria had identified as a girl, even when she was no more than a toddler. She said the whole situation developed into a love-hate potion, a mixture of pure joy and excruciating sadness. On the one hand, she said, it was like having a gifted child in the house. On the other, it was like having a son who was a vampire or a werewolf, or something. Both he and the whole family were busy at all times attempting to keep the terrible secret hidden and the appearance of 'normality' intact. A small village in Macho Spain was not the ideal place to raise a girly-boy who'd undoubtedly and inevitably want to blossom one day into a transgender butterfly. Maria's Mam must have seen it all coming and wept heavy, muffled tears in the dead of night.

Maria went to school and played with the other kids as a boy. In the sanctuary of the home, she was allowed to dress as a girl. However, the tension of 'the situation', as Maria's father referred to it, hung over the family like a spectre. By her teenage years, Maria's father couldn't take it any longer. So he moved into his tiny workshop at the end of the garden where he made exquisite cabinets and drank himself into an early grave.

By the time Maria was twenty, she had gravitated towards Madrid where she lived as a *trans* woman and worked in a gay café. She created an outrageously carefree exterior, which belied an often troubled sub-stratum of anger and resentment. This usually co-manifested as loud-mouthed, confrontational bitchiness. Contrary to her own expectations, the cutting side to her persona actually made her more and more popular with the gays, so she indulged it to the Nth degree.

One day, alone in her tiny flat in Chueca, Maria was waxing her legs and half-watching a French TV documentary about primary schools in Thailand. She was suddenly transfixed by the image of a little boy living openly as a girl. The narrator explained that even in small villages, these *Katoey* children were fully accepted and even considered a blessing in some families. Maria couldn't believe her eyes. She wept so uncontrollably she actually howled like a crazy woman. She watched the young Katoey going out of class to use the bathroom, which had been especially designated for this 'third sex'. Wiping away a steady torrent of tears and snot now, Maria watched and watched as she inhaled every last detail of the child. Right there and then, she vowed to save the money for a sex change and go to Thailand. Within a year, she had gathered enough for the operation and the cost of living there for more than a year if necessary. Her friends and family were extremely generous. Her boss at the café offered Maria her job back whenever she wanted to return. Her mother insisted on going along to nurse and support Maria every step of the way, saying *I created you, brought you into this unforgiving world, Darling. I've been here with you through all your good and bad days, and I want to see your true blossoming find its ultimate resolution.*

But Maria managed to dissuade her loving mother from actually having to accompany her, saying she wanted to face the newness of Thailand and the whole experience by herself. She said not to worry, that she would stay in regular contact.

Still forced to travel on a passport that stated Maria del Mar was 'born a male', she arrived in the fabulous new airport at Bangkok late at night. The air was very hot and humid outside the arrivals terminal as she paused for a cigarette before dragging her bags to the taxi. She promised herself that the new Maria would quit smoking, although she doubted the strength of her conviction as she knew they were only a euro a pack.

The taxi took her along the super fast highway, through the toll-booths, and down into 'The City of the Angels' (*Kreung Thep*, as the Thais know it). She'd once heard an ex-junky friend refer to it as 'the city that never weeps'. But Maria was really impressed by the twinkly skyline and how surprisingly modern and futuristic and clean it all appeared. She was also impressed with the taxi man's perceptive and forthright questions. He enquired first of all if he was correct in thinking she wasn't on holidays but moving there temporarily, his friendly eyes sparkling at her in the rear-view mirror. Then his very next question was, *Are you a woman or a transsexual?* Far from seeing this as a rude invasion of her privacy, Maria actually relished the thought of speaking the truth to a total stranger in this strange, foreign land. His English was so good compared to Maria's that they chatted for the 25 minutes or so it took to get to the Malaysia Hotel. She had pre-booked a room for the first few weeks as gay friends had recommended it. The Malaysia was cheap and close to everything and was just a five-minute taxi ride from the Bangkok Nursing Home hospital (BNH) – one of the best medical facilities in the world.

The next few minutes of her full immersion into Thai reality was something she'd reflect on time and time again. Really, it said so much about Thailand.

As she got out of the taxi and walked across the car park to the entrance she noticed some young men – Thais, presumably gay – gathered by the open air restaurant belonging to the hotel. Maria felt drawn by them, compelled to stop and chat for a minute or two. A very brief exchange of pleasantries, cigarettes and small change occurred. It would become an almost daily ritual of mutual interest and respect.

Having sized each other up in an instant, they all knew exactly where they stood. *They* were on the game, some nice, some not. *She* was a pre-op tranny who wasn't going to take any nonsense. They would always subtly try to assert their superiority over a *farang* ('white foreigner'). And she was a pre-op tranny who wasn't going to take any nonsense.

In truth, Maria considered them potential friends – no better nor worse than anyone she'd been close to in Spain – and the 'boys' considered her extremely beautiful, strong and glamorous – like Rihanna, Whitney or J Lo.

The check-in procedure proved problematic. The Lufthansa trolly-dolly previously occupying the room 'reserved' for Maria was having such a good time that he decided to cancel his scheduled trip to Chiang Mai in favour of another week in BKK. *So sorry*, the desk clerk said, *but there is nothing we can do.* Maria was invited to take a seat either in the lobby or the air-conditioned indoor bar-restaurant. The idea was to wait until such time as someone previously intending to stay longer decided to check out unexpectedly, thus freeing up a room. Maria couldn't believe her ears. Surely this was no way to run a business. After 20 minutes of complaining about such an unworkable system, the check-in lady looked up at her, and smiled a panoramic, beatific smile. She pressed her palms together, touching the tips of her fingers to her chin. *This is Thailand, Madame*, she said. *Please be patient and take a seat. Don't think too much. Maybe something will change soon.*

As she sat, Maria recalled reading about 'The Malaysia' in a guidebook a few months earlier. The hotel was originally intended for Thais, not foreigners. Subtle details, on closer inspection, attest to this peculiarity: doors open outwards into the corridors, rather than inwards to the rooms. Each floor has its own small team of ladies in uniforms who clean and prepare rooms and run room service. They are kind and motherly. Even when heavily pregnant, they still show up for work. Siam, always an enigma to Westerners, always somehow fresh and unexpected, usually preferred to do things its own way. Establishing strong trade and cultural ties with strange bed-fellows is the hallmark of an Asian miracle in the ascendant. Thailand rapidly became skilled at sliding its tongue down a twin-edged, honey-coated blade (that unholy three-way alliance she still attempts to juggle with arch-enemies America and China). Like a mistress with two feuding lovers, The Malaysia Hotel had to choose – however temporarily – and subsequently reincarnated as a quasi-doss-house-cum-knocking-shop for U.S. soldiers on leave from the Vietnam War. There was a vivid story in Maria's guidebook about one fateful night when under-cover Vietnamese assassins crept into the hotel and killed some of the Americans as they slept. When Maria found it, though, The Malaysia was coming to the end of its honeymoon period  with a new market: foreign, gay, single men of a certain age and a handful of straight tourists who didn't quite see what was going on around them but who booked online because it was quite cheap. In time, no doubt, she will clean up her act and fling her doors wide open to China, whose nouveau riche travellers seem set to descend on the region like the next wave of incomprehensibility.

But for the moment, at any rate, the Queers still ruled and one was permitted 'without the slightest embarrassment', the guidebook said, to have a newly-made acquaintance join you overnight in your room if you wished. These temporary roommates, it continued, were known locally as 'joiners'. They were usually Thai people of either sex who, having surrendered their I.D. card at the desk downstairs, could accompany guests to their rooms. Whenever the joiner was leaving, the desk clerk would telephone the room to check that everything was OK and nothing unfortunate had happened. Then, all being well, the joiner would have their I.D. returned to them and the guest's final bill would be increased by 100 baht (2 Euro). Americans, Chinese, faggots... Business is business.

Maria noticed with more and more curiosity the various discreet comings and goings through the lobby.

After a further 40 minutes a huge Texan silver daddy, no less, complete with flawless Thai girlfriend and mountains of faux Vuitton baggage came from the lift and swiftly checked out.

*Madame, please come.* The check-in lady motioned Maria to approach the desk. And 30 minutes later Maria del Mar, 'born male', was happily ensconced in her room on the second floor with cable TV, minibar and a view of the pool and car park. Seems 'Old Silver Daddy' and his girly had grown tired of the city and decided to take off to Samui instead. Maria had a triple Jack Daniels and a long shower. She winked knowingly at the long, thick penis and big, shaved balls that smiled back at her from the mirror as she dried off. Then she put the 'do not disturb' sign on the door and waved goodnight to the boys downstairs in the car park before drawing the total-black-out curtains. She slept for about 10 hours straight and awoke to a bright new day.

Over the weeks that followed, for a small fee, the boys from the car park became her trusted helpers and allies. At first she wondered if they'd ever re-emerge from the city's grip with her change and whatever she had dispatched them to find for her. She needn't have doubted or worried. Half-priced beers from 7 Eleven, mobile phone credit, pizza for everyone, even hair-removal wax accompanied by a small packet of Imodium all appeared without fuss, in good time. Maria was learning to be patient and not to think too much... a lot.

Nothing was too awkward or too difficult for them. Although they quickly accepted the existence of certain necessary boundaries and limitations, the truth of the matter was they also provided Maria with a ready-made circle of friends, which included people from all walks of life. There were even some *katoeys*, who would stand the test of time and come to be counted amongst Maria's lifelong soul mates. In what seemed like no time at all, these boys had helped Maria achieve so much, and all with such panache and a sense of fun beyond price. They secured meetings with top surgeons for her at the BNH hospital. They cheered on as Maria bought a whole new wardrobe at the markets in *Pratunam*. The sight of a six-foot Maria in killer heels strutting through the market, followed by her coterie of bag-carriers clad in singlets, shorts, and flip-flops, was actually not at all unusual for BKK.

Eventually, her posse of new-found bosom buddies selected and moved her into a fabulous one-bed condo around the corner. Complete with tropical plants on the 28th floor balcony, and its very own panoramic view of the Chao Phraya river and Kreung Thep's twinkly skyline, it quickly became home.

8

As soon as possible after settling in Bangkok, Maria tried her hardest to cultivate connections with fellow transgender women. She felt hearing their experience would be of great benefit to her.  But the katoeys she met were, at first, completely uninterested in knowing her. Perhaps they'd had their fingers burnt before by a stream of neurotic, cross-dressing 'farang'. Or maybe they didn't want to get involved in witnessing someone else's costly transformation when they themselves couldn't even afford a new bra or a slap-up meal.

Many of the katoeys Maria was meeting were either 'working girls', or 'ladyboys' who performed in shows, or glamorous opportunists who just hung around nightclubs. Some of them had outrageously fabulous names while others were known by relatively masculine, terse names such as Ben or Champ.

In reality, practically one hundred percent of the ladyboys in Bangkok had grown up in small towns and villages buried deep in northern rural Thailand, generally known as 'Up Country'. And that's how they began to connect with Maria too. To them, she was not superior.

Maria was just another trans country bumpkin who gravitated towards the big city to see what's what.

However, when Maria thought deeply about the new people she was getting to know, she found it hard to infer which ones were prostitutes or performers, and which were pre-op or had already completely transitioned. She even struggled to ascertain who had retained their male genitalia as a matter of choice and who was basically just a gay man in drag. In Bangkok, all of those lines are blurred... just as it should be.

Some breast implants she noticed were quite excellent and had either been paid for by wealthy 'sponsors' or by the girl herself after many years of shaving and slaving and saving. Other boob-jobs were so cheap they'd gone horrendously wrong. Maria lit a penny candle for those girls in the Roman Catholic Cathedral of The Assumption down near the majestic river. She offered some incense for them too at the busy Hua Lamphong Buddhist Temple on Rama IV Road.

But, there was no denying it. Most ladyboys Maria knew were really living the life. They fell into two broad categories: those who were glamorous creatures of the night, and those whose sole aim as women was to appear, and just BE, as natural as possible.

Maria adored those precious moments, while moving about town on the Sky Train or in the Metro, when she found herself sitting opposite one of the more 'ordinary' looking katoeys. She would observe their every move and note every detail of how they were dressed. Being natural it seemed was a very subtle, fine art. Maria knew that this was the kind of trans woman she wanted to be. A woman who could blend into a crowd. A woman who was just on her way home from work, probably as a check-out girl in a supermarket like Tops, or as a sales assistant at one of those fancy clothes shops in Siam Paragon. These were ordinary women who could conceivably have straight husbands and modest families quietly tucked away somewhere in the outer suburbs. Of course their true nature would be no secret. No one would be too bothered either way about a woman like that, provided she was a good wife and loved whatever children the Buddha had miraculously somehow managed to send her. There is no shortage of children to love. Previous relationships, the extended family, the streets... If you are open to it, there is love and a ready-made family around every corner.

On the other hand, you could easily find the first type of ladyboy all around town by night. These 'glamorous creatures' were in practically all the gay venues, out socializing with friends or lone she-wolves, stalking. The bars in Soi 4 on Silom Road, the famous DJ Station and G.O.D. nightclubs down the road, and in all the many eateries around the area... They were everywhere.

These ladyboys were so confident, and often so showy and flamboyant they were a really striking addition to any establishment. But rarely did they come across as divas. Somehow they just seemed to fit in. You could find them working in lip-sync and cabaret venues across town. There was also a quota of katoeys in those bars and clubs that sell sex in the hetero ghettoes like Soi Cowboy and Nana Plaza. Apparently they're very popular with 'straight' men who for whatever reason like the novelty of having 'a chick with a dick'.

However, it's worth noting that only around five per cent of all prostitution in Thailand is for the tourist market. The rest is strictly for Thais and remains largely hidden from public view. Those places are almost impossible to find, even with a map. And then having found them you wouldn't be allowed in anyway, as a foreigner. There are also several bars around the city where 'off-duty' ladyboys would go before or after work for a quiet drink and a chat together, without the added bother of having to impress anyone.

After a few months of running with her regular crew, Maria was really starting to look the part. She'd chosen a 'role' for herself. She looked quite ordinary by day, but still very beautiful. And by night she was glammed up to the nines for going out. Her breasts were really starting to show with all the new hormones and preparatory medications her consultant at BNH had given her. They were not very big yet. But they still managed to look voluptuous and soft as silk. She'd probably have implants when the time was right, and a bit of surgery on her face and tummy. Her breasts were tanned, of course, and her nipples were slowly becoming super-sensitive. She'd often become aware of them unexpectedly getting hard as a faint breeze passed through the humid air, caressing her moist skin. Inwardly, she would gasp and release a little sigh. Occasionally, she'd even dare to imagine some hot night in the future when a dark Spanish lover would hold her with thick, strong arms and lick those nipples while his soft moustache brushed against her breasts.

Eventually, Maria became so accepted by the katoey regulars on the scene – and their katoey housewife friends in the suburbs – that over one ordinary yet momentous weekend, Maria finally became friendly with two very different, really amazing katoeys who would change her life completely.

Wen worked in Maria's local 7Eleven of all places, and had a husband and two young daughters. And then there was Mae. Meaning 'Mum' in Thai, Mae was true to her name. Despite being younger than most of them, Mae liked to take care of everyone she met. She was a regular at DJ Station and was the spitting image of Rihanna. Mae showed up late at the club to see friends or hoping to find a 'customer' whenever she hadn't been lucky at the go-go bar she danced in.

It was because of Wen that Maria networked with a small group of trans women living exquisitely ordinary lives. And it was thanks to Mae that Maria was accepted into the intimate circle of katoeys that met for drinks and a laugh in *Hot Bar*.

Near the Skytrain stop for Sukhumvit 22, and long past its prime, in its hayday *Hot* had been a lively katoey go-go bar where stocky English lone wolves went anonymously in search of company. These days, however, Hot Bar was just a drinks bar mostly frequented by working girls on their night off. *Farang* were no longer welcome really, other than part owner George from Newcastle and his close drinking-buddies.

Maria told them about a Bear Bar near where she lived in Madrid called *Hot*. But the coincidence made absolutely no impact on her new friends. Apart from the usual gossip between girls, they seemed to have a pact to leave all talk of bars and clubs and men at the door as they entered their tatty little oasis from all the neon and glitter. For them, Hot Bar had become just what they all needed from a bar. It was a local where a girl could get a cheap drink, bring in some take away food, and chat, and laugh. It was the one place they were sure to get the much-needed energy boost required for going back out. A real woman-to-woman timeout, buoyant and profoundly nourishing. Within just a couple of weeks of going there regularly with Mae, it was in *Hot* that Maria first met a rather unusual-looking cross-dresser from Tibet named *Jalu*... Me.

At that time, I had beautiful long hair tied in a topknot. I still looked quite masculine but I'd learned to carry myself in such a way you'd still believe I was a woman, if you didn't already know otherwise. '*Jalu*', I told her, means '*rainbow*' in Tibetan.

I explained I'd come from a Himalayan kingdom called Sikkim. I said I'd chosen to go to Thailand because I wanted to explore my feminine side in a relatively safe environment, and because it was also a Buddhist country. Bangkok was the only place on the planet where I could totally immerse myself in the trans world, and learn from the experts themselves. They knew exactly how to 'bring out' what was naturally inside all of us. And *that* was the most exciting process for me. Not just for femininity. My whole life has been devoted to finding how to go inside and bring out what is naturally already there, in abundance. The greatest question Buddhism has ever asked is this: *What if whatever we are looking for outside is already inside?*

I loved that group of katoeys. We usually seemed to bring out the best in each other. But, as Thais, they were very direct, very honest... I was told early on by one of the quietest that none of them could quite work me out. She said they considered me dignified yet aloof. No one could ever quite pin me down, or deduce anything much about me. They quickly concluded I was not trans at all, and they were left wondering what I was really up to there.

I've always appeared to be what the British call 'something of an enigma'. Neither one thing nor the other... That's the way I like it. I seem to know a lot about the teachings of the Buddha. But I am definitely not a monk. I wanted to experience the process of living as a katoey, but I would not be doing it afterwards. I am gay, but rarely find other gay men sexually attractive.

For the others, perhaps the strangest thing about me at that time was my own curious version of how a woman ought to dress. Of course, when I say 'curious' I mean 'wrong'. It really did take me a long time to 'get' how to dress. It was months before I found a look that suited me, a look I could reproduce by myself and with enough variety and adaptability for day-to-day living.

My katoey friends never really understood. I wasn't so interested in learning how to *appear* feminine. I wanted to learn from them how to BE your true self. As a Buddhist, I believe we are all Buddhas deep inside. We just need to awaken that dormant perfection to find true happiness. Before I ever went to Thailand I'd heard that the katoeys in Bangkok knew how to go deep inside and awaken what is sleeping there in all of us. That's what I was learning from them. Many deep and lasting friendships blossomed in my life at that time. I'd become so used to being alone that I found all the company quite novel.

Eventually, after lots of requests, I reluctantly agreed to meet Maria away from Hot Bar, just the two of us. She was always drawn to me. I must admit I'd always suspected Maria was a little too hungry to find out whatever she could about me, and Buddhism, and Tibet. I suspected her of being superficial. She'd just satisfy her curiosity and move on. I have no time for such games. So I'd been avoiding her. The Buddha's teachings are not something you can just nibble. Neither should they be devoured.

We sat opposite each other in the restaurant, *Vincent's* on Sathorn Soi One, around the corner from The Malaysia. The owner and his staff were charming in the extreme, as usual. They obviously thought nothing in the slightest about Maria or me, or the sophisticated cocktail dresses we had chosen to wear that night. The food was a fine mixture of Thai and European cuisine, and the atmosphere in the small dining room was private and intimate. Lightly spiced fishcakes, Paneng Gai, Sparkling Water, coquettish glances around about and at each other, followed by Vincent's own homemade cheesecake and strong black coffee. Yet, no matter how Maria tried to open up a meaningful conversation, I decided to keep my distance really. Ever polite, but erudite and aloof as expected. Playful and evasive. I just wouldn't be drawn out. Looking back, I must have seemed so cruel. But I was reading her; how persistent, how serious she was.

As soon as Maria accepted how it was going to go, I used my eyes and a smile to reveal some of the truth to her. The penny dropped. She could see I was simply relishing being in the moment without too much chatter or probing questions. She began to do the same.

Maria realized she'd been too over-zealous from the beginning. That she was grasping at clouds as they passed in the sky. It was only when she relaxed into the moment, simply being with me, that we finally met. Our eyes met often, as we enjoyed our food. We met each other on a very profound level. Maria felt an upswelling of limitless wisdom and compassion that came from within. She no longer wanted anything from me nor wondered what on earth I made of her. From then on we understood our connection. I was able to see deep inside her. And that was that. Who she really was. Not *what*, for a change. But *who*?

There was no need for much conversation at all. We were happy simply being.

We both understood that the person sitting opposite already knew everything. The bond was made. I could sense she imagined I knew all her past and future lives, and all the variety of experiences of her present incarnation too.

Maria felt like a huge social burden had been lifted. For once, she didn't have to analyze or explain a single thing. Maria would later describe the occasion as the first time in her whole life she had the experience of being truly *known*.

We quickly became friends.

Maria would soon discover who *I* was too, and ask to become my student.

# 9

The next morning, all three musketeers had agreed to meet for brunch in Gini's apartment on Gran Via. They needed to discuss her assignment before going over to the private mansion belonging to the British Embassy in the afternoon. Their openness the previous evening had watered the seeds of a far more profound bond between them. There was a freshness in the air that day. They all commented on how it felt like a new beginning. And the two women seemed to have by-passed their usual frosty treatment of each other in favour of a more useful entente cordiale.

As he had promised, Pedro was busy preparing his world-famous spicy sausage risotto with side salad and grilled wild mushrooms. Virginia and Maria sat at the small breakfast table in the kitchen observing his every move and discussing the nature of dreams.

*Why do we have dreams?* Gini wondered.

*Yes, what do they mean? Are they really supposed to mean anything at all, do you think?* Maria asked. *I have been thinking recently about the power of recurring dreams. Do you dream much Virginia?*

*O Yes, Dear, Gini said emphatically. I think I must dream at least two times a night, if not three. In fact I find it increasingly difficult to distinguish between my dreams and this so-called reality!* They both laughed heartily. *I seem to be losing my grip on 'reality' to the extent that I don't really care if what I experience is a dream or being awake, good or bad. If I don't particularly like what's going on, I simply try to 'change channel' – cut through the energy of the situation, and move on. It's when you let yourself get stuck that you have problems. Keep moving, that's what I always say.* Directing her voice across to Pedro, *Isn't that right, Consuela love? Keep moving, that's what I always say, isn't it?*

*Yes Mama,* replied Pedro. Virginia seemed slightly shocked.

*You almost never call me Mummy anymore, Darling. Why have you suddenly started again today?*

*Because we have spent so much time not calling each other Mother and Son over the years. In the spirit of last night's exchanges at Mastropiero, I wanted to use those words again to resurrect the truth of who we really are to each other. Don't worry, I would never embarrass you in public with it, but you are my Mum after all.*

Maria re-entered the busy soundscape, *O isn't that just the sweetest thing,* she mocked. *Yeah-yeah. Whatever! You're his mother, he's your son. Get a room, for Buddha's sake! Meanwhile, back to me. HELLO! I was talking you know... I asked if you had any re-CURRING dreams, Gini. But you never really answered. You just went off on one of your little tangents, Dear.*

Pedro came over and kissed Maria on the head saying; *Now that's the Miss del Mar we all know and love. The bitch is back! Wondered how long it would take.* Then he kissed Gini on the cheek and said, *I love you so much Mum. And I miss you when you're off in your own little world, however momentarily. I miss you, Sweetheart.*

Choking back a very un-British tear, Gini moved swiftly on and began telling Maria of the recurring dreams of Jelly-Yoghurt she's had most of her life. She described the scene with all the rainbow light. How her imaginary friend and guide has always been like a spiritual teacher for her. Virginia confided how, rather than diminishing over the years, the dreams of Rainbow Man have actually increased in frequency. Especially more recently, for some reason.

Maria could hardly contain herself! She launched into a florid explanation:

*'Jalu', my Buddhist teacher's name, actually MEANS 'Rainbow'. 'Jalu Yogi' sounds too close to 'Jelly Yoghurt' to be a mistake!* Maria pleaded with Gini to try to meet me in person as soon as possible as I was obviously meant to be her spiritual friend too. *There ARE no coincidences in life, she continued. Everything happens for a reason – as a teaching.*

Maria was getting busy writing out all my contact details. As a taster she shared the web address of the online talk they'd read about on the flyer in the restaurant. Virginia, feeling a bit manoevred, decided to cut in and distract her by changing the channel: *Tell me about YOUR recurring dreams then Maria. What preoccupies your little bundle of neurotic, grey cells while YOU sleep?*

Maria, now fully distracted from writing, listed a few standard recurring themes that almost anyone might have. But then she brought herself quickly back to centre by sharing that she hardly ever dreamt of her teacher directly, as such. How she envied Gini.

*I sometimes feel I receive profound teachings INDIRECTLY from Jalu through my dreams, but I don't really understand them,* Maria explained. *For example, recently I was dreaming over and over of needing to get away from crowded situations where I was in great danger. The weirdest thing was that people in the dream would whisper 'Ave Maria' into my ear as they brushed past. Over and over, always the same thing... 'Ave Maria, Ave Maria'.*

Gini thought this was absolutely hilarious, that Maria must be suffering from some sort of Messiah Complex. But Maria was unperturbed by such jibes. She insisted, *No! It's something much more important than that. It's another of Jalu's coded messages. I'm certain of it. It's as if my life is in danger – all our lives – and the solution is 'Ave Maria', somehow.*

*Don't think too much, Maria. You'll make yourself ill,* Pedro said.

*You see. You SEE!* Maria cried. *That's what the receptionist at the Malaysia said to me too! I'm convinced of it now. There ARE no coincidences! I'm really beginning to believe that practically everything is some kind of spiritual teaching.*

*If Jalu really were trying to contact you,* Gini interjected, *and teach you through your dreams – but you say you have each other's contact details – wouldn't it make far more sense for Jalu to email you or pick up the phone or something? And why the hell does he have to be so cryptic all the time?... 'Ave Maria', I ask you! What the hell is that supposed to mean??*

*We DO have ordinary, direct contact too, Gini. Sometimes we text one another to say 'hi' or if I have a particular question or something. But the indirect approach seems to be how these things work with Jalu. He's extremely perceptive, you know. One day, I got the most bizarre text from him when we were staying at the beach in Phuket for a little holiday after my surgery. It read, 'Big wave coming. Fly. Fly!' He went missing. So I jumped on the next available flight back to Bangkok and narrowly avoided the Tsunami! Jalu had decided to stay behind to warn anyone who'd listen. And to simply be with the survivors afterwards... I told you that, Pedro, didn't I?*

*OK, OK ladies, Pedro said. That's enough of all that for one day. Lunch is ready. Please set the main table and help me bring it all through to the dining room.*

Over lunch, the talk meandered back and forth from Gini the 'sleeper' and her brainwashing/training in Kent, to the basic human need for sleeping and dreaming. From precisely why British Intelligence was involved in the transit of a man from South America, to stories of other times when spiritual teachings had brought profound meaning to Maria's life.

Virginia and Pedro touched and held hands across the table a couple of times and really appeared to rejoice in the lucidity of this particular juncture in their often fragile relationship. At one point they even ignored Maria altogether as she explained what meditation really is. Gini reminded Pedro that she never knew which of her lovers had made her pregnant with him. And Pedro reassured Gini that he loved her madly and always would. Meanwhile, Maria continued to talk and talk... and talk and talk, effectively missing the power of the present moment entirely. *Meditation and mindfulness,* she explained, *is a powerful tool for living life to the full. It could release all of one's natural, innate potential for awakening in a flash. Or it could prove to be a much longer process, one that may even stretch across many lifetimes.* She noticed how physically close Pedro and Gini were and ventured: *You don't believe your connection with each other has only been established in THIS lifetime, do you? Or that we three have not run about together many times before?*

"The vast ocean of time and space", Maria finally concluded (obviously quoting from some book or other), "whether by enormous wave or tiny ripple, brings flotsam and jetsam together which clings and remains together, sometimes for many aeons".

The next hour or so was spent, in relative silence, doing the washing up and getting ready to go out for Gini's mind-boggling afternoon tea date. Before they had the chance to jump into a taxi outside, Virginia announced she wanted to go for a very strong coffee with brandy (strictly for medicinal purposes) at Chicote, just down the street, to steady her nerves. After quickly checking their watches for time, Pedro and Maria agreed and soon they were all sitting opposite each other again in the window of what has to be one of the finest café-bars from the 1930s, anywhere in the world.

The three sat silently for a while, mustering all their strength. The room has a beautiful combination of original period features with some modern touches. Lovingly maintained in the Art Deco style, Chicote is wall-to-wall class. The signature wood-panelled walls are magnificent. Unfortunately, they're almost entirely covered with framed photos of Celebs nowadays. But the eye finds peace elsewhere. There is so much dark hardwood, juxtaposed with beautiful chrome trim. Even the original seating is intact. This particular haunt has always been popular with celebrities, artists and writers. Virginia had sat there on many a previous occasion and imagined around her such luminaries as Frank Sinatra, Orson Welles, and Ernest Hemingway. She even envisioned such inferior, contemporary creatures as Catherine Zeta Jones, and the once ubiquitous Hugh Grant. She also loved to evoke the buzz of the world's Foreign Press Corps gathered there to bear witness to the Spanish Civil War and, later on, the frivolous frolics and hijinks of the many prostitutes who took refuge in Chicote during the Franco era. Above the door outside it still said Museo Chicote, for reasons unknown to Virginia, but this was no museum. It was very much alive and continued to encapsulate the vibrant spirit of Madrid. Though slightly too expensive for the pocket of the ordinary Madrileño, a cocktail and a snack at Chicote was so sumptuous it was universally considered worth every penny.

After a bit of a chat about the weather, Gini noted she was still understandably feeling quite apprehensive and it was time to get going. So, while Virginia took her medication, Pedro paid the account and left a good tip for their waiter José, whom they'd come to know very well over the years. Moments later, they were headed across town for that little piece of Britain in the sun.

10

I have always been considered an unusual bird, even by those who really know me. But not many people get that close.

I live my life practically incognito, preferring to wander from place to place, without roots. I suppose I am something of a rare breed. As an adult, my life aspires to echo the mendicant tradition of Tibetan Buddhist saints such as Milarepa, Shabkar and Patrul Rinpoche.

Mine is the path of a meditator, a yogi. So, I often spend extended periods of time doing personal retreat in caves, monasteries, hotel rooms. Outwardly, I display a carefree, 'crazy-wisdom' streak, which has drawn me to unusual, often dangerous places and situations. I am drawn wherever I feel I can be of some service, just by being there. That's how I went to Phuket. It's how I ended up in Spain. I need to learn. I need to be where the people are.

Emulating the path of an irreverent warrior, I had originally confined myself mainly to the East. But recently I found myself drifting Westwards, visiting some of my students in Europe and America, to see where that might lead. Sometimes I am invited. Other times, I arrive practically unannounced. I sometimes travel anonymously and take part-time jobs in unusual settings, or I go homeless. Anything to meet and observe the needs of people. The countries I choose are based on my own instincts about what is happening there (or is about to happen). I pray to see if my presence might help shed some light. It would never be my style or intention to make a big splash. Far from it! I simply want to be present with whatever is going on in the world. Just as I did in Thailand during the Tsunami, I've always been committed to drawing attention and bearing witness to events. But I'm no saint either. I simply intend being with those most affected by suffering, and to help if I can. Above all else, this particularly vague path is exactly how I want my life to unfold for the next few years.

Once, feeling daunted by the true meaning of the Buddha's teachings, I asked my master precisely how I could show love and compassion to all beings. In characteristic form, he simply replied the only way to love them all was one being at a time.

A key part of my new life is to go out into the unfamiliar world and learn as much as possible about people. My hope is to put myself in as many strange and new situations as possible, often at the very edge of society, in order for my personal experience of life to expand and grow. Really, I have so little experience of what is out there. It was for this reason too that I'd gone to Thailand. The ladyboys of Bangkok were showing the world how to transform from within. Whether bringing out our inner lady or our inner Buddha, the route is the same; From outside, look in. From inside, bring out.

Through meditation and sustained effort, each one of us has the opportunity to go inside and awaken our own Buddha Mind. Our innate qualities of wisdom and compassion are lying practically unused just under the surface, and we only have to tap into them and they will flow limitlessly for the benefit of all, like a river of healing light or an inexhaustible shower of blessings. I went to be with the katoeys to learn from their wisdom.

Because I am not a monk, I was not bound by any code of how to dress or act, as such. And because I am gay, I was already quite comfortable moving around the margins. As a single man, I was always free to stay or go as I pleased. But my greatest freedom stemmed from being a Buddhist yogi, a practitioner of The Way. I am familiar with the many pitfalls, but also the innate power of the human mind. It is this, the Greatest of All Freedoms, that affords a small town boy such as me all the carefree, crazy-wisdom, and the enlightened courage needed to navigate the world and its ways.

I was born to doting Tibetan parents living in exile in India. They'd been nomadic yak herders on the fertile plains of Tibet all their lives until one day my mother had a vision. Mum was a very ordinary, simple woman. Her only spiritual practice was the repetition of the 'Mani Mantra': *Om Mani Pémé Hung.* But she did it so continually and so purely that the mantra suffused her entire being with stability and blessing. Mother's vision was of Chenrézi – the Buddha of Compassion – and he appeared to float in the ripples on the surface of the lake. He warned her Tibet would soon fall to the Chinese invaders and that she had to gather her family, just a handful of their most treasured possessions, and flee to safety over the snow-peaked mountains to a new land in the south. In the event, the whole extended family fled over the Himalaya on foot. Extreme terrain and weather conditions claimed the lives of many of them. It is nearly impossible for us to imagine their great suffering and tremendous courage. The journey took many months and brought them down to India where so many of them lived and died in squalid, disease-ridden refugee camps. The Tibetans didn't know how to look after themselves in this new land. They didn't speak any of the languages, and even the food was so alien to them. If they found something raw thrown in the gutter they took it back to their tent but didn't know what to do with it.

Eventually the young couple, who would later become my parents, heard of a Tibetan community gathering in the borderland Himalayan Kingdom of Sikkim. The kingdom is wedged between Bhutan, Nepal, and their own beleaguered Tibet. The exiled Tibetans were drawn to this high place for a variety of good reasons, not least of which was they wanted to be as close as possible to the Tibetan border in order to facilitate a swift return once the free world had intervened and liberated Tibet. Tragically, decades later, their pleas to the international community continue to fall on deaf ears. Even now, the descendants of those first Tibetan refugees still dwell in mountainous border regions and pray to return one day soon to the homeland they have never seen.

My parents were quite invisible in this new world inhabited largely by other Tibetans. They had no status and no skills for making money. So they set up a roadside stall selling tasty momos and other Tibetan favourites on the path between the Royal Palace and the monastery of the revered Buddhist master, Dzogpa Chenpo Rinpoche. This monastery, in so many ways, was the major focus for all Tibetans living in and around the Sikkimese capital Gangtok. The small town clings to both sides of a ridge that runs along the top of a steep mountain. The monastery perches on a ledge, just below the town, that juts out and seems to float above the valley far below.

It was into this tiny cosmos, this lofty exile from which you could peer longingly and anxiously back into Tibet, that I was born. Just one child among many, my given name was Péma. And, in the traditional Tibetan way, my date of birth went unrecorded. No one ever really knew or cared exactly how old they were. I worked hard for my parents running errands and helping in their tiny makeshift kitchen by the side of the road.

One day, as a very young boy, I was standing to attention in a small crowd by the dusty roadside as the King's mother passed by... I gasped and, thinking I was talking to my mother behind me, exclaimed: *O how wonderful it must be to be Royal!* When I turned to look for a response, an old man standing behind me said: *O Yes, child. But how much more wonderful to be a Buddha!* That was the beginning of a lifelong connection with my first spiritual guide, Dzogpa Chenpo Rinpoche. He said we had been master and student, student and master, for many lifetimes. I was to be afforded every courtesy at his monastery from that moment on. I didn't know how to respond. I was in shock. This was the most saintly master in the region; his very name meant 'Great Perfection, Precious One'. The whole of Gangtok and the surrounding countryside buzzed with the news. A complete nobody, a random vagrant, had been plucked off the street – practically out of thin air – I was to be ritually recognized and installed as the reincarnation of Dzogpa Chenpo Rinpoche's former master.

Soon after, as my astonished, tearful parents sat in the place of honour in the front row at the Temple, Dzogpa Chenpo Rinpoche (known as 'Dzogchen' Rinpoche) made the formal announcement in public. He had done this on many an occasion before and was famous for identifying reincarnate lamas as very young children. To everyone's amazement I, the scruffy kid formerly known as Péma, was scrubbed to within an inch of my life, and dressed in monks robes. They smothered me in the finest silk brocades with fur trim, and seated me on a high throne facing a beaming Dzogpa Chenpo Rinpoche. There was an enormous gold statue of the Buddha and several hand-painted images of Padmasambhava, the Indian saint who brought Vajrayana Buddhism to Tibet in the Eighth Century. From the ceiling hung long tubes of elaborately embroidered silk, and all around the walls were pictures of the most ornate Peaceful and Wrathful Deities imaginable.

*I have found my teacher's 'tulku'*, Dzogchen Rinpoche declared to an incredulous crowd. *Henceforth the reincarnation's name shall be Rangjung Long Gyé* (Spontaneously-manifesting Vast Expanse). The temple musicians began playing their shawms and horns and drums. The sound filtered through the crowds standing outside and off into the surrounding hillsides and valleys beyond.

I don't really remember much of it. But I'm told that suddenly, and at little more than ten years old, I rose to my feet and descended to the ground below our host's high throne. There, I proceeded to make three perfect prostrations before Rinpoche. Though I say it myself, the exchange that followed quickly became the stuff of legend. It was high drama, like a blockbuster or an Indian soap opera. A microphone-type contraption was passed to me as I began to address the great Rinpoche, and the expectant assembly behind me:

*I am just an ordinary boy. I'm not the one you say I am. If I am a baby-buddha, I am so because I share the same potential as every other living being to become Buddha. I am nothing special at all. As my given name Péma suggests, we are all like a 'lotus blossom'. Our roots are firmly planted in the filthy mud. But, given the right circumstances, we bloom into magnificent flowers. It is indeed my heart-felt aspiration to become an awakened, fully enlightened being. But it is not for my own sake – or because of who I may have been in a previous lifetime – but for the sake of others, that they may also find the true path to liberation. With your loving help and expert guidance, Rinpoche, I know I can do it. So I most humbly request that you accept me as your student. Please take me not as a monk – for I have to continue working for my family – but as an ordinary boy who wishes to tame his mind and open his heart by following in the footsteps of all the buddhas and bodhisattvas. I'm so sorry if this offends or upsets anyone, but I am convinced that this is my true path. If you don't mind, I would like to go now and spend some time alone, away from all this noise and fuss. But I have to ask again: Will you still take me under your wing and nurture my progress, Rinpoche?*

The venerable lama, Dzogpa Chenpo Rinpoche, was completely unsurprised and unshaken by the declarations of this young boy, whom he joked had come as a wise old wolf dressed in the clothes of a lamb. He looked me straight in the eyes and said, *What you say is so typical of you, you little rascal. I KNOW you are him. You were always such a rebel. You say you're not him, but I know what I know, and that's that. Anyway, the outcome is just the same. I have found you and you want to learn the practice for awakening the Buddha Nature within you. It is no surprise at all that you want to do it all your own way. That's nothing new to me ... Master. So, once again old friend, I agree to be your guide this time around provided you agree to do the same for me in a future life. You're a funny, funny little man. Always were and always will be. It has forever been your habit to suddenly come into my life and disappear again just as quickly. It is so like you to arrive mysteriously and unannounced then, having shone your light for a little while, to go off again. For that reason, this time around, I shall name you 'Jalu' ('Rainbow'), and with your parent's permission you will call me 'Pa-la' ('Father'). Together, we will see just how far along the path to awakening a so-called 'ordinary boy' can travel.*

As the weeks and months rolled by, most people eventually stopped talking about me altogether and I melted back into the fabric of everyday life in Gangtok. Of course, I continued working at my parents' dumpling stall and went to school, where I quickly learned to read and write. I consumed my education with great gusto. And soon enough I also had a functioning knowledge of Tibetan, Chinese, Sanskrit, Hindi and English. The neighbours were amazed.

It was hard work at that age, learning languages and the sacred texts. Science and philosophy blissfully stretched my thinking mind beyond its limits. But my favourite time of all was practising meditation with Rinpoche. I loved walking through the pre-dawn twilight over to Pa-la's monastery. Once admitted to his cozy room, I would sit on the floor beside Rinpoche's bed. He'd already be sitting upright, meditating, ready to begin. That was how, at 4 o'clock most mornings, I received the spiritual teachings from Dzogchen Rinpoche, while the town still slumbered, before the so-called 'normal' day began and it was time for me to return to work on the momo stall.

Months turned into decades, and gradually the tried and tested path of Awakening was lovingly transmitted to me. Both Rinpoche and I could sense the teachings and the practice gradually illuminating my core being. With ever-increasing gratitude, I received all the teachings and mind-to-mind transmissions. Sometimes, not as student and teacher, we would simply take tea together and chat before having a quiet stroll in the gardens at dawn.

But there were also periods of intensive meditation practice. Sometimes I would be sent away for months of solitary retreat in isolated places far away from home. But I always felt cherished and sustained by the loving presence and constant blessing of my mentor, no matter how tough the going was or how alone I seemed to be. In time, I came to experience the loving care of my master in all situations and regardless of circumstances or where I was. Whether together or far apart, we had become – just as Dzogchen Rinpoche intended – father and son. Inseparable, either by life or by death.

My growing determination to fully awaken didn't even falter when Rinpoche sent me away to the far-off, ancient city of Varanasi on the banks of the holy mother Ganges.

A disciple's devotion for his Guru should never stray into the mire of attachment or aversion. It must transcend all superficial reactions and habitual tendencies. Of course, one's Root Guru – your first master – will always have a special place in your heart. But it is so important not to become too attached or needy. That's dangerous territory indeed, for all concerned. It's only a hop, skip and a jump from joining a 'personality cult', which could never lead to true awakening, or even ordinary happiness.

Wisely, the Root Guru often dispatches disciples to go finish their studies with other masters. So it was that I was dispatched to Varanasi on the Sacred River, a place older than history itself.

I was sent there to study under another great lama, an elderly layman called Nyima Özer Rinpoche ('The Sun's Rays'). He lived in a tiny monastery, up a narrow laneway. It was just a stone's throw away from the famous Deer Park at Sarnath where the recently enlightened Buddha had been persuaded to give his first teachings, over 2,500 years ago.

In time, I also came to perceive this humble, almost magical, old man as inseparable from my root master, and all the Buddhas. I stayed there for many years. Our connection ran so deeply, I never wanted to leave him and only agreed to go away for short periods of time. I was always by his side.

By the time he passed away, sitting upright in profound luminosity, the precious one known as The Sun's Rays had transmitted to me all that he'd come to realize himself.

However, without my anchor, I began to drift. And within a few short months I found myself in the Kathmandu Valley. There was a long-term retreat centre at the far end of the valley, with a small group of advanced meditators from the West doing intensive practice there. I was invited to remain with them and share in turn what little I had come to embody as a yogi. They were in the middle of a strict retreat that would last the traditional three years, three months and three days, so I stayed. The day after the retreat finished I visited the famous Stupa at Boudhanath. Transfixed by its enormous eyes, I prayed: *O Precious Awakened One. Please hear my deepest aspiration... Bless me into usefulness.*

A couple of days later, just like a rainbow, I simply disappeared into the landscape and began my wandering ways.

# 11

At the gate of the British Embassy's private mansion, the security guard advised Virginia and her two confidantes to send the taxi away as the car didn't have clearance to enter. Gini paid and thanked the driver. Then she, Pedro and Maria were invited into the gate lodge to sit while their security passes were verified. From the outside, the lodge appeared like a small concrete bunker, which almost blended into the high fortress wall running around the perimeter of the large grounds. Judging by what little they could discern from their vantage point, it was a strange kind of place. It was not the residence of the Ambassador. Neither was it the main public office for visa applications and consular services. Their best guess was that they were about to be allowed into a large English stately home, set beautifully in a rolling landscape. It was a world apart from the ordinary. A private domain in which the cogs of International Relations ground and whirred to the sound of their own self-created self-importance.

Of course, the name Virginia Blake-Léon was on the list of those to be permitted entrance for that day but she still had to provide passport identification to confirm who she was. Gini joked that she hardly knew herself who she was these days. Pedro and Maria were only cleared to enter certain parts of the main building while Gini was reminded that her meeting was to be held in absolute privacy, over tea in the 'Churchill' drawing room with a certain Mr Brown. Interestingly, formally identifying Maria was problematic, as usual. But, with true British flair, the functionary at the lodge rendered it a minor issue. Maria was cleared to enter, but not before she and the middle-aged lady doing the clearance appeared to have a very brief and mysterious private chat.

Maria had been dreading the moment she'd have to present her passport again to someone whose duty it was to go over it in fine detail. Maria still feared awaiting rejection or approval more than almost anything else in life. She just objected, with every fibre of her being, to elevating others to a height from which they could look down and judge her. Her passport continued to identify her as male and, as far as she knew, even officially changing her name to 'Maria del Mar' wouldn't solve the *problem* as her gender would always indicate 'born male'.

As she awaited permission to carry that particular passport whilst wearing that particular low-cut, Prada summer dress, Maria said a quiet little prayer to the Universe. In time-honoured tradition, imagining her master radiating rainbow light, inseparable from all the buddhas and bodhisattvas, opening her heart Maria prayed: *O Lama, Care for me. In circumstances good or bad, in situations high or low, I completely rely on you. Please help me now.* It was just then that the clearance lady leaned in close and had her private moment with Maria.

As they were all led out of the gate lodge, the first thing Pedro asked was, *Well-well Mata Hari, what was all that about? Was she looking for a date or something?*

*No no, baby,* Ms del Mar beamed. *I can't believe it! That nice lady is gay! She gave me her wife's phone number over at the Spanish department of Foreign Affairs. She said she believed  my passport could be legally altered to include the name-change and OMIT all reference to birth gender! This is what I've been praying for all these years... I can't believe it actually happened because of our little day out with your mother, of all people!*

They chatted away as they meandered along the drive up to the main house. Gini seemed preoccupied, naturally enough, but appeared none-the-less to adore the walk through the English country garden that stretched out around them. *This is gas,* she commented. *You might as well be strolling through the grounds of a country mansion in Wiltshire.* The icing on the cake was a huge British flag, the 'Union Jack', billowing in the soft Spanish breeze above the fantastic portico. The mansion had been built by British labourers in the nineteenth century, in the style of Inigo Jones and Robert Adam. As they were led into the vast, opulent entrance hall, a Third Secretary who introduced himself as Stanley Crawford, invited Pedro and Maria to tea with the admin staff. A Miss Evans ushered Virginia through various security check-points all the way along the main downstairs corridor. A short ascent followed in a super-modern, six-person lift. Gini noticed the manufacturer straight away, Schindler. *Schindler's Lifts? Really?* Then Miss Evans walked Gini into a very large upstairs drawing room. It was set out like a grand hotel suite with a sitting room at one end and a library, complete with enormous antique desk, at the other. Miss Evans announced Mrs Virginia Blake-Léon's arrival. In the distance they could see Gini's host was still speaking on an old-world telephone resting on a Queen Anne side table. Beneath a curiously grotesque portrait of Sir Winston Churchill, a well-dressed gentleman in his late forties mumbled, *She's here. Have to go now. Talk later Sir. Cheerio.*

Then, walking towards Gini with an outstretched hand – perfectly manicured fingernails and glittering cufflink – he finally addressed her: *Ah Mrs Blake-Léon. Welcome to Her Majesty's home from home in the sun. May I call you Virginia?*

*You most certainly may not*, she grinned a very British smile, the likes of which might conceal anything from utter contempt to intent to marry. *And who might YOU be, Dear?*

*I'm Brown. Mr Brown*, he said rather apologetically for somewhat jumping the gun. It hadn't gotten off to the flying start he anticipated. Apparently, he noted, his usually disarming diplomatic charm wasn't going to win over this particular old bird.

*I have to tell you Mr Brown, I am not particularly impressed by very much these days, so please don't stand on ceremony. Just get to the point, if you don't mind. I've only come along to hear what The Crown would have me do by way of service at this late stage in my life. To be perfectly honest with you Dear, I could just as easily have been persuaded that day on the bridge in Cambridge to become a Communist spy. Lucky for Her Majesty, your man got to me first, eh?*

*Quite*, Brown smirked. *Mrs Léon. I see you rather enjoy playing the loose canon. What fun. So I'll press on if that's OK with you.*

*Oh please call me Virginia, Mr Brown. And by the way, I KNOW that's not your real name either. Oh, and another thing Dear, you haven't told me WHAT you are supposed to be yet. I mean your rank, your function in this 'Palacio de los Gringos'. You do realize that's what the Spaniards call this place, don't you?*

*Yes Virginia. I had heard a whisper to that effect alright. As for my identity, my name is Mr Brown and I am the 'high-up' in charge of – O let's say – paperclips, and photocopying. Petty cash, that sort of thing. But don't underestimate my influence. I may just be the man who saves your life one day.*

*As you wish, 'High Up'. Let's get on with the business of the day then, shall we?*

*Virginia,* he finally began. *Make no mistake – as we sit by the window at this exquisite occasional table and share high tea, while your amigos are downstairs having coffee and biscuits with the typing pool – what we are asking you to do for us is no small thing.*

*We want you to sign the Official Secrets Act again, after we do a brief Psych Evaluation to establish how far your condition has progressed. We must assess your suitability for the mission. We also need you to sign a waiver, should everything go horribly wrong and you suffer injury or death in the service of Her Majesty.*

Once agreed, all the formalities were dispensed with. Gini's Early Onset Alzheimers/Vascular Dementia was re-confirmed and she was cleared for active duty provided she continued to take her tablets. Although she felt vaguely upset at having her 'condition' referred to at all, Gini accepted the mission as if she were still that young woman at the training facility in Kent. She felt her consciousness was being catapulted back across the decades and she had just volunteered. Gini felt again all the sublimated ego that accompanies the *caché* of being in the Secret Service rising up within her. So she just managed to catch it in time, before it got out of control.

Gini wanted to regain control over her mind – her life – more than anything. She was sick and tired of behaving, and being treated like, a woman in her eighties especially as she was still only in her sixties.

But there was an upside, for once, to Alzheimers. Gini's illness had rendered her brain more comfortable dwelling in the past than the present. And all this talk of service and missions brought her back to a time when her mind was crystal clear and her youthful energy was high.

Brown outlined the mission in general terms at first, just to recap what she was getting into. Then he went into much more detail so Gini understood exactly who she was meeting, where and when, and the limits of what she was allowed to discuss with him before putting him on the plane that would carry him on the next leg of his journey.

The name of the man she was to meet was Karl Weithaler and he was a Roman Catholic priest, of European decent. He was born and raised in South America. His native tongue was Spanish, but he also spoke English and two other languages. He was expecting take-away coffee and a small cake, and a lively discussion about his favourite subjects: Liberation Theology and Revolutionary Politics. And, since that was such a huge part of who Virginia was, that's why she'd been the perfect choice for the job. Father Weithaler was travelling from Argentina to Rome for a very important meeting. Nothing was to prevent him from arriving there safely. As previously promised, there would be an inconspicuous, armed security presence at the airport. This was to be provided by a number of different governments, who would remain nameless. The British Government in particular, had a very high stake in his safe transit. Therefore they were co-ordinating the entire operation. The only thing Gini had to do was chat away as if they were old friends and see him to the boarding gate for his onward flight.

Virginia expressed mild excitement at the prospect of meeting someone with similar interests to her own. But she also disclosed a little concern she might get caught up in some danger beyond her control if anything went wrong. 'High Up' reassured Gini she was still well able for the task at hand, and anything unforeseen beyond coffee and a chat was *their* department, not hers. Before she left, Gini was to be given a file. It contained all the relevant details including background biographical info, maps of the airport, and a return ticket to London in her name. The idea was she'd pretend to be flying to the United Kingdom in order to gain access to the airport's internal, more secure, transit areas. There she would meet Fr Karl at the designated point. Then, having completed her mission, Gini was to simply leave the airport without flying. She joked she might be tempted to travel to London for a short break, but High Up countered that the ticket would be cancelled before the London flight boarded.

Warming to each other slightly now, the two briefly discussed the layout of the airport, and their 'Plan B' if anything unexpected should occur. Fr Karl would be whisked away by the special operatives, and Gini was to go her separate way and take the Metro home where she should await further instructions. Obviously, neither Pedro nor Maria would be able to accompany her to the actual rendezvous but they were permitted to wait for Gini at the nearest staircase that leads to the Metro below.

Perhaps the funniest thing about that day was, once the official part of the meeting was concluded, both Gini and High Up tucked into the traditional afternoon tea like two English Public School boarders allowed to join the Head Master in his private study. Never before had an assortment of sandwiches with their crusts cut off tasted so truly scrumptious. Nor had miniature confectionaries followed by fruit scones with raspberry jam and clotted cream ever gone down so well. So typically English, so polite and socially versatile, the two nattered away like old colleagues about current affairs and the weather. They didn't even seem to notice the time until the last drop of the second pot of Darjeeling was gone.

Practically one hour to the minute after the meeting had begun, the *three amigos* – as they'd come to think of themselves – were in the back of a chauffeur driven Embassy car headed back to Gran Via. Asking politely if he had time, Virginia requested the driver to bring them on a little tour of the centre of Madrid. It was rare that any of them travelled in such style and they really wanted to make the most of the moment. Gini commented how she hadn't actually been through the streets of her adopted city for many years. Of course, she had. But Gini wanted the moment to be special. She opened the window on her side of the car, put her head back, eyes closed, and simply inhaled the smells and sounds of each place as they passed.

Outside, all life was going on around her. But in her mind Gini was deeply rooted in the past, holding her husband Benjamin's hand.

From time to time, she opened her eyes just enough to note where she was. It appeared they were gradually spiraling around the city and inward. Virginia saw the *Retiro* as they turned one corner, the Fountain of the Earth Goddess on her chariot at *Las Cibeles* after another turn, the *Circulo de Bellas Artes* and the *Telefonica* building. The Royal Palace and the Cathedral were next. Then *Plaza Mayor* and *Puerta del Sol*. Finally, Gini had the driver go along the *Calle Espoz y Mina* – where she'd first lived with Benjamin – to stop outside their old flat and beep the horn for the neighbours. Of course no one came out to investigate. Most of the people from her time were long dead. But Gini imagined her old nemesis, the Señora Garcia-Martinez, glaring at them in their fancy car from behind her filthy lace curtains. With a triumphant air, Virginia imperiously commanded the chauffeur to move on.

She told him he could drop them off on Gran Via, as they would be going to *Chicote* (for the second time in one day). There they basked in the early evening haze and enjoyed a few rounds of Brandy Alexanders. *Chin-chin Darlings*, Virginia said as she toasted her two comrades. *These are on The Queen.*

*Anyone we know?* chuckled Pedro. *You do realize Gini,* Maria laughed out loud, *you probably aren't supposed to drink alcohol on those tablets of yours? Ah, don't think too much Sweetheart,* Gini replied as they fell about laughing. *You only live once, right?*

*Really?* said Maria.

## 12

Pedro and Maria escorted Gini, arm in arm, back to her place and got her to bed. Gini had coined a new catch-phrase during the evening and their friendly waiter didn't seem to mind how many times she said it, provided there would be a good tip at the end of it all. It was Gini's last garbled utterance before falling into a deep sleep: *José, Alexander me!*

Maria whispered, almost wetting herself, *Just as well we weren't drinking 'Screwdrivers' all night. 'José, Screw Me!'*, she cackled.

Like two drunken schoolgirls trying not to get caught sneaking back into their dorm, Pedro and Maria muffled their laughter with both hands clasped over their mouths. They crept through the dim, dappled half-light of the beautiful old apartment trying to get out without waking Gini up or knocking some sentimental ornament or other crashing to the ground.

As they passed through the corridor towards the hall door, Maria pointed to her left remarking that it used to be Pedro's bedroom when he was a boy. She asked if he'd been happy living there again and if he missed his father Benjamin through all this drama. Pedro didn't want to get into all that again. Although he loved him dearly, Benji wasn't his real father anyway. He believed Gini wouldn't have gone quite so doo-lally if Benji hadn't passed away so suddenly and so young. However, Pedro had to concede he was at a total loss to imagine what Benji would have made of Gini's forthcoming Secret Service activities.

In the small square in Chueca, Pedro and Maria made arrangements to meet the next day, kissed their goodbyes and went their separate ways.

Maria's apartment was on the third floor. As she entered her 'little nest' she switched on the TV for company, as was her habit. Then she opened all the windows and doors to create a refreshing airflow and put the kettle on to make tea. The TV newsreader was saying something about the anti-government marches and riots that were happening in Madrid and Barcelona. And Maria watched in disbelief as the police appeared to use excessive force and teargas to disperse the crowds. The protestors were carrying banners with slogans against the government's continued cuts and other 'austerity' measures. Some young men wearing balaclavas were throwing stones and debris at the police in what looked like an attempt to provoke a violent reaction. Maria wondered if they were actually just reacting to the brutal tactics of the police. She dreaded where all this fear and dissatisfaction must inevitably lead.

In the kitchen, Maria spied a single avocado, perfectly ripe and resting on a spectacularly simple cobalt-blue Japanese plate... *Just ideal*, she thought, *for a light supper*. She passed through the living room again, continuing to think about what would go well with avocado, and what she had in her fridge. On entering her boudoir, Maria straightened the bed and fluffed up the Thai silk cushions that were scattered on her antique chaise longue by the window. Then she joined her palms together over her heart and made a deep bow in the direction of a modest Buddhist shrine she had established in the corner of her bedroom.

The shrine was very simple and mindfully put together with lifetimes of accumulated loving care. It consisted of a low coffee table with a glorious, Chinese lacquered box placed in the centre. She'd brought it with her from her parents' house for keepsakes. The box contained some of her most private things, including a photo of her as a little boy.

It was entirely covered by a medium-sized square of fine, golden silk from the Indian shop around the corner. On top of that – at eye level – Maria had put a 60cm high Buddha statue that had come all the way from Kathmandu. He was demonstrating perfect meditation posture. His legs were crossed and folded in what is known as 'full lotus', and his magnificently sculpted small hands rested naturally on his knees. The Buddha's robes were so well carved that the detail of every individual fold in the material made it look like he was wearing real cloth. You could discern each and every curl on his head, all the way up to the tip of his majestic topknot. But, ah, his face said it all. His lips were gently parted as if he were smiling; he was exhaling limitless love and compassion to all, and his eyes were blissfully half-open. His gaze was truly something to behold. His expression embodied such natural, great peace that he appeared to radiate all the sublime comfort and ease of a fully awakened being.

Arranged around the elevated base of the Buddha were some photos in gilt frames. As is the tradition, in front and centre Maria had placed a picture of her master's face, with eyes looking through the camera lens and out into the vast reaches of space and time that lay beyond. For her, it was just like there was a presence in the room, showering the blessings of all the buddhas on whoever should happen to glimpse the picture. Maria often imagined the shower of blessings cascading in the form of pure rays of magnificent, healing rainbow light. To the right was the photo of my root guru, the Great Saint Dzogchen Rinpoche. And to the left sat Nyima Özer Rinpoche, The Sun's Rays.

In a line along the front edge of the shrine were placed five objects, every one of them something from Maria's own life that represented each of the five ordinary senses. In the centre, there rested a beautiful cut crystal that Maria's ladyboy friend and mentor Mae had bought for her in *Chattuchak* market. This represented Sight; it also made Maria consider the Clear Light nature of mind itself. To one side of the crystal lay two other objects – a Ferrero Rocher chocolate, to represent Taste, and a mini-CD of the Gyuto Monks chanting prayers to represent Sound. On the other side of the crystal, lay two more – a small piece of finest velvet for Touch, which Maria had cut from a curtain she bought at auction that used to hang in the Palace of the Kings of Spain, and for Smell a little bottle of Maria's favourite perfume, Coco Chanel's *31 Rue Cambon*.

Behind the shrine table itself, right into the corner of the room, Maria had placed two long mirrors at 90 degrees to each other. They enabled her to see the Buddha from all angles at once, and flooded that whole area with such shafts of reflected light it became all the more spacious an environment for meditation to naturally arise. She could also see her own reflection inter-mingled with the host of enlightened ones populating the shrine. This gave Maria an inspiring sense of fearlessness that empowered her to begin to dare to believe – if only for one instant per day – that she too was imbued with the same potential, the same Heart Essence, as all the awakened beings.

Maria lit some incense and a tiny candle, and sat down on her cushion before her perfect little shrine and meditated just as I had taught her all those years before in Bangkok's Lumpini Park.

All her senses open, Maria simply observed her breath entering and leaving her body. Just as she watched the natural flow of the breath, without manipulating it, so too Maria left her mind *unaltered*. Unstirred, she found the mind naturally settled down to find its own level of peaceful clarity and openness. Observing and maintaining her mindfulness, awareness and spaciousness in this way, there was only the present moment, none other. The past had gone, and the future had not yet arisen. Only the Moment remained. Joyfully and peacefully remaining like that, Maria found twenty minutes had easily passed. She felt happy, well and safe.

Spontaneously her heart opened wide and she recited a few prayers of great aspiration and dedication for the benefit of self and others. The superstitious little Catholic boy, still somewhere deep within Maria, wanted to thank his Buddha-God from the bottom of his heart, perhaps with a prayer, or a hymn, or a donation. But the adult Maria understood – at least intellectually – that each one of us is responsible for our own awakening.

Having risen from her meditation cushion, Maria was careful not to then go rushing about like the Spanish, peasant tranny she allowed others to perceive her as. Instead, she mindfully prepared supper: a lightly tossed salad of avocado, vine tomato and crumbled salmon from a tin, drizzled with extra-virgin chilli-infused olive oil and a liberal splash of fresh lime juice.

After supper, Maria watched some more depressing TV news about the government's threats and promises to utterly extinguish the rioters and stop the wild fires in their tracks. Then she cheered herself enormously by watching the recording of her favourite soap opera, which she'd missed earlier in the day.

Eventually, Maria decided to do some emails and enjoy an extra-long shower before going to bed.

Maria decided to briefly email me before bedtime with the good news that she may soon be able to get a new passport, a real passport, her first true passport. She would also admit, superstition or not, that she firmly believed it was all thanks to me.

As she stood naked in front of the mirrored bathroom wall, Maria scanned and admired her female form: her hair, her face, her ample bosom and her slender waist. She marveled at her feminine hips and her glamorous legs, which seemed to have manifested as if by magic.

Maria rejoiced in her perfect vagina, so smooth and full of life.

As she dressed for bed, Maria reminded herself for the thousandth time of the Absolute Truth. As if intoning a primordial mantra, The Truth Beyond Concept flowed through her mind-stream from a source transcending time itself:

*A layer of fabric covers a layer of woman covers a layer of boy. A layer of thoughts and emotions covers a layer of ignorance and delusion. A layer of habitual patterns covers a layer of Karma which all covers a baby Buddha-to-be.*

Pedro, having scoffed a quick sandwich at his place, got ready and disappeared, full of longing and expectation, into the night. Passing by the door to Maria's building, he turned the corner into *Calle de las Infantas* where he bumped into some friends chatting in the street. Like most of Pedro's friends, they were all single gay men. They were also of a similar age and build. Being *'bears'*, most of them were stocky, rugged-looking types. Their hair was either shaved or cropped tight and their tanned faces bore a couple of days' stubble or a full beard neatly clipped. The most common attire for bears was the 'American' look. The spectrum of choices is quite limited:

You can wear a tight t-shirt to show off your pumped, upper-body muscle tone, complete with obligatory tribal tattoos. This is usually finished off with shorts whose legs end just below the knee, plus trendy trainers or work boots.

Or you can do as Pedro had done and wear a nice shirt open to the third or fourth button to display your magnificent chest-hair. A pair of combats or workman's trousers adds the finishing touch. Maria always teased Pedro by calling it his 'uniform' and claimed they were all just doing 'male drag' really.

As they were going to the same place anyway (*Hot Bar*), and for the same reason (to find sex or a boyfriend, whichever came first), they agreed to go in as a group, have a few beers and a laugh together, then go their separate ways inside and hope for the best. As was the tradition, each man went up to the counter, shouted his order above the pounding house music, and paid for his own. Then, having secured a spot big enough to accommodate them all, they'd stand facing each other in a circle with their backs to all the men they claimed they wanted to attract later on. Appearing friendless or too keen was always considered the worst of the seven hundred gay deadly sins.

Pedro observed all these details each time he went out with them. But, even then, he refused to break free of it all or transgress in any way, even for fun. And he rarely, if ever, remained anywhere alone. He never ceased to be amazed by the endlessly limiting carry-on of it all. The clothes, the look, the choice of beverage. The familiar barman who shook your hand firmly, 'like a real man', and offered to sell you cocaine or marijuana with your drink. Then who, squeezing through the jammed crowd later to collect bottles and glasses, squealed like a girl secretly wanting to be groped and behaved like an off-duty whore or a b-list celebrity diva hairdresser.

Like clockwork, after the second or third drink they all dispersed to the four corners of the bar, the downstairs bathroom and the adjoining 'dark rooms' and private cabins. They promised hope to the hopeful and a very temporary brand of relief for those whose engorged loins were bursting with the milk of human kindness or whose inner void was simply aching to be filled.

Once again Pedro passed through it all, practically undetected, involuntarily passing judgement on this one and that. It was perhaps the only part of that life he truly hated. Not the sex or the longing. No, he loved that. But the labeling of people as they entered his radar: Like. Don't like. Like. Like. Vile. Had. Had. Had. Not sure. How should *I* know if I had him or not? Wouldn't touch him with a barge pole.

Pedro particularly hated the way they'd made sex so readily available, any hour of the day or night. The dreaded internet's ubiquitous, bastard offspring (the 'smart' phone) had created a brave new world of such depraved dimensions, you could now see with your own eyes – and at a single loving stroke of an L.E.D. screen – just how large a man's penis was, what his open anus looked like, what he wanted you to do with either or both of them (all going well), and how close or far away from you he was at that very moment. Pedro felt the wonderful world of gay 'cruising' for sex was perilously in danger of total implosion. It was reducing men to little more than pieces of meat: extra large, uncut, too fatty, past its sell-by date, prime beef, hung, well-hung, hung like a gerbil.

Having been singularly unsuccessful in finding *Mr Right*, yet again, Pedro settled for Mr *Right Now*. He sucked something that had just been sucked by someone else, whilst he shot his load on the dark, hairy chest of some other guy that he couldn't even see lying below him.

Terminally disappointed – the very definition of what suffering is – yet somewhat relieved at having scored nonetheless, Pedro strolled home alone, again.

As a budding writer, he mused to himself whether this kind of sexual encounter could or even should be written about appropriately. What would ordinary, straight people make of it all? What would Maria's enlightened beings say? ... *How tragic*, Pedro thought to himself as he opened the door to his bachelor pad. *All that barely existing on a stodgy, super-saturated diet rich in sex, but only sex. While what everyone secretly yearned for was a good old-fashioned, home-cooked three-course meal of Love, plus fantastic Sex of course... Oh and a bit of Extra-Mural Sex, on the side.*

Tucked up in their beds that night, as Maria dreamt scenes of future chaos and carnage on the streets of Madrid with a chorus of *Ave Marias* conducted by yours truly, Gini dreamt of devouring her usual mountains of jelly and yoghurt with High Up, in the Churchill drawing room, surrounded by glorious shafts of rainbow light that whispered words of wisdom and compassion in her ear. In *his* bed, Pedro dreamt of escaping the city for once and for all. Of living in a small mountaintop village where he'd write sublime poetry, the likes of which would cause even the coldest, heaviest heart to melt and rise and soar. Somewhere with an uninterrupted view of the mountains and an enormous bed where he could sleep like a baby in the strong arms of a broad-chested lover. A place he could finally call home.

## 13

As agreed, in the early afternoon of the appointed day, Virginia, Pedro and Maria took the Metro out to the airport together.

From the moment they sat down in the carriage to the moment they arrived at the terminal, all three of them were very nervous and tried to chat away about whatever came to mind. They appeared to have no control whatsoever over their blabber-muscles. It was like there was an unspoken pact in place.

*Don't say anything about where we're going or what we're up to. Don't even pause for breath. Whether you know what you're talking about or not, just Keep TALKING!*

Virginia spoke at length – being an Englishwoman – about the weather, the weather forecast, and weather systems in general. Pedro replied in turn with an in-depth monologue about the various woes and pitfalls of being a part-time barman and an, as yet, unpaid writer of love stories not based on personal experience. He confided in them about his thoughts of sex without love on the way home from the bar the other night. Then Pedro told them of his dream about living in the little mountain village and sleeping in his lover's arms. That prompted Maria to speak of her dream. She inferred I was trying to warn her of the mortal dangers of being on the streets at this turbulent time in Madrid. She told Pedro and Gini that the meaning of my cryptic message, *Ave Maria*, completely eluded her for the time being and wondered if either of them had any insight they wished to share. Pedro said he believed it could simply have a very literal meaning; 'Ave' was a salutation in Latin meaning 'Hail', or maybe even 'Holy' in certain contexts, he ventured. And, of course, Maria was her name. Or was the dream literally singing the praises of Mary, mother of Jesus? ... Unlikely, he concluded, completely side-tracked now.

Gini jumped in with both feet, impatiently insisting if this Jalu Yogi person was all Maria claimed him to be, if he did have some paranormal premonition of what was about to happen, and felt the need to warn her in advance, then why on earth would he not just use technology to contact her directly, and quickly? Why wouldn't he simply dispense with all the third-rate hocus pocus and amateur dramatics altogether if Maria was really in danger and may not live long enough to decipher his secret codes?

Just then, Maria's smart phone bleeped loudly to inform her she had a text message. They all jumped. Maria exclaimed, *O.. My ... BUDDHA!!!* (Her eyes rolling in Pedro's direction, like a mad woman) *I can't freaking believe it!* (Now glaring at Gini) *It's Jelly Yoghurt, I mean Jalu Yogi !! NOW do you fucking believe me??* Maria opened the message on the large screen for all to see... they stared at it in total disbelief! There it was. In plain sight! Two words... *Ave Maria.*

Virginia and Pedro were dumbfounded. They both sat frozen to the spot, in utter shock, slowly, quietly mouthing the five syllables, *A-ve Ma-ri-a*, as if their lives depended on them. *O for fuck sake!!* Maria screamed, under her breath. *I'm going to ring him right now, wherever the hell he is, and cut through all this code bullshit. It's totally wrecking my head, do you hear me?!!* In an instant, I answered her call. She put me on speaker phone so they could all hear for themselves. There was a lot of noise around me. *Not now! Too crazy here,* I shouted, cutting through the madness. *They're killing each other here, right beside me. I'll phone or reply to your email when I get a chance.*

*Maria,* I altered the tone of my voice to gather gravitas, *Listen carefully. You're all in grave danger. Get out of Madrid, baby-buddha.. NOW!!* (I roared like a lion. Then hung up).

The three amigos sat there in stunned silence, not knowing how to process this information.

*I don't think I really believed he actually existed till now,* Pedro said.

*What danger? Where? On the train?* Virginia bleated like a lamb.

The phone rang... *O fucking hell! I'm shitting myself!!* Maria cried aloud as she answered the call from the undisclosed number, re-activating the speaker phone.

*British Agent Green here. I'm on the train watching you. What on earth just happened?*

*O nothing,* Maria replied (not trusting anyone now). *We just received some very bad news from a friend.*

*How did those bastards get your number Maria?* Gini said.

*Have you got me on speaker phone??* Agent Green asked politely. *Please turn it off, immediately,* he commanded.

Doing as she was told, but placing her hand over the mouthpiece, Maria answered Gini. *Of course I did. Pedro won't carry a mobile phone. You don't know how to work one. What other choice did I have? They needed a number to contact us. And the nice lady said she'd help me get a passport.*

*Very well then,* said Green. *Keep the noise down and don't attract any further attention to yourselves. You're undercover, for God's sake.* The phone went dead.

The next fifteen minutes passed glacially. Hardly a single phrase was uttered that made any sense. Their blood ran cold.

Safely off the train and up the silver escalator to their designated meeting point for later. Pedro and Maria watched in near horror as Virginia walked alone from the check-in desk towards the departures area, through security and then out of sight altogether. This rather frail, old-ish lady, living with premature dementia, Pedro's mother, had marched purposefully into God only knew what. Either extremely brave, or extremely stupid, Gini proceeded like she had been transformed into the young, self-assured Virginia Blake of times gone by. In her head, she was invincible. And being innocent of any crime, she had no reason to believe her life was in danger. In fact, Virginia rather relished the thought of the mission. It could be the quiet crowning glory of her whole life. Plus, she was actually looking forward to meeting Fr Weithaler. She hadn't found anyone even vaguely interested in *her* kind of stuff for decades. Gini was looking forward to a nice day out. *Why not? She thought. What could possibly go wrong?*

While safely ambling through the duty-free arcades, she constantly reassured herself that she was possibly in one of the safest places in the country at that moment. The 'secure' zone inside an airport is supposed to be the best place to be if anything untoward were to happen. Feeling increasingly at ease, Virginia focused on the task at hand. Ignoring all the signs intended to guide her to the London flight that she was meant to board in two hours, Virginia found her way to the café nearest the gate through which Fr Karl was going to arrive. Checking her watch, she noted she had just under twenty minutes or so to purchase the cakes and coffee, and get herself to the specific brushed steel bench assigned for the great meeting of minds. As she approached it, in perfect time and right on cue, the young couple wearing denim shorts and tie-dye t-shirts she was told would be holding the bench for her stood up and disappeared with their bags, leaving the seats free for Virginia and Karl.

Seeing through the huge panes of glass that the flight was in, and people were already disembarking, it wasn't long at all before the priest from the photo they'd given her appeared and walked straight up to Gini. They embraced fondly, as instructed, like old friends or aunty and nephew reunited in transit. Taking their seats, only separated by a small table built into the centre of the bench, they took the lids off their coffees and opened the wrappers on their cakes like nothing the slightest bit unusual was taking place... the stage was set.

14

Virginia was determined not to get too distracted or drift off into the past as she usually did when feeling disconnected from present circumstances. Having watched some of my 'Real Revolution' teaching on YouTube with Pedro and Maria, she was now beginning to understand the radical sanity of dwelling in the *present moment,* and how even she might come to manage it.

Gini observed how her mind drifted towards something – say, some past event – and clung on to it for a sense of comfort. As she chatted with Fr Karl she was looking directly at him but in her mind's eye she was seeing her deceased husband's face, or some man from decades ago in Trinity. Or she was speaking with the man from British Intelligence that fateful afternoon in Cambridge. But she was coming to realize that habitually going back to her 'special places' and favourite moments from her past was just a fantasy, fraught with all manner of psychological complications it would create for her present condition.

The only way, 'YouTube Jalu' said, to find true comfort and ease was to somehow bring herself back into this present moment. Regardless of whether it is a 'nice' moment or not, the present is a far healthier place to live, psychologically speaking. Anyway, compared to living in a fantasy land of half-remembered truths, what other option do we really have? The past is gone. The future has not yet manifested. The present is all we truly have. But it completely passes most of us by.

I had taught in the online clip quite a bit about gently bringing the mind into the present moment. Gini was learning, hard though it is, to allow the mind to drift habitually into the past without chastising herself or suppressing anything, but not to allow her mind to *get stuck* there. She was learning to think of her breath as her main anchor in life. Without thinking 'Oh No! There I go again, drifting into fantasy land', Gini was starting out on the path to Awakening, using the present moment as the portal. The path that all the fully awakened buddhas had walked. The path that begins with just one breath.

Without altering her breath in any way, Virginia just brought her mind gently back to the present by becoming aware of her breathing. She was patient and loving with herself. If her mind got distracted again, she simply brought it back to centre, time after time. Like training a puppy not to wander off but stay by your side as you sit on the floor, Gini was training her mind not to wander too far, or for too long. Neither suppressing the mind by forcing it nor giving it too much freedom to roam, Gini was gradually waking up to all the potential of living in the present. It was a skillful act of juggling three balls at once: mindfulness, awareness and spaciousness. No more, no less. Pure and simple!

The method was working. Virginia was slowly becoming more able to remain in the moment. She used the breath, her coffee cup, Karl's face as an anchor. Of course, they chatted about the weather at first. Then about life in Madrid these days. All the while Gini was observing the natural flow of her breathing in order to keep herself grounded. She remembered how she could be quite the actress too, if needed. At one point she found herself ad-libbing rather outrageously:

*Tell me Karl, how is that old dog Juan Ramon Jimenez? Does he still ask for me? And the widow Estefan? Is she still alive?* The poor Fr Weithaler tried his level best to keep up with her but knew when he was beat. They both collapsed with laughter. The ice was broken at last. Gini and Karl were now connecting on a deeper, more natural level. To avoid flying off into the realms of the imaginary again, Virginia suddenly took a more serious approach and brought everything back down to earth. *Tell me about your parish work. I'm really dying to hear all about how you are putting Liberation Theology into action out there in the hill towns of Argentina.*

Karl charmed and regaled Gini with heroic tales of priests, sisters and brothers all working the land together with the villagers, living in ordinary houses with their own families and friends. Above all else, he explained, they were serving the poor and disenfranchised just as Jesus would have done.

The pair discussed the grass roots theology of the Peruvian radical Gustavo Gutiérrez. Without him – they both agreed – the Roman Church might have disappeared altogether in the early 1970s. Once they heard about it, Catholics all over the world became deeply motivated by the new Liberation Theology. But, fearing they would lose control of their grass-roots rank and file altogether, Rome more or less steered the Church completely away from the 'new' ideas. Of course, there were many meetings after the second Vatican Council, and the Church promised to move with the times. But they could never deliver that sort of reform. Rome feared a schism, and had clamped down.

Gini was in her element and she waxed lyrical about Gutiérrez and the whole school of thought that had evolved. She exclaimed that a major revelation for her had been when she embraced the idea that sin manifests in the world primarily in the form of unjust social structures. If the Churches uphold that satanic edifice, then they themselves are the agents of Evil. They become the problem not the solution.

According to the Liberation Theologians, if Jesus were here today he would side with the world's poorest people, whose dignified struggle embodies all that Jesus taught and was put to death for over two thousand years ago. Virginia quoted Gutierrez directly: *Hunger for God, Yes. Hunger for bread, No!*

Karl brought proceedings to a natural pause for reflection by summarizing that poor people are so rich in other ways. Their generosity of spirit, and how they offer love and caring to one another so freely, he said, truly creates the Kingdom of Heaven right here and right now. In the gap that followed, without feeling at all contrived or awkward, Gini and Karl both became very silent and still. They inhabited the space they had created and in that perfect moment they just rejoiced and smiled, inwardly and to each other. The invisible entourage of assorted international security operatives dotted about the place wondered what on earth was happening. They spoke via microphones concealed in cuffs and lapels to their various national 'bases' who, equally baffled, advised their agents to stay calm.

Karl then began speaking of non-violent revolution within the Church. He described these remote, Latin American hill-towns and villages as the ideal environment for the radical teachings of Jesus to be tested and to grow and flourish freely. He told Gini that priests and religious community leaders up there simply ignored the directives from 'Mother Church' that the people didn't agree with. For example, he said, they made sure that local health clinics were well stocked with free condoms since that empowered ordinary people who wish to limit the number of children they have. It also enables people to take responsibility for their own sexual health, people who might otherwise have been condemned to death from AIDS or consigned to the wasteland of other sexually transmitted diseases that could so easily go untreated.

Karl spoke of entire religious communities who were being led by women priests. These extraordinary women had been chosen by village elders and had even been fully ordained by a sympathetic bishop. Gini clapped and laughed gleefully when he said these women were often married with children, and who better to lead people in the ways of loving kindness than a mother. Finally, lowering his voice a little, Karl confided that he too was a married priest. He said his wife was also a priest and that they had three children – one girl of their own making, and two little boys they had taken in when a local single mother had died in an accident.

He reported a real world, with real people struggling to move forward together.

Fr Karl said he was not describing a 'Utopian' existence. Communal life doesn't come without the occasional serious difficulty. He said a Latino, rural, macho environment was still not the ideal place to grow up if you were gay or transgendered, but they were committed to working on equality for all nonetheless.

Virginia, now with tears flowing down her face, had absolutely no difficulty staying in the present moment with this wonderful man. Through his evocative and provocatively vivid descriptions, she was effortlessly being transported back and forth through far-away fields and villages, to the opulent palaces of The Vatican. From the now hidden accounts of past priests, bishops and popes that included the married, the gay, even the female, to the slums of the present moment where über-conservative papal ordinances are dictated from ornate pulpits to an ever-dwindling congregation of ordinary folk who are simply looking for some small flicker of hope.

Both Virginia and Karl acknowledged that they had agreed not to speak too personally but, since they were such *compadres* already, they decided to go a bit deeper and tell each other a little more about themselves.

Gini enquired, since Karl was of German descent how his people had ended up in South America. Curiously, Karl began rattling off some story or other that started out like a script he had memorized but which, on closer inspection, proceeded to unravel. He didn't make it clear whether his father had been German or Polish. He stumbled over answering whether he himself had been born in Europe or

Argentina. Although he was obviously not of Latin stock, he seemed to be saying at one point that his mother was. The more Gini looked at him the more she realized you couldn't tell from his face what nationality he was at all. She commented on it. One minute he appeared dark and angular. The next, fair and bronzed. She wondered if he sometimes resembled his father but looked more like his mother at other times. Maybe that explained it.

Karl looked straight into her eyes, as if apologizing for being so unavoidably vague. He said not to think too much about it and maybe one day soon all would become clear.

Trying to draw him out some more, but alas to no avail, Gini volunteered some pseudo-autobiographical old guff of her own. It was a clever tapestry that started in her new favourite place – the present – and which wove its merry way backwards through the annals of time into her murky, distant past. It was a multi-layered confectionary of fact dipped in fiction, rolled in blatant lies, sprinkled with fun. En route, Virginia mentioned she had been married to the legendary conductor Daniel Barenboim but he had run off with a prostitute he met in a public toilet.

On and on, the train of consciousness led her further back along the path of hilarious happenstance and finally up to the lofty peaks of pure invention that culminated in telling a red-faced Karl, now holding his sides with laughter, how her mother had in fact been the Queen of Sheba and how unfortunately she'd met her untimely demise when her gas oven exploded. They both laughed so much that Gini belched quite loudly and they held onto each other's hands as they completely disintegrated into total chaos.

15

An enormous explosion ripped through the entire length of the waiting area. Most of the windows and doors simply blew out and disappeared in an instant. Flames and smoke rushed through the space like a tsunami in search of the nearest exit. In that moment, Virginia observed many people including nearby undercover security personnel being completely lifted into the air, dismantled limb from limb, their all but liquidized body parts blown outside onto the tarmac. Those who had randomly and inexplicably not been killed or mutilated picked themselves up and scattered throughout what was once the safest place on earth.

There was no point trying to *understand* what was going on or what had happened to cause the explosion. Gini and Karl found themselves still holding onto each other and running down the hall through the thick smoke and the stench. They could hear their names being called from somewhere within the hellish mass of torture and death behind them. But they kept running. Moving with the flow seemed the best strategy. Provided there wasn't going to be a second blast somewhere else ahead of them, getting away from the scene of the first explosion and out of the airport altogether appeared to be foremost on everyone's mind.

They found themselves re-entering the duty-free shopping arcades. But, far from being safer there, total bedlam was breaking out all around them. People from all over the airport, in a high state of panic and aggression, were being funneled into one very tight space. There was lots of shouting and pushing. Somebody even grabbed Karl's arm and commanded him, by name, to follow them to safety. Karl flipped out and pushed the man to the ground in order to free himself. The crowd surged suddenly and trampled him underfoot. When the man finally jumped to his feet Gini and Karl could see he was waving a gun which caught the attention of the armed police nearby who shot him in the hand to disarm him. More and more people were flooding into the arcade from every conceivable direction. The very old and the very young were being crushed by the sheer force of the crowd and it appeared that looting had also begun.

Police marksmen perched on balconies overhead used megaphones to pierce the din. Foolishly, they were calling for calm. But what else could they do. Then the shooting started in earnest. Echoing the brutality of the anti-riot police on the streets of Spain, snipers actually began picking off the unruly and those who seemed to be unwilling to follow orders. Those undercover agents who were still alive, having seen what happened earlier to their colleague, put their weapons away and moved stealthily through the throng trying to gain higher ground and await clearer instructions.

Karl had a sudden flash of inspiration and, pulling Gini along with him, started wading towards the security scanners near the main public area beyond. Of course the place was in a state of total mayhem and disarray with people dashing in and out past the armed guards. Alarms were going off everywhere around them and staff just had to stand back to facilitate the flow. They pushed and pushed their way until *their* turn to pass through finally came. As they squeezed through the mass of bodies and booty going in both directions Gini became suddenly disoriented and unbalanced. Her mind seemed to dislocate temporarily and she became obsessed with having to find her passport in case somebody needed to check it on the way out. Karl just persevered and, without saying a word, held on tight and marched her through the security doors and out into the sea of screaming people beyond. Some were 'departures' now outside again. Others were 'arrivals', outside without their baggage and on the wrong floor for meeting their loved ones. Many people, not travelling at all, were at their wits' end trying to find out if their loved ones had been caught up in the explosion.

Unable to form any words at all now and appearing to be suffering some kind of mini-stroke Virginia, with Karl's loving support, gathered all the British bulldog resolve she could muster and somehow navigated them both by the signs for the metro to the top of the moving stairway where she fell into Pedro's arms. Maria, quite hysterical by this stage, shook Karl's hand and said *You must be the priest. I'm a transsexual, Maria del Mar. Jalu warned us about all this you know. Now. Let's get the fuck out of here, Father. For Jesus' sake!*

The four of them disappeared down into the metro – which was astonishingly still running – and collapsed in a heap on the first train. Just before departure, Maria's mobile phone rang again. All she could catch was *Control here! Very dangerous situation! Karl is in grave danger. Stay in crowded public places. There's safety in numbers. Blend in. Lie low. Don't be afraid, Maria. Keep this line free for further instructions.*

The line went dead. Someone tried to snatch the phone from her hand saying she also needed to call home. Maria called her a bitch and snatched it back shrieking there was no coverage anyway. She jammed the phone down the front of her jeans thinking nobody would dare go after it without a written invitation.

Two of her pills and some borrowed water later, Gini was starting to pull through without any apparent lasting signs of stroke damage, to her face anyway. Her three carers lavished lots of attention on her and pretty soon the whole carriage was involved in looking after one another. Maria managed to convince Karl to get out of his priest's 'uniform'. And, telling him of the danger he was in, both she and Pedro used whatever they could get their hands on to disguise all four of them, at least temporarily.

Before they reached their stop, they got a text saying to stay on the train and not go home. They got another one, almost straight away. It said to get off immediately and take a taxi to the *Museo Reina Sofia*, where they should stand right in front of Picasso's *Guernica*.

# 16

In the back of an over-sized, rainbow-coloured, wheelchair-accessible taxi, Gini, Pedro, and Maria sat with their lovely new friend, Fr Karl Weithaler – just in, from a hilltop village in Argentina – on the way to the museum.

Yet again – and perhaps for the ninth or tenth time in recent days – a stunned silence descended upon the 'three amigos'. So great was the fallout from their earlier shock and awe, that the resultant profound confusion hovered over the layer of silence like a fog. There just didn't seem to be any point in talking about it. So they whispered. But only questions. There were no answers yet.

*What the hell was THAT all about!?*

*Was the explosion a terrorist bomb?*

*How come we survived a bomb that exploded right beside us?*

*Why is Fr Karl in such danger?*

*If we're supposed to hide in plain sight, just blend into crowded places, what happens late tonight when everyone goes to bed? Where are we supposed to find a crowd to hide in?*

*I'm so nervous, I'm starving.*

*Let's find a crowded restaurant somewhere instead?*

*What happens if we disobey Control?*

*OK Karl. Who the fuck are you? And what the COnyo is going on?!!*

*Driver,* Gini finally said out loud. *Please could you turn on the radio? We want to hear the latest news.*

... The newsreader was announcing that the blast at the airport had ripped through one of the busiest terminal buildings at *Barajas,* killing 42 people. The massive explosion itself, and the chaos that ensued, had also caused serious injury to hundreds. A government minister was busy reassuring the public that the airport at Madrid was now a secure place again and that flights in and out would resume early tomorrow morning. Specialist teams were beginning the long process of clearing debris and trying to locate the last few people that remained unaccounted for. It was a public relations smokescreen, of course. How could they have accounted for almost everyone already? Most people just ran away.

A search and rescue expert, not directly involved, commented with great caution that it was very early days indeed to say *anything* with certainty about the situation. Such was the huge disruption at Barajas that one couldn't possibly say with confidence whether a missing individual was lying dead under rubble or sipping *café con leche* somewhere in the city. Interestingly, Maria remarked, the government and the media's current pre-occupation with spinning stories about the rioters was so unstoppable that there was already an estimate of several million euro specifically related to the cost of all the looting and rampaging that had followed the blast. There was an implied undertone that rioters had even caused the explosion.

Another government minister was quoted as saying that all the evidence pointed to the explosion being caused by a very specific kind of bomb. And that this particular bomb was a favourite of almost everybody currently wreaking havoc on the world stage. Al Qaeda, Hamas, ETA and the continuity IRA were all linked to such devices. He said you couldn't rule out any terrorist group with strong financial support.

For that matter, playing devil's advocate, the interviewer enquired whether there were any *governments* with a known penchant for that sort of bomb. Could a foreign government have been responsible for detonating the bomb? The Russians? The Americans? The Israelis? Or what about the Spanish Government itself... Do the Spanish have access to that kind of bomb?

The minister, of course, declined to comment further. And terminated the interview with a plea for peace and calm on the streets. He requested a bed-time prayer for the dead and the injured.

On returning to the live component of the news, the principle anchorman allowed the next studio guest (a pro-riot political commentator) to preface his first response with a very telling comment. He noted that the minister hadn't mentioned the reasons *why* there was unrest on the streets. And how curious it was that he hadn't asked for prayers for those Spanish citizens murdered by their own police and army during the protest riots in Sevilla the previous night.

Listening to the appalling accounts of the riots, the driver said how shocking the news was of today's explosion.

Then – as if it had already become old news – he informed them they were just minutes away from their destination, *Reina Sofia*. In case they were tourists, he also told them the museum's name meant *Queen of Wisdom*.

Maria's phone rang. It was me.

I still didn't have much time to chat but, addressing her as *Baby Buddha*, I told Maria that I was in Spain and had already been down south in Sevilla for days, witnessing the official massacre of protesters there. I told her it was like the end of the world, a real Hell on Earth.

*And 'Ave Maria'?* (enquired Maria, rather impatiently).

*O that. Why are you always so slow, Darling? It's not the Times Crossword. I want you to stop ignoring my instructions and get out of Madrid. Come down South to me. Take the AVE, Maria? The fast train, you know?!!*

*You want me to drop everything and everybody here,* Maria said, *and run headlong towards the gates of hell just because you say so?*

*Yes. That's right,* I replied. *Not just you. I want you to bring everyone you can with you. Is the Argentinian priest still with you? And the Madonna and son? Bring them too. Do as you were told for tonight. The AVE is booked solid for the rest of the day. Stay safe. Lie low. Unless you are rioting, there's supposed to be safety in numbers. Stick to crowded places. Don't go to bed tonight, it's not safe. The priest is a sitting duck and you're his minders. Plus Madrid is about to erupt! You have no idea how far the armed forces have been authorized to go. Spain doesn't want another Greece. Those with their fingers on the national purse strings will slaughter everyone before they allow another Greece to happen here. Take the Ave to Sevilla first thing in the morning. I've booked the tickets. Just pick them up. You can take turns sleeping then. I'll be there to meet you when you arrive. I'll probably be dressed in my Mata Hari get-up. You should all completely transform yourselves as well. Disguise yourselves overnight. I'll be waiting, Baby. Don't worry about clothes or money. Mommy will take care of everything, Sweethearts. Just stay awake. Stay alive. Get down here as soon as possible. Don't worry. We won't be staying in this hell hole either. I'll have a super-fast getaway car waiting outside. Oh, this is SO exciting, isn't it? Happy days! Ciao.*

## 17

They stood shell-shocked and raw before *Guernica*, Picasso's iconic mural.

Surrounded by a coach-load of new-money Chinese tourists, the four stayed very close together. They surveyed the vast surface of it with a foreboding sense of the abyss. Almost nothing about it was as expected. In her mind, Gini was back in Trinity College's Spanish Department, where she was presenting a short talk to her peers. It was a small tutorial group held every Thursday in a windowless room on the second floor. Another November downpour was freezing hard on Front Square, and it was Virginia's turn to give a fifteen- minute talk. The topic was *Guernica*.

As she began speaking to the surprised assembly of friends and holiday-makers, Virginia moved confidently through the crowd and stood side-on to the painting in case she wanted to illustrate her presentation by pointing to the great work. To those who knew how rapidly her mental health was deteriorating, Gini appeared suddenly fresh and clear. A woman transformed.

Her short talk was very thorough and succinct. Every relevant piece of information was included. Virginia held nothing back.

The mural measures 11 feet from top to bottom, and 25.6 feet from left to right. An impassioned Pablo Picasso painted it in June 1937 after he read George Steer's newspaper article alerting the world to the vile atrocity that had been visited upon the Basque city of Guernica on April 26. Of course, the Spanish Civil War was already raging by 1937. Earlier that same year, the Irish poet Charles Donnelly had been killed fighting against the *Francoists*. His last words were '*Even the olives are bleeding*'.

Meanwhile Picasso – living in exile in Southern France – was commissioned by the beleaguered, legitimately elected, Republican government of Spain to paint something extraordinary for the forthcoming International Exposition in Paris.

He'd been struggling rather reluctantly to paint a different project altogether. But once Picasso became aware of what had happened in Guernica he switched his focus to capturing the horror and redressing the apparent hopelessness of what had taken place there: A rag-tag coalition of Nationalist, right-wing groups in Spain had joined forces and were committed to overthrowing the Republican government. Of course, by 1939, history would come to record their total victory under the dictator, General Franco. But in 1937 Franco needed desperately to do something on such a large scale that it would help his opponents understand how serious his Nationalists were in their pursuit of absolute power in Spain.

Recognizing a kindred spirit in Franco, both Mussolini and Adolf Hitler pledged support. The people of the northern Basque region of Spain had always proved a serious obstacle for any government trying to establish a new order in Spain. So it was, in April 1937, that Franco invited Hitler to practise his new *blitzkrieg* methods by bombarding the strategic Basque city of Guernica. Total destruction and misery! By June 1937, the extraordinary painting we now see was complete. And by July it was hanging in the Paris Expo.

Astonishingly, Picasso's *Guernica* made little or no impact.

At first, the horrendous event itself was considered just one more instance where the Spanish got away with massacring their own people in the name of progress and stability. The world continued to cast a cold eye on Hitler's meteoric rush for dominance. Franco was even portrayed internationally by many as a man of the people who was simply helping the downtrodden overthrow their cruel overlords. Franco went on to rule Spain with an iron fist – and with the help of the Roman Catholic Church and other right-wing interest groups – until his death in 1975.

*When we first look at Picasso's Guernica* – Virginia flourished her left hand elegantly across the face of the enormous anti-war icon – *we are shocked to see such a huge work, painted entirely without colour. Comprised solely of black, white and grey, Guernica is a stark cataclysm. At first glance, it is an unforgiving portrait of inhumanity. Parents, children, soldiers and animals ... all fall to the ground in agony, slain. However, Picasso doesn't actually depict a world entirely without hope or the possibility of a better future. Because the artist has not allowed himself to use red, the gaping wounds flowing with blood do not have the impact one would expect from a painting of such carnage.*

*Buried within the symbolism of Guernica, Picasso has offered us several glimmers of hope. We notice the soldier's dismembered arm is still clutching a sword. And furthermore, from this deadly weapon we can clearly see a flower blossoming. Whilst Spain's most noble creatures, the bull and the horse, are depicted in utter panic and terror, a small bird – perhaps the dove of Peace – perches defiantly on a shelf in the background. The electric bulb suspended from the ceiling looks more like a massive explosion than a light. Whereas a simple lamp held aloft beside it appears so much more illuminating by contrast. It seems to possess the power to dispel the darkness of the entire universe. Guernica shows – no matter how bad things may appear – that all is not lost.*

When she had finished her presentation, Virginia's mind came crashing back to the present. Becoming more frail and exhausted suddenly, she scanned the faces of the mystified Chinese and cried out a warning not to repeat the sins of the past, and never allow politicians to commit atrocities in our name. Catching Pedro's eye, Gini could see that his face was drenched in tears. As he mouthed the words *I love you*, she directed her final comments to him personally:

*Just look at what's going on in Spain right now. The past, the present, it's all the bloody same. Even if you manage to end up living in a gorgeous tiny house in a hill-top village paradise, with the love of your life wrapped around you, never forget the ways of the world. Keep yourself informed. Watch the TV news when you can. And if you write, write poems of such spectacular beauty that they'll awaken people from their long sleep of ignorance. Compose words that will move people to take action in the world.*

Fr Karl's phone vibrated to say he had a text. It was from Control:

*What's going on? What's she DOING up there pontificating? I said LIE LOW!*

*Just an elegant bit of a rant, from a wise old soul. She's finished now,* Karl texted back.

*We're watching you all. Very closely! Remember your commitment to us. Keep moving. Crowded places. Await instructions.*

Meanwhile, I was calling Maria again ...

*From now on,* I warned, *totally disregard absolutely everything you are told by British Intelligence, or anyone appearing to be in authority. I'm the boss now, Dear. When you get the chance later on, confiscate everyone's mobile phones, including your own. Remove the batteries and SIM cards to avoid the phones being located and hide them somewhere in Madrid before you leave. Night-night, Princess. See you in Seville tomorrow morning.*

# 18

An all-nighter gradually unfolded the likes of which none of the *'Fabulous Four'* had ever experienced in their lives. Pedro, Maria, Gini and Karl had embarked upon a bizarre, uncomfortable, yet often hilarious white-knuckle roller coaster ride that would prove to offer little respite before dawn. A journey none of them had actually signed up for.

The nocturnal Madrid they were about to encounter bore no resemblance to the city depicted by the writers or movie directors of the past. Most *Madrileños* themselves never get to experience the city in this way either.

Granted, the average person in Madrid liked to stay out late. Students would often party all night. Young parents might take their baby out for a midnight stroll. Elderly men and their squatting dogs, floral-smocked grandmothers sweeping the dusty pavement are all fairly common sights. However, once exhausted, an ordinary person could always go home to bed when their bodies demanded.

But our four were considered to be in such grave (though invisible) danger that they'd been ordered to stay awake, stay safe and stay out in crowded places until they could board that high-speed, south-bound train the next morning. So, with the exception of piling into a taxi, they managed to busy themselves going from crowd to crowd throughout the night.

As a matter of priority – and before it got too late – both Pedro and Maria called in sick and told their bosses they didn't know when they'd be fit for work. Then, as instructed, Maria somehow managed to convince those who had phones to hand over their mobiles. Once in the relative, but temporary safety of a friend's bar, she dismantled and promptly hid them, and her own, behind the counter. In a corner of the bar, they all agreed to abstain from alcohol for the night as a strategy for staying awake. Although they all wondered just how much fizzy water and soft drinks they could bear, it seemed to be the ideal solution.

Maria was determined to alter everyone's appearance, so she dispatched some friends from the bar to go and get an assortment of clothes and accessories they could borrow. Actually, this caught their imagination to such an extent that the whole process took up a few hours and provided everyone with some much-needed light relief. Pedro was transformed from a clichéd bit of a scruff in a check shirt into a splendid beatnik student-type. Karl shaved off his beard in the toilet and emerged unrecognizable as a handsome businessman on his way home from the office. Gini, with the assistance of just a few skillful alterations and additions, blossomed into an elegant lady of means. And Maria herself assumed the role of a sophisticated *cougar* – an old personal favourite. Whatever clothes and other objects they needed to cast off were placed in bags labeled with their names and stored in the same locked cupboard as the phones.

As time was moving on, Gini momentarily asserted control suggesting they now move on to another venue via the laneway to the rear. Even though Gini had no experience in this field, everybody agreed and the four moved as one out the back door. Once in the lane, Gini admitted she was merely going on instinct.

*Just because we have no obvious evidence we are in danger,* she advised, *we should still proceed with extreme caution and never allow ourselves to fall into a false sense of security. Until we actually understand how and why we are in danger, we have to trust that Jalu knows something we don't.*

*That's right,* Maria added. *If it comes down to a question of who we should trust more – Jalu or the Brits? – I'm afraid I have to go with Jalu (Sorry Gini. No offence). I know Jalu wants to keep us out of danger. But all I hear from British Intelligence and Control is that they want to, well, control and manipulate us. As you can imagine by now I'm sure, THIS lady is not going to be controlled by ANY man ever again.*

As if temporarily leaving their former selves behind in that little bar, they crept along the dead-end back alley. And, soon realizing they had very few real options, entered the restaurant a few doors down through the kitchen. Nevertheless, they had made a clean break. If anyone *had* been following or observing them, they'd probably shaken them off for a while. As they passed through, one of the waiters said hello to Pedro and the Kitchen Porter said: *Hey Maria. How are you, Gurlfriend?*

*Ssshhh! Will you STOP that?! We're supposed to be in disguise, for Buddha's sake,* Maria giggled under her breath.

*I'm fine. We're all fine. Just passing through. JESUS, is nothing ever simple?!*

*Well that's that,* Gini said. *Our cover's blown. Yet ANOTHER triumph for the Buddhist Tranny.*

*Oh my God,* Karl interjected. *Are you trans-sexual, Maria?*

*Yeah, I am. What about it?!*

*No, nothing. Nice job. Great boobs.*

*Oh give me a fucking break! Just keep it in your pants, Father.*

By the time they found themselves standing in the middle of the busy dining room a concensus was emerging that they should just keep moving.

*This place has gone right off. We won't be staying,* said Virginia in her best fake posh-lady accent. *I don't much care for the standard of hygiene in the kitchen either. I sincerely hope you're not thinking of eating that salmon, Dear?*

Between them, in what must have amounted to no more than three and a half minutes, Gini and Maria had caused quite a stir, as usual. Then they were out in the main street once again.

*Funny thing is,* Gini chirped, *I was actually feeling a bit peckish. It's way past dinner-time. Can't we pop in somewhere for a bite to eat?*

Another minute or so and they were seated in a late night place around the corner looking at menus. It wasn't actually so late. Time was really dragging. It was going to be a long, long night.

As they ate supper, Pedro broke the silence by asking Karl if he knew what was going on and why they might be in danger. As Karl began to speak, the sound of the music playing around them and the TV news with more reports of rioters being battered began to merge and fade into the background.

They were extremely patient with Karl. Anyone else in that situation would've demanded to know whatever *he* knew. But his monologue was allowed to proceed without interruption, just as they had each taken turns that night in *Mastropiero*.

Karl began by explaining that he wasn't so sure how much detail he was permitted to go into, but he would tell them as much as he dared for the time being.

*My name is Karl Weithaler*, he said. *I am an Argentinian priest, living and working in a small community in the Andes. It's a bit complicated to explain it all – maybe Virginia can fill you in on the theological background another time – but I am a married priest. This is not so unusual in that region. In fact, we are actually so out of step with the main Roman Catholic Church that we take advantage of our geographical remoteness by simply getting on with our ministry unfettered. We're really quite rebellious. We not only allow priests to marry, we welcome women priests too. My own wife is a priest. We have three children...*

(Maria is thinking: *Don't tell me. THEY'RE all priests as well?*)

*... Our daughter is our own biological child and we have 'adopted' two small boys who were orphaned when their young mother passed away.*

*Almost everything about my early life was so strange in the extreme – to say the least of it – that being a mountain village priest, married to a female priest, with a whole bunch of kids plus various waifs and strays is completely unremarkable to me. Actually, it is a very grounding, ordinary, uplifting day-to-*

*day existence. I have a blessed life; I am both a simple Daddy, and a religious man. I am a humble servant overflowing with the love of God for his marginalized and forgotten people.*

*But the main thing you are asking about right now is why we are in danger – and for that, I must offer you my heart-felt apologies.*

*We are in danger, because of WHO I am, and because of what I am about to do.*

*I've been branded a 'renegade priest' by Rome. But that has very little to do with why we are in such danger.*

*I am in possession of certain facts and information about the Vatican's secret activities over the decades. I've been re-called to Rome to hand over the files in my possession.*

*Although I say it myself, this hand-over will be an earth-shattering event. It has to be. It mustn't be allowed to occur under the guise of the Church reprimanding a rogue priest behind closed doors. The dark silence of the Vatican is not a fitting resting place for my documents.*

*Therefore, I fully intend to use the proposed handover as a bargaining chip to make my case, and the case of priests like me. Not just married priests, but priests dedicated to serving the poorest of the poor. The voiceless must be heard.*

*But there are many people and agencies that don't want me to make that case, to make that handover, because it reflects badly on them. Very badly indeed! The poor, it turns out, are not the main problem. It is the contents of the scandalous files themselves and how I (of all people) came to own them.*

*Not just for the Vatican either. Foreign governments, intelligence agencies. The whole slimy house of cards. There are so many elements involved here... none of which will tolerate being named and shamed in public for what they have been a party to.*

*There are those who intend to prevent me from ever getting to Rome. Some would even have me assassinated. However, there are also those who would do everything in their power, albeit from afar or at least from a 'discreet' distance, to see to it that I travel safely.*

*Then there are others to whom I owe the highest allegiance. Loved ones and comrades. Plain, ordinary country folk. My heart goes out to them. And it is for their ultimate benefit that I will make the greatest possible use of this bargaining chip – this poisoned chalice – that has miraculously landed in my lap, thanks to genealogy and the hand of God.*

*There are those at the highest levels within and behind the Vatican who suspect – who KNOW – I will not just hand over my files without them first having to set in motion major church reform. I wouldn't be surprised if they are merely tagging me along until they get the files. But I have surprises of my own in store for them too.*

*We all know that before things can re-form and rebuild, they often have to utterly disintegrate. That is my role at this time in the history of Christianity, and no amount of counter-espionage or threats of violence will stand in my way.*

*I have made doubly certain that I have a few aces up my sleeve. So you must forgive me if I don't tell you everything about my mission or about who I am. But I do apologize that you've all been dragged into it. I can just about cope with my own life being in danger, but I can't bear the involvement of innocents such as yourselves. You will soon discover that you are up to your eyes in this mess and there's no going back.*

*I thought I could trust the British, or at least my own government, as they are both so mutually tainted by the cesspool I am keeping secret. But I was wrong. They are all incompetent, corrupt fools, waiting to see which way I am going to jump next. The Argentinians and the British between them have brought so much avoidable suffering to the world over the years. It is unforgivable.*

*Your Jalu Yogi is right. He is a wise man. Forget them all! We're on our own now and we will just have to produce a diamond from a pile of shit by ourselves. Maybe Jalu will have some clearer guidance when we meet him tomorrow. Dear Buddha, and God in Heaven, I hope so. Until then we'll just have to huddle together and keep our heads down. I suppose, longer-term, the main objective for me is to simply keep moving until it's safe enough to fly to Rome.*

Just then, the TV newsreader interrupted the scheduled bulletin to announce that Madrid's Counter-Terrorism Police had stormed a small bar in Chueca and closed it down indefinitely. They had hoped to intercept a foreign agent suspected of inciting anti-government rioters, who was thought to be hiding out there. But, by the time they arrived, he had gone.

As the man's photograph was being displayed on screen, there was also an implication he may have had something to do with the recent airport bombing which had claimed so many lives.

The photograph had obviously been taken in a remote, mountainous region.

It was of a rugged, heavily bearded man...

Karl.

# 19

Karl reassured his companions he had nothing to do with bombings or rioters. He took a moment to explain how things are rarely how they seem and that the announcement on the TV news was more likely to be the authorities trying to rediscover his whereabouts so they could protect him from those who wished to harm him. Somehow Pedro was not entirely convinced. But he kept his mouth shut for the time being.

After long silence, they were on the move again. Outside, in the small street, they could see the little bar they were in before. It was indeed closed down. Police were everywhere and flyers with Karl's photo were being handed out to passers-by. A discarded flyer blew along the path towards Maria: *Have you seen this man tonight?* She wondered if her friends at the bar would be able to stay quiet about meeting Karl earlier. Then she consoled herself they probably would. After all, most people in that little subset of the bohemian gay scene tended to stick together. They also despised authority, especially in the current climate. With newly transformed appearances, the four simply drifted down the road and followed the dwindling crowd around the corner.

Feeling somewhat panicky, Pedro's nerves got the better of him and, perhaps out of instinct, he convinced the others to get in somewhere else with a good crowd as soon as possible. A creature of habit, for better or worse, Pedro decided to bring them to *Hot Bar*.

As soon as they crossed the threshold, a big old Daddy-Bear who often did security as a favour to the owners looked as if he was about to say *'Sorry, regulars only'*. Karl was halfway through saying: *What kind of place is this?* Maria was primed to launch into an old script entitled *How fucking DARE you! Is it because I'm a woman?!* While Pedro, realizing their disguised appearance had temporarily rendered him unrecognizable as a regular, started to whisper *Hey, hombre. It's me. Pedro...* Simultaneously, Gini hoisting herself up to full height, pushed her way gracefully through the whole tableau announcing: *Finally! So THIS is the place my son has been hiding all these years! Step aside young man. We know our rights. There are no 'men-only' spaces in Madrid, BY LAW! Now. Fr Karl, follow me. In case you require either, I have it on the highest authority that the bathrooms are downstairs to your right, beside the dark-rooms, and the bar is just straight ahead of us here. Now what should we drink, Pedro? Do you boys still adore those Cock-sucking Cowboys? Or is it all Cosmopolitans these days?*

Surfing Gini's intoxicating wave of self-confidence, Maria dragged a mortified Pedro up to the bar and soon all four were sipping *Mocktails* and *Coke Zeros*.

*Pity about the no-drinking-tonight rule. I feel like getting pissed*, Gini sighed into her *Shirley Temple*. Popping another one of her brain pills, she admitted she wasn't feeling so hot and needed to sit down somewhere quiet to take stock.

Maria popped one too saying *O Fuck it! It won't kill me, will it? And you bitches have my head melted with all this fucking drama. Honestly, a high-speed motorbike taxi ride across Bangkok pales into insignificance by comparison.*

Gini and Maria took their glasses and made their way arm in arm across the packed bar room and down the winding stairs that led to the labyrinth below. Reluctantly, Pedro and Karl followed close behind.

Of course, there was no *Ladies* toilet and the *Gents* was occupied. Gini remarked that the stench would have killed a large cat. She said she really just needed to sit down somewhere for a short while and get her head straight before another mini-stroke took hold. She asked if they'd like to spend the night in Accident and Emergency instead. It was always an option. Her consultant had explained to her that, with her particular type of early onset dementia, every time her condition worsened and actually culminated in a stroke-type event she would plunge irretrievably to an even deeper level of dementia and her lifespan would be shortened. Consequently, Gini was continually trying to prepare herself for passing away after a mini-stroke one day. Hopefully that would be in the very distant future. She never discussed such matters with Pedro for fear of mounting hysteria, on both their parts.

Maria disappeared momentarily into the darkness of the basement and returned promptly with news. She grabbed Gini and the others and guided them through a dark-room filled with heaving sexuality and slippery condoms underfoot. No sooner had Gini asked *O Dear Jesus. What fresh hell is THIS? What's that shitty smell?!* and they'd crossed the *Lubricon.* They were now in a darkened corridor with tiny rooms on either side ... A luminescent sign read *'For Relaxing'*. They all entered the same cubicle. Hoping there was nothing too contagious or filthy lurking on the leatherette bench provided, our four fugitives perched on the edge of it and sat speechless in the darkness. Maria was last in. She locked the door behind her and lit a cigarette.

Eventually Maria broke the awkward silence: *At least we got away from that fucking horrendous disco-remix of Adele upstairs!* Sounds of coitus interruptus emanated from the cubicle next door, and the voice of what could only have been a heavily mustachioed purveyor of fresh cut flowers screeched through the wall: *No smoking allowed! Can't you morons read?!!*

*O shut the fuck up, Fidelma!* Pedro snapped. *It's me, Pedro! We're having a bit of a crisis in here. My Mama's not feeling too well.*

*Your MAMA's in there with you?!*

*YES. And, as I said, she's not feeling very well so PLEASE would you just this once mind your own fucking business and stay out of it?!* (Pedro *Sotto voce* to Maria: *I swear that Cuban queen just gives me gas!*)

*Do you want me to come in there and do CPR or something?* Fidelma replied. *You know I trained as a nurse back in La Havana... Or I could just sit with her for a while, maybe tell her some stories to take her mind off it... How we kept the dead pig in my mother's bath-tub for two weeks, Life in a Cuban Gulag, that sort of thing?* Fidelma's offer sounded quite genuine if somewhat unhinged.

*No No. Thanks, Love. It's OK. Everything's under control. Go back to your whatever-that-was before. Have fun.*

*OK Pedrito. Chat later. I'll call you tomorrow, Angel.* (The manly sound of rutting resumed).

*Can you 'imagination-that-one', if she knew there was also a tranny and a priest in here?* Maria said. *Nosey cow! Hostia!! She'd have a fucking stroke (O Sorry, Gini baby. No offence. Are you OK? Feeling better now, Mrs Léon?)*

*Sorry about all that, Mum,* Pedro murmured through the darkness, tenderly caressing Gini's hand. *Welcome to my world,* he added with a chuckle that reminded her of Benjamin.

*Darling. What kind of prude do you take me for? I tried to tell you lots of times before but you just won't listen to that sort of thing about your mother. I was quite a 'goer' in my day too, you know. I was having raunchy sex in public places before you were born... quite literally!* A hearty chortle slowly began to brew and rise from deep inside her.

In the smelly darkness, in a cubicle intended for 'manly rutting', *The Fabulous Four* had no choice but to sit there on the *faux chaise d'amour* rocking with stifled, contagious laughter. They were slowly bonding.

2 0

Virginia was recovering.

Feeling like he owed them a fuller explanation, thanks largely to a lengthy interrogation from Maria, Karl decided to share exactly what he'd been authorized by British Intel to say if he was ever captured. Previously, he hinted that they were being pursued both by his enemies and his protectors. And that it was because of who Karl was, and what he knew.

In the alien anonymity of a dark-room cubicle, in one of Europe's premier gay bars for bears and their friends, Karl visualized himself in a kind of confessional. Recognizing he was not the first man within those walls to quietly share his secret truth with another – he probably wasn't even the first Catholic priest – in the darkness he finally began to shed a layer or two.

*As you know, my name is Karl Weithaler and I am from Argentina. But I was not born there. I was born in Poland in 1967 to an unmarried woman.*

*My mother was a simple, devout woman. She worked as the house-keeper for a wonderful, vibrant, young priest. She said he took her in when no-one else cared and that she would stand by him through thick and thin. She ran the house. Cooked and cleaned for him. Eventually, she gained his confidence to the point where she also organized his weekly diary. He was so kind to my mother. He called her by her first name, Marion, and treated her like his own family.*

*He quickly rose through the ranks becoming Parish Priest some years later and then Bishop. He was elected Archbishop of Krakow in 1964 and Cardinal in 1967. Mother took care of him all that time. But she also realized she may not be able to stay with him forever. So she made tentative inquiries with distant relatives about making a new life for herself in Germany some day in the future. Then disaster struck. Mother got herself pregnant by some man who couldn't marry her, and I was born.*

*The Cardinal never spoke about the pregnancy or the baby but saw it as his Christian duty not to insist that my mother leave. So it was that she and I lived in two small rooms in a side annex separate from the main mansion with access to a beautiful scented garden filled with summer roses. He brought us along with him on skiing holidays and short trips abroad. The life we had together when I was still only a child was a curious kind of idyll.*

*I don't remember him as a Cardinal at all. When the three of us were together, time stood still. We were just ordinary. Mother shopped and kept house. I went to school and did homework. And 'The Father' – as we continued to call him – said Mass, heard confessions, and immersed himself in some of the most incredible social work projects in Krakow. He didn't seem to have so much 'Cardinalling' to do apart from regular meetings, which he hated, and the occasional civic function to attend.*

*He used every opportunity to speak out on behalf of the poor and the marginalized, and soon became well-known as a champion of the people. For a genuinely spiritual man, his was a dangerously high profile. Remember this all happened during what was, of course, yet another horribly dark time in Poland's history. I was still very, very young. So I don't recall much about the times. Even those early days when we still lived with him are little more than a warm, distant blur.*

*By the early 70s, Mother and I were living in Germany. She was working in a hospital, cooking and cleaning of course. I attended school and – though still only a boy – became very interested in politics and religion. From time to time, the Cardinal would write from Krakow with small gifts and news about his social work. I didn't know it then, but Mother also received money to supplement her small income. He always made a point of sending me his love and encouraged my mother to make me into a fine man. 'Someone who would love others more than himself. Someone who could change the world'.*

*Life in Germany plodded along. An un-married mother pretended her husband was dead. There were picnics on hillsides and school trips to the lake. But I kept a close eye on the Cardinal's activities through newspapers my mother got sent to us from Poland. Although I never knew any of this, around the same time I was born the Cardinal had been instrumental in formulating the Papal Encyclical 'Humanae Vitae'. It focused on the sanctity of human life and forbade artificial birth control and abortion. Apart from being a champion of the poor the Cardinal, it seemed, was also a champion of The Church. For this great loyalty he had been rewarded with meteoric upward mobility.*

*I also now realize he would have been very much in the forefront of Rome's official response to the growing popularity of the Liberation Theology movement which was sparked by Gustavo Gutiérrez in 1972.*

*When I was eleven, Mother sat me down and told me all about sex and mortal sin. I remember how excruciating it was. It seemed to go on for hours. Yet the worst was still to come, the following day.*

*Mother took me into the garden where she'd set up a jug of lemonade and two glasses on a rickety table that'd seen better days. She began to weep and finally broke down entirely. She told me she had to share with me her darkest secret and I was never to tell a living soul. She threatened me with eternal damnation and hell-fire. She said she would haunt me all my days if I ever breathed a word of it. The Cardinal had requested a private meeting with me in a summer lodge high up in the mountains... He was my Dad.*

*Within a matter of days, I was in a simple sitting room on top of a great mountain. The sun was shining in from across a deep valley and Mother was outside waiting. I was sitting face to face with the Cardinal from Krakow, Karol Wojtyla, after whom (in the German form) I had been named.*

Karl went on to tell the spell-bound assembly how the meeting with his biological father only lasted one hour, and how he never met him again. He said the Cardinal hadn't once referred to being Karl's father or his relationship with his housekeeper, Marion. The reason for their meeting was, at least for him, far more important. Cardinal Wojtyla gave the young boy details of how to gain access to a safety deposit box registered in his name in Switzerland.

The box, the Cardinal confided, could only be accessed by either himself or the boy, since they both bore the same name. It was not to be opened unless Karl was instructed to do so, or in the event that Karl deemed it necessary to move its contents to a safer place at some future time due to 'perilous circumstances'.

The Cardinal told Karl the safety deposit contained copies of 'top secret' Church files that he called his Insurance Policy. He said the documents attested to many of the numerous 'unsavoury' events and situations the Church had been involved in, over the centuries. He said he had made his own personal peace with having documented proof of such abominations and that Karl shouldn't become obsessed or disillusioned by such matters. The Holy Church of Rome, he said, was man-made after all. Even though it is inspired and guided by God, foolish men had occasionally misled it and brought it into utter disrepute. The files were the sordid evidence of their demonic work.

He concluded the meeting by telling Karl of his growing fear that certain 'elements currently controlling the Church behind the scenes' might do very bad things if they didn't get their way. Sometimes he even feared for his own life and the lives of other Cardinals and bishops. Even the Holy Father, the Pope himself, was not entirely safe.

A bewildered young Karl Weithaler left the alpine lodge never to see his father again, apart from on television.

At the end of Summer, and without any discussion whatsoever, Karl was sent to a Protestant boarding school, of all things, in England. Far away from his beloved mother, and still reeling from all that his young mind had recently learned, he prepared himself to settle into this new place and all the lonely, anonymous isolation that came with it.

## 21

By around 1.30am they'd all moved back upstairs to the bar. Still numb from Karl's revelations, they hardly spoke at all.

Sebastián, the volunteer doorman they'd encountered earlier on had joined them for a drink. The crowd was beginning to move on so they were sitting at some high stools around a circular table near the entrance chatting pleasantries about the riots and the weather. Gini seemed to be recovering well, and she and Karl started talking directly with Sebastián about politics or something.

Pedro took the opportunity to move close to Maria for a more private exchange.

*You do realise Karl was saying he is the son of Karol Wojtyla, don't you? The Polish Cardinal who became John Paul II ... the Pope?!*

*Yes. I'm not an idiot. I DID manage to grasp that subtle detail all by myself, Maria groaned. What about it anyway? We all have our back story. You yourself don't know whose son you are. What if you found out it was someone famous or something. What if people didn't believe YOU? Think how that would feel.*

*Yeah yeah, I know. Being the secret son of someone famous is one thing. But the POPE! Come on! ... I don't believe a word of it!*

Maria turned to Sebastián and said, *Sorry to interrupt Big Man. But we were just wondering what it would feel like to discover you were actually the son of someone famous and no one believed you.*

*What do you mean?* Sebastián looked puzzled at such a bizarre interjection. *Personally I wouldn't give a damn who believed me or not. If it is true, it's true no?* A couple of beats passed as the others stared at Maria for being so indiscreet. They looked to Karl apologetically. Sebastián, picking up on the obvious, addressed himself directly to Karl: *Jesus! Have you just found out your biological father was someone famous?!*

*Not quite famous,* Karl retorted dismissively (feigning modesty, and glaring at Maria who pouted back at him like a scolded child). *I haven't just found anything out. I was just telling the others that many years ago, my mother told me I was the son of a well-known folk singer in Argentina. That's all.*

Pedro whispered out of the side of his mouth to Maria: *You see. I told you. It's all fantasy with him. Another tall tale. And so easily manufactured on the spot. Habitually evasive to the last. He'd lie his way out of anything, that one.*

The conversation was allowed to quickly flow towards 'safer' ground via a river of trivia and social commentary such as what celebrity had a secret love-child, who is having an affair with whom, and who might be going to win Celebrity Big Brother this year.

Before long, all four of them were being driven by Sebastián in his massive, luxury 4 Wheel Drive. He was taking them to a private all-night party that was already in full swing out at his place in *Salamanca*. As they cruised along at some speed, Sebastián asked if anyone minded some music. *Anything but that bitch Adele*, whined Maria from the back, raising a laugh. Catching the moment, Maria ventured to ask how Sebastián could afford such a fabulous motor and what he did for a living.

*Apart from fucking the right guys, I haven't really worked for years,* he ricocheted (sticking his long fat tongue out at Maria in the rear-view mirror). *Actually, I got this particular vehicle as a gift from a very grateful person who wanted me to keep our secret love secret... Julio Iglesias. Ever heard of him??*

A millisecond passed while the penny dropped. Then they all fell about cackling and snorting with laughter. Before it fully subsided, Sebastián chuckled devilishly: *Ah no, Darling. That's not true. I'm only pulling your leg. Julio didn't give me THIS car. I bought it myself. How rude are YOU anyway, asking such personal questions?! You don't really think I'm going to tell you all my sordid little secrets do you? We've only just met. Try me again after a few whiskey-cokes at my place and I might open up to your incessant probing!*

More laughter. Amazing to think this guy seemed so different when they first laid eyes on him, and now he was the life and soul of their night.

Maria leaned in to Pedro saying: *See, Conseula. People make up stories about themselves for all sorts of reasons. It's not always lying. Maybe it's just for fun, something to say. To smooth things along, you know?*

*Actually, you're simply reinforcing my basic point, Maria. What I'm saying is, Karl could tell us anything at all just to smooth things over and we'd be none the wiser now would we?*

*What if the newsflash was right and Karl IS dangerous to be around?*

*Jalu knows more than you think he knows. He wouldn't tell us to look after Karl if he was a bad person. Just wait till we meet him tomorrow. Let HIM put your mind at rest.*

Soon they were driving through Salamanca, around by the famous university and out a bit further where a leafy avenue opened up ahead of them. As they turned into a quiet side street, Sebastián used a remote control to open the enormous security gates. They were in.

The house was actually more like a palace. All very modern and spacious. Downstairs was like a New York loft. Hard wood and chrome, with floor to ceiling windows that slid and folded to join the interior seamlessly with the exterior. From the outside there was a touch of the Orient about it all. Subtle architectural details and cross-cultural references combining Modern Spain with Bali or somewhere. And the garden! As you walked towards the entrance hall, a tiny path meandered through such planting as you'd only find in a 6 Star hotel in Phuket. The stone garden walls overflowed with fragrant tumbling blossoms of every imaginable origin. Gini and Karl lagged behind a while, taking it all in. As they mooched from this to that, Gini informed Karl of the importance of the place that Salamanca's great university occupied in world history.

*The grand old University of Salamanca, she imparted, was established in 1134. It was the first institution in Europe to be awarded the designation 'University'. There have been numerous professors and past pupils of great note. Foremost among them perhaps is the Christian mystic St John of the Cross, whose life and work kept true spirituality alive throughout the Counter Reformation. And Miguel de Cervantes who of course went on to write the legendary 'Don Quixote', which I myself had the great pleasure of translating into modern English when I was a young women at college and still knew nothing of the world.*

For what seemed the longest time, until Sebastián came back out to fetch them in, Virginia and Karl moved about the exquisite moonlit garden together chatting like two old friends. They shared their ideas about foreign travel and exotic flowers. Which windmills *The Man of La Mancha* and *Sancho Panza* might have tilted at, and how a *Dark Night of the Soul* could lead to a rapturous merging with the Love of God.

On entering the house proper with Sebastián, they could clearly see that a party of sorts was indeed in full swing. There were stocky gay men who for the most part seemed very friendly and appeared weirdly similar. There were also several women, some of the 'classic beauty' variety and others who were either considerably larger in girth (and laughed a lot at the men's antics) or who appeared more the creative, 'free-spirit' type of gal. There was drink and lots of food to nibble. Some people were chatting together. Others were dancing to the minimalist chrome stereo that was turned up just loud enough to enjoy but not so loud as to intrude too much on others. All in all, Gini thought, it looked like a perfect evening. Karl wasn't so sure, but was glad of a safe environment to pass the last few hours before boarding the train.

Maria was standing at the kitchen counter with Sebastián making him belly-laugh to the extent that he dribbled his *Rioja* down his chiseled chin. It was all she could do not to lean forward and lick a droplet or two before kissing him full on the mouth. She imagined his thick member. She wondered if she'd last the rest of the night without alcohol.

Pedro was in a corner chatting to an old friend from his school days, who he also knew from the bars. They didn't look the same age, perhaps because Pedro didn't buff and preen himself enough to compete at that level. Maybe, in truth, he was now so jaded with the search for *The One* that he was very close to giving up altogether.

Gini and Karl made a bee-line for the food platters. Gloriously fresh, carefully prepared *tasties* would not normally make sense at such an ungodly hour, but tonight (or was it this morning already?) somehow they made perfect sense. *Eat when you're hungry,* Gini said. *And drink when you're dry,* added Karl completing the old adage. They continued picking and munching, drinking wildly over-priced *Badoit* fizzy water from France and chatting with whoever passed by.

After some time, Gini felt tired and resisting the urge to go lie down in a spare bedroom made a throne for herself in an armchair next to Pedro. From there she could observe almost everything without effort. And she could do her most favourite thing, in such a situation: Magnetize the people she was interested in meeting so they would come to HER and sit around while she held court. *All these people are so young,* she thought to herself. *I doubt if any of them are over seventeen.* As they each began to speak about themselves, and their full and varied lives, she found a wry smile settling on her lips. *Sweet Jesus, these kids haven't lived at all,* she heard her own voice say inside her head. *I've probably already forgotten more than they will ever know.*

It was clear to see that Sebastián was a rough diamond, perhaps even with a murky past. But he had a really pure heart and was also a wonderful host. As time progressed, he moved about chatting and topping up drinks, offering more food and joining others in the garden for a sly cigarette. Gini also noticed people discreetly slipping away, and spending a very long time in the bathroom. *Maybe they're having sex, or doing coke,* she mouthed over to Maria, who had also noticed and raised an eyebrow in Gini's direction.

*Maybe I should go investigate,* Maria mimed.

*No. Don't you dare, Missy! That's ALL we need,* Gini hissed under her breath. She attempted a comical mime of Maria being found passed out on the bathroom floor, her knickers around her ankles. Suddenly, they realized the whole entourage had stopped talking and were completely agog, staring quizzically at their carry-on.

Pedro said: *Mother, stop that right now. You're embarrassing yourself. Why can't you two play nice?*

Virginia pretended to turn her head aside in blatant disregard. While that got a good laugh, and she could hear one friend saying to another how cute Pedro and she were together, she glimpsed Karl out of the corner of her eye replacing the receiver of the house telephone and nodding an almost imperceptible thank you right across the room in Sebastián's direction. She mentally filed it away under '*WHAT !!??*' (while wondering simultaneously if she would remember to bring it up again later).

The night was almost over and Sebastián, recognizing their deep need for no-questions-asked, agreed to have them driven to the train whenever they were ready. At 6 o'clock, another silver chariot, this time with black tinted windows and an even bigger, thuggier driver, pulled up in the secure driveway. The '*Fab Four*' made their goodbyes quickly and stylishly. All of a sudden in the near twilight the Tibetans call Vajrasattva's Dawn, looking like they *had* actually been disguised by a rag-tag bunch of beatniks and drag queens in a Chueca speak-easy and spent the whole night on the town, they slipped quietly out of Salamanca.

They agreed they were still pretty much undetected. At the station, an envelope with tickets for the AVE awaited them, as if by magic. And soon, with no phones and no luggage, they were on their way. South.

## 22

Twenty minutes or so into the two-and-a-half hour journey, Gini was already asleep. She was dreaming of a sunny afternoon she'd spent on a hillside high up in Nepal. She was lying on a tartan blanket with her head in Benjamin's lap and the infant Pedro was sitting upright against her hip. There was a picnic of quaint little sandwiches in the English style, some china cups and a flask of hot tea, all arranged around a small Everest of jelly and yoghurt. A local driver sat dozing in the shade against the side of his jeep. It was a scene she'd revisited many times before except this time the sky around them was replete with double and triple rainbows that spoke to her. She heard the voice say she should never be afraid of her mini-strokes and, if it did occur unexpectedly, that death was just like walking through a doorway; Virginia was being lovingly counseled to prepare for the unexpected. *Yeah-yeah, Jalu Yogi. That's easy for YOU to say,* Gini found herself grumbling.

Maria, sitting opposite, checked the reflection of her hair and makeup in the window.

The two aisle seats were taken by Pedro who sat beside his Mam and Karl who sat opposite reading a pamphlet he had picked up at the station in *Atocha*.

Without thinking it might present a source of irritation to others, Karl began reading aloud some 'interesting' passages from it.

*"Alta Velocidad Española (AVE) is a service of high-speed rail in Spain operated by RENFE, the Spanish national railway company, at speeds of up to 310 km/h (193 mph). The name is literally translated from the Spanish 'Alta Velocidad Española' ('Spanish High Speed'), but its initials are also a play on the Castilian word 'ave', meaning 'bird'. As of December 2011, the Spanish AVE system is the longest High Speed Rail network in Europe with 2,665 km (1,656 mi) and the second in the world, after China."*

*Karl, please. Do you have to do that?* Pedro was trying not to snap.

*Oh, I'm sorry Pedro. Am I bothering you?*

*No. Go on,* Maria announced. *Personally, I find it quite interesting.*

Karl sent a sheepish glance in the direction of Pedro, who was fixing Gini's blanket. Then he recommenced scanning the page and reading in more hushed tones (summarizing for the sake of brevity as he went).

*There was a courtesy lounge at Atocha Station in Madrid (Oh I guess we missed that one), which is available to those holding First Class tickets. On the train itself there are dining and bar cars, which are open to all passengers regardless of class. It looks like there are two classes: 'Preferente' (that's us, First Class) and 'Turista', which must be a kind of Second Class, I suppose. Oh, poor them. Condemned to languish away in some kind of hellish 'cheap seat' no doubt. Discrimination... Will it never end, I ask myself?*

A wry, self-mocking grin crossed Karl's face momentarily. Maria, warming to him more and more, caught his eye and grimaced in recognition of his little joke. Pedro gave a childish, huffy sigh and held Gini's hand.

As if having no awareness of what could be on Pedro's mind, Karl continued:

*The AVE can travel at 300 km per hour, and the journey from Madrid to Sevilla can take as little as 2 hours 30 minutes, if you don't stop at Córdoba. (Scanning forward apace) Oh, let me see now... Ah Yes, here it is. The first train to Sevilla is 7am (that's the one we're on). And it should arrive at 930am (All going according to plan, 'God Speed')... Oh and Yes (the icing on the cake): The wonderful RENFE says that if we are more than 5 minutes late arriving at our destination, we can have our money back. Isn't that simply marvelous? Hurrah!*

'Hurrah'? 'Icing'? Gini said, rousing from her snooze, her eyes still closed. *Did you say something about cake, Fr Karl?*

*Now you see what you've done?! You've woken Mother up,* Pedro glared. Fixing Gini's fringe back into place, he continued in a baby-voice that made the others squirm: *And she was just having a lovely little nap for herself, poor lamb. You must be exhausted, Mummy?*

*Oh will you please just stop fussing, Consuela! I'm not a child! Going senile and being infantile is not the same thing!*

*No, not at all,* Maria added.

*Will you just give me the common courtesy of at least TRYING to decipher the difference and allow me some dignity, Darling. Is that too much to ask?*

*No, Mother. You're right. I'm sorry.*

*What's up with you this morning anyway? Is little Pedro cranky because he's tired? (You see how patronizing it sounds now, do you?)*

*Yes, I DO see. Thank you, Mother. Thanks ever so much for pointing that out. And no. There's nothing wrong with me. I'm perfectly fine. As you say, I think we all just need some sleep.*

Her eyes wide open now, Gini looked across at Karl saying, *Everything alright, Karl? What's that you're reading from anyway?*

*Yes fine. Thank you, Virginia. What, this? Oh it's just some pamphlet about the train I picked up.*

*Please continue,* Gini commanded in a very regal tone, which matched her *rich-lady-about-town* disguise. Then looking to Maria in her *Cougar-Par-Excellence* get up, Gini smiled graciously and pronounced: *Personally, I find that kind of thing quite fascinating... in the EXTREME.* (Now turning back to Karl) *Please DO go on, Dear. You're exotic 'timbre' is very much to my liking.*

Feeling a little embarrassed and put on the spot, Karl glanced through the remaining paragraphs for something 'fascinating' to share:

*Em. Let me see now... Aha! Got it: The journey from Madrid to Sevilla is 536km long and we'll be there at 930 am since we are not stopping in Córdoba.*

*You said that already,* Pedro moaned in the background

*Incidentally,* Karl soldiered on regardless, *I just happened to notice it is also possible to return to Madrid via Córdoba starting at Málaga. If all goes well down here, and I can book a new flight to Rome from Madrid, I think I should very much like to go that route.*

*We will pass through La Mancha (à la Cervantes, don't-ya-know!) and cross the Sierra Morena, eventually arriving at Sevilla (the capital of Andalucía, 'El Andaluz').*

Periods of silence interspersed with sunny spells of polite chit-chat ensued for much of the journey as they took turns napping and admiring the majestic views that rolled by their tinted window on the world. Nobody seemed too pushed about going for food or drinks. Pedro shared bottles of water he had bought, and that was enough to keep them going.

At one point, after Córdoba, Gini needed the loo. So Maria accompanied her whispering, *Why do you suppose Pedro is so grumpy with Karl? I don't think he likes him very much.*

They each used the bathroom, Gini first then Maria, still continuing their analysis of the situation through the closed door. Not having arrived at any real conclusion – neither one had said what was really on their mind – the two ladies came back to their seats to find Pedro *arguing* with Karl. He sounded just like Benjamin, cautious yet passionate. His voice was not raised, but his point was being firmly made nonetheless. Both Gini and Maria knew from experience not to get involved. They excused themselves and squeezed into their window seats, and observed the one-sided mini-drama unfold.

Pedro had obviously been telling Karl he had difficulty believing his story about who he was and what he was doing in Madrid – and who would blame him – it did sound too outlandish for words. Karl was in the process of trying to comfort Pedro when the others got back. He was saying he couldn't prove anything there and then. And how fact is often stranger than fiction anyway.

*But the Pope's son? Are we really expected to believe you are the son of the man who later became Pope John Paul II ? And because of the Church secrets he entrusted to you, that we are all now in grave danger?? Come off it, Father! We' don't even know if you are a priest. Or if you actually flew in from Argentina. We don't know anything at all about you now, do we?*

*I AM my father's son. There's no denying it, even if I can't prove it to you right now. Forget about the Pope for a moment... THESE are the important facts: I know dangerous stuff. Seriously dangerous! I have dropped into your lives from somewhere, en route to somewhere else. You wouldn't even have met me had your mother not been who SHE is. My mission is to make maximum use of the knowledge I have when I get to where I am going. Hopefully it will benefit many, many people. That's what I am up to, Pedro. I am not some shady character in a cheap spy movie. I'm a good person, who is doing his best with what life has dumped on him. That's all! Plain and simple! So now, we are all on this kind of journey together. None of us know where it will lead or how it's going to end. It's not enjoyable. It's not fun. And there is no room for error.*

*I could go it alone, I suppose. But it's too late for that. You're all in it with me now – up to your eyes in it. You COULD go home and leave me to it. But my guess is you all have your own individual reasons for continuing on this path with me. Virginia is here because of her connection with my mission. You are here because of your mother's ill-health. And Maria is here because of you and because she is going to see her Buddhist teacher again when we get off this train. At every single moment, you each continue to make the choice to stay. The choice is yours. I, on the other hand, HAVE no choice. This is my life now. This is MY choice. You might say the day I get to Rome will be the culmination of my life's work...all that I am. WHO I am. What I know. And what I must do with my life. It all comes together once I arrive safely in Rome. That is why so many are protecting me, and why there is so much danger from others.*

Gini, also using a hushed but intentional tone, asked: *Why did you ask to make a personal phone call last night from Sebastián's place, without telling any of us about it?*

*You SEE what I'm talking about??!!* (Pedro gestured to the four winds) *And you're shocked when we don't believe you? Don't trust you?!*

*Stop it, Pedro. That's enough now!* Gini turned and directed her gaze at Karl once more: *At least tell us YOU are not going to harm us, whatever other danger we may be in.*

*I called Rome to postpone my meeting with the mandarins at the Vatican and to alert some third parties in the media that I wanted them to be aware of my difficulty getting to Rome. Unknowns to the Vatican, as I already told you, I have some aces up my sleeve that I fully intend to play when the time is right.*

The final stretch of track towards Sevilla felt quiet and lonely.

It wasn't fear or distrust, or even the unknown that hung in the air. There was a kind of separation between all four of them, the likes of which normally follows a massive stand-off or a family screaming match.

Just as the *Three Amigos* had come together, then dissolved and morphed into the *Fabulous Four*, now the

*Four* were completely disintegrating somehow. They were soon to become an entirely new entity:

*Five*.

Part Two

# PLEASE. CALL ME JALU.

2 3

As they walked down the platform and through the barrier, I was standing there to greet them. I caught Maria's eye and waved.

*Rinpoche, it's so wonderful to see you again!* Maria said, joining her palms together at her heart and beaming from ear to ear.

*I told you before, please don't call me that,* I said. I pulled her close and held her elegant shoulders with both hands as I kissed her on each cheek. Extending my hand towards Gini, I looked deeply into her eyes saying, *And you must be Mrs Virginia. So lovely to finally meet you. Please. Call me Jalu.*

We shook hands warmly. She didn't seem to know what to say and simply stood there, rooted to the spot, her mouth open. A tear inexplicably dropped onto her ruddy cheek.

Still holding her hand, I smiled at each of the others and used my free hand to make contact: *Young Mr Pedro, with his whole life ahead of him,* I said. *And the intrepid Fr Karl, with so much important work to accomplish.*

They seemed a bit shocked that I addressed them by name. I could see Maria wasn't in the slightest bit shocked by anything I could do or say. We had history and a profound heart-connection we both knew transcended space and time.

Maria was scanning my attire to check out what I had chosen to wear for the occasion. She could see I was also in a kind of disguise; I had flip-flops, beige shorts and a jaunty mauve polo shirt. She recognized the look immediately. I was obviously in *tourist drag*. We had both discovered in Bangkok that every 'look', every conscious choice of clothing, is just another sort of *drag*. An image we wish to dredge up from within and project to the world for a day.

Composing himself, Karl greeted me quite formally and thanked me for intervening. Searching for common ground, he added how much he respected Buddhism and felt deeply for the plight of Tibet. He confessed that he had photographs of the Buddha and His Holiness the Dalai Lama in his daily prayer book back home.

Pedro continued to say nothing but was clearly moved by something. He held Maria's hand to ground himself. He was taking everything in. I could tell he was comparing me to himself; both of us were *out* gay men, of a vaguely similar age. But on the face of it we couldn't have appeared more different (I suppose he'd become accustomed to thinking of gay men as having only one generic appearance). He could see I was neither hairy nor muscled. I was nicely kempt but not prissy about it. I suppose to him I just looked like any foreign tourist; maybe I look a bit Japanese or Mongolian to Westerners who know nothing of Tibet. But, as a generic tourist, at a train station, I just blended in... Exactly the look I was going for today.

Although in reality only a few minutes had passed, I was keen to get them moving. So I quickly explained the lay of the land in Sevilla:

*So nice to meet you all. But I need to get you out of here straight away. There'll be plenty of time for chatting once we get on the road. As you are probably already aware, Seville is one of the major flashpoints for the current spate of rioting and civil unrest in Spain. The authorities are terrified it will escalate even further later today. So far, there has been a whole week of what can only be referred to as out-and-out war on the streets here. That's why I came.*

*The citizens are rising up against the police and the army. Banks, Government buildings and essential personnel have all been targeted and this has prompted the army to take to the streets, even in the daytime. They have used brutal, excessive force against their own people; water-cannons, tear-gas and taiser baton-charges at first, but now they have resorted to gun fire and tanks on the streets. There is even a rumour that last night they entered a new phase and are now using snipers on tall buildings to pick off the supposed ring-leaders and minor incendiary devices have been put into bins and bus shelters to get people off the streets.*

*Right now, the crowds have gathered in their tens of thousands to block the airport. And they are outside here too in an attempt to disrupt the normal flow of people in and out of the city. There's a tank blocking the main road up to the station and a cordon of army and police securing the perimeter. I'm sure they must have announced something on the train before you got off, but I need to tell you that your AVE was the last train to enter Seville. The station is now closed until further notice and they are advising all remaining passengers to exit by the side door and get the hell out of here. So now… stay calm and follow me. I have a rental car waiting in a side street around the back. Try not to draw any unusual attention to yourselves as we walk. I'm afraid that 'other elements' may detect Fr Karl and use the smoke-screen of the civil disobedience to cause us all major harm.*

It was a terrifying walk across the marble hallways. It took us around by the closed cafés and news-stands, and out into the searing sunlight. I crossed the tiny street into the shade, all the while shepherding my companions like a line of trusting goslings.

In no time, and apparently undetected, we were all in the relative safety of the car, *air-con* blasting, heading out of town. We then made a three-quarter circuit around a kind of ring road till we were pointing in the correct general direction for where I wanted to go. We appeared to pass through a shimmering heat mirage that hovered above the highway and, having crested a tiny hill, were finally out in the open. The majestic, scorched countryside unfolded and sprawled out before us. The spacious grandeur of *Andalucía* lay all around.

We felt self-liberated and reborn.

**24**

As we left the utter chaos and injustice of Seville far behind, I turned the radio down and began asking Karl some leading questions to get to the heart of things and clear the air.

Karl said he would already have arrived in Rome by now, had the explosions not occurred in the airport at Madrid. He added he probably would've been in the thick of it all with the Vatican at this precise moment.

I decided to cut through his evasive tactics from the start and lay my cards on the table saying, *We are all in this thing together now, Karl. You owe these good people an enormous debt of gratitude for taking care of you so well this far. Look around you. It is thanks to these three that you are still alive. Don't you think it's time to tell them a bit more about what's going on? I suggest you start somewhere near the beginning, and take it from there little by little. I find bite-size chunks of complex information are always easier to digest. Tell us about what happened at Madrid airport.*

Karl slowly began piecing a story together about how he got off the plane and walked over to Virginia. I hurried him along  saying it'd take an aeon if he was going to include every detail. Encouragingly, I prompted him: *Tell us about the explosion. Why do you feel it happened? ... Honestly, please.*

He seemed to be preparing himself to tell something at least resembling the truth so I backed off to give him the space he needed.

*Because of the nature of the Vatican secrets I possess, there are certain nations who are implicated and they are the ones who are protecting me. All they want is for me to get to Rome and hand over what I've got so the secrets can become hidden again. They will do whatever they can to make sure the truth doesn't come out or fall into the wrong hands.*

*AND...,* I said.

*And, then there are those who would most dearly love these secrets to actually come out.*

*BUT MORE THAN THAT...,* I said.

*But more than that,* Karl continued carefully, *there are those who want to kill me for who I am more than anything else I suppose.*

*YOU SUPPOSE...?*

*Sorry. I KNOW. Being the biological son of a father such as mine means I have been a target all my life. It would benefit people greatly to have me killed so they don't have to face the truth about my existence. If it were widely known who my father was, there would be a queue around the block with people who want me dead.*

*When I arrived at the airport there had been a catastrophic breach of security. Despite all the efforts and planning of the British and Spanish governments, one of those parties who want me dead knew where I would be and when. They detonated a bomb right beside me and Gini as we sat talking.*

*Miraculously, we were blown clear of the devastation and escaped with our lives. Many innocent people were not so lucky.*

Pedro became very animated suddenly: *I can't take any more of this bullshit! You almost got my mother killed, you fraud! And for what?! I can't take it! This is all just BULLSHIT!!*

*You'd better learn to 'take it', Pedro. Believe me,* I said, *resistance to the truth will only make you suffer more. This is just the beginning of it, and there's plenty more to come.*

*Jalu's right,* Virginia finally entered the moment. *If that bomb, or whatever it was, was intended to kill Fr Karl you must at least take it as proof that he has some very powerful enemies...*

*And some very powerful allies,* I added (smiling in Karl's direction).

*OK. That's enough truth-telling for now,* I suggested. *Let's try to simply drop it for a while, and we'll take it up again later if you like.* Judging by their jaded silence, I inferred a resounding affirmative.

*What we need now is some Group Therapy... Retail Therapy, Darlings!*

*WHAT??!!* Pedro groaned with the habit of many lifetimes.

*Oh isn't he simply wonderful, Gini? I knew you'd like him,* Maria chirped.

*Like him?* Virginia, sitting in the front passenger seat right next to me, directed her conclusion to the panoramic view: *I think I'm going to LOVE him.* I kept my eyes on the road ahead and waited for a signpost that suggested so-called 'civilization' and shops.

*You see... Excess baggage, you can live without. Even mobile phones, in this instance, proved to be more of a hindrance than a help (We can't have various government officials tracking you and contacting you willy-nilly calling the shots, now can we? To say nothing of would-be international terrorists also with tracking devices and what not). No. That's not what we need. What we need is Fashion! Drag! As the Buddha always used to say: You can never have enough hats or gloves ... Honestly, what a Drag Queen SHE was...* That got a good healthy laugh out of them. Spirits needed to be raised, so I made a joke at the expense of the one person I knew wouldn't take offence, and who always told the truth. Simple.

*You need clothes and... well, stuff really. Girly stuff. MANLY stuff. We all need to get into a town, soon, and go SHOPPING!*

Pedro, starting to ease up a bit more now: *I would actually LOVE to get something else to wear, and some toiletries. But we have practically no money between us. How can we pay for clothes, or anything for that matter?*

*Worry not, Little Squirrel*, I said. *Jalu Yogi to the rescue!*

*That's what I used to call him when he was a little boy and in need of reassurance*, Virginia whispered to me. *I know*, I replied. *I picked that up the minute I met him.*

*Don't worry about anything to do with money while we're on the road together. I have a very wealthy benefactor. He gave me a Visa Debit card in my own name for his personal bank account some years ago and trusts me completely with it. He knows I would never abuse his great kindness. And that I'd only access his apparently limitless billions of 'Lovely Lolly' if the need arose... And today, mi amigos, the 'Famous Five' NEED to go shopping!*

*Now Maria, I said. I trust you can take care of co-ordinating all this? When we get into a town, Miss Virginia and I will sit somewhere quiet sipping coffee and nibbling something incredibly delicious and lo-carb. You will take my bank card – the usual pin number, Dear – and bring the two boys and yourself off shopping for enough clothes etc to last a few days on the road. Virginia will tell you every intimate measurement of her youthfully blushing body before you depart. So surprise her with a collection of fabulous new looks that'll make her the envy of anyone from the world of Espionage Internationale who may pass by.*

Arriving in the centre of the first suitable town, I parked the over-sized, over-priced people-carrier.

*Get some brekky for yourselves while you're at it. Then head back here to me and Virginia so we can get on the road again. You have an hour.*

*O please call me 'Gini'. Nobody's really called me 'Virginia' since I was in Cambridge. 'Mizz Virginia Blake', they would say.*

*Yes, but that's where it all started, didn't it? In Cambridge? ... Let's grab a couple of comfy chairs under the collonades, near the plaza. We can have a lovely cuppa together and you can tell me all about it.*

## 25

The 14th century little town of *Utrera* clusters around a Moorish castle. There are some fine churches from the Renaissance and earlier, and the town is peppered with many Baroque mansions. Surrounded by vast olive groves and fields dedicated to cereal production, Utrera is also famous for raising some of the best cattle and fighting bulls in all of Spain. There is a strong tradition of Flamenco dancing and song stretching back across the mists of time. And once a year, in June, *Los Gitanos* (*Gypsies*) gather from all around to hold a great festival there.

Young birds were singing the news of the day from ancient tree-tops and steeples. And the intoxicating smell of citrus and fresh bread baking hung on the mid-morning air.

I sat with Gini in *Plaza Santa Maria de la Mesa*, sipping from fine, gilt-edged cups. I allowed space for her story to emerge.

*I was reading for a post-graduate degree in Philosophical Theology at St John's College, Cambridge. It was the early 70s. But apart from drinking a bit, and sleeping around a lot, I was completely out of step with the times. My passions centred mainly on the new Liberation Theology coming out of Latin*

*America, namely the paradigm-shattering work of Peruvian Gustavo Gutiérrez. I was also steeping myself in classical music, especially choral music, since the choirs at St John's were so exceptionally good. That's how I met Benjamin Léon. My life changed forever... Oh, why is it so easy for me to recall the past so readily? Yet this sick and tired old brain of mine still finds it so difficult to remember ordinary pieces of information? I find it virtually impossible to live here in the present moment with all of you for any significant amount of time. I just drift off too easily.*

*Maybe that's because your brain disease is rapidly worsening, I suggest truthfully. And you feel all you have access to are your memories. Maybe it's so many factors. Anyway, you must realize most people find it hard to live in the moment. You're not the only one, Gini. But try we must. For the present moment is all we really have. If you like, I can help you with some of that. It's never too late to wake up, you know. Even on our death bed, being firmly rooted in the present is the best way forward... But, do go on. Please. You were telling me about meeting Benjamin Léon.*

*Yes. Benjamin was an incredible musician. He was coming to the end of his stay in England – a kind of scholarship scheme whereby the Spanish government paid for him to hone his considerable talent abroad. He conducted the famous choir at St John's. I spent many rapturous hours enveloped in the heavenly music they produced together. Watching him from afar. And slowly falling in love with him.*

*When we finally met, face to face, it was at a faculty cocktail party and he was with another woman. Undeterred, I pursued him relentlessly over many weeks. Finally, I charmed him into my bed, and he took me into his heart.*

*Soon we were an item. We began making plans for the future together. But his father, also a well-known musician in Madrid, fell ill and my darling Benji had to return to Spain in a hurry. His father passed away and he never came back to Cambridge. Oh, we kept in touch by post and the odd phone call. But it wasn't the same and we began to drift apart. He had his professional life in Madrid, conducting and teaching. And I had my studies to finish, not to mention a dance-card simply burgeoning with suitors, only too willing to feed my compulsive sexual addiction. You see, my relationship with Benji was never exclusive – at least not on my part. I assumed he had young women throwing themselves at him all the time. So I forgave myself for all my ongoing indiscretions.*

*Eventually, mad with jealousy, Benji wrote from Spain pleading with me to become monogamous and keep myself only for him. He said he couldn't live with the idea of me sleeping with other men anymore. And he couldn't live another second without me by his side. He said he couldn't work. He couldn't eat. He said I was ruining his life and the only solution was either to break up completely or for me to drop out of Cambridge and move to Madrid straight away.*

*Not knowing how to respond, I chose to ignore the letter and carried on around college regardless.*

*I picked up with an older student who was reading Russian and Politics. He was nothing like Benji. He always seemed to have an axe to grind, and was rather furtive about his agenda. But worst of all for me, perhaps, was having told him almost everything about myself I didn't learn a single thing about him. I got bored, and eventually dumped him.*

*I was fully prepared never to think of him again and try to mend my bridges with Benjamin when I discovered I was pregnant with Pedro.*

*The very same day I received a telephone call from Benjamin's mother saying I should come immediately as he had attempted suicide over me. She said I had to go sort things out with him, one way or the other. She accused me of being a very cruel young woman, and utterly stupid to have passed up the chance of a fine man like her son.*

*I said I'd moved on considerably since Benji's premature departure from Camridge. And, I must confess, to put Benjamin right off pursuing a wretch like me, I blurted out that I was already pregnant with another man's child.*

*There was silence at the other end of the phone. Then Benji's tortured, beautiful voice came on the line.*

*I'll never forget his words that evening. I was pretending to be so strong and resolute. But I hadn't the slightest clue which way was up. His words were so devastatingly full of love (and compassion). They blew my mind wide open, and melted my frozen heart:*

*'Do not worry about a thing, my darling Gini Blake. I love you so much. And I know you love me too, from the bottom of your heart. We both know we were meant to be together, through thick and thin, come hell or high water. Any child you bring into this world would instantly become my child. I'd love and cherish it as much as I love you, my angel. Please, Gini. I can't live without you. I know it's the most selfish, self-centred thing you've ever heard, but please just drop everything and come to me here in Madrid, as soon as possible'.*

*So, one month later to the day, that's what I did.*

*What an incredible love you two must have shared,* I said as we finished our brunch. *Thank you Gini, for giving me hope. Because I am supposed to be a Buddhist master or something, people forget I'm not a monk and may also wish to find a Great Love of my own.*

*You will, Jelly Yoghurt,* Gini consoled. *And when you do, he will turn your supposedly grounded, allegedly omniscient head inside out and upside down.*

*Oh I do hope so, Gini. I really do.* I felt her hand reach across the tablecloth and caress the back of mine. *You see, I* continued, *one of the many strange things about the brain that I inhabit is that – no matter how much insight and intuition I may get into the lives of others – I have little or no clue about where my own life is heading. I consult my master regularly about where exactly in the world I should go next, and for what reason. But, to be perfectly honest with you, if the man of my dreams were to fall out of the sky right now and land on top of me, I probably wouldn't recognize him. I'd say something inane like 'Oh I am so sorry. Please forgive me for getting in your way'. I'd probably walk off without a second thought. Sometimes being like me is just so ridiculous, you might as well just burst out laughing.*

*Don't worry, Rinpoche,* Gini whispered. *Your secret's safe with me. Could be, we have a lot to learn from each other. Let's always stay close.*

*Thank you, Virginia. I'd like that,* I said.

*Before the others come back, let me just share with you one essential piece of advice I have about your condition. If all you have is memories, but you wish to live more in the present, then you must make use of the cards you're dealt: use your memories to bring you to the present. While there's still time, let's try this exercise together:*

*Recall that special person or situation from the past: a time when you felt really loved and cherished. Really go there. Soak it all up. Breathe it all in. All the love. All that unconditional love. Limitless love.*

*Now hold it in your heart. Nurture it and cherish it, like a new born child. And bring it back with you to the present moment.*

*Start to notice more and more about where you are and who you're with. Little by little, come back to the present moment and simply notice every thing and every one.*

*With each out breath, you can share the limitless love you contain in your heart. Breathing out, you send it over here. Breathing out, you send it over there. This way. And that way. Breathing out, you send infinite love to this one, and that one. Send your love to each and every one of them. To all beings, one at a time. One by one.*

*Not labeling at all. Not thinking 'Ah, I like this one' or 'Oh no, I don't like that one'. With no distinction or judgement whatsoever, simply gaze lovingly towards all beings, as if they were your children and you were their mother.*

*Remain in the moment. Open and content. Sharing your loving presence with all.*

## 26

Back in the 'people carrier', all the shopping and some cheap mini-backpacks were loaded on top of my own stuff in the boot, and we were on the road again.

For the moment at least, the air appeared to have well and truly cleared. I flicked between radio stations: some news in English about the current state of emergency, interspersed with pop tunes. Eventually we hit on a nice classical station. The 'highest common denominator', I thought to myself. It was the Guitar *Concierto de Aranjuez* by Rodrigo.

The drive was not very long but it took us through the most spectacular hills and valleys and impossibly vast expanses.

I told everyone the plan. We were going to tour around some of Andalucía, changing the hire car every day and staying in rooms I had already booked online. Our first overnight was going to be in an exquisite mountain town called *Ronda*. I reminded everyone that we'd no idea if we were being followed or not. So they should not let their guard down. And making personal phone calls was certainly out of the question.

Gini said she and Benjamin had made a similar road trip many years ago and, although he wouldn't remember it, they'd brought Pedro with them too. She said she had such fond memories of that trip and that she was actually looking forward to seeing some of the places again.

*It's so funny how the mind works, Gini said. I seem to recall, out of all the magnificent things we did, that there was this little village or town way up in the hills. It had the most amazing natural hot spring. I can still see Benji sitting there, soaking in it, with Pedro on his lap laughing and kicking his little legs in the hot water. I would dearly love to revisit that place if it still exists and we can find it.*

I kind of half-promised to research it and do my best.

*While you're in the mood for remembering stories, Gini... why don't you tell us all the one about how you got involved with British Intelligence in the first place? Not to put too fine a point on it, but it's really all YOUR fault we're in this mess in the first place* (I chuckled involuntarily. She knew I meant no harm by it).

In the background, the famous guitar concerto was already well into the vibrant, opening movement. Listeners were being transported into another world, long ago. A beautiful garden landscape with birds and heavily-scented magnolia flowers and flowing water.

*I was out for a walk in the gardens at St John's College, Cambridge, Gini began. It was so beautiful. Full of flowers and birds, and the river flowing through it. As you know, I was studying there in the early 70s after my time at Trinity. But circumstances changed and I decided to follow Benjamin Léon back to Madrid, instead of finishing my post-grad. You see – sorry you have to hear this Pedro, but I DID visit your darkroom and cabins at Hot Bar – I was a bit of a trollop in my youth, and had managed to get myself pregnant by another man. Oh it was not so bad really. Benji forgave me and insisted on me joining him in Spain anyway.*

*It was right then, at that crucial juncture in my life, I was standing on the Bridge of Sighs looking down at the River Cam flowing beneath me. In fact I was remembering a much earlier pregnancy which miscarried. I was becoming quite emotional about it, actually.*

*I was also wondering if having this baby would help me settle and stabilize, finally. And then there was this whole new life in Madrid ahead of me. But as what? The wife of a famous conductor? A mother with a new-born child, stuck in an apartment somewhere, waiting for Benjamin to come home?*

*Just then, a familiar hand tapped me on the shoulder. It was some guy I had dumped. A mature student of Politics and Russian. I've forgotten his name. And he had a friend with him he wanted me to meet.*

*He said his name was White and he had an interesting proposition for me. So the two of us continued to walk and talk alone, through the squares and gardens of Cambridge. I must admit, by the end of it I was totally convinced by the case he was making. And I was ready to sign up.*

The first movement of Rodrigo's concerto was gathering pace and Pepe Romero was really thrashing and rasping those climactic chords.

*Mr White said I was an ideal candidate for the job. I had no family ties, was cultured and inoffensive, and my interest in fair play meant I was already well-disposed to committing myself to acts of public service. He said my plan to settle into a ready-made new life in Madrid meant I would blend in perfectly, ready to answer my country's call if it ever came.*

*I was assured time and again that he was not suggesting I become a spy for British Intelligence. It was quite possible, he said, I might never be asked to do anything at all. But what I WAS being asked to do was to become a 'sleeper'. An unpaid volunteer, who would make their talents available to the Crown at short notice, if the need arose. Otherwise, I could expect to live a normal life and just get on with things.*

*But there was, White concluded, the little matter of spending some time at their training camp in Kent before I departed for Spain. So that's what I did.*

The slow, instantly recognizable Second Movement drifted into our group consciousness. Its haunting melody charted a sonorous course from a rather pensive, even doleful mood, towards a higher, transcendent place. The kind of elevated space from which one could envision overcoming anything.

*The training 'camp' in Kent, it turned out, was actually a beautiful but small stately home situated on a grassy hillside looking out across the sea to Europe. I was only there a week or so. But I thoroughly enjoyed the break from my so-called reality. Most people there were in the same boat. We were all just about to embark on new lives in foreign countries. Some were en route to far-flung places such as Leningrad and Shanghai. Others, like me, were simply hopping over to Paris or Rome.*

*Our morning 'lessons' covered many areas. We learned all about the structure of the Foreign Service, and our place in it. Spying was never mentioned, although we did learn the standard techniques for gathering information, writing reports, and sending them back to our nearest Head Office. We were informed that 'sleepers' were not in danger. And we would never be called upon to take unnecessary risks. As a precaution, there was a half-hearted attempt to teach us some self-defense. I remember quite vividly laughing out loud and being told off.*

*In a one-to-one interview, shortly before the end of my time there, I was actually reassured to hear that I was not entirely of the right temperament for becoming a fully-fledged 'sleeper'. The lady said Britain's relationship with Spain would almost certainly remain stable for the duration of both our lifetimes and I might not even get a single call to serve. But just in case I did, she said, I would have to undertake the final day of what she called Mind Training.*

*Interesting, I said. Buddhism is all about that.*

*I know. Fascinating, isn't it? But I imagine your kind of 'mind training' has nothing to do with 'brain-washing', does it?* Gini seemed to be recalling an unpleasant moment. Then she was completely thrown off course altogether. Distracted by the music, Gini came back to the present.

*What an incredible melody that is. I've always adored it, though I sometimes find it too painful to listen to.*

*You know,* Gini meandered down one of her famous sidetracks, *after this concerto was composed Rodrigo spoke readily about the scenes the first and last movements evoked. But neither he nor his wife ever spoke about the middle one, at least not for many years. People began to infer it was all about the recent massacre at Guernica, so that's what became the accepted truth. But, Rodrigo's wife wrote years later that while the beginning of the Second Movement evokes the joy of their honeymoon and subsequent pregnancy, the path it takes after that is all about the sadness of her miscarriage and how utterly devastated her husband became. Nowadays, many people imagine the child's soul ascending to heaven as the final arpeggio slowly causes the closing notes to rise and soar as if to infinity.*

*Oh, there it goes again. It always seems to move on to the last movement far too quickly. I usually stop the recording there. I don't much like the Third Movement... Something twee about country dancing, or a party or something. Ghastly anti-climax, if you ask me. Rodrigo should've stopped while he was saying something meaningful.*

*Speaking of which,* Karl interjected. *What about the day of Mind Training? I'd love to hear something about that.*

*Ah Yes. 'Mind Training: Sessions 1 to 4',* Gini was back in the saddle.

*The whole week, they had us memorize a short script in our free time. It was easy enough to learn off. A sort of conversation where each phrase would trigger a pre-programmed resulting phrase from the other person. It was all in a kind of non-sensical jibberish... Pedro, Maria, you heard some of it when 'London Calling' triggered it that day in my apartment... To an ordinary person over-hearing the exchange, it would sound like nothing important. But basically it translates as 'Hi it's me. Long time no see. Remember your promise? We have something for you to do. Are you in a position to proceed?' Then you would either say Yes, and arrange to get further instructions, or No, and await a minor slap on the wrist.*

*Yes, but 'mind training', Mother,* Pedro said. *That sounds like something far more sinister. 'Brain Washing', you said?*

*The last day in Kent, Gini continued, was divided into four sessions. The first and second were very similar. I remember they used a kind of hypnosis technique on us individually, in separate rooms. They told us in advance they were going to program our brains to recall the script we'd been learning so we could reenact it with ease, even under duress and after many decades. First they tested their 'trigger-response' technique on us with an innocuous series of paired words such as black cat, white shirt, red rose, and so on. Then they spent the rest of the day 'planting' the other far more important exchange deeper and deeper into the psyche of each potential sleeper.*

*What concerns ME is we relinquished our free will to such an extent that we actually have no idea WHAT else they planted in there while they were at it. Under hypnosis, the subject has no real awareness of what is going on, and no lasting memory of it either. In theory your average, harmless, little old granny could be brain-washed to assassinate on command. And she wouldn't know a thing about it. She wouldn't know she was doing it. And she wouldn't remember it afterwards. Everyone would think she had just gone ga-ga.*

The Concierto de Aranjuez had long finished its final flurry.

According to most of the guide books, we had just driven some of the scariest roads in Spain on that short journey. But Gini's story kept us firmly glued to our seats.

Climbing to a respectable elevation of 750m above sea level, we had twisted and turned our way over hills and along steep mountainsides, which opened up evermore breath-taking vistas and vertiginous drops to one side of the car.

Levelling out to a sprawling high plateau, and just in time for lunch, we paused to acknowledge *Ronda* reclining in the middle-distance, waiting patiently before us.

27

We checked into our hotel, which was perched dramatically on the precipice of the deep, narrow gorge that drops perilously away from the edge of the old town. I had chosen to opt for a configuration of three rooms that made prudent economic sense: Gini and Pedro in one twin room, Maria and myself in another, and Fr Karl in his own single room. While everyone settled in, I took the opportunity to drop off the car and order a different one for early the next morning, thus saving the unnecessary extra cost of a day.

While I was out, I also decided to use *Skype* to phone the saintly being I call my master. Still only a teenager, he is the reincarnation of *Nyima Özer Rinpoche*. 'The Sun's Rays' had been the second precious lama to take me under his wing, all those years ago in Varanasi.

A few well-focused minutes cost little more than a Euro. We only covered the essentials: *How's the weather in Varanasi, Rinpoche? And your family? Did you get my email about Andalucía, with the link to the map you asked for? What should I concentrate on over the next few days?*

Rinpoche advised me to make sure I prayed strongly for all beings in Spain and elsewhere who have been through unbearable suffering. In particular, he said to focus on the places I was passing through.

*Not just the current 'difficulties',* he warned. *The whole region is steeped in centuries of 'nightmarish atrocity'.* Almost joking, he finished by saying: *And we think the history of Asia is bad. Oh man, just take a good look at where you are now! ... Unearth and reveal the truth, Rainbow Man,* he said. *Then let it settle again.*

As I left the internet café, I resolved to quietly investigate each port of call as we went, and to discreetly do prayers and practice. Not just for the victims, but for the perpetrators as well.

Back at the hotel, I chatted briefly with Maria in the room.

*Alone again, Darling. Finally!* I said. *How have you been? How is your meditation going?*

Although by now we were old friends, Maria knew that in this context getting right to the point was the order of the day. She shared how her practice was developing and told me what was foremost in her heart. She had one thing she wanted to run by me. And I simply replied, *Why not? If that's what you want to do when this is all over... Just do it.*

I told her I'd bought cheap mobile phones with pay-as-you-go *sim cards* for each of them and asked her when would be an appropriate time to trust the others. She said to hang onto them for another while yet. But I should consider giving everyone some daily pocket money right away.

*Of course,* she added, *if you have a few cents in your pocket you can always make a phone call. And the rooms have phones too, remember. But at least for now we won't be getting calls telling us what to do next. Or (Buddha forbid!), Vatican terrorists or whatever trying to get to Fr Karl.*

*I don't think the Church will be doing anything of the sort,* I said.

*Don't be so naïve!* Maria howled with laughter. *Just look around you, old friend. You're in Spain now... you know: home of The Spanish Inquisition? The Spanish Civil War? ... HELLO?!*

We collected the others from their rooms and began a lovely stroll through the narrow streets over towards the main square in search of a late lunch and a well-deserved glass of ice-cold beer.

I didn't say anything, but I knew Karl had made more phone calls while I was out. I knew Pedro was worried sick about his mother dying suddenly. He was also racked with guilt for wondering how he would ever get to live his own life again if she didn't.

I was aware that Gini was secretly using the methods I had shared to stay present. And I feared Maria had come to the false conclusion that it had all been a big mistake to get a vagina. I planned to bring it up later when we were alone together.

We sauntered along the cobbled alleyways, past the ornate *Casa de Don Bosco*, and further still towards the famous *Palacio de Mondragon*. Then, having paused to drink in the glory of what is Ronda's most beautiful public space, the leafy *Plaza Duquesa de Parcent*, we entered the *Plaza de San Francisco*, where we enjoyed a good lunch.

Surrounded by ordinary people going about their ordinary lives, it was easy to forget what clandestine forces were following in our wake. For all we knew, someone was watching us right now. Maybe even planning to kidnap us or assassinate Karl. But I couldn't feel any sense of impending danger, so I said nothing. What else could I do? Anyway, the platter of mixed tapas looked so inviting. Served with a local baked rice dish, creamy garlic potatoes and, of course, a few glasses of *vino tinto*, it was all too easy to pretend we were just tourists.

On the way back to our hotel, Gini was in grand form. She and Karl were chatting as they strolled arm in arm. Maria struck out ahead of the group alone. Pedro and I lagged behind and took the chance to get to know each other a bit better.

As we walked, Pedro uncharacteristically decided to open up to me. Completely.

He said he didn't know what it was about me but, like all the others, he felt it was safe to talk openly with me, if I didn't mind. A quick smile, some reassuring eye contact (I was sending him Love and Light on every out breath), and the silence that followed opened up the space he needed to talk freely.

As I suspected, he was terrified about Gini passing away prematurely from her illness. He was also ashamed of feeling trapped by the role of 'primary care-giver'. Just because he was an only child, and a single gay man with no children of his own, that shouldn't mean he had to give up his whole life or any prospect of finding a man, did it? I simply remained silent and encouraged him to follow his train of thought. He said he wished there was a better way for his mother to get the proper care she was going to need, without her having to leave her home, or without him having to give up his whole life to provide it. He said he was at a point, as a gay man and as a creative artist, where he really needed to meet the right guy, leave Madrid and settle down somewhere quiet.

*And another thing... he said, Karl seems very nice and all, but there's something about his outrageous backstory that just isn't – well – it just sounds like one enormous cover up. A big fat lie he rehearsed in case of capture or something.*

*Do you know, Pedro whispered, I've been thinking about little else since we met him. And I know it sounds mental, but I actually suspect that Karl's true story is even MORE outrageous than the one he told us about being the Pope's son.*

*I think he is in danger – we all are in danger – because of some deeper truth about his identity.*

*Well well, Miss Marple. Now aren't YOU the perceptive, intuitive little squirrel?* I joked, shocking him by taking his hand in mine as we ambled along side by side. *I can already see I have a potential ally in you, Pedro.* He was completely thrown by me holding his hand, so I let go: *Relax, will you? We'll never be lovers – we may not even see each other again after this little road trip of ours – but I do feel a very strong simpatico between us. Yes, we're two gay men, who have probably been around the block and through the mill a few times. Both hoping to find love one day. But – more than that – you have insight. And without insight about the true nature of things, we remain in darkness.*

Pedro, jumping in: *I know I come across like a narky, disgruntled c-u-next-tuesday sometimes...*

SOMETIMES??! (I said mockingly)...

*O Shut up, you Tibetan Witch! I'm trying to bare my soul here (I preferred you when you were simply a silent, holy know-all),* he jibed, now with insuppressible friendship in his gaze.

*Aahh... Two insightful bitches with a past, going head to head for dominance. Didn't you just LOVE Dallas and Dynasty?* (I began to laugh. We both did)

*No, seriously* (I reeled it back in). *You may be onto something there. As I said, you have insight and intuition. Without that, we are lost in a sea of illusion and lies. Let's continue to have these little chats.*

*I'd like that.*

*Me too.*

We walked on to catch up with the others. Maria had stopped just before the bridge and was soon joined by the Gini and Karl. As we re-entered the fold, we all walked together till we got half-way across. We stopped to peer over the edge into the abyss. Our minds were drawn way, way down into the stomach-churning depths of the gorge far below.

To break the ice, I said I'd been reading about it in my guide book and thought it was perhaps the quaintest name for such an ancient bridge:

*'New Bridge'*, I smiled. *What a great name for an old bridge... Well, I suppose it WAS new at one time.*

Gini caught my eye with a gleefully mischievous grin.

*I don't wish to introduce an unnecessarily macabre air to such a wonderful afternoon,* she said (obviously intending to be as macabre as possible). *But you do know the story behind this bridge, don't you?*

Seeing that none of us had read that far into the guide book, Gini launched into a Spanish Civil War story about how this little town exemplified the torment by which Spain had torn itself apart at that sad time. 'Neighbour against neighbour. Even brother against brother', she told us, a grim tone descending into her normally chirpy voice.

Although it must remain apocryphal hear-say, as the townspeople understandably never really spoke much of it afterwards, it transpired that a whole load of the fair people of Ronda from one side of the Civil War had chased a whole load from the other side. Arriving at the New Bridge, they battered them and threw them down into the gorge below.

*They tumbled and fell,* Gini drawled hauntingly, *down the terrifying 120 metres of limestone rock that creates the walls of the narrow canyon, all the way down to the gushing River Guadalevín, which appears little more than a harmless babbling brook from up here... Inside the bridge itself (another sidetrack), just below our feet in fact, there is a prison cell built into the bridge's structure that was used on many an occasion. So, you see, one way or another, to these people the New Bridge has always stood as a symbol of justice being served... By the way, I think Ernest Hemingway mentions that Civil War massacre in one of his books. There's a street named after him around here somewhere...*

*Mother. You're beginning to sound a bit like a 'babbling brook' yourself. Let's get back to our room for an hour of telly and a nap.*

As we traversed the New Bridge, making for our hotel, all Karl said was: *Dear God! Man's inhumanity to man!*

*I know,* I said. *I'm a Tibetan in exile after all, remember?*

*Poland, Germany, England, Rome...* Karl eventually spoke up again. *Every corner of South America too. Sometimes I feel like 'The Evil that men do' is actually following me across the globe... And, instead of running away from it, what I must do is face and avert it for once and for all.*

*That's it,* I said quietly. *Maybe so... Sounds like a plan to me.*

Following Gini and Pedro, Karl disappeared through the hotel doors and entered the lift. Maria and I remained in the lobby, where we sat on two big armchairs by a palm tree in a quiet corner, and started to chat.

# 29

*S*o. *Maria,* I began. *How is your vagina?*

*Rinpoche, PLEASE!* Maria scolded me like a naughty school-boy. *I know you were there with me through all of that in Bangkok, but I haven't really discussed it with anyone for YEARS. And I'm not about to start now, and with YOU of all people.*

*Maria, you are not only my disciple. You are my friend too. I hope you recognize that. And ANYTHING that is on your mind is an appropriate topic for discussion. I only bring it up because...*

*Yes. I KNOW... I know... You've picked up on something, with that spooky radar of yours, and you've decided to bring it up now – before it becomes an obsession with me. Am I right?*

*Quite.*

*Yes, quite. And you're not going to give up until I go through the whole psycho-drama with you, are you?*

*Well. That's entirely up to you, Maria. You are entitled to your private thoughts and emotions. I just wanted to see if I could help. That's all...*

*I know you only want to help. I'm sorry. Please forgive me, Jalu.*

*So, if there's anything you'd like to share about your vagina, please feel free. Now is the time...*

*Ok,* Maria conceded. *But I DO reserve the right to keep some thoughts private – and I will be absolutely MORTIFIED if I talk to you about this and you have nothing to contribute – but here goes anyway:*

Maria's gaze drifted out the window. Her eyes widened as she tried to form the right words to express what was going on for her.

She told me her vagina was doing alright, actually, overall. But in the last few months, it seemed to have become a little, well, depressed.

*Oh, you mean like Carrie's friend Charlotte's vagina in Sex and the City?* I offered by way of showing I understood where she was 'coming from'.

*Why do you always have to make light of everything?* She said. *But YES. A bit like that...*

*When I admire her in the mirror, she is really beautiful. VERY beautiful indeed. And so perfect. A beautiful, perfect vagina. But you see – and I think this is the main obstacle I have – she, my vagina, is not 'real'. She is cosmetic. Fake. A 'designer vagina'.*

*What do you mean?* I enquired further. *Are you becoming upset and obsessed with your vagina because it – I mean 'she' – is TOO perfect?*

*No.* She replied, becoming a bit tense. *That's not really it either. When I first made the transition in Thailand, and even long after I came home to Spain, I couldn't have been happier. She was everything I'd ever dreamt of. Trans Heaven, you know? But now – and I don't know why – all this time later, the 'reality' is only just beginning to dawn on me.*

*My vagina is so perfect; absolutely no man, and practically no woman could tell if she is real or fake. Believe me, I've tested my theory. A lot. And they can't. But the difference is that I know. And that's what the problem is. My vagina is a combination of my old, unwanted dick and ball-sack, recycled and reshaped. It's not that hard to do really. A vagina is just a penis turned inside-out and pushed back into a newly-constructed cavity. The new clitoris is made from the most sensitive part of the old head gland of the penis, with its original blood-flow and super-intense feeling still intact. Sexual stimulation can still be good – it can still be pretty damn good. But – I don't know if you know this – a 'real' woman is many orders of magnitude more sensitive 'down there'... So, my dear Jalu, sorry if you find all this shocking. But you did ask. And there it is: I am not a real woman. Never can be. You can't tell by looking. But I know...*

*... Now, there IS another aspect to all this (which is perhaps equally important in exploring the problem).*

*I thought there might be,* I cringed. *Please be gentle with me, Maria. You know I'm not a big fan of visiting 'Lady Gardens'. A woman's 'down below' has never been my forte. I've never even seen one up close and personal, like.*

*No. That bit's over, Dear. Relax. God, you're such a fag sometimes. No, THIS aspect to my problem is to do with men.*

*Men are always 'the problem',* I say. *First, you can't get one. Then you can't get rid of him!*

*PRECISELY!* She proclaims. *That's totally it! You just completely brought my entire drama down to one.. concise.. phrase: I can't get a man (Oh you are clever). That's it: I can't get a man... I simply CANNOT get a fucking man! Oh, believe me Jalu, I'VE TRIED. Either you can't get one at all. Or you get the one you don't want (And apparently it's a crime to murder them too. Did you know that?). OR... You actually DO manage to get a good one, but he won't stay – not even for a month!*

*I hear you there, Sister!* I say. *Can I get an 'Amen' from the choir?*

*AMEN!!* Maria replies... *What's wrong with me right now is I am in a head-spin because I'm worried I will NEVER find a good man to share my life with. I'm not talking about an 'other half' here, or someone to 'make me complete'. I know that's all BULLSHIT, Jalu. I really do. But I can't see myself finding a man in Spain – one who knows I'm a transsexual and who doesn't care, maybe one who's even into that, God forbid* (Maria blesses herself with the sign of the cross)... *Sweet Mother of Divine God, I can't BELIEVE I just did that!*

*Are Spanish men too macho or something? Why wouldn't a single ONE of them go for a gorgeous girl like you, Maria? Really? Not ONE? In all of Spain?*

*No. I told you. Not ONE! I've searched high and low. Under every rock and behind every sofa. I've LOOKED, OK? And there isn't one!*

*So what's the answer then? Have you got any ideas?* I said, aware all along that Maria obviously had a plan in place, ready to put into action at a moment's notice.

*Oh, you! YOU!! ...You KNOW there is! Anyway, I told you earlier, more or less... It all started to fall into place one afternoon when I was over at Gini's apartment on Gran Via with Pedro, watching British telly on satellite... and what should come on the old jelly box? Well, I'll TELL you... Only a documentary called 'Ladyboys of Thailand'! ... Ten minutes in, and I was hooked. 20 minutes in, and I was in floods of tears. The fantastic thing about the Sky Living channel is they show all the episodes of a series back-to-back. So! While Pedro cared for Gini, I just sat in her living room with a box of tissues and an enormous tub of ice cream and basked in the whole thing from beginning to end. It reminded me of the first time I ever saw anything about sex change operations on TV, and the huge impact it had on me. It gave me New Hope.*

*By Episode 3, I think, there was this whole segment about a 'straight' guy from England. George or Tim I think his name was. And he was stocky, good-looking (Chiseled, FIT!)... Totally macho – a real 'bloke' – and with such a heart of pure gold! (Ai, Dios! Que bonito!! Que guap-ÍS-imo!!!). I immediately wanted to go right back over there and find me a man just like that!*

*Here in Spain, the kind of stocky straight guys I go for might hook up with me in private, but they wouldn't be seen out in public with a girl like me. They wouldn't want to know me, if anyone were to discover our little secret.*

*It could also happen that once they discovered I was transsexual, they'd dump me anyway. Long before you got to bed, there are always tell-tale signs for those who know where to look: the Adam's Apple, the shoulders, the hands, the hips. No matter how much I turned them on. No matter how much they wanted to. Most Spanish men just couldn't take the risk or find the courage to say 'No! Fuck the rest of the world, and all their judgemental bullshit! THIS is the woman I love! Mind your own god damn business!!'*

*But over there... in Thailand... I KNOW I would fit right in. Nobody would give a rat's arse, or even bat an eyelid... I would be free again, Jalu. FREE! ... I'd open a bar or café somewhere. Maybe in the city. Maybe on a tropical island (You could come and visit) ... But sooner or later, Darling. Sooner or later, my working class hero, my Blue-Collared Prince would walk through that door. I'd be waiting for him. And he'd be looking for EXACTLY a girl like me... So what do you think, Rinpoche? Do I have your blessing? ... Even as a friend, Jalu? Tell me. Am I barking up the wrong tree here or what? Should I withdraw my savings, pack up and move back to Thailand?*

*I told you earlier, I said... Before you expressed it in those terms exactly... If it's what you really want... JUST DO IT!*

*Oh thank you, Jalu. Thank you for everything. You must think I'm totally de-RANGED – going on and on about my vagina and all like that – but I really do appreciate it. I love you SO much (I never get to tell you that, but I DO). I love you, Rinpoche.*

*And I love you too, Ms del Mar... Go to Thailand. Open a café-bar somewhere. I'll be your first customer, Sweetheart... As the song says: Go before you break my heart. Go before I get down on my knees and beg you 'Please, don't go' ... Go.*

3 0

After dinner, I decided to hand everyone some cash and their new phones mainly so we could keep in touch. Maria was right, you can't prevent people from making phone calls nowadays anyway. There's always a way. Everyone was exhausted, so they retreated to their rooms for an early night. All I could do was hope nobody would make a call that would put us in jeopardy.

Maria wanted to do her evening meditation followed by some TV, a long shower and bed. So I left her to it and decided to go for a walk.

Before I left our floor in the hotel, I looked in on Gini. Pedro was writing at the dressing table. Gini said she was feeling quite well. But she seemed to be babbling a bit still. My gut feeling was her condition had deteriorated considerably. And, although quite interesting and pleasant to listen to, she was hard to follow at times (drifting in and out of past events and books she had read). I asked her to try come back to the present as much as possible. As a method of achieving that, I got her to describe the hotel room to me in as much detail as she could. She became much sharper and seemed to enjoy the exercise. Then I asked her to describe Pedro without looking at him. At first

200

she said '*Who?*' She was mortified not to have remembered his name. Then, covering her tracks as if she hadn't heard me correctly, she did her best:

*Pedro is still quite young. About 40. He is medium build with well-defined muscles on his upper arms. He goes to the gym, you know. Funnily enough, he has Benjamin's colouring. His skin is dark and his hair is brown...* Oh my goodness, she confided, *I am actually finding this game very difficult. It's like painting a portrait with very broad brush strokes. I can't seem to focus in on any of the detail... My own son. I'm so ashamed. I'm so sorry, Pedro.*

*Don't worry, Mama. You're probably sick of looking at me by now,* Pedro joked to ease the tension.

*Gini. Why don't you look at Pedro's reflection in the mirror there? It's almost as ravishing as the real thing,* I continued with the light-hearted tone. *Describe Pedro's face for me...*

*Oh yes. Good idea, Jalu. Yes, I can see him clearly... He has beautifully tanned skin. A good strong jawline and high cheek bones, like his father* (Pedro blanched and became slightly tense).

Seizing the chance on Pedro's behalf, I said (quite matter of fact): *Now, Virginia. Close your eyes again. Go back into your memory and see the face of Pedro's father... OK. Quick as a flash, tell me, what year was it?*

*1972 I think.*

*Quick as a flash, now. What is the man's name?*

*Leonard Cavendish, of course. That's common knowledge. Everyone knows that. What a silly question.*

In Gini's deteriorating version of the truth, she'd never hidden the fact that she DID know which man had been

Pedro's father. Worse again, she now seemed to believe she had already told Pedro who he was.

Pedro looked at me, slowly turning round on his stool: *Oh My God* (he mouthed the words without making a sound).

*... Oh, and, just two more things about Leonard: Did he know you were carrying his child? And what colour were his eyes?*

*No, he didn't have a clue. I really didn't like him at all. He was cold and slimy... His eyes were dark brown.*

Bringing Gini back to the present: *And Pedro's eyes? We completely forgot to mention them earlier...*

Still with her eyes closed, drifting somewhere in the past, Gini seemed to hazard a guess at their colour:

*Blue?... Yes, pale blue.* Gini opened her eyes again. *Most unusual in a dark man. Pedro has MY eyes. Pale blue. Sometimes piercing, sometimes soft. He is his mother's son, no doubt about that.*

Gini's pale blue eyes pierced through the dimmed, golden hue of the hotel room and settled on Pedro's. For a moment, there were no secrets between them, and their bond was stronger than ever. Perhaps not since she held him in her arms as a new-born baby had their eyes locked like that.

Shortly after, I said my goodnights and went for that walk.

I was suddenly struck by how quiet and peaceful the town was after the devastation of the riots in Seville. I recognized that I too needed to unwind. I soon found myself sitting in an old church, quite amazed it had been left unlocked at that time of night.

I simply sat there, taking it all in. The Renaissance décor, the ornate stained glass, the many religious paintings, and the flickering candlelight. My gaze settled on a wonderfully simple statue of the *Madonna and Child* that stood majestically on a side altar. My mind turned to Gini and Pedro again for a moment. Then I allowed my awareness to open to the Vast Expanse, leaving all my senses open and content. No longer labeling or fixing on anything.

I prayed for all the people who had died on either side of the Civil War. I gave special attention to praying for those who had died in this area, during any of Spain's dark times. I prayed for my four companions, each with their own particular futures ahead of them. And I prayed that I'd continue to be blessed into usefulness. Then I allowed the mind to rest. Simply be, in its Natural State. Open.

After a period of meditation, free from all concepts, I joined my palms together at my heart centre and dedicated the merit of my prayers and practice towards the enlightenment of all beings, everywhere.

Back outside, and in another side-street, I saw Karl.

He was sitting in an empty bar. I could plainly see him through the window, so I went in to see if everything was OK. He was sipping a fine brandy from *Jerez*. Almost everything about this picture looked wrong to me; a champion of the poor secretly quaffing a very expensive night cap, out alone at night without the comfort blanket of crowds to blend into or comrades to watch out for him. I sat down beside him and ordered a beer.

We did the small-talk thing for what seemed like an age until I began to get a clearer insight into what had happened to him. I wondered if my meditation in the church had been a little too 'non-conceptual' and profound. Had I inadvertently put Karl at risk during that gap? What Karl told me next was alarming in the extreme.

He said he'd decided to risk going out alone for a stroll. He'd stopped at the New Bridge to reflect on the gruesome murders that had occurred there. He said while he was praying for their souls two darkly-clad henchmen approached from behind and rushed him. While they were trying to lift him off the ground, presumably to push him over the edge, it suddenly dawned on Karl that they were not going to kidnap him but send him hurtling to his death. He said the only thing that crossed his mind was how his death would appear to have been a tragic suicide.

My jaw dropped in horror. He quickly added that three other men suddenly appeared, just as unexpectedly, from the far end of the bridge. They simply chased his attackers away. All of this had been achieved in total silence, with the minimum of fuss, and without firing a single shot. Fr Karl's saviours then jumped into a car and drove off into the darkness in hot pursuit.

*It just makes no sense,* Karl said.

*No sense at all,* I added (hoping not to offend him after such an ordeal). *Why didn't they just shoot you if they wanted to kill you? Why didn't the two factions just shoot each other, for that matter?*

I told him that sooner or later he was going to have to tell us the whole truth about what was going on. He said he was frightened, and could only divulge what he'd been authorized to say.

*Authorized by whom?* I asked.

*British Intelligence.*

*But if British Intelligence really cared about your safety at all, they would have simply lifted you long before now and gotten you to your destination.*

*I know. But they can't. They only agreed to operate from a discreet distance. It was all settled beforehand. The plan was, if something should go wrong, I was only allowed say certain things about who I am and what I'm going to do in Rome. And they would monitor from a distance until things calmed down and I could continue on my way. Think about it. You're right. All they'd have to do is air-lift me from here to their base in Gibraltar, then fly me privately to Rome. They just won't do anything at all that could be traced back to them. The British are already up to their eyes in this.*

*So what on earth was all that about on the bridge, then? Who was protecting you, if not the British? And who were your attackers working for?*

*Of course, the Intelligence world is based on secrecy, lies and double-bluffs. So you never really know who is who anyway,* Karl said. *But I'm still pretty certain it wasn't the Brits who came to my rescue. The attackers are a mystery too. It could be any number of agencies. I can't be any clearer than that at the moment. Not even with you, Jalu.*

We let the matter rest awhile and finished our drinks. Then, after another long silence, Fr Karl began to think out loud:

*One thing I CAN share though... What absolutely mystifies ME is... If the bomb at the airport was indeed an attempt on my life, why didn't they just shoot me on the bridge tonight? Why the need to have my death conveniently look like suicide all of a sudden?*

*... Could be*, I concluded, *the two events are not linked at all. Different attackers, different agendas, you know? The world is a CRAZY, mixed up kinda place, remember. Maybe the airport was Basque separatists, or the anti-government rioters. Nothing to do with you. Maybe the attack on the bridge just now was something else entirely...* (I dared to lighten the mood with a nervous joke) *The Prada Fashion Police, perhaps?*

Mission accomplished, the dark veil lifted. We left the bar giggling and chatting.

Karl was off the hook, again ... for now.

As we walked along the back streets together, I began to feel that Karl was protected by forces greater than he knew. Guardian spirits even more powerful than the Archangels themselves were keeping him alive. I didn't judge him for it, but I was beginning to detect a certain arrogance in him. A single-minded determination that amounted to blind stupidity at times. Increasingly, it was becoming clear that his story was false. Deliberately misleading. A cover up. He probably knew who his attackers and his defenders were. The only thing he said that rang true that night was he couldn't understand how he was still alive.

*You're Guardian Angels were working overtime tonight,* I said. *You're lucky to be alive.*

*I know... Blessed.*

*You do understand that it's only a matter of time before I fully realize the truth behind all your stories, Karl. Don't you?*

*I know.*

*And that, once I do, I'll have to force you to tell the others?*

*I know that too.*

I watched him for a minute or two as he walked back alone towards the hotel entrance. Then I instinctively went in a different direction.

I followed a road that took me down to the legendary Bull Ring, the *Plaza de Toros*, and sat on a bench outside.

As I rested there, gazing wide-eyed at the crumbling exterior wall, my insight arose and glowed with such clarity I began to perceive sounds and moving images. It appeared as if they were being projected, like in a darkened cinema, onto the flaky façade opposite.

I saw men on horseback going through their paces. They were riding around the vast ring inside the mighty edifice before me, like they were training in the art of hunting on horseback. Their movements were very precisely choreographed, almost ceremonial. It appeared to have been the original purpose of this building.

More images came of a later time when the same kind of men on horseback, wearing incredible silks and brocade, were displaying their great prowess and riding skills to an enormous crowd. But it wasn't *Dressage* they were engaging in. This time there was a wild bull in the ring with them. He was nervous and extremely angry, having been tortured and goaded for some time before. The men were using weapons that looked like long swords or spears which they thrusted into the bull as they made their 'courageous' passes. The bravado of the riders knew no bounds as they flourished and pouted to the adoring hoards. Occasionally, the terrified eyes of the horses would lock with the bull's. Only the kicks and spurs of the riders could snap them out of it. Of course, the object of the inglorious pageant was to wear the bull down over an hour or two by taunting and stabbing him repeatedly. He had to lose just enough blood to become ever weaker, but not so much as to lose consciousness altogether. Finally, the senior-most assassin would move in close and, stretching his long arm down from his lofty mount, deliver the terminal thrust of his sword. The crowd goes ballistic!

Then a new film began to play on the crumbling wall. This time it looked more like old *newsreel*. A momentous day indeed for the history of Bull Fighting! On this occasion a rider was inadvertently forced to dismount, either by error or unforeseen circumstance. Observing a golden opportunity, the bull naturally began to charge him.

The fighter stayed calm and stood his ground. Removing his cape, he used it as a decoy to confuse and distract the bull from being able to ascertain with any accuracy the exact location of the man's torso. Not only did the new technique of cape-waving and twirling prove an excellent strategy to avoid being gored or trampled on the spot, it was a very effective way to further rile and exhaust the valiant bull. The crowds loved it! Combined with all the grandiose posturing and strutting it facilitated, the accidentally-dismounted, cape-flapping executioner went down in history as having given birth to none other than the 'art' of modern bull fighting.

As the *cinéma vérité* eventually began to dissolve and fade to black, my mind's eye glimpsed residual images of old *YouTube* clips and photos I must have stored away for just this particular moment...

I saw a 360 degree view of *Michelangelo's* famous *Pieta*, the statue of Mother Mary holding her dead son Jesus across her lap. Then, a vintage comedy clip of Bob Hope or someone like that prancing around a bull ring with his red cape. I saw a bull-fighter on some special night recently in Ronda's Bull Ring wearing an ornate costume covered in lights, designed by Giorgio Armani. And finally, an image of a repentant, broken down bullfighter slouched at the side of the bull-ring. He is distraught with the cumulative remorse of all his past negative actions. As he sobs into his hands, the bull approaches slowly to investigate, with equal measures of disbelief, curiosity and compassion.

As the last picture lingered, then drifted away, I walked the remaining two blocks or so to the hotel. When I got into the room, Maria was already snoring, fast asleep.

Next morning after breakfast, we checked out and slowly gathered in the lobby for our departure. Despite the beautiful day, dark forces gathered all around us. Nobody to trust. And nothing as it appeared.

By the time I paid the bill with my magic card and walked over to where the others were sitting I could hear Gini was in flying form. Karl had obviously told everyone about his brush with death on the New Bridge, and they'd just finished going through all the process of doubt and analysis I had navigated with him the night before.

*But I simply don't follow the logic,* Gini was saying. *If they wanted you dead, you'd be dead long before now.*

*And the bomb in Madrid?* Maria declared, with controlled exasperation. *Was that about you or not?!*

I sat down and decided to let it play out a little further without getting involved, just to see how Karl would react.

Pedro was looking straight into Karl's face as he addressed the group: *I'm sorry but I'm having a really hard time believing anything you say, Karl... About your attack, your identity, why any of us are here at all. I'm just not convinced. For example, when I dig deeper into your 'back story', my impression of what I hear is that you're reciting a pre-*

*rehearsed script. A tale so unnecessarily elaborate and grandiose, I can only assume the real truth behind who you are is even more outrageous and outlandish if it requires such an intricate red herring to cover it up ...*

*Let's try this,* Pedro continued, *as an example of what I mean: Karl, your story thus far ended with the Cardinal of Krakow, Karol Wojtyla no less, telling you (a young boy, his son) to open the safe deposit in Switzerland if the need arose and remove the secret papers... Please tell us the next chapter so we can follow it, not as friends or fellow-travellers, but as we would listen to evidence in a courtroom. What happened next?*

Karl was indeed well-rehearsed and immediately launched into it, as you would when picking up a child's bedtime story from the night before. But his face told a different story. Pedro, and now the others too, could see something was amiss. Whenever Karl's eyes met mine I got fleeting glimpses of the true nature of his past. He could detect it, so he avoided further eye contact to remain undistracted in the web he was so busy spinning. But my insight radar was switched on now and the truth indeed came trickling slow.

He said the Vatican had chosen the Italian-born Albino Luciani, Patriarch of Venice, to be the next Pope in 1978. In homage to his two predecessors he took the papal name John Paul. Everybody loved him. The people called him the 'Smile of God'. But he was a reformer and a forward thinker. Once in office, he began to put in place a series of radical changes. The Cardinals who elected him were not surprised. But those who really control the power and the purse-strings of the Church were not at all happy. They advised him to slow down and consider the conservative elements more. He ignored them. They warned him to respect those who had allowed his rise to the papal throne. He obviously didn't show enough respect, because after only one month in office Pope John Paul was found dead. 'The Smiling Pope' became known as 'The September Pope'.

Karl told us his father got a message to him which simply read *'Act now'*. So he and his mother made a hurried journey from England by boat and train to the Swiss bank where they accessed the vault and removed the secret Vatican files.

The episode ended with Karl fast-forwarding for brevity:

Sensing he might be the next man for the job, and how dangerous it could be for your health, Karol Wojtyla had young Karl move his insurance policy to safety.

Within a fortnight he was installed as Pope John Paul II (even the name was a Public Relations master-stroke).

The mystery surrounding JP I's untimely demise was never properly investigated as the Vatican is a State unto itself and its laws come from God, not Italy.

In choosing Cardinal Wojtyla of Krakow, the powers behind the 'Holy See' had given the flock their man of the people, a hero fit to succeed a smiler. And the movers and shakers got someone who, despite all the waving and hand-shaking and baby-kissing, was a true conservative at heart.

But more than that, John Paul II was someone who could easily be manipulated. They knew his dirty little secret... Karl. All the new pope had to protect himself with were those files.

Almost as a throw-away tag-line, Karl happened to mention that John Paul II's rise to the papacy had been orchestrated from the early days, and micro-managed in almost every detail, by one Cardinal Joseph Ratzinger. He was the faceless mandarin behind it all. He controlled almost everything: the rules, the agenda, the Pope's speeches. He got to codify church policy on a vast array of matters from the personal and sexual morality of the sheep in the fold, to suppressing the many scandals and misdemeanors of the shepherds, to shrewdly investing the enormous wealth of The Vatican in God-only-knows-what. In return for all his years of humble service Ratzinger, the shy theologian from Bavaria, was later selected as the next pope.

*You see what I mean?* Pedro summarized. *The plot just gets thicker and thicker; all the convoluted twists and turns, the mesmerizing allure of the conspiracy theory... Now THAT's what I'm talking about. The way you just churn it out like that. And just imagine the even MORE mind-boggling truth that lies behind it all... I can't listen any more.*

As Pedro moved to get up and leave, an elegantly dressed man in his early 40s appeared, as if by magic. He approached the group, and invited himself to sit down. He was an English, Oxbridge, Last-Night-of-the-Proms kind of man. He wore a very expensive open-necked crisp white shirt by Hugo Boss, cream linen pants from Gant in Knightsbridge, and some deep-tan Prada loafers.

Acknowledging each of us, by name, he scanned all the faces and finished by extending both hands to greet Gini more personally, taking her fingertips between his manicured thumbs and forefingers and pressing quite hard till she landed in the moment with a jolt and slipped free.

*Please allow me to introduce myself... My name is Leonard Cavendish from Head Office in London.*

The very sound of his name rang so true, it reverberated several times around the foyer, up the grand sweeping staircase to the room where Gini had spoken it only hours before, and back down again to Gini, where it hit her like a ton of bricks in the back of the head. The crystalline build-up in her diseased brain began to cause acute pain and short circuits all around.

She said, *But it can't be! I don't understand. What a wicked trick to play!*

*I'm afraid it IS my name, Mrs Blake-Léon. Your old acquaintance at Cambridge was my father.*

*So we're – no wait, let me get this – we're biological half brothers?* Pedro said, as the penny dropped.

*Quite. Same father, different post-grad mothers at St John's. Same year probably... But that's not the point, Virginia. Do try to keep up. Sorry for the shock just now. And yes, my name is Leonard Cavendish... But you can call me LC if you like. Most people do, one way or the other...*

*What on EARTH is 'one way or the other' supposed to mean, young man?* Gini groaned, holding the back of her head with one hand and the crown with the other. *Maria, be a dear and get me my pills out of the bag. If I have a stroke and die now, I'll never forgive myself. I have to get to the bottom of this enigmatic intrusion... Go on. Do, pray tell, enlighten us as to why people call you 'L C'... and why 'one way or the other'?*

*Oh, it's just a joke. An attempt to be clever and mysterious, I suppose. You know: Leonard Cavendish (L C), 'London Calling' (L C)... ...* (Now putting on a fake British Spy accent from an old black and white film) *'London Calling... London Calling'* ... (Holding an imaginary telephone up to his left ear) *'London Calling' ... ... 'London Calling' ...*

*Young man. Do YOU mean to tell me not only are you another offspring of Leonard Cavendish but you're also the voice of 'London Calling' ??*

*Well.. I was actually trying NOT to say all that. You know, codes, secret passwords, international espionage... That's precisely what I was trying not to say... Let me start again... ... Oh, Virginia Blake I presume. What a great pleasure it is to finally meet you face to face... And your lovely son Pedro too, and all your interesting friends... I am 'LC' from 'Head Office in London',* he said with a sarcastic tone, miming quotation marks with his fingers in the air, and a protracted comedy wink of his right eye.

## 32

The whole assembly took an instant dislike to LC. Virginia had described his father at Cambridge as cold and slimy. But the son had taken that to an even more unpalatable depth. He knew the difficulty we all found ourselves in. He knew the truth about Karl. He was obviously aware of Virginia's terminal illness, and its rapid deterioration was plain to see. The only new element of *The Famous Five* that Mr Cavendish wasn't familiar with was me. And that disturbed him. I think that's why he paid us a visit in person.

He continued on his cruel course, attempting to passively exert his aggressive superiority over us. He had an unsettling talent for exuding *faux* charm and his saccharin smarm was of the highest order, as only his type could be.

Karl was reflecting on how LC must have emerged from the primordial slime and made his home in a sickeningly privileged echelon of society. *They* – as Karl had come to call the enemy of the poor – actually contributed very little to society. Yet *they* controlled practically everything. And now that LC was high up in a top secret, shadowy stratum of puppet masters, Karl was determined to disabuse him of the fallacy that he was going to pull our strings a moment longer.

*Mr Cavenidish, Karl said. Sorry to interrupt, but we haven't actually met in person yet. My name is Fr Karl Weithaler. I was briefed by your team in Buenos Aires before my departure...*

*Ah, Yes. Of course. Fr Karl. So nice to finally make your acquaintance, he replied. You didn't seem to be receiving my calls, and I was on holidays with family down the road in Marbella, so I thought I'd just pop up and...*

*Never mind all that, Karl cut across his blabber with deliberate rudeness. The reason you are here is to try and reassert control in a situation over which you have lost all control. That much is now plain...*

The rest of the group sat up eager to bathe in Karl's new-found ballsiness.

*... Now listen here. I am certain last night's attack on the bridge was an attempt on my life, with the intention of making it look like suicide, for some reason. In the event, the attempt was foiled and here I am. I'm also pretty sure that British Intelligence had nothing to do with it either way: From what little I could see, my attackers, and my rescuers for that matter, appeared far too dark-skinned and interesting for MI6. The good people you see around this table have become my closest friends and confidantes, and I think you owe us all some explanation of what is going on... if you know yourselves, that is. Beyond that, please get on with it! The last communication I had from your office was: 'Have a good flight. And DO give our best regards to the Holy Father'. So say whatever it is you've come to say and, with all DUE respect, take your iPhone and your concealed binoculars and just fuck off back to whatever bush you and your chums are hiding in.*

Maria grinned from ear to ear. Gini perked up considerably and chuckled to herself thinking, *I love this guy*'. Even though he wondered if it was all just a big act, the ever-skeptical Pedro considered the outburst an extremely positive development.

A mildly shocked LC, recomposed himself and feigned upset by pressing his palm to his heart:

*Fighting words indeed, Father* (he whimpered). *I didn't quite understand all of them. But so nice to see the Church of Rome is still using Latin in its communiqués ... I simply wanted to check in with you all and remind you that Her Majesty's Government wishes you all the best. Our role in this affair has only ever been that of Facilitator. It is in our best interest that you get to your destination and do what you have to do. Even with the full endorsement of the American and Argentinian governments, our remit here is extremely limited. We must maintain our distance from you and your dirty, dirty little 'secrets'. We cannot be seen to be associated with them or get involved in any way whatsoever. Therefore, we feel we must remind you that you are on your own, essentially. We can't intervene at all. Only observe and, well, 'Facilitate'* (more airborne finger quotes).

*Does this mean you have no control over what happens next?* I eventually choose to interject. *And if something goes badly wrong you can't fix it?*

*Ah, our foreign friend. Asian is it? No, Mongolia perhaps?* (He can't help sniping, not realizing his bad attitude only serves to create more negativity for *his own* mind-stream, rather than anyone else's)... *Or, is it Samoa?*

*No, it's Jalu actually. My name is Jalu.*

*Ah yes, Jalu... From?*

*From the Present Moment, Sweetheart. Ever heard of it? It's right at the heart of a remote place called Samsara, just before you get to Nirvana.*

*Oh yes, TRES DROLE. But who are you?* (It only took a few phrases of unforeseen jargon to rattle his cage)

*Jalu is our friend from India,* Pedro gasps impatiently.

*He is my spiritual teacher,* says Maria... *And mine too,* adds Gini. Now looking from Pedro to Karl, she explains: *After all, I'm not getting any younger, or healthier. And I want to be prepared for the great transition when my time comes...*

*The Great Transition,* smarms LC. *I love it... So that's why you're here on this exciting little road trip then, Mr Jalu?*

*Of course. Yes, that. And so much more. You have absolutely no idea... So many concepts, but no idea. Tragic, isn't it?* (I say in a genuine attempt not to wound him but to awaken him)... *Have you ever heard the story of a frog who lived his whole life down a well? And when his friend finally brought him for a stroll one afternoon, he saw the vastness of the ocean for the very first time ... And his head exploded!*

*That's hil-ARIOUS!* (says Karl)

*I know, right? Totally hi-LE-ro!!* (says Maria) *I LOVE that one!*

*But...* (I regain my centre and return to the original question) *... At this particular moment in time I am asking you – a high ranking agent on Her Majesty's Secret Service – if you actually imagine you are really 'in control' of ANYTHING* (I relish the chance to do air-quotes) *or if you can 'fix' anything when it goes wrong...*

LC, now on a defensive slippery slope, replies: *Precisely. That is exactly what I am saying. Given the 'Observer' nature of our official stance here, we have no powers to control or fix.*

*That's a good start, I say to the group. At least you accept that we're all equals here. Sometimes there are things we can control and fix, and sometimes there are things we can't. Virginia knows this only too well... No matter who you think you are, we are all just the same. 'Observer' is actually the perfect word to describe our preferred role in life in such uncertain, turbulent times, isn't it Maria? ... We simply remain grounded in the present moment, and OBSERVE... Better to do nothing at all, than make matters worse, isn't that right Pedro?... Just observe ... But! – and this is an even more important point, Fr Karl – when we observe that there is a subtle shift in the delicate balance of things, in our favour, and we CAN actually act decisively and make a big difference, then that's the time to act for the benefit of others. We can, and we must.*

*What the Devil are you prattling on about now? asks LC.*

*Oh, I was just saying that we may not be in control of events right now, but at least we're not entirely alone. We are together. We have each other. We just continue on our journey as we are. And, when the moment's right, we take appropriate action ourselves... A wise man understands, from personal experience, when to rest and when to move. A wise woman knows what cannot be changed at the moment, and what can.*

*Is that it? LC chirps. That's the sum total of your Eastern Wisdom?*

*Yes, I smile... For now...*

He smirks, not sure if he's won or lost.

*So, I conclude, without further ado, Mr Cavendish, we must bid you a fond farewell and gather our belongings.*

*Comrades, I look around our little dysfunctional modern family, Our new rental chariot awaits. Let's continue to give our friend Karl the benefit of the doubt, for he IS a good man. Of that I am certain. We may not know everything about him yet, but we can at the very least walk alongside him for a few days more, until it's safe for him to be on his way again.*

*Return to the shadows, Mr Cavendish... Mr London Calling... Return to the sidelines of history and observe this drama you have set in motion but cannot control or fix. Whatever it is your government has done in the past – whatever it is the U.S. and Argentinian governments have been up to – to warrant you all monitoring the outcome of this perilous charade – it must have been beyond shameful. No doubt we'll find out in due course. Or maybe we won't, and that's what you want. Either way, the truth is the truth. And neither The Pope nor Her Majesty can outrun the eventual ripening of past negative karma.*

So it was that we headed out the road, south-east towards Málaga, leaving Leonard Cavendish's 'other' son sitting in the hotel lobby, alone. The last we ever saw of the meticulously dressed, reptillian LC was him using his phone's LED screen as a mirror to check his teeth for food debris and to pluck a rather stubborn rogue hair from his left eyebrow.

In this Dark Age, the grotesque may hold power but it will not triumph. Yet it continues to lurk everywhere you investigate. Truly, nothing is as it appears.

A happy town is not a happy town. A bridge is not a bridge. And Karl is not Karl.

# Part Three

# THE PRESENT TENSE

*33*

On the road again, and sensing a renewed air of firm resolve and togetherness, we choose to remain as much as possible in the present tense. For only in the present moment do we glimpse the truth.

We can feel its grounding effect on each other. Although still clueless, we peacefully remain. Quite content. And open to change.

Eventually, though, Pedro understandably succumbs to a momentary lapse and voices a realization as it passes through his mind-stream:

*I just can't believe I share the same DNA as that creep. He is so vile!*

*Don't forget you share my DNA too, Sweetheart,* Gini consoles. Then realizing that may imply a future filled with Alzheimers she adds... *All the good stuff, I mean.*

*I know, Mother,* Pedro reassures. *It's not that. It's just he is so awful.*

*DNA isn't everything either, Darling,* Maria consoles. *Modern Science will soon catch up and discover that consciousness and intention account for so much more of our true potential than a double helix of proteins or whatever.*

*That's right, Karl continues. We may share 98% of our DNA with a monkey but it doesn't make us one... I read somewhere we even share seventy-something percent of our DNA with a banana! What does that say about our mind or our spirit?*

*Nothing much,* I venture. *Maria is right. It's out of the infinite space that we currently refer to as consciousness that EVERYTHING arises: matter, energy, time, thoughts and emotions; all simply the fizz that naturally and effortlessly arises from deep within the primordially perfect Champagne of Bliss... Now THERE'S something to ponder, if ponder you must (I add with wide eyes and a mischievous grin) ... I'll leave it with you.*

*Maria, can you call to mind the words of the Buddha on this very topic?* I say, as a little test.

*Yes. I think so.* She suddenly becomes crystal clear:

"We are what we think.
All that we are arises with our thoughts.
With our thoughts, we make the world."

*Just perfect,* I pronounce. *Thus it is, O Daughter of noble family. Thus it is.*

*If you'll permit me to expand a little,* I continue... *We are all constantly learning from personal experience – the Greatest Teacher of all – that we create our own future in the here and the now. And that begins with the mind itself. Whether we are on a hazardous mission to change the world, living with terminal illness, or simply planning a new life, it all starts with this thought we are having right here, right now. To really shape the future, we have to remain firmly rooted, undistracted, in the present. That's why we train the mind in meditation. So we can stay present and open for longer and longer periods of time. So we can stay free.*

*Every breath we take, I summarize, is a kind of 'little death' followed by a tremendous rebirth. The trick is to master it so we don't cling to the past and don't grasp at the future. By simply remaining open to the infinite possibilities the present offers us, we always have a choice: We learn to 'respond' to life, rather than 'react'. As the Buddha said, we make the world we want ourselves.*

Soon we are driving along main roads with spectacular vistas on either side as we make our gradual descent to the coast of *El Andaluz*. I observe with immense rejoicing that everyone's minds are open and content. There is neither too much planning nor too much worrying. Nobody is passing the time by labeling or judging each phenomenon as it passes. They simply glide by our windows.

We are like the sky itself. Everything is just passing through. There's no need for running commentary. We are not running at all. We are *journeying...* together. For this moment at least, there is very little hope or fear arising. Just being... Perfect... *Thus it is...* And that's OK.

Several transitions occur as we go. Maria slips off her heels and drives for a while, barefoot. She and I quietly discuss meditation and the mind, Buddhisty things like that. Karl apologizes, again, for all the intrigue and secrecy, and for the mess he's gotten us into. Gini dozes off. Pedro's heart opens a little more and his mind goes through the long process of profoundly settling. All this 'spiritual' stuff is awakening something new in him. Something fresh. He feels like he's about to write something major. We briefly consider re-routing up to *Mijas* for lunch, but then change our minds again; we acknowledge the freedom of our situation and rejoice in the power to make decisions for ourselves, as we go. When Gini wakes up, she announces two requests:

*When we get to Málaga, I wonder if we could pay a visit to the hospital? I want to have a quick check-up. And I'd dearly love to visit the Cathedral again.*

*No problem at all, Ms Virginia,* I say. *Your wish is our command. Our very great pleasure.*

Our new rental is so roomy and spacious. It would easily accommodate six or seven people and all their baggage. We joke for a moment about the possibility of picking up a hitch-hiker. How he would have no idea what on earth he was getting himself into, poor thing. But, in the end, we think better of it concluding that one of us would have to bring him up to speed with our saga. And we might then have to kill him, to shut him up.

After a while, I go in the back to be with my newest student, Gini, and Karl moves to the front to get to know Maria better as she drives. Pedro is now sitting alone with his legs stretched across the remaining two seats at the very back of the vehicle. He is scribbling a new story in a notebook he bought in a tacky souvenir shop. There is a dark, handsome gypsy cutting wood on the cover. Though it's only a water-colour, you can clearly see his bare chest is massive and has some light fur on it. His incredible arms are taut and strong, all the way from his thick neck right down to his rough finger-tips. I'm thinking it was no mistake that Pedro chose the one with that cover. And you don't have to be *Miss Marple* to work out what kind of new life he's envisioning in those lines.

Gini and I steal the chance to discuss the *dharma* quietly together, and to meditate a bit more.

She is bright today. And she recognizes she may not have acres of time left to play with, in this life. We quickly develop a hybrid contemplation practice. It makes clever use of her stories about her past experiences and flows easily back to the present. We can harvest the fruits of those positive memories, thus creating a more powerful environment for meditation in the here and now.

It's similar to the method we used before. But this time Gini herself suggests it's not so good to dwell too long in the past for fear of distraction. Therefore, she resolves to revisit brief moments – beautiful, tender moments – from her life. And, having captured the vibrant essence of that love, bring it back to the present to share. It is like a torch which dispels the darkness and all the misery of the world.

Gini is extremely keen to try it straight away, and for the rest of the day if possible. At the beginning of each attempt, she closes her eyes to help her focus on one incident or another. But after that, she knows that keeping her eyes open orients the practice towards the present. It also keeps the *mind* open and spacious, which is what we all want. In a very short time, Gini's natural ability for retrieving and sharing love and light is radiating brightly like the sun.

Sometimes she whispers to me what particular episode she is recalling. Sometimes she just basks in it, and I sense what joy she is rekindling. She is becoming increasingly adept and focused. Always positive and warm. Always primed to share the limitless light she awakens.

At first, Gini is harvesting the obvious: She's reliving a moment spent in her beloved Benjamin's arms in Madrid in the early days. There is a rich, inexhaustible seam of such precious moments to mine.

There are stolen kisses and unexpected caresses on airplanes and in taxis. Backstage before important concerts. Beaming smiles dispatched across crowded parties afterwards.

There are cuddles and tight hand-holding with Pedro as an infant. There are family daytrips and foreign holidays: a glorious picnic in the majestic Roman theatre at *Segóbriga*, which culminated in a long snooze at sunset after a couple of bottles of *Tempranillo*.

Of course there are favourite snapshots from that villa in *Positano,* and the incredible view from their hotel's rooftop 'infinity pool' in *Montalcino*. And from such far-flung places as the Kathmandu Valley and the Zen Garden at *Ryoanji* in Kyoto.

In just a very short period of time, and despite being in a moving car, Gini rapidly becomes an old hand at diving into the ocean of the past and returning once more to the present – not to mourn, or to yearn – but to exhale Love to all: her companions in the car, workers we pass on the road, animals in the fields. Sunflowers, grapes and olives, and the insects who make them their homes. Those who wound and oppress ordinary folk, enemies of the Truth, biggots, dictators and abusers. Without feeling extra love for this one, or less love for that one, Gini's light becomes *all-pervasive* and *unconditional*. Hers is the love of the *Great Mother*. Faced with a universe populated by so many beings, no other response would seem adequate.

Virginia is feeling more alive than ever. Her heart-breakingly fond memories of the past are finally being put to good use. Her consciousness is rapidly purifying and transforming. She is making the giant spiritual paradigm shift that we all must make, if we truly want to experience lasting happiness.

Gini is moving from past to present. From self to others.

She is Shining in a Dark Age.

34

Pedro has made a good start on his new story. The world he is creating is full of vision and beautiful imaginings. He is driving now as he's familiar with Málaga, and knows the way to our hotel.

Karl has been reading his guidebook so we ask him to give us a quick summary.

He reports that Málaga is one of the world's oldest true cities. Founded by the Phoenicians over 3000 years ago, it was named *Malaka*. In many of the ancient languages, this means 'salt' and refers to the high quality salt that was harvested from the sea there. It was widely used all around the famous port area to preserve the super-abundance of fish that Málaga used to be so famous for.

Later captured and further developed by the Carthaginians, Romans, Christians and the Moors, Málaga is best thought of as a city within a city within a city.

Perhaps the most influential period for Málaga's architecture and culture was the period under the Muslim *Moors*, which lasted for 800 years. It's still considered to have been the greatest flourishing of beauty in all of Southern Europe. Málaga was the principal bastion from which the Moors colonized Spain. It was also the last place to fall to the Christians who only managed to triumph by laying siege to the citadel and starving the population to death. Those who did not die were captured and sold into slavery, or given as gifts to the Church's wealthy benefactors.

*So many coincidences,* Karl continues. *Málaga's famous Cathedral of the Incarnation was built on the site of a fabulous Mosque, which they demolished. Close to the Alcazaba and Gibralfaro, the Cathedral's construction was begun in the Renaissance but completed in the Baroque by the same architect who built the New Bridge in Ronda. And – yet another coincidence – Málaga's grand old theatre, Gini, is named for your beloved Cervantes.*

Karl concludes by saying that Málaga is, of course, the birthplace of *Picasso* who – he imagined – could never have guessed as a little boy what horrors were to befall his beloved Spain during his own lifetime. In the final *Battle of Málaga* alone, the Civil War claimed over 7000 lives. Many of their bodies are interred in a mausoleum inside the Cathedral itself.

The hotel I chose is in the centre of town, just down the road from Picasso's childhood family home and a short stroll from the museum dedicated to him. Pedro tells us the museum has a beautiful internal courtyard that's cloistered and, if memory serves, has quite a good restaurant. So we agree to lunch there after we settle in at the hotel.

As we enter the grand foyer to check in, we all remark how fancy it is with its opulent plasterwork and exquisite chandeliers. We agree to keep in touch by phone and to avoid being alone if possible. This time we allocate the rooms as follows: Maria in a single, Karl and me in a twin, and Gini and Pedro to share a twin as before. Karl and I go drop the car at the rental place, which is handily nearby. That's what influenced me most when choosing the hotel, though I did think we all deserved a bit of a treat too. We arrange to rent a new car for late afternoon the following day. But in the back of my mind I am wondering if we might need to stay two nights, depending on how Gini's hospital visit goes.

Pedro confirms that Gini has brought her Hospital Services Card with her. And within thirty minutes, he has arranged the appointment by phone. Everything should be free of charge, and all of Gini's personal details and 'on-file' medical history will be in front of the consultant before they meet. The consultation is scheduled for tomorrow morning so we still have the option to move on in the afternoon, all going well.

Having freshened up, Pedro and the ladies are already downstairs in the lounge. It is elegantly modern with hints of former glory peeping through here and there. Karl receives a call from Pedro to say they are ready and waiting. I switch off the BBC World News. The civil unrest is ripping northwards through Spain. Every city and town from Sevilla to Madrid to Barcelona is set to explode with a rage that will dwarf the carnage that already ignited. In other news, I note that Greece is still in utter turmoil. Protests and street violence continue to erupt. On the other hand, the Irish economy and political situation is in just as bad a state, but the people are already so down-trodden and disheartened that they barely raise a finger. The voice of rebellion is fast-becoming extinct in Ireland.

We pass a very pleasant hour or two over lunch. We are sporting daywear that's sensible but sophisticated enough to see us through to dinner, if we decide to stay out all day. I am wearing *chinos*, the colour of faded sandstone, and a crisp pale-blue shirt from Ralph Lauren. A very light sweater draped around the shoulders to accessorize (lambswool, rich charcoal). A pair of plain dark shoes from Marks, completes the look. I leave the others chatting over coffees while I slip outside to a quiet corner to connect to the internet on my phone.

I call my master on *Skype*.

He is sitting in a café in Kathmandu, directly facing the incredible *Stupa* at Boudhanath, playfully locking eyes with it.

He tells me he's having a short holiday away from Varanasi with some family and a few monks as chaperone. Disarmingly, he sometimes speaks just like any teenager: He says the long journey was '*lame*' but the famous eyes painted on top of the Stupa are '*cool*'. I often just can't believe he is the same being who blew my mind all that time ago.

But then, all of a sudden, *Nyima Özer* of old re-emerges taking my breath away. He says I am probably in Málaga by now and I should remember to take Virginia Blake to the concert in the Cathedral. He tells me that, for some people, music heals everything (especially the mind). That the Greeks at one time used the same verb, *Therapeuo*, to mean both 'heal' and 'sing'. They got the concept from the Egyptians, who got it from The Ancients of Pre-Antiquity.

Before I get a chance to ask any questions about how to proceed with Karl, Rinpoche instructs me to ask Gini if she knows she's related to the famous artist and mystic poet *William Blake*. And to inform her that she'll find some fine words of wisdom and solace in his poems.

Finally, he tells me to grow up and trust my instincts about Karl and his story. To see through the fog and help Karl reveal at least *some* of the truth that lies beyond.

*How is your insight going?* ('The Sun's Rays' enquires nonchalantly). *Have you seen those Swastikas yet?*

*You do* realize – he continues – *you are going to lose Maria and Pedro too, before all this is over, don't you? No, I don't mean they're going to die or anything (Not for a long time anyway). That would be so 'uncool'. Calm down, Dear. No, what I'm saying is: Don't forget about them in all of this. Look after them both, and remember to water the seeds for all THEIR dreams too.*

He says he's thinking of changing his name to *Lama Sunshine*, then hangs up.

*35*

As is so often the way with miraculous insight, it just happens there *is* a choral concert starting at 4.30 in the Cathedral. Timed to display the magnificent, luminous interior as the afternoon sun dissolves. It's a joint affair with two of Gini's all-time favourite choirs: *La Capella Reial de Catalunya* and none other than *The Choir of St John's College, Cambridge*, both conducted by Jordi Savall (an old friend of Gini and her beloved Benji).

As we approach the Cathedral's vast, almost triumphal edifice, we walk through a quiet garden of ancient pines and palms. They disperse the subtle scent of late afternoon as we enter the comparatively arctic stillness of the enormous interior.

Settled in our seats, Karl asks if we noticed the two bell towers outside; one was left unfinished. He says the locals nicknamed the Cathedral *'The One-Armed Lady'* with reference to its lop-sided appearance. The money allocated for completing the second tower was redirected to America in the late 18th Century, to assist with the effort to rid themselves of the occupying English during their War of Independence.

As we look around us, there are few words to adequately describe the space we find ourselves inhabiting. I am wondering how fabulous the original Mosque must have been if this is what the Christians had to construct in its place to rival it. Where did the money come from? Was there no poverty in Málaga at that time?

The vaulted ceiling alone has all the appearance of pure gold, and floats so far above the people it seems to offer a glimpse of heaven itself. No matter what direction you look, the space revealed stretches out and opens up as if to infinity.

The altar, and even the original area for the choir to sit, appears so far removed from the public that I question if it was the designer's *intention* to make them feel inconsequential and separate. Who paid for all this, if not the people?

The main organ has pipes that are so huge you can hardly see where they end, so richly ornamented with carved wood and gold leaf that you get the message these people took music very seriously indeed.

It's a wonder the Cathedral was able to stand at all under the weight of all that embellishment. Structurally too, there's a game being played out here; what exactly IS supporting this church? The ceiling appears to hover independently, and the walls seem practically non-existent; there are massive stained-glass windows everywhere you turn. Enormous Renaissance panels of glass depicting Jesus and the saints, great iconic flourishes: the symbols of a complex, intricate Theology of The Elite.

While we simply marvel and gasp at it all, I notice Gini sitting beside me has a distant, thoughtful air about her. I rub the back of her hand and remind her to stay with us, remain in the moment.

*I know,* she whispers. *It's all just too incredible for words: the atmosphere, the programme of music we're about to witness, and all my favourite performers from the past. It's nearly impossible not to drift ... I miss Benji so much.*

*Benjamin never left you, Gini,* I remind her. *Death is not a defeat or an abandonment. It is just Change. Your Benji is always with you, whenever you dwell in the here and now. He is not just in your memory or your heart. He has been liberated from his old, diseased body to the extent that he's totally free. Free to float in the air you breathe. Free to travel along those shafts of light you see. He is free to permeate every fibre of your being, coming to you in every single note you are about to hear. Don't miss him because you are off somewhere else, in your head, feeling melancholy. Don't miss him. Stay here. Use your breath to anchor you. Open your heart and just see what miracles the music brings you.*

The main lights of the Cathedral are fully extinguished. All that remains is a multitude of tiny candles flickering in every corner. And, of course, the Sun's Rays as they lovingly illuminate whatever they touch.

Bathed in the half-light, we are first treated by St John's to a slow, heart-melting rendition of Victoria's *O Nata Lux.*

The two choirs perform separately at first, each taking turns to offer choral wonders from a variety of Spanish composers. There are examples of the finest Renaissance and Counter Reformation *polyphony* ever written. *Victoria, Guerrero,* and *Morales* nurture and sustain us, interspersed with short organ works by *Milán, Mudarra* and *Narváez.* To further enhance and augment the splendour, we are treated to a sprinkling of lesser-known choral gems by *Albéniz, Granados,* and *Sor.* Time stands still. Almost two hours pass imperceptibly. We hover and float like a melisma, like we inhabit the flow of the music itself.

But the crowning glory is saved for last: As a *finale*, the two choirs combine, under the expert guidance of Savall, to produce a numinous rendition of the *Mass for the Dead* by Morales. Its magnificence is beyond description, and nobody wants it ever to finish. However, after what seems like an eternity of pure perfection, the choirs' deep, resonant voices bring the closing cadence to its final resting place and finish it does.

The remnants of the last chord hang on the quiet air, then slowly dissolve into space. Time has been transcended and all is well in the universe.

The sun has moved around to illumine the earth's dark side and an aeon of silent afterglow settles upon the audience.

Although the glory of every rapturous syllable has long subsided, nobody dares to shatter the natural great peace with anything as mundane as applause. So we simply sit there. Suspended. Open and content.

Eventually a ripple of applause begins somewhere far behind us. Its slow, gentle contagion spreads like the energy of Compassion itself to fill the entirety of the cosmos.

When we finally join in, and look around at each other, I can see Gini is calm but awestruck, her mouth wide open. Karl is hiding his face behind his hand and appears to be praying. Myself, Pedro and Maria are in floods. Joyful tears.

For an instant, we are completely and utterly inseparable. We are indeed *'The Famous Five'*, united in our mysterious journey towards the truth and whatever peace of mind it brings.

The conductor, Jordi Savall, stands in front of the two choirs. His palms joined at his heart in gratitude for this great moment of healing, which we've all been so privileged to share.

As the ecstatic applause turns to cheers and roars of immense gratitude, we are no longer in a church. Nothing sacred has happened here... Transcendent LIFE has happened here. We are alive in this very moment. And we want to shout it from the rooftops!

Only in Spain can quiet *Glorias* and *Halleluias* turn so quickly to great cries of *Bravo* and *Viva! Maestro!* As the cheers are carried on the four winds and rebound defiantly off every wall and barrier they encounter, I thank Buddha for the Spanish. I thank *God* for them too! Every last one of them.

With a swooping, theatrical gesture *El Maestro* Savall moves aside and gets the combined choirs to take a bow in unison. Bow after bow, their talent is celebrated and causes an upswell of tremendous gratitude and rejoicing. Without these particular human voices, at this particular moment in time, perhaps it wouldn't have been so incredibly beautiful. Without this vast cathedral being filled with these *particular* souls, would the great beauty we just witnessed have happened at all?

Sometimes, when the causes and conditions are just right, things simply come together and manifest for a while. Like a rainbow.

And when the moment has passed, it's gone.

We all leave our seats and turn to make our way out of the great *Cathedral of the Incarnation*. Just then, the enormous pipes of the organ resound with a rousing postscript to the concert. The famous *Miguel Perez*, a young Málaga-born-and-raised organist of growing international repute, treats us to one of his own compositions. The full spectrum of sound the organ emits raises the roof off the place and blows away all the cobwebs from every heart and mind.

The call is *Wake Up! Wake Up! This day is not finished yet!*

When we get outside, an incredibly beautiful young woman approaches at quite a pace from behind and gently places her hand on Gini's shoulder.

*Sweet Mother of all the Buddhas and Bodhisattvas,* I think to myself. *What a fright! I'm assuming they don't make assassins THIS gorgeous nowadays, do they?*

*Aunt Virginia,* the young lady says in perfect English, with all the grace of an angel. *It's me. Arianna*

It's the daughter of Maestro Savall and she has been dispatched by him with the express purpose of catching Gini before we leave.

*Jordi may be older now, but he doesn't miss a trick you know. Father saw you from up there as the choirs were taking their bow. He sent me to invite you and your friends to dinner in our suite at the hotel.*

*Well, dear God in Heaven. But Arianna, you are the image of your mother,* Gini declared. Turning to the rest of us, Gini explained that Arianna's mother, the incomparable soprano *Montserrat Figueras,* had recently passed away. And that the

Savall family and their circle have been great friends of her and Benjamin for many years.

*Although WE were in Madrid, and you lot were always splitting your time between Switzerland and Catalunya and France, I always felt we remained very close,* Gini says to Arianna.

Becoming a little confused, Gini can't remember when she last saw them all or whether she'd attended Montserrat's funeral. So she decides to say nothing. What's more, for fear of becoming increasingly vague as the night goes on – and it being the night before her check up – Gini decides to turn down the invitation to dine with Jordi saying they must surely have far more exciting things to be doing after such an amazing concert than to sit and chat with a dotty old bag like her.

Crest-fallen, Arianna pleads with Gini saying nothing would make her father happier than to share a meal with her. After all, they'd *both* now lost the great loves of their lives and only they would really know how that felt.

That said, plus the bizarre 'coincidence' that we're all staying at the same hotel anyway – I know, like *HELLO!* – Gini can no longer refuse. It turns out we're on the floor beneath the whole entourage, including *La Capella Reial*. And the choir from *St John's* is on the floor beneath us.

Gini vows to do her best and not go to bed too early. She jokes that, even if it kills her, she will party with Jordi until they sample all the desserts on the menu and consume at least a barrel of Brandy Alexanders.

*Arianna,* Gini says rather feebly after all that bravado, *I know my Benji has been dead for some time now, but I still can't believe that Montserrat is gone too...*

*Not gone Aunty Gini*, she quickly steps in. *Death is not 'gone'. Just changed, Darling. That's all. Just listen to that music we heard inside. Does each note mourn the death of every other passing note? Even the notes they found themselves so well-suited to? No. Music is Change. So is life. We must learn to move with it. Benji is never dead, and neither is Mother, as long as we hold them in our hearts. That's what I think anyway.*

We all just gape and gawk at her, each stunned to varying degrees by her beauty or her wisdom.

Arianna tells us the number of the suite and makes a seamless retreat. Her slow-motion hair bouncing in the cool evening breeze, she turns one last time to say: *See you all at 8.30. OK?*

Left standing there, in a small circle, we recompose ourselves...


*If only Benji could be here for one last dinner with Jordi*, Gini sighs.

*If only I were ten years younger*, Karl thinks but doesn't say out loud.

*If only I were straight*, both Pedro and I say in unison... *Snap!*

Gini turns to a grinning Maria: *Well then, Miss del Mar? What witty remark have YOU got to offer?*

Barely able to contain herself, Maria finally manages to blurt out: *...No SERIOUSLY. I was just thinking: 'If only I were a MAN!'*

36

It is about 9.45 and we're just finishing the main course. The suite is extremely plush. You could live there quite comfortably. As well as a large double bedroom with windows on two sides, there's a small study as you enter, which leads onto the sitting room. There are beautiful sofas with low, occasional tables at either end, large high-backed armchairs and, of course, a baby grand piano in the corner. Very expensive embroidered silk cushions are scattered around as a finishing touch. They pick up the gold motif from the heavy, floor-to-ceiling drapes that run throughout. Then double glass doors open into a gorgeous, private dining room. The only art worth noting hangs on the wall at the end of the dining table. It's a rather large reproduction of Rembrandt's *Lamentation of Jeremiah*. It is all the more striking at this scale. The colours in the prophet's robes radiate so vibrantly from the darkness that surrounds him.

Jordi really is the perfect host. Even his seating arrangement reflects great awareness. He has placed Gini at his side, and Pedro beside her, should she need any special care. The rest of us have been interspersed around the table, alternating visitors with family. Of course Arianna is there, next to Pedro. Then Maria, Ferran (Jordi and Montserrat's son), Karl, Michael from Ireland (Jordi's assistant), and yours truly. Jordi is naturally at the head of the table. And because I am sitting on his left I can easily share in his conversation with Gini and Pedro, who are opposite me.

The meal has been served by waiters who effortlessly glide in and out of the suite like nymphs. And, I must say, the stimulating conversation around the table is a welcome relief for us all, having been cooped up together for days.

It's most interesting to observe tender moments between Gini and Jordi. They have shared so many moving experiences in the past. And now they share grief too. Gini and Montserrat had been extremely close and really bonded over raising their children in such a strange environment. Jordi is probably the only person still alive qualified enough to have recognized Benjamin's genius. Although head and shoulders above him, career-wise, Jordi always made sure Benji knew how much he admired and relied on him, both as a musician and as a man. I can clearly see how much it means for Gini, and Pedro, to hear such praise reiterated by one who knew and loved Benjamin as much as they did.

In recent years, and largely because of Gini's fixation on the past, Pedro has been so busy trying not to mention his father Benji too much for fear of further upsetting her mind. On some level, as a result of habit, he now finds it hard to face talking about Benji at all. But he's glad to hear Jordi speak of him so warmly. At this table, Benjamin is not a person to be mourned. His death is not a problem to be faced or solved. Benjamin is a real, living, flesh and blood man whom they all knew and loved. Someone to be celebrated.

Arianna and Ferran are both a bit younger than Pedro, but they remember family holidays together with them all. They tell such sweet stories of two ordinary families on holidays together. They recount the good times as if they were yesterday. Then the juicy stuff starts to come out. Maria's ears prick up. She loves gossip, even if it's about a dead person she never met.

Ferran remembers discovering Jordi and Benji drunk one night at the bottom of the garden in Switzerland. They were fighting, and their shouting had woken him up. By the time he snook down to see what was going on, they were rolling about on the ground laughing and singing to each other.

Arianna spills the beans about another time there was a row brewing between Montserrat and Gini. It was over some childish fight or other that she and Pedro had gotten into during the day. She remembers how both mothers were so protective of their children and could see no harm in them. The cold silence lasted for days. Both women were a real force of nature in those days.

We haven't needed to explain much about our little group or why we are on the road together. Once Gini said that Karl and I are new friends she's made, that seems enough for Jordi. But he's curious nonetheless.

Noticing at one point that Karl is mesmerized by the painting of Jeremiah, Jordi engages him more fully. Addressing himself down the full length of the table to Karl, Jordi asks him directly what it is he sees in the picture that holds him so spell-bound. While Karl is still forming a response, Jordi presses him further. He asks what exactly Karl imagines is going through the prophet's head at that particular moment.

Karl responds straight away this time:

*He is thinking about Justice, or INJUSTICE rather. He is calling for a total overhaul of human society. He's crying out for a rebellion of sorts. A quiet revolution of the heart... He speaks out against a world where people are treated unfairly: by their religion, their state, in their own homes by their own family, but especially at the margins of society. Jeremiah's main thought is for the marginalized and the poor. He gives a voice to the voiceless.*

*Sorry Gini,* Karl says. *I don't mean to bring the party down, and I'm sure you're all tired of hearing me go on about all this stuff by now...*

*No. Not at all,* she replies. *You know how much I share your sentiments. Anyway, how could you possibly bring the party down any lower?* Gini jokes. *The main theme so far has been our dead spouses and how much we miss them.*

*Celebrate them. Rejoice in the memories of them,* I interject.

Jordi quite agrees and turns his attention to me. He asks semi-probing questions about my private life: if I have a wife, whether my parents are still alive, the 'situation' in Tibet. I tell him I am gay and still single. That my parents live in Sikkim, though they are very old now. And that I've never actually been to Tibet myself, but I plan to make an extra-special effort to go there once my travels in the West have finished.

Ferran says a photographer friend of his has just returned from Kham in Eastern Tibet. I say that's where my family originally came from.

Arianna says she longs to go there to collect the music of the people, their Buddhist chants and folk tunes. I tell her to stay in touch, that I can easily arrange a guide for her if she is serious about arranging a trip. She is thrilled and remains very animated on the subject for some time. As she speaks, we all notice how her beauty (and that of her brother) runs far deeper than their skin. They are wonderful people. The product of positive past karma, which has ripened into being born to wonderful parents. Neither of them is as young as we first thought. Though their youthful energy is light and clear, they are 'old souls'.

Pedro enjoys meeting them both again, though he still holds some small vestige of resentment that the Savalls' contact with his family had fizzled out in recent times. He always felt it was because of his mother's dementia and how difficult she could be at times. But nonetheless, Pedro is really enjoying the evening. Everyone feels so safe and secure in the suite. And being close to Jordi – whom he'd always held as another kind of father figure – is so comforting, warm and familiar. From time to time, Pedro even finds himself thinking he would love to have a hug.

Gini doesn't quite make it through the entire dessert menu, but she does insist on a few rounds of Alexanders before she has to – as she puts it – *'go up the wooden stairs to BEDfordshire'*.

I'm very curious about Jordi's assistant Michael who hasn't said much all night. He apologizes for being so quiet and tells me he's exhausted. He organizes practically everything in Jordi's schedule. He has to remind himself that his greatest joy is helping Jordi in all aspects of the music too. He is something of an expert on Early Music and relishes those rare days when his work centres mainly around arranging and transcribing what Jordi has left for him to do.

As if by way of apology, Michael suggests we all adjourn to the living room with our *digestifs,* whereupon he miraculously perks up and offers us a request at the piano. Anything we like, he says, and he'll have a 'fair *ould stab* at it'.

Maria, always the joker who likes to disrupt class, requests Abba's *Dancing Queen*, which he instantly launches into. By the chorus, Michael is actually extemporizing on the theme in the style of *Rachmaninov*... The man's a freaking genius!

While he's still playing that, Karl requests the famous Socialist anthem, Beethoven's *Ode To Joy*, which he interprets in the style of heavy rock. Incredible!

On and on it goes, for nearly an hour. We have *Kylie, Bach, The Carpenters, Frank Sinatra, Handel, Scarlatti, Bon Jovi*... then he draws the musical odyssey to a close with Abba again and a monumentally over-ornamented *Tierce de Picardie* finish (Classical Music's version of the ultimate happy ending).

We applaud outrageously as Michael rises to his feet and flourishes the exaggerated deep bow of a court jester. He looks over to Jordi who, knowing Gini's musical tastes as well as his own, has one final request that will finish the evening off to perfection.

As Michael plays his own wonderfully poignant transcription of Bach's *Sleepers Awake* we're all profoundly transformed, and our minds settle on an entirely higher plane.

37

The next morning, we're at the hospital.

Gini's had another episode during the night. Both she and Pedro are exhausted. Having completed a whole list of standard tests plus a deep scan of the brain, which normally takes months on a waiting list to get, we're all sitting around a kind of private lounge area outside the consultant's office, waiting.

Surprisingly, Gini is in very good spirits. All the music of the previous day and the wonderful evening with the Savalls has boosted her no end. She chats intermittently about nothing else. It must have been marvelous to reconnect with Jordi and the family. And remembering Benji in such a positive way was so uplifting for her.

A male nurse finally opens the door and invites Gini in to meet the consultant. She insists that Pedro and I accompany her for moral support and to take notes on what is said. Maria keeps Karl company outside.

The consultant is a woman in her fifties. She has a very warm, motherly approach but is capable of being quite direct too. Her time is precious and she doesn't flinch from telling the truth as it is.

As a kind of opener, the consultant chats informally with Gini about how she's feeling, and how her family is coping. Then she asks Gini to answer some routine questions, to check how her mind is functioning. Amazingly, Gini gets many of them wrong. She mis-spells her maiden name. She can't remember what year it is. She lies to cover the fact that she can't recall her own telephone number by saying she never knew it. Eventually, feeling under tremendous pressure to pass the test, Gini becomes totally confused and exasperated. When asked who Pedro and I are, she says he is an old friend she met recently on holidays and she has no idea who I am.

How unpredictably fragile we are. To think the brain can so easily pop in and out of gear like that. Makes you wonder why we rely so heavily on our thoughts and emotions in the first place.

*OK Mrs Léon,* the consultant pronounces. *That's very good. Our little test is over. You've passed with flying colours.*

*Oh Thank God! That's a relief,* says Gini with all the helplessness of someone who really was trying her best to please.

*Now, for the results of your medical tests this morning...*

The consultant reports her findings directly to Virginia, but continually glances at Pedro and me, to check if we are following.

She reminds Gini that her particular strand of Early Onset Alzheimers – some precise medical term that I cannot remember, because I've never heard of it before, and which Pedro still can't spell correctly – is an extremely aggressive disease of the brain. *The main symptoms you are experiencing are dementia (short and medium-term memory loss, clinging to the past, confusion bordering on bewilderment), and catastrophic events in the brain itself that cause permanent, chronic damage.* I don't recognize the proper term she uses there either, so let's call them mini-strokes.

The consultant is very kind and compassionate but presses on with her assessment, determined to come to her considered conclusions.

She says that what her tests and the brain scan have found is nothing new actually: Gini's condition is very serious indeed. Nothing can be done to halt the deterioration or the decline. Medication merely tries to mask the uncomfortable symptoms. But it will gradually become less effective.

She says the worst thing about the strokes is that, after each one Gini suffers, her brain function plummets to a new, even lower, level. Little by little, stroke after stroke, she will inevitably get to the level where her brain functionality is minimal.

Furthermore – and this is the thing the consultant obviously found the hardest to say – most people actually pass away before it ever gets to that stage. They have a stroke one day. Maybe it's no worse than the other mini-strokes they've been having, or maybe it's a massive stroke event.

*The fact is, Virginia,* the consultant bluntly summarizes, *one of these days – and maybe sooner than you think – you will have another stroke and pass away. If you haven't done so already, I strongly suggest that you gather your family and friends and tell them how your disease is going to deteriorate rapidly from here on in, and clearly tell them (while you can still express yourself) what your final wishes are.*

Virginia gains a penetrating clarity of mind:

*All the people I truly love in the world are here with me today. They're the only ones willing to put up with me, I suppose. (Her memory clicks back on) My son Pedro here, and our travelling companions. That's it... They already know about it all. Just not how it may happen so soon.*

*The next thing I must do, she said turning to me, is live my life – every moment of it – to the full. One moment at a time. To the full. And, with your continued kind help and guidance Jalu Yogi, prepare for the moment of death.*

By lunchtime, Gini is playing it all down and joking about living forever, like a shaft of light or a musical note hanging on the air. But she is not avoiding the truth. On the contrary. She's simply making it more palatable for everyone else.

At one point, when a waiter or a doorman or someone asks Gini 'And how are YOU today?', she answers with a wry smile: *Ah. I'm dying, Love. No big deal. We all are.*

In the room, she tells Pedro she doesn't want her deterioration or her passing to hold him back from finding the great love of his life. She urges him not to wait a second longer. To be free. And go fall in love.

She says that, ultimately, everyone dies alone anyway. Like birth, it is the one journey nobody else can accompany you on. Whenever Pedro attempts to interrupt or contradict her instructions, she simply says No. Her mind is made up.

Her insight is growing clearer as she reasons it out with him.

*Look at it this way,* she says. *Even if you are living with me and caring for me twenty-four hours a day, chances are I would have a stroke and pass away the moment your back was turned anyway. That's often the way with these things, Darling. People die at the strangest of times: during the night when nobody's watching them, when they are alone on the loo, when their loved one has just popped out of the room to make some tea.*

She is very persuasive. She even says she might actually prefer to die alone, with her music and her memories. She concludes that it's totally stupid at this point for Pedro to even consider putting his life on hold, to make a grand plan around Gini's care and her passing. After all, she points out with all the cutting wisdom of a great Zen Master, she could die tonight in her sleep! And where would that leave all their plans and soul-searching?

Pedro never really stands a chance. Without actually agreeing to anything, the effect is the same: he seems to have agreed to everything. As a joke, he even agrees to go with the first eligible bachelor he meets. But he says the falling in love part may take some time. Gini laps up his wicked sense of humour and jumps on the band-wagon saying her greatest wish is for him to cut those apron strings and fly, be free, head for the hills. She doesn't want to see him again until her funeral where he should be so distracted by his new love that he even forgets to cry.

By two o'clock, everyone's bags are packed and loaded
into our new chariot. We say a last goodbye to Jordi and the
clan, and we're on our way.

38

Pedro is at the helm again. He's researched a special treat for Gini. And, with my assistance, we've arranged to visit the place she mentioned was an old favourite of hers.

Slowly coming back to a more grounded awareness, after all the upset of the morning, Gini is sitting between Maria and Karl who are caring for her (without too much fuss, at her request). I'm in the passenger seat flicking through the guidebook and keeping an eye on Pedro, who is understandably still feeling quite raw.

*So where are we off to today?* Gini asks. *Granada, I imagine?*

*No Mama,* Pedro replies with a gleeful air of delight and anticipation. *We're off to your old favourite, Alhama de Granada – the place you mentioned visiting with me and Dad when I was a kid. I want to try and find the Banos Thermales (the thermal springs).*

Gini is quietly thrilled beyond belief. She doesn't remember saying anything about it the other day. But, just then, the clear image of Pedro sitting on Benji's lap in the naturally hot rockpool returns with great gusto. Maria and

Karl are also delighted for her. They take one of Gini's hands each and rub and squeeze it gently.

*Yes indeed,* I join in. *Today we're taking a break from the world of International Espionage. A little family holiday in the countryside, away from it all, by the river.*

*Alhama de Granada* is inland and up. More or less equidistant from Málaga and Granada, as the crow flies. With Pedro's excellent driving, we'll get there in no time at all.

The road takes us up, up, and up again. We drink in the spectacular views, as always. There are periods of light chit-chat alternated with healthy silence. The further we all get from the hospital, the more our minds open out, release and relax. We're not running away from anything, or trying to forget. No. In fact, it seems the spaciousness of nature is helping the mind, left unstirred and unaltered, to find its own natural great peace. We all sense it opening up around us as we go. The uncertainty of the hour of death, even if it's close at hand, is no longer a daunting prospect. It is clear for all to see that Gini herself is leading the way. For today at least. For this precious moment. There is no fear.

With Karl's permission, eventually I take on the role of tour guide and report my discoveries from the travel book about Alhama.

The old Moorish town of *Alhama de Granada* is perched on a high, strategically important location for the province. From there, the Muslims had a perfect vantage point from which the entire region could easily be surveyed. The thermal baths, called *al Hammam* in Arabic, are what gave *Alhama* its name. It had always been such a beautiful place to live that, when it was finally conquered by the forces of the Catholic Monarchs in 1482, the Sultan himself is said to have cried out: *¡Ay de mi Alhama! (Woe is me! My poor Alhama!).* So powerful and evocative an utterance was it that the Arabic phrase has actually entered the modern Spanish language. To this day, people still use the very same exclamation to express profound sadness and regret.

But before the Moors, of course, there were the Romans. They captured the power of the natural hot springs and created a magnificent vaulted bath-house in the heart of the original town.

Before the Romans, there is archeological evidence of continuous settlement stretching back across the mists of time, deep into pre-history. Good land for hunting and growing, the pure fresh river, the hot springs themselves, and the panoramic views all combined to make this an irresistible spot to put down roots and settle.

On the other hand, Alhama is actually fairly remote. We have to turn off the *Sat Nav* in the car as it's no longer making sense. We twist and turn so frequently on the final approach that reading our road map becomes such a juggling act we abandon that too. Suddenly, we feel all at sea without a compass and drift along a small country back-road for a while. This route briefly reveals majestic little Alhama to us in all its former glory, then snatches it out of sight again and takes us into town the back way. There are ordinary buildings of no special character. Grandmothers hauling shopping up a steep road. Then a clearing. We're not actually inside the old town itself yet but we park up anyway to ask for help.

There's a small café-bar, mainly with men standing at the bar and sitting at tables in the shade outside. Taking the bull by the horns, Maria decides to jump out and go over.

As she walks towards the bar we watch in quiet amazement as the spectacle unfolds.

Maria is wearing tight, faded jeans, that stretch all the way down her incredible legs and partially cover the tops of her patent leather *'strappy sandals'* which, of course, have four inch heels. Her tanned midriff is exposed as she hitches up her floral shirt and ties the two corners firmly just below her more than ample bosom. Her dark hair, originally tied up, is now set loose upon the world. Her long, silky locks are floating on the gentle air as she bobs along. I can't see her face but I just know her expression is all *lovely lashes* and full, *pouty lips* which (if needs be) are parted momentarily, to devastating effect, revealing her perfect pearly white teeth. The killer blow – though she rarely has to call in the cavalry – is to slowly lick across the edge of her front teeth with the tip of her sensuous, pink tongue. I've seen it all before. Maria is back! (And all that talk about her depressed vagina... *Schmajina!)* When Maria really turns it on, she really turns it on.

Apart from one old guy, who obviously couldn't care less who the new person in town is, most of the men at the bar see Maria the second she starts to walk towards them. By the time she gets half-way across, they are grunting and fixing their hard-ons. By the time she walks through the parting crowd, they are in love. What can I say? This part of town seems to be like that: Rough. And ready.

Naturally they contain themselves. They are also men of the modern age. Most of them have wives or girlfriends already. They may be manual labourers on a quick break – intoxicated by the overwhelming femininity of this exotic creature we otherwise know as 'Maria' – but they behave like gentlemen.

Even the old man who was previously oblivious turns round to investigate the subtle disturbance on his radar. Apparently he's the owner.

In less than five minutes, Maria has landed on this sleepy little town, exploded all over the place, and extracted from the indifferent head-honcho a detailed map of Alhama with all the local info. She knows where 'people like us' would stay in the town. Where we would eat and socialize too. She's discovered all the places of interest. Which ones are interesting, and which a waste of time. For example, she's ascertained where the *Roman Baths* are located. But, apart from taking a photo of the beautiful arches holding up the roof, the locals tell her to go down to the river and sit right alongside its cold waters, in the open-air, in the makeshift thermal pools the townspeople have created with their own hands over many centuries.

The old man summons his young grandson, who is off school sick, to escort Maria and her friends directly to the right spot. He says he'll make arrangements for us to stay at the hotel he already recommended. If we go down to the people's *Banos Thermales* right away, he promises us a treat, the likes of which is rarely found these days... With a wide grin, he says the people from the factories are not there to bathe yet so we'll have it mostly to ourselves. Dusk slowly falls, he says, and you simply sit there under crimson skies in the hot water and soak to your heart's content. And it's free! Just as Mother Nature intended.

The boy arrives, nursing a slight cold. He's immediately dispatched to borrow towels from somewhere. He returns quickly with them and a little plastic bag full of something he calls 'secret'.

In just a few short minutes, the *'Famous Five'* are being carefully guided down a small track through a forest of poplars and pines to the river's edge.

When our eyes adapt to the dappled light we notice there is a pleasant hue of turquoise mixed with chartreuse all around. The woodland setting, by the strong river, is simply wondrous. The boy stops and stands to one side to present the town's pride and joy. There are three rock pools that seem so natural they appear to have always been there. He explains that everything is inter-connected. The hot spring rises in the first pool, so that is the hottest. It overflows and empties into a second pool, which is less hot but still *hot*. And that empties into the third and last pool, which has a very enjoyable *warm* temperature. He says we are free to do whatever we like, except bathe naked. The accepted protocol is to strip to your underwear, or put on swimwear. Then, the idea is to wash your feet in the fast-flowing, cold waters of the river, enter the third pool for comfort, and graduate to the other two as and when ready.

It all seems so civilized. Although shy to undress at first, the mounting anticipation is infectious. Before any of us have gotten our trousers off, Gini is standing there in bra and bloomers saying she just doesn't care anymore. She has no more shame left in her. And she simply has to get in.

Driven forward by Gini's gay abandon, we all follow suit. She washes her feet in the relatively icy water. She even sits down in it for a moment exclaiming: *O Dear God! Sweet Mother of Jesus, that's FRESH!*

With whoops and howls of laughter, we do the same and soon we're all in the first pool, immersed to the neck. There are groans of pleasure and much needed release. For the longest time, nobody says a single word.

The kid says he feels too chilly to join us. So he appears to fade into the background and drift away, leaving us to it.

After some time relaxing, and soaking, and smiling across at each other, we notice the boy is sitting at the side of the hottest pool chatting to someone we hadn't even observed before. It is a man. He's submerged right up to his lips and his face is so dark and rugged-looking, he just seems to blend into this enchanted place.

The boy calls down to us: *This is Salvo. He's a barman in the town. He comes here almost every day at this time before he starts work.*

A giant hand appears from the water, and waves a rather lazy hello to us. He has a dark handkerchief spread over what appears to be a shaved head. Both Pedro and I sit up to wave back. Even from this distance, his arm looks massive. Raising an eyebrow and darting a knowing smile across at Pedro I slink back down into the water like a happy baby hippo.

After a respectful time has elapsed, Pedro tells Gini he's moving on to the next level and slides himself over the rocks to the middle pool.

We chat amongst ourselves – our eyes closed in sheer ecstasy – about everything and nothing, giving Pedro some space to explore further.

The boy goes over to the trees where he has carefully hung his 'secret' bag on a branch. He obviously has something in there he needs to attend to.

Pedro and Salvo instantly strike up a conversation from one pool to the other.

*Salvo. That's Italian, isn't it?*

39

Salvo is half Sicilian. The other half is peasant, Spanish gypsy stock. His father's story is fascinating and Pedro hangs on every word:

*Boiko,* Salvo's Dad, somehow ends up in the south of Italy where he gets a seasonal job on Salvo's mother's family farm. Her name is *Silvia.* At first she detests and looks down on Boiko and the other gypsies who work for her father, thinking them an uncultured and brutish lot. But then, as these love-hate things so often go, Silvia and Boiko have the most incredible sex one day behind a tree. And the rest, as they say, is history.

A familiar tale, as old as the hills: Silvia's father forbids the union with Boiko. She gets pregnant. They run away together back to Spain, where they settle below the slopes of Alhama. And Salvo is born.

His name is short for the Italian *'Salvatore', Saviour.* Silvia always felt that running away with Boiko and giving birth to her baby in Spain had been *her* salvation. It saved her from a life of comparative drudgery in Sicily. Headscarves and black lace. The abbreviation 'Salvo' has a special connotation of feeling 'safe'. And that's how people always feel around Salvo.

He is strong and very handsome. He looks to be in his late forties/early fifties. He has 'Special Operations' Military training.

But Salvo also has a razor sharp intellect and a very talented creative streak to match. He speaks a fist full of languages including his native Spanish, Italian, English, and the gypsy hybrid *Romani*. Although he's never once exhibited his work, he is also an excellent painter of landscapes with vast, expansive skies.

He could've been married a hundred times. All the locals continue to call him by his schoolboy nickname *El Muchachón, Big Boy* (or *The Big Fella*). Salvo's had the name ever since they glimpsed the size of his manhood in the shower. He says he doesn't like the name much, though it did make him extremely popular with the girls for decades. He casually drops into conversation that to be hung like a horse isn't all it's cracked up to be, and that he's not that interested in women any more anyway. He says he prefers to work at the bar nights, keep himself to himself, and live alone with his art and his books... until the 'right person' comes along.

Needless to say, Pedro is well and truly in hot water now. To smooth over the awkward silence that's about to befall him, he makes Salvo shriek with laughter by confiding in him that his mother was the only person ever to see his 'manhood' as a boy, and that her nickname for him was *'Little Squirrel'*. As Salvo's laughter begins to subside, he adds: *It's not all true, you know – what you hear about squirrels – some of us are Big Boys too.*

Soon, they're sharing the same pool and talking quite openly about their hopes, their dreams, and aspirations.

Salvo is indeed a fine, big man. Of epic proportions. Ruggedly handsome and strong. His shaved head is deeply tanned from an outdoors life. His broad face looks like he's been sculpted from stone. He is visibly beaming as they get to know each other better. Salvo is quite smitten with Pedro too.

They say opposites attract. And, to Salvo, Pedro comes from Madrid and must therefore be the very epitome of learning and sophistication. When he discovers Pedro's passion for writing, he throws a huge arm around his neck and shoulders. He is completely natural and uninhibited with him.

Salvo pulls Pedro into his chest, squeezes him tight, and gives the top of his head a big, loud whopper of a kiss. It's impossible to distinguish whether this is an overt *move*, or a rugby thing. Pedro has spent too much time in gay bars, dreaming of being somewhere else, to interpret what is actually going on. Moving away to an appropriate distance, Salvo settles himself again low in the water. He stretches a long leg across to Pedro's space, where he rests a heavy foot on top of a bewildered Pedro's thigh.

*I think we are going to become the best of friends,* Salvo announces with a flash of his blue eyes and that killer smile.

*I certainly hope so,* sings Pedro under his breath.

Meanwhile the rest of us have drifted up to the second pool, and Gini is already moving up towards the hottest one, to the boys.

Pedro introduces Gini to Salvo as '*Virginia*', his mother. And Salvo immediately responds in perfect English what a great pleasure it is to meet the woman who produced such a wonderful son. Shaking Gini's hand almost clear off the end of her arm, but looking at Pedro now, he grins almost triumphantly: *You see, Little Squirrel. We've only just met and already I've been formally introduced to your mother. I can tell that she's going to be wild about me. Be careful what you wish for, Pedro. I told you. Everyone's after me. I'm a 'keeper'... Your move.*

Pedro breathes a huge sigh of relief. 'Well at least that's abundantly clear now', he hears my voice say inside his head.

Before we know it, we're all in the hot pool chatting and laughing about everything under the sun, which is just about to set over the hill on the far side of the river. Pedro and Salvo are sitting very close indeed, holding hands under the water.

The boy, who has finally introduced himself as *Juan-Martín*, reveals the secret treat his grandfather told him to offer the new guests in town. He walks around the three pools and lights what seems like thousands of little *tea-light* candles he's been randomly placing around the edges, and on the forest floor. Then, bidding us a good night, he takes a bow and goes home to his mother in time for their favourite TV programme.

We are so filled with awe and gratitude that we don't know what to say, and he's gone before we even think of thanking him.

*Oh don't worry about him, Salvo says. He's such a good boy and doesn't perform this kindness in search of praise or thanks. Look how magical it all seems tonight. The fairy lights, the indigo and scarlet sky...all of US. You'll see Juan-Martín again later anyway. His parents own the best little hotel in all of Alhama. It's the place you'll be staying in tonight. He's the bell boy.*

We stay submerged in the soothing waters that never cool, chatting effortlessly, and watching the early night sky for signs of the first stars as they pop their heads out. We watch and observe them as they appear one by one. And then a billion, all of a sudden! Only when our shoulders and faces start to feel cold do we realize that night is falling fast. So we agree to get ready and head back to the car.

When Salvo stands up to get out of the water, it is evident for all to see that he has retained the body of a military beefcake. He is wearing skin-tight, wet, black speedos that leave nothing to the imagination. The material is old and worn to near-transparency in places.

Then, we all notice Salvo unselfconsciously looking Pedro up and down too, without giving it a second thought. Salvo looks him straight in the eye and makes an adorably cute, yet totally macho, face at him. His lips are pursed and dragged upwards towards the tip of his nose. And his eyes are screwed tightly shut with a popeye-esque grimace of sensual expectation. It embodies all his combined approval and desire.

On our way up the darkened path, we pass the factory workers who've just knocked off and are looking forward to a nice bath in the pools. One of them runs by calling behind her: *Hey look. That kid has put the lights around the place again. Oh, he's so cute.*

Another voice from the shadows in the crowd acknowledges Salvo as we pass:

*Hola Salvo, El Muchachón.*

*Hola, Diego.*

We drop Salvo to work in plenty of time. Or rather *he* guides *us* to our hotel, which is just across the square from the bar.

We arrange to go over there later for a few drinks after showers and a late dinner somewhere. Pedro walks with Salvo to the door of the bar, but doesn't go in.

*I can't believe we just met,* Pedro says.

*I know,* Salvo replies. *Some things are just meant to be... Wait in one place long enough and trouble will eventually find you and come knocking at your door.*

*So this means trouble, does it?*

*Could be... Or it could be the 'Real McCoy'.*

*But we haven't even, you know... kissed or anything.*

*No. Not yet... Later,* Salvo says with a cheeky grin. *You boys in Madrid get it all backwards. Talk first, then kiss... By the way, have you noticed the name of the bar I work in?*

Looking up, he can't believe his eyes: It is called *Pedro's.*

*Pedro died over fifty years ago, but they still keep the same name... Magical, isn't it? The whole thing... I guess we were ALL just waiting for you to come along one day... It's for sale, you know...*

*Later then. I'll see you later,* Pedro says choking back the tears.

He walks over to the hotel. At the door he looks back across the plaza.

Salvo is still standing there, watching him.

40

By the time Pedro arrives at check-in, we've already repaired to our rooms.

Juan-Martín's father, *José*, is on duty at the desk. He tells Pedro he's in room 9, on the same floor as the others. He calls his son out from the family's private sitting room to take the room key and show Pedro upstairs.

It is only once Pedro is in the room alone, and closes the door behind him, that he realizes he's been allocated a double room to himself. He grins and wonders which one if not all of us had the bright idea of being so kind and understanding. He takes it for the sign of quiet approval and encouragement that is our joint intent.

A quick shave, shower and change of clothes. Then Pedro phones Maria to find out the plan for dinner.

*You dirty DAWG!* Maria taunts, lovingly. *No, really. I'm totally over the moon for you two. I just can't believe you met like that...*She sings a childish little ditty to the words '*Salvo and Pedro, sitting in a tree. K-I-S-S-I-N-G*'.

Pedro doesn't rise to the playful bate. Eventually Maria gives up joking around. He knows that in her heart Maria *is* really thrilled for him. He can sense we all are, especially his mother. However, Pedro is trying not to think about it too much, for fear of putting a jinx on it. At the very least,

Pedro wants to enjoy having a good time with Salvo. Beyond that, whatever happens happens. For now, he's resolved to stay cool, calm and collected. He's promised himself not to get too carried away with it all in advance. In particular, Pedro promises himself not to get into petty gossiping or analyzing the whole thing to death with his girlfriend Maria...

*Oh my God!* Pedro blurts out, uncontrollably. *I just can't believe I met him like that! I have to talk to someone about all this. What room are you in? I'm coming down right now.*

In a nano-second, Pedro is sitting on Maria's bed, holding his head for joy and fearing it will explode. Gini is at the mirror in the ensuite, looking back at the scene.

*Now you know how MY head feels most days. I'm all over the shop usually...* Gini says. *There there, now. Poor Baby. Mama's here for you too,* she adds, meaning every heart-felt syllable. *A major crush like that can really hurt. I know... Just give yourselves lots of space, Darling.*

*She's right, you know. Mothers usually are,* nods Maria, reassuringly cradling Pedro's head and stroking his fine, silky hair. *Your Mam is an incredible being, in her way. It was all her idea to get you the double room. She simply spoke up at reception. Took over the whole thing she did, saying: This is what's best for Pedro right now. Pedro gets a double to himself tonight. He'll need his privacy. Maria and I will have some girly time in one twin, and Karl and Jalu can discuss whatever floats their boat in the other.*

*Thanks Mama,* Pedro calls in to Gini. *Thank you for everything, I love you so much.*

*You're most welcome Dear,* Gini replies, tying the exchange up in a nice neat bow.

Pedro looks at Maria and whispers: *Thank you, Gorgeous. I don't know what I'd do if I didn't have you to run to. I love you so much too, you know... You're like the older sister I never had.*

*What do you mean, 'OLDER'?* Maria hisses. *I'm at least ten years younger than you, you be-atch.*

*Touché.* Pedro admits defeat. *By the way, you were incredible today, strutting over to that bar full of ogling men. In-cre-di-ble!*

*Thank you, Sweetheart... Yes I WAS, wasn't I? ... I'm back!!* Maria cackles insufferably... Lifting Pedro's head off her lap to stand up, Maria stares through him, deep down into his soul: *I hope all goes well with this one. You deserve it, Baby. Jalu's right. Live in the moment, and make every second count... Life is just too short.*

*I hear you Sister,* comes the refrain from the ensuite.

*Mother! Were you listening to mine and Maria's private conversation?* Pedro whines, pretending to be annoyed.

*I may be near death, Son. But I'm not deaf!* Gini giggles at her own reflection in the mirror.

The *Three Amigos* knock at our door as they pass by, and soon Karl and I join them in the lobby.

Our shadow for the day, Juan-Martín, is charged once again with guiding us down the street to the restaurant they've selected for us. It's not far, and is run by the boy's Aunty Rosario. The food is very fine indeed, and really inexpensive. We have a mixture of cold meats with fried aubergine and courgette to start. Then there's a delicious baked rice dish with chicken and garden veggies. Next, a kind of lasagne with tons of shredded garlic and ginger cooked into the mince-meat beforehand. Finally there is a break of 30 minutes. We're told by the locals that the men use this much-needed gap to go to the bathroom, have a walk, a smoke or a stiff drink. The women usually jump at the chance to be free of the men, and do exactly the same things without them.

Reconvened, we are treated to strong coffee or sweet tea and dessert. I say 'dessert', which brings to mind perhaps a slice of cake, maybe with a scoop of ice cream if you're lucky. But *Aunty Rosario*'s dessert course is legendary in these parts and consists of two trolleys that are wheeled into the dining room with great pomp and circumstance. The tradition is to respond with rapturous applause and whistling while the precious cargo is loaded onto the great serving table, from which everyone helps themselves.

One trolley has a vast array of cheeses and fruits to cater for every palate. There's also a platter of assorted crackers and breads with nuts of every variety sprinkled around and in between them. The second trolley is laden to the point of collapse with large gateaux, smaller confectioneries, and biscuits. A veritable cacophony of ice cream! Every flavor known to man, all scooped randomly into one enormous glass serving bowl. From the outside, it looks like a rainbow has exploded in there.

Of course there's extra-thick whipped cream and – wait for it, I kid you not – two great presentation molds she inherited from her Granny: One is filled with jelly, the other with yoghurt... *Jelly Yoghurt*. Gini is pointing at them and laughing at me across the table, teasingly. She's having a wonderful evening. The second in a row. But this one is extra special to her. For Gini, today started out all about her, and her memories of Benji in the thermal pools of

Alhama. Now it's become a celebration of life, and the possibility of new love waiting around every corner. In Gini's mind, the day is now all about Pedro. She goes out of her way to cuddle and kiss him at every opportunity. He is mortified, but secretly loves it.

Maria is loving the food and the festive nature of what is after all just another ordinary night in Rosario's restaurant. Karl is agog at the spectacle and the excess of it all. To him, it feels more like a whole village has brought together all their communal resources to produce a wedding banquet.

Pedro's actually having a blast. He really appreciates what Gini is doing. And he's very grateful for all the freedom and the support. He is still a bit nervous, though. He can't remember having a real shot with a guy like Salvo before. He's excited and nervous and just doesn't want to mess it up. He is shocked and surprised too at his own reaction. He hasn't eaten much; he doesn't want to be too full or bloated when he gets to see Salvo later.

*Pedro,* I say, taking him by the arm as we return to our seats. *Give yourself a break, man. Relax and enjoy. Don't think so much. Don't worry anymore. Just follow, and see where it leads... Enjoy.*


Over an hour later, we finally get to *Pedro's.*

The place was packed earlier, but is starting to empty out a bit now. Salvo is at the far end, near the big window with the view of the valley below, tending bar.

At first, he doesn't notice we have arrived. So we take a table in the middle of the rather large room. There's a very big wood-burning stove right beside us. The flue goes straight up and out through the roof. It's not lit. But it serves as the main focus of the bar in winter. The tables are arranged around it, and people either go to the bar themselves for drinks or get served at their table by one of the barmen.

The floor is old and kind of dusty. There is a large manufacturing plant nearby and the workers from there are the bar's main customers. Entry to the Ladies and Gents toilets is gained via swinging saloon doors, like you'd see in a cowboy movie. Outside the Ladies there's a sign with the silhouette of a lady and the word *Nuestras,* meaning *Ours.* So there was obviously a powerful lady with a good sense of humour behind this bar at one time. On the Gents, there is a silhouette of a bull's head and the words *Los Otros,* meaning *Others.*

Pedro strolls casually over to Salvo's end of the bar to catch his eye and place our order, for which Gini insists on paying.

Salvo lights up and reaches across the counter with both his hands to hold and shake Pedro's. It's like the reunion of two lovers separated by war. Something has happened in the intervening few hours. 'Smitten' is no longer the word. It is no longer a massive crush. They are *besotted.* Hungry for each other.

They chat briefly. And once the order is ready Salvo brings it over to the table on a large tray. The span of one enormous, thick hand, placed dead centre underneath the tray, is more than enough to stabilize an entire planet. The group is thrilled to see his smiling face again, and all his cocky antics make us laugh. For such a quiet, soulful man he's quite a performer. Of course, Gini enjoys making a big drama out of paying for the round. She even flirts with Salvo, and slips a 5 Euro note into the front pocket of his denims. Maria joins the friendly assault by bringing up the rear as Salvo bends over the table to place the drinks. She whistles like a docker and smacks his bubble butt with the full of her palm. We fall into hysterics with the unexpected carry-on. Maria whimpers saying his ass is so rock-hard it nearly broke her hand in two. Salvo, loving all the sudden attention from the ladies, says Maria wouldn't be the first woman he made scream like that. More howls of laughter.

Before going back behind the bar, Salvo squeezes Pedro's shoulder and says: *If it's not too rude to drag you away, why don't you come over and have your drink with me? Sit at the end of the bar and we can chat some more.*

It's already quite late and there are fewer and fewer customers in the bar now. Realizing it's quiet enough for an intimate chat over there, Pedro moves to a high stool down by the big window. The second barman is very understanding. He even appears to know what's going on. He basically does all the serving and cleaning, while Salvo and Pedro get to know each other better. At first, the whole bar notices what's going on. 'Salvo has a new *friend*' seems to be their way of explaining the obvious to themselves.

Within a very short time indeed, Salvo is caressing the back of Pedro's hand and they're clearly talking like lovers do. It has gone way beyond a first date. Something far more profound is taking place. No one can really take their eyes off it. The simple honesty and sheer beauty of what is unfolding is mesmerizing. This little country town, full of tough guys and straight-talking women, is so spell-bound by it all, they're powerless to stand in its path. Just then, Salvo raises his hand and softly lays it on Pedro's cheek. Ourselves included, every customer in the place averts their eyes and launches into fascinating conversations about the latest sports results and the perfect weather for drying clothes.

Pedro says to Salvo: *What are you doing? Aren't you worried about your customers seeing us like this? The whole town will march to your door bearing torches and burning crosses on your lawn.*

Salvo looks him deep in the eyes, with a soft openness that's so arresting in all its simplicity:

*I'm 'The Big Fella', remember? I'm pretty sure nobody will ever challenge me on this, or anything much. Anyway, I've never hidden the fact I prefer men. In school, they all knew it but chose to ignore it. You see all these men? Half of them have touched my cock at one time or another. Half their wives screamed – when they were with me – how they'd never had such good sex. And when they finally settled with their men, they told them about how good it was with me. All those women know I am gay. My only problem in this town is my mythological reputation as a big boy, a hard man, a good lay, a real nice guy. It prevents everyone from actually getting to know the real me, from believing I'm gay. I told them all. They know. And they simply don't believe it... Perhaps they're so concerned I might take their wives away that it hasn't even occurred to them that it's THEM I like...*

*Leave the torch-wielding villagers to me,* Salvo says. *I would never rub this in their faces too much anyway. I'm too private for all that. But tonight belongs to us. It's the night Salvo and Pedro met. I wouldn't let anything mess that up! Life is too fucking short to let you slip through my fingers. And I just know you feel the same way.*

Pedro's response is so perfect, it takes Salvo's breath away. He's been doing most of the chasing so far. Now it's Pedro's turn to show his cards...

*You're right,* Pedro asserts himself finally. *Life IS too short. And this could be something real, you know? Between us... To be perfectly honest with you, I'm crazy about you already: You're my type, all the way down to your dusty boots. I can't wait to be alone with you. And I know the sex will be fantastic. But much more than that... I just KNOW something real is going on here, you know? Something without precedent, for BOTH of us. We're both in uncharted territory here, and all we have for navigation is each other and the stars. I know I'VE certainly never been blind-sided like this before, have you? And I've been around the block a few thousand times. In your way, you probably have too, right? I'm in my early forties now and you're in your whatever YOU are... But sex is sex, man. No matter how much or how little of it you have, it's still just sex. But this... THIS is.. I don't know what the fuck 'this' is.. It's something totally different. You know, I actually laughed at friends in the past when they said this happened to them. They couldn't sleep. They couldn't eat. I thought they were exaggerating and dismissed it. But all the while I was secretly waiting for it to happen to me too. I've been thinking and dreaming about it. Writing and writing about it. But, wouldn't ya just know it, the second I take my eye off the ball – the first time in maybe 20 years I stopped looking – and here you are, with your hands and your speedos and your smiles and your everything.*

Salvo agrees. He says he feels the same.

*When you're right, you're right,* he says smacking the counter top. *Sex is great – and our sex will be amazing – but this is THIS. I've never felt it like this before, and that's the God's honest truth of it. Oh sure, there were huge man-crushes in the past. In the army. Around the town. But those guys weren't really gay. And there wasn't this natural, this emotional thing allowing itself to properly come to the surface. I like it. A real life is what I really want with a man. It's what I've been waiting for all these years... I'm 50 by the way... (I know my skin looks like an old leather sofa. But you have to remember I've had a hard life, man. A lot of work. A lot of sun)... It's the emotion I've been missing all this time. And now YOU'RE here...*

The word they're both appropriately trying so desperately not to say is 'relationship'. Oh and 'Love', that's another one.

Speaking as a practicing homo-sexual myself (well, more theory than practice really), I have to hold my hands up and admit that I find the whole gay thing a total mind-fuck...

We have constructed this crazy *scene* for ourselves, this gay ghetto, based on sex. When what we really want is Love. The bars, the clubs, the saunas, the toilets, backrooms and steamrooms... They're all fantastic. Don't get me wrong. I'm not saying they're a *total* waste of time. Great sex is amazing, and extremely good for you. But all the rest of it?

So, while we wait for Love to walk through that door, we form other bonds. There's friendship, support, camaraderie. Safety in numbers. On some level, there is even spiritual fellowship, political activism: anything that takes the focus off *Self* and transfers it to *Others* is a good thing, right?

But make no mistake, gay people are just like straight people. We're all just hoping for that special connection to manifest. We are vulnerable and bolshy. But we all just want to share love...

My whole life, after I left Asia, has been a steep learning curve. I've travelled extensively and deliberately put myself in situations where there was something to learn from the world about the very essence of what it is to be human. The gay world has taught me so much too. I've worked all over the place: in gay saunas, as a barman, as a toilet attendant. I have worked as a group counselor for gay men, and taught meditation in LGBT drop-in centres. I've even swept the streets at night to learn more about the homeless ones, the addicts, the runaways, and the sex workers... And I can summarize all I've learned in one sentence: Most of the people I ever met are just looking for love. Sometimes I just wish they'd cut through all the bullshit and settle for each other.


After Salvo closes the bar, he and Pedro go for a stroll around the old town before going back to the hotel room. We've already said our goodbyes, without making it too obvious that we're cheering them on from a distance.

Perhaps it's the honesty of Salvo and Pedro's heart-to-heart that inspires us; As the boys pass along ancient streets and alleyways way after midnight, sharing and dreaming together, two other conversations are already in full swing.

## 41

Gini and Maria are sitting up chatting about recent developments. They have the pillows of their two single beds piled up against the wall behind them. The TV is on low in the background. It's some 'reality' programme.

Maria asks Gini what it feels like to have her disease. She says it's like living in a dream. The conversations she's had with me have been very helpful. And she's determined to live in the present moment as much as possible; the mindfulness meditation and sending love exercises are a revelation.

But, even so, Gini says the dream-like quality of *her* reality is disturbing and is taking a lot of getting used to.

She feels kind of disjointed much of the time, like nothing is real. For Gini, the fluid boundaries between past and present are the main issue. She finds it far too tempting to just settle in her memories and relive the past. Staying in the present is far more difficult than you'd think, she says, as it's near impossible to control or predict what will arise next. And without control, there's fear.

Maria agrees and says she couldn't have put it better herself.

*What do you mean?* Gini asks.

*It's just that remaining present is really hard for everyone,* Maria explains. *That's why so few people find it a workable option. We're all so easily distracted from the here and now. It's often easier to just give in and veer towards our memories of the past or our plans for the future.*

*Are you saying everyone feels like I do? I certainly don't remember feeling the draw to the past so strongly before I got sick.*

*Maybe everyone experiences that pull but it's so normal for them that they don't think of it as a problem. They aren't aware of any alternative way of being.*

*But, the future... We all have to make plans, don't we?* Gini posits. *It's only natural to make plans, isn't it?*

*Of course we do. Everyone wants to have an active role in what is going to happen next in their lives. We all make plans. We have to. But I suppose what the Buddha's teachings are saying is that we shouldn't become so trapped. Always plotting and scheming, to the extent that we've no time left to be in the present. It's in the here and now that all the good stuff happens anyway... We only have this moment, when you think about it. The last one is gone and the next one hasn't arisen yet. There's only now... A constant stream of present moments. Don't get me wrong. I'm no expert on all this. I'm no spiritual teacher or anything. I'm just starting to see things that way myself.*

*Well Dear,* Gini says, *I want to use this present moment to chat to you about MY plans for the future, if you don't mind.*

*No, not at all. Please go ahead, Gini.*

*Ok. I will then. Thank you for listening, Maria... You asked me how it feels to be me right now. So here it is: I often, quite naturally, feel overwhelmed. Not just by the illness or how my brain is mis-firing or stroking or whatever. I feel overwhelmed by almost everything. It's all just too much for me to handle: sights, sounds, sensations – the whole lot.*

*Have you ever heard that song by Harry Nilsson from the late 60s?* Gini asks. *It goes something like this:*
"Everybody's talking at me.
I don't hear a word they're saying,
Only the echoes of my mind."

*... Well that's how I feel. It's very hard to take anything in. It all just seems like a dream that floats by me.*

*I see,* Maria says with genuine compassion arising. She wishes she could just take Gini's suffering away completely.

*I wish I could help,* Maria adds. *If you can think of any way I could be of benefit, please let me know.*

*Well, as it happens, there is,* Gini comes to the point. *I want to tell you what I hope will happen in the future. And I want to know if you'll help me bring that about. We'd be like undercover agents together.*

*OK... Go on,* Maria says tentatively. *I can't promise anything till I hear what you want, though.* Maria's concerned suddenly that Gini is going to ask for help to commit suicide. She is embarrassed by such a weird thought occurring. But she now feels she's in a corner, and a little bit panicked.

Bizarrely, Gini somehow picks up on the thought and immediately reassures her: *O No, Sweetheart. Not that. I'm not going to ask you to get me a pamphlet on Euthanasia or anything. I'm not asking you to smother me in my sleep tonight. O you poor thing. No. Not that... I want to tell you mainly how I want everything to pan out – not just about my death, if it happens suddenly one day very soon, but about what I want for Pedro and his life too.*

*OK... Go on,* Maria feels somewhat relieved but still unsure where all this is going.


Pedro has brought Salvo back to his hotel room. They are both in the shower kissing. They're very excited but really don't want to rush anything for fear of spoiling it.

Salvo is a big man but underneath it all he's really just a *teddy bear.* As they wash each other, Pedro takes the lead and brings up the subject they're both wondering about. Most heterosexual people would have no idea whatsoever about what that subject is. It never arises for straight people.

Pedro says he is '*versatile*', which is internet gay-speak for someone who likes to have sex both ways; as far as penetration is concerned, he is both active and passive. Salvo says that's perfect for him. That he is actually the same. He says most people assume he is just a 'big old top'. And that he finds what he calls 'greedy bottoms' so boring anyway. They just lie there making fake porno sounds, calling the shots. They confide in each other how they both find kissing the most satisfying part of sex.

*Sounds like we're perfectly suited then,* Pedro says as they dry themselves off.

*Nobody's perfect,* Salvo says. (Pedro laughs in agreement). *No, seriously though... It's not fair to expect perfection from sex, or a man, or anything for that matter. That's just setting ourselves up for a fall. Agreed?*

*Agreed,* Pedro shakes Salvo's hand and pulls him close. He really gets what Salvo is saying and greatly appreciates his insight and courageous honesty. They allow themselves to fall on the bed and begin to enjoy each other's bodies, as God intended.

It dawns on them simultaneously that they're both having sex like it's their first time, ever. They're somewhat shy and tentative. It's as if nothing they did in the past had actually happened. The big difference about this time is they're not having sex at all.

Pedro and Salvo are making love.


Karl and I are sitting at the table in our room talking and drinking some tea we've made. We have the latest news updates on the television in the corner. But our conversation has moved from the civil unrest in Spain, and elsewhere in Europe, to the many full-on revolutions that are happening in the Arab states. We are mostly in agreement, but there's an unusual tension too. The kind of energy that exists when two people are discussing something they're very passionate about. Our exchange flows freely, and without hindrance. We are carefully navigating a common stream of consciousness. It feels more like surfing one of those rare tidal waves that surge up-river.

He's saying that the Arab people deserve so much better from their lot in life, and from their governments in particular. His impression is that the average person in one of those countries is no different to someone from anywhere else. They are incredibly loving and loyal people who simply want happiness for themselves and their families.

He suggests, Islam itself is terribly – almost willfully – misunderstood by people of other faiths. From his study of it, he's learned that the Muslim religion is very much about inspiring people to think spiritually rather than materialistically. Islam, Karl concludes his train of thought, is about bringing the Love of God to everyday life, into society. It's not about making extremely conservative laws or waging Holy Wars against non-believers. That, he surmises, is one strand of Islam that only seems to have taken hold of the Arab world in recent decades, and which emanates mainly from the very rich and powerful leaders in Saudi Arabia.

While Karl is speaking, I can tell he's about to change tack completely and launch into another spiritual matter he has secretly been longing to bring up with me.

After a short silence between us, Karl asks if it's true what Maria and Gini have told him. That I have the power of *Clear Seeing*. What he really wants to ask is where does that kind of *Insight* come from, and what have I come to understand about *him*. He seems paranoid. I remain evasive.

I tell him if someone had such a power they'd probably deny it anyway. They would certainly never discuss it. I tell him that that's also my response to his question.

He pushes me further on the matter and asks:

*But what is it? Where does it come from, exactly? Is it like clairvoyance, something one is born with?*

*No Karl*, I insist. *I really don't want to go there with you, OK? Anyway, let's call it a day and get some sleep.*

*I hope I haven't offended you,* he says, doggedly keeping the subject alive. *I'm just trying to understand you more, I suppose. At any rate, you brought it up yourself. The other day when you implied you were getting a clearer picture about my identity and the mission I've unfortunately dragged you all into. In fact, you were quite explicit about your powers of insight with me on that occasion. You said, when you had a clearer picture about me – or words to that effect – that you'd be confronting me about your findings. And that I'd have to tell everyone the truth about what's really going on here... That's what you said, Jalu. Your words, not mine.*

I feel I'm being badgered. And that doesn't sit well with anyone, insight or no insight.

*OK Karl,* I say. *Here goes. I don't know, maybe this IS the right time to say all this anyway. But I'll be very brief about it. And remember, you asked and asked. You just won't let it go. So here it is...*

*By the way,* I say by way of clarification, *the Insight or Clear Seeing you're referring to is precisely that. It's when a person has developed their mind through spiritual practice to see things as they really are. These abilities are not parlour games or gimmicks. They're real. And they arise as a direct result of the practice...*

*Attaining special gifts is not the goal of the practice, however. The only goal of genuine spiritual practice is to end all the suffering that beings endure. No, they're not the goal of the practice but a BY-PRODUCT of it. As a person develops and becomes more and more Awake, sometimes they find they have certain special abilities that they never intended to have. But they're now there nonetheless. Clear Seeing is like that. It's an involuntary side-effect that some people get from lots of*

*meditation. I can't put it any simpler than that, I'm afraid...
The insight that comes from Clear Seeing is precisely what it
says: You see things clearly, very clearly indeed. Your
perception of phenomena around you becomes very, very clear.
You see through people too. You see the Truth of things. You
see things as they really are.*

*The Truth can dawn on you in a flash, or it can take some
time to emerge, that's all. But when it does – and this is what I
was referring to – there's no mistake. What you see IS the
Truth. Not the superficial gloss, or even the complex details
that float around it, surrounding what appears to be the truth.
But the Truth itself, with a capital 'T'. You see right to the very
essence of what is going on before your eyes.*

*WOW! Karl says. That's how you really perceive the world
and its inhabitants? That's miraculous!*

*You haven't been listening at all, Karl, I reply. Insight is the
result of hard work. You're not born with it and it's not a
miracle. It is training... And NO! For the last time Karl, for the
love of God, I'm not saying I have this ability. I don't have it. I
never did enough meditation anyway. I HAVE no Insight, got
it? ... Into you, or anything else. So let's just drop it now, OK? I*
decide not to say more.

Then after a respectful period of reflection, and thinking
that I'm simply being humble and appropriately evasive,
Karl has another stab at it. He decides to appeal to my
Eastern mindset, the Asian DNA which I carry in the body I
currently inhabit. Karl attempts to build a bridge between
us (while really trying to get what he wanted all along). He
wants to know what, if anything, I've worked out about
him.

Presenting me with the only road he can find that may lead out of this impasse, Karl finally asks the magic question:

*What if someone – not you, not you at all – actually DID possess such a gift... And let's say for argument's sake that they encountered me and everything I have told you to date... What would they see clearly about ME?... Jalu, please. Throw me a bone here. I'm really, really interested to know because I need advice about how and when to proceed.*

*Alright, I pronounce. Precisely how and when you should proceed is entirely up to you. It always has been. That's MY advice... But someone who could actually penetrate all the layers of mystery and subterfuge, all the superficial crap, and mirror back to you the Truth about who you are and what you are doing... That's a BIG question, Karl... Such a being would probably tell you something like this:*

*You are a good man, a very good person indeed. And a lot of good will come from the dangerous mission you've embarked upon.*

*The documents in your possession were an Insurance Policy. That much of your story is true.*

*But practically everything else you have told us is lies! A smokescreen. Just an elaborate cover story you've been trained to regurgitate if captured or if you feel under pressure to explain yourself. I'm sure no one blames you for telling us lies. In any case, who are we? Just some random collection of misfits you ended up with on the run, right?*

*Such a being would tell you to give up the charade. Nobody's going to be that impressed by the lie, or that horrified by the truth anyway.*

*He or she would remind you that you're not the son of Pope John Paul II. The documents you have in your care are not Church documents, copies or otherwise. What you have was not given to you by your father. Your biological father was already dead before you were born. Your mother gave you the files because she knew they might keep you alive someday. And because she truly believed that only you could find a way to turn all the horror into something good. So that's what you are doing now.*

*You were not born in Poland. You never even set foot in Germany, or England, or Switzerland. Your mother WAS German, though. Not Polish. Now THERE was a woman to be reckoned with. She must have seen all this coming, didn't she? All those years ago in Argentina, as she cradled you in her arms. She must've known that, one way or another, the truth would finally come out about everything one day. Her only concern was that you'd get away with what you're about to do in Rome. That you would bring the truth to light, and live to tell the tale.*

*Oh yes, you ARE a priest. That part was true... Liberation Theology, breaking Church rules about married priests and women priests, your children, and your remote country parish tucked away high up in the Andes. THAT is all true. However, it's actually neither here nor there really, is it? You didn't have to conceal it so you just told us the truth there. Now that's a novel idea. Telling the truth.*

*But what you don't realize is, you didn't have to lie about all the rest either. You could've told us the truth about EVERYTHING, Karl. Neither Gini nor any of these good people would have abandoned you if you'd told us the whole truth yourself. If only we didn't have to play this stupid game of dragging it out of you!*

*Tell the truth, Karl...*

*If YOU don't – I mean it – I will.*

*If you really need proof that I know what I'm talking about, let's continue with this little hypothetical game you've started:*

*If there WERE a being who could look at you and see the Truth, they'd see the huge flags with Swastikas blowing in the wind, Karl. They'd see Nazi propaganda films being projected in every cinema and in every school across Germany. Do you want me to go on, Karl?*

*Such a being would see exactly why the Vatican and the Sovereign governments of some of the main democracies on the planet are up to their eyes in all of this, and shitting themselves that you're going to fuck it up for them, Karl. Will I go on?*

*Such a being would see the Death Camps being opened by Allied soldiers, piles of emaciated bodies, Nazi escape routes...*

*Ultimately, they'd see a syringe full of semen.*

*Do you really want me to go on, Karl?*

## 42

Gini is growing very tired but she and Maria are still propped up on their beds chatting.

Maria is extremely perceptive at times. Although Gini is wandering around what she really wants, Maria brings the subject back to her plans and aspirations for the future.

*What was it exactly that you wanted to ask me to do for you, Gini... You know, about what you'd like to happen next?*

*Oh Yes, Dear. Thank you for keeping me on track,* Gini says with a sweet smile. *I wanted to tell you that I really do now believe I might die soon. Or at least I must proceed as if it were a very strong possibility indeed. I can feel it my bones.*

Maria has been making a study of Shantideva's *The Way of the Bodhisattva.* Straight away, she has an intense glimpse of one of the phrases from it. She clearly sees the image of a lifetime flashing by as quickly as a bolt of lightning in the night sky. Maria now *understands* what she's been contemplating for months. It has become *real.* Gini's terminal illness and being faced with the prospect of sudden death, perhaps sometime soon, has convinced Maria of the importance for a proper practitioner to live in the moment;

*Death is real. It comes without warning. This body will be a corpse.*

With all this in mind, not skipping a beat, Maria encourages Gini to say what is really on her mind.

Gini starts slowly and somewhat falteringly. She says she doesn't want to die alone. Neither does she want to die on the road with all of us. She's thought long and hard about it, but knows now she doesn't necessarily want to die in her own home either. If Gini had a choice, she says she just wants to be somewhere (hopefully an inspiring place) where she can simply relax and release, as the teachings say. She'd love to be so natural and open she'd simply *let go*. When her time comes, Gini says she would like to have the dignity and the privacy to pass away in the spirit of *spaciousness* that we have been discussing so much in recent days.

She says dying on the road wouldn't be so bad. But she couldn't bear all the fuss of being surrounded by people, even a small group of friends. So, if she had to choose just one person to witness and support her passing, she tells Maria she doesn't want it to be Pedro.

*My thinking, Gini says, is I am completely determined not to hold Pedro back in any way. My greatest wish is that he's so pre-occupied by life – and perhaps even new love – that his vital energies continue to flow in that direction. I don't want Pedro's life to be ruined either by me dying or by being with me when I go. I want his new life to already be in full swing.*

*That all sounds really beautiful, Maria says pressing her hand to her heart. But how can I help make it come about?*

Gini says she's going to do her level best to ensure she doesn't get so worked up over the next few days. She'll use the meditation practices to keep her grounded and spacious, as much as possible. The last thing she wants is to stroke and pass away while we are all still around.

Finally Gini drops her bombshell, with all the matter-of-fact-ness that only the elderly, the dying or the plain mad possess:

*So. Maria, Sweetheart... I want YOU to organize the end of this saga so that we all go our separate ways as soon as possible, and in total safety. I want you to promise me, if things are going well for Pedro and his new beau, that he feels compelled by love to go to the ends of the earth with him and let me go back to Madrid to get on with whatever's left of my life...*

*Oh, and one more very important detail, Gini requests... I want you to make sure that Jalu comes to stay with me in Gran Via, and that he's there with me when I die. He's the one I have chosen to accompany me to the departure gates for my final journey. It is Jalu Yogi I want by my side. Him and only him... I am asking for your help to shape my future in this particular way because I KNOW you are a very determined and focused person when you put your mind to something. Just look at the miracles you've performed in your own life! Unfortunately, I don't have that kind of skill anymore. That's why I am reaching out to you like this. Now, do you think you can organize all that for me?*

*Jesus Christ, Gini* – Maria blanches. The logistics alone for carrying out such a mammoth last request – *How am I supposed to do all that?*

*You're a very clever girl... I'm sure you'll find a way.*

*Yes, I know. But it's only a week ago that you and I didn't even like each other that much. And now all THIS?*

*Oh please, Maria.* Gini smiles the helpless grin of a master-manipulator commencing her *swan song. You CAN do it... Anyway, all that animosity between us is in the past. I only live in the Present Moment now... You heard what the consultant said: I must avoid stress at all costs. I really need to rest... I need my beauty sleep now more than ever. If I'm going to meet my maker, I want to look my best. I'm sure you can relate to that, Dear.*

*Oh You... YOU! You're a real piece of work Ms Blake, aren't you?* Maria says, smiling too... *And you want me to arrange all this without compromising the safety of anyone in the group? That alone is something the United Nations couldn't guarantee at this stage. Our situation IS dangerous. We don't know what'll happen next.*

*Just do your best, Maria. I know I can completely rely on you,* Gini says fluffing up her pillows before turning towards the wall to try and sleep.

*And what about Fr Karl? You haven't mentioned how you want his story to end,* Maria adds (a hint of sarcasm mixed with idle curiosity).

*Oh, Karl... He'll be OK, I hope. He just needs to get to Rome without being followed. The rest is up to him. After all, he started all this. We just got roped in. Fr Karl is responsible for himself. Imagine if that bomb at the airport hadn't exploded beside us that day? Imagine if ETA, or whoever, hadn't just happened to plant a bomb the day I went to meet Karl... We'd all be in our own beds tonight. He would be in Rome. And the whole road trip wouldn't be happening at all. He'd probably have already done whatever he is going to Rome for... Ah, Karma is indeed a many-splendoured thing. I just love all this Buddhist stuff. Don't you?*

*Alright Gini,* Maria surrenders wearily. *I'll do my best to make your plans a reality. It'll be far from easy, but I'll try my hardest for you.*

*I was hoping you'd say that, Darling... I really have come to like you very much. Like the daughter I never had... Goodnight, Maria. Sweet dreams,* Gini says with a huge yawn and a stretch.


Pedro is lying on his back with Salvo by his side. He is holding Salvo's beautiful head on his chest. Salvo's arms and legs are wrapped around his entire body. They both feel totally spent, and safer than either of them have ever felt before. Something as natural as the sunset, and as profound as love itself has occurred between them. Somehow, in an ocean of time and space, they have met, connected, and bonded... all in one day.

They're so content. But neither one knows what to say next. It's almost too painful for them to contemplate shattering what's newly come together by uttering a single word.

They doze and cuddle. Turn, and turn again. The way they fit together is so gorgeous, and so perfect after all.

Eventually, Salvo clears his throat and speaks up.

He says he doesn't want Pedro to go with us when we leave tomorrow.

Pedro says he doesn't want to go either. But he feels he has to.

Salvo suggests he convinces the rest of us to stay one more night. That he'll show us around the town. We can revisit the *Banos Thermales* too. He asks Pedro to seriously consider staying, just one more night. He even invites him to come stay at his home. To cancel the hotel room, and stay in his place with him. He says he'll take the night off work and the whole group can join them both for dinner up at his house... He'll cook his signature dishes. He'll make us all really comfortable. Then he'll kick us out by 10 so the lovebirds can have their privacy.

Pedro, almost weeping for joy, says he'll do his best. But he signals the chance it may not be possible. He says there's lots and lots he wants to tell Salvo but cannot, yet. Pedro rules out the possibility of letting the rest of the group move on without him. He says it just isn't on the cards.

Salvo says he's only asking for one more night together ... on this occasion. He encourages Pedro to say whatever is on his mind. Without fear of shocking or disappointing him.

Finally Pedro agrees to tell him some of what is going on.

He says we are a group of his mother's old friends, on a final road trip around Andalucía. He says he used the word 'final' because Gini is dying.

Salvo is shocked and very moved. He sits up in the bed and cradles Pedro into his body, kissing his face and hands. He understands only too well what Pedro is about to go through. He nursed both his parents in their final days, one soon after the other. When he tries to communicate this to Pedro, he says the next weeks and months will be very hard for him. Hard to watch. Hard to let go.

Pedro tells him of the nature of Gini's illness and how death could happen unexpectedly at any time. Salvo's shock deepens. His mind goes into freefall when Pedro says, as a final act of compassion, that Gini has requested he get on and make a new life for himself as soon as possible. That she

doesn't want him to nurse her or even be there when she
dies.

*That's fucking awful, Baby. All of it! I can't believe it,* Salvo
says, like he's just been given a terminal diagnosis himself...
*But, you do realize she doesn't mean that? Maybe she's so ill
she has no idea what she's saying?*

*When you get to know my mother better, you'll understand
that Gini always says what she means, and means what she
says.*

*But still... Even so,* Salvo tries to reassure Pedro from the
heart to the heart: *Your mother sounds like she just has your
personal happiness in mind. But that doesn't mean she actually
wants you to keep away altogether.*

*We'll see,* Pedro says with the wisdom of experience.
*We'll see.*


Karl finds the directness of my approach more than a
little uncomfortable.

He's thinking this isn't how one would normally expect
a Buddhist to behave.

I tell him I am sorry if what I've said, or how I've said it,
is shocking. But sometimes it's better to cut right through
the dense fog to get to the light beyond. Sometimes it is the
only truly compassionate response.

Reading the signs, I decide to go a little further and
inform him that his attackers on the New Bridge were not
*Mossad*, as he suspected, but trained brutes acting on behalf
of the *Vatican*. He's shaken to the core. I remind him, if
Mossad knew his whereabouts and wanted him dead he'd
be dead. I say the heavies were sent by Rome to scare him

to within an inch of his life, to force him to comply with their wishes and remind him who's boss.

Before he has the chance to ask any more awkward questions, I conclude by saying his saviours on that occasion were not the British – that we now know the Brits are mere by-standers in all this – but agents of *Islam*, who will not declare their interest until we get to Granada.

I sit back in my chair and observe Karl's reaction... He is understandably quite stunned.

After some moments, he asks: *But what of this place, then? Are we safe here in Alhama?*

*Apparently so, I say... It seems we are. I'm not quite sure why, though. But I think it's something to do with the Karma of Pedro and Salvo meeting... Love always conquers Evil. Ultimately, Darkness can never win. Light will always triumph in the end. That's why we're all supporting your attempt to get to Rome, after all. We believe in you. We appear to have shaken off those who are pursuing you. Not just the Vatican thugs, but all of them. You have many enemies. Thankfully for now, though, the trail that leads to our door seems to have gone cold.*

*But once we move on?* Karl requests yet more 'advice'.

*When we move on... we move on,* I reply with all the annoying wisdom of a Chinese Fortune Cookie:

*Yesterday has gone. Today is all we really have anyway... Tomorrow is another day.*

43

We are just about finished breakfast when Pedro and Salvo come back from an early morning stroll down the town.

No sooner have they joined us at our table than Maria strikes up a conversation with Salvo (obviously intended to glean whatever she can on behalf of the group about how last night went).

Gini dispenses with the round-the-houses approach. She comes out with it directly and asks Pedro if he'd like to stay another night with Salvo. Under his breath, Pedro tells his mother it's going very well and Yes, if nobody minds, he'd love to stay at Salvo's home tonight before moving on tomorrow.

Realizing the plan has already been set in motion, Maria turns down the intensity of her inquisition a few hundred notches thus allowing Salvo to re-enter the group.

Salvo is chatting to me and Karl about how we must all go with him for a little tour of the old town. But he can't take his eyes off how close Pedro and Gini are. He can't get over the news about Gini's illness, and for one awkward moment his eyes meet hers. In an instant, Gini understands everything: Salvo knows all about her prognosis, he's

302

already head over heels in love with Pedro, and her master plan has well and truly been set in motion.

On the surface we continue to discuss the history of the old town and agree a schedule for the day's activities. Various glances and wordless, subtle eye contact around the table expresses far more:

Maria's expression tells Gini that she imagines the sex was incredible between Salvo and Pedro.

Gini replies they're completely and utterly in love.

Karl tells me, with just one look, he's very grateful after all for my disarming directness with him last night.

I flash back at him there's plenty more where that came from, and he'd better get on with it and give the others a clearer picture of what's going on before he gets us all murdered in our beds.

Salvo and Pedro are over the moon to be spending another twenty-four hours together and how spontaneously the change of plan manifested. In fact, for the rest of the day, every little glance they dart at each other says '*O Dear God. I'm falling so in love with you*'.

Although she's actually done very little yet to set Gini's plan in motion, the look in Maria's eyes as she proudly surveys the assembly announces that she's got everything under control and things might really work out as Gini intended.

My expression catches her on, and warns her not to be so cocky. Not even the Buddha himself could control *everything*.

With one last piercing stare, Gini's pale blue eyes tell me we need to spend some quality time together as soon as possible. I smile, and blink in agreement. She only has to say the word and I'm there for her.

So much cumbersome interaction conveyed subliminally, and with so much ease. The power of the Mind is even greater than this too. We have no idea. We could move mountains if we'd only dare to let go of our egos and dream a little... Sublime indeed!

However, some things cannot be communicated without the help of embarrassing mimes or just plain saying it out straight. Thank Buddha for the direct approach too. At times it's your only man.

Gini reaches over to Maria and asks her to accompany her to the bathroom.

Once they're inside, Gini says:

*Maria, thank you for everything last night. It all seems to be falling into place quite beautifully. Brava! Well done, Girly. I knew I could count on you... But there's one more little thing I have to ask you to do for me. Immediately, in fact. Right now, I'm afraid... I don't quite know how to say it, so I'll just come right out with it if you don't mind...*

Virginia Blake – who had prided herself all her life on being so in control – was about to say one of the most difficult things one human being ever has to admit to another:

*I'm incontinent,* Gini says to Maria (they're standing side by side, looking at each other in the bathroom mirror).

*No problem,* Maria replies, quick as a flash (sensing she's on a roll: trouble-shooter *extraordinaire*).

*Maybe it's not a big problem for YOU, Dear. I'm the one pissing myself. This morning I soaked the bed, and I don't know what to do. I'm so mortified. I normally carry adult incontinence pads with me at all times. I just happened to have a pack in my bag when we went to meet Karl at the airport. But now they're gone and I don't know if they can be got in this small town...*

*OK Gini,* Maria springs into action. *It's like this... When I say 'No problem', I mean, woman-to-woman, heart-to-heart, 'Don't worry about it'... Meditator-to-meditator, I mean 'Don't even think too much about this, Baby Buddha. I've got your back. I've got this. Thank you for offering me the chance to help'.*

Maria's a natural *Bodhisattva.* She is becoming a great saint, disguised as a very ordinary yet extraordinary woman. Literally translated, the term implies that someone is *Awake.* But it also carries all the connotations of someone who is a true *Warrior.* Someone who acts directly for the benefit of others, rather than themselves. Someone who acts from a space that lies way beyond the realm of Fear. In this precious moment, Maria is utterly transformed. She displays the Ultimate Compassion in Action. She is radiant! Maria removes Gini's suffering and takes it onto herself:

*You go back up to our room,* Maria says. *Go to the loo. Have a shower. Whatever you need to do. I'll say you're a bit tired... Then I'll go to every pharmacy and supermarket in the town until I find the right pads you need. I'll tell the housekeeper here at the hotel it was me who wet the bed... Too much drink (It could happen to anyone)... Watch some TV, have a nap, do some meditation. I'll be back before you know it.*

The boys take Karl and I to do a little sight-seeing. We arrange to meet the girls later on in an outdoor tapas place on the upper side of the *Plaza de la Constitution.*

In less than an hour, Maria has sorted everything without the slightest embarrassment or fuss. The pads she found, as it turns out, are even better than the brand Gini usually carries in her bag. They're ultra slim and the whole affair is easily concealed beneath the average-sized knickers. For all intents and purposes, these pads are a very light nappy that's worn in case of sudden leakage from either orifice. Thus giving the wearer a chance to get to the bathroom.

Gini is so grateful. And Maria won't hear another word said about it.

After we meet to sample the tapas, we're led by Salvo on a whistle-stop tour of the town. It is really enchanting in its way. Very old buildings lining narrow streets and alleyways. The old walls are so bright you really do get the impression it must shine to the heavens on all those sunny days they get up here. Many of the streets end suddenly on a precipice, with spectacular views of the gorge below or the great mountains in the distance.

We have a quick look at the original Banos Thermales that the Romans embellished in their own style. They were first built by the Moors in the Arabic style. Nowadays, we see a powerful combination of two great civilizations in one magical space. The cistern is still there filled with water. Above it rise the beautiful Roman horse-shoe arcs that support the earlier Moorish vaulted ceiling. The ceiling itself still has all the original star-shaped, tiny holes. They were cut into it to allow glorious shafts of sunlight to stream in and illuminate the baths below.

We stand motionless in the cool air.

Sensing the wonderful acoustic created by the sacred geometry of the *Banos*, Karl spontaneously and unselfconsciously begins to sing... His tenor voice is a pure revelation of all that is beautiful and true in this moment. The melismatic stream that emanates from his soul sounds ancient. Yet it's an original creation. His plainchant flows unhindered:

*Glória in excélsis Deo*
*et in terra pax homínibus bonae voluntátis.*
*Laudámus te,*
*benedícimus te,*
*adorámus te,*
*glorificámus te,*
*grátias ágimus tibi propter magnam glóriam tuam...*

The divinely inspired chant fills every nook of this exquisite temple, dedicated to purification. We sense ourselves hovering, suspended in space and time. The sonorous energy cascades and tumbles effortlessly. It rises up through every star-shaped portal and out into the vast skies above Alhama.

The birds, like little angels, resonate and sing *Sanctus, Sanctus, Sanctus* in refrain.

Instead of lunch we take another small snack and a cold drink outdoors. We sit in quiet amazement as we scan the wonderful panorama of the rolling landscape and the vast expanse above it all.

Salvo tells us his plan again. He's so happy to be with Pedro one more day that he's taken the day off. We can go back to the hot springs we all enjoyed so much the day before, and then over to his humble abode for dinner. We're all delighted to accept, and make our way back to the hotel for a little *siesta*.

He and Pedro go straight to Salvo's for an hour or two so Pedro can finally see the place, and they can begin the preparations for the evening feast.

Karl has a nap in our room while I accept Gini's invitation to join her and Maria in theirs, for some meditation and a short Dharma Discussion.

As a beginner in the *Dharma* (The *Path* to Awakening) – or even as an intermediate practitioner – there's great power and support when sitting in meditation with others.

When I'm with my students in this context, I always begin by sitting quietly.

I tell them to forget any meditation 'method' or 'technique' they normally use. I always quote the great Tibetan masters of the past: *Meditation is not about 'doing'. It is about 'getting used to' things, as they really are.*

Today is no exception. I begin our short meditation session by inviting Gini and Maria to *Simply Be*.

I try to awaken in them this simple yet profound state of being by reminding them of three of the most beautiful words in any language: *Natural... Open... Awake...*

First I invite them to remain *Natural*.

In meditation, there should be no sense of doing anything 'extra'. Just *being*. And allowing one's *Natural State* to arise from within.

The biggest mistake made by practitioners of The Way is to think that all the busyness and craziness we normally experience *is* our natural state. It is not. That's only the habitual disturbances that persist on the surface of the mind. The waves on the ocean. Underneath all that – and not too far below it, for that matter – is a much calmer simplicity. We must remember at all times that we're already perfect and pure, to the very core of our being. Happiness and Enlightenment are not destinations we try to reach. We do not have to un-do or get rid of anything from the surface of the mind. We simply accept what is on the surface, and rest our attention at a deeper level, where the habitual turbulence no longer exists. We should always remember that we are *already buddhas...* Remember, remember, remember. That is our *Natural State.*

The second word I invoke is *Open.*

We remain in the present moment, with all our senses Open. We do not block anything out, or keep anything in. We just practice accepting everything as it is... All phenomena, the so-called 'good' and the 'bad' and the 'indifferent', are natural in their own way. So we train on letting them be. Whether these phenomena arise from inside or outside us, we allow ourselves to '*get used*' to them. We become like an *Open Gate,* through which anything and everything can flow with ease.

All the senses are left *Open.* Our eyes, for example, are left open with a soft focus that doesn't fixate on anything. Similarly with the ears, nose, tongue, physical body, analyzing mind. We learn not to suppress or indulge anything that flows through those gates: hearing, smell, taste, physical sensation, or assigning judgemental labels. We leave it all, as it is, without watering those seeds. We are Natural and Open. Nothing is held tightly. Even the muscles in the face and mouth are released and relaxed... As if we were about to exhale the primordially pure syllable *Ahhh.*

Thirdly, I offer the word *Awake.*

Even the word itself can be a profound teaching; it contains *Everything.* To hear it, and eventually realize that our natural state is to be *Awake...* I always hear my *inner-buddha* saying: *Rejoice! All beings are naturally open and awake!*

*Remembering* we have within us the spontaneously present jewel of being *Awake* is so profound. It's as though we have within us a light switch that can turn on the *Clear Light* of Mindfulness, Awareness and Spaciousness at any time. Yet we've forgotten it is there at all.

These three key words are the *Heart Essence* of all the Buddha's teachings. We must train ourselves to recover completely from our mysterious amnesia. And remember we are *already* buddhas indeed.

We are *Natural, Open* and *Awake...* All we have to do is *remember.*

During meditation, Gini and Maria are having glimpses of the *Natural State.* One day the light switch will be thrown to the '*on*' position, and remain there for eternity. That is *Enlightenment.*

When we have such glimpses of our *Buddha Nature,* we simply remain in that state, *undistracted* and *unaltered.* And radiate the limitless Loving Compassion that overflows from within us.

After 20/30 minutes, I invite the girls to chat with me about whatever observations or questions they may have today.

Maria starts by saying how grateful she is for having the practice in her life. How optimistic and empowered she is becoming because of it. She vows to bring the qualities of being natural, open and awake into her daily life as situations arise. She makes a promise to herself to 'remember'.

Gini says she is amazed that such a simple practice can be so profound and transformative. That real Compassion would imply the longing for all beings to attain such lasting happiness free from suffering. She says she only wishes she had come to it much earlier in life, instead of reading all those books.

I remind her it's never too late to live in openness and contentment in the present. Even with her illness of the brain, she always has access to her *true nature*. It is never stained or damaged by illness, dementia or anything at all.

Buddha Mind is not produced by the brain.

The brain is a product of Mind. Everything is.

Gini asks about the moment of death itself.

I tell her the important points from what my masters taught me.

She's pleased to hear once more that the Buddha Nature never dies. That dying in the state of *undistracted awareness* is something we can train for and perfect in advance. I tell her that in such a wonderful state there is *NO FEAR*, and we possess a great capacity for letting go. I tell her the physical shutting down process is accompanied simultaneously by a great liberation and opening out of the ground of our consciousness. We experience a physical swoon into darkness, followed by an awakening into light... I quickly remind her that this is not about going to heaven. I tell her that all the cumulative effects of our life's activities – carried out by our body, speech and mind – create what is referred to as a 'Karmic Wind'. And this propels us through the transitional state of dying towards our next incarnation. Becoming expert in the practice, *while we are still alive,* means it stays with us as we make the transition from one life to the next. If we're open and stable enough, we can even experience a profound Awakening as we go.

*I want you to be there with me when I pass through that transition, Gini says... I want you to be at my side guiding me all the way, even after my body has died. Will you do that for me, Rinpoche?*

*I will,* I reply without hesitation.

44

We're sitting in the middle pool in the dappled woodland by the river.

Maria and Gini are becoming extremely close, now that they share not only the practice but some personal confidences too. Karl and I are bonding cautiously; we both know this road trip is about to accelerate towards his ultimate destiny. Pedro and Salvo seem to have always been together. Today Salvo has brought his dog, who also now loves Pedro. He's a wonderful old soul. An adventurous, independent Cairn Terrier named *Tano* (short for *Gitano*, Gypsy).

Alhama has provided us all with a very pleasant interlude in what is otherwise an extremely stressful and potentially hazardous sojourn. We're so grateful for the refuge this place has offered us. But we know we must make a move soon, before trouble comes to *us*.

The transition our little group has made from three to four, to five, has been fairly easy. The main thing has been to stay united and focused on our task. The secret we share has been the one thing that's kept us so close and well motivated. We all feel that we are OK provided nobody we meet on our trip finds out the true nature of our mission.

Yet here we are... Salvo is fast becoming part of Pedro's life. Surely it's only a matter of time before he finds out or is told what's actually going on. Maybe it's inevitable. Perhaps it's even the right thing to do. Either way, there's really no avoiding it. As far as having to accept a new member into our little gang is concerned, Salvo is actually a perfect fit. Anyway, it's only the espionage and the subterfuge stuff he doesn't know about. All the important things, he already understands: Gini's condition, Pedro's heart, various essential points of interest about Maria, Karl and yours truly.

It looks like – without any of us noticing or minding – our 'family' unit has just expanded.

The *Famous Five* have become Six.

Maybe we should rename ourselves 'The Secret Six'? But then again, no. Wasn't that the adjective Enid Blyton reserved for her 'Secret *SEVEN*'? Maybe we should save that one in case we ever get another member.

Then, looking around, I remember *Tano* is also with us. It's perfect! That's that then. *Secret Seven* it is.

How funny, to watch the ebb and flow of the Superficial Mind's  thoughts and emotions. The machinations and whirrings of the chemicals and electrical pulses of the brain.

No sooner have I hit on the ideal name for the group than I observe myself wander down yet another synaptic back street.

Imagine – I think to myself – if there were a certain magic number, as it were, that connects all of the world's *minorities*... For argument's sake, let's say 10%. This statistic could represent so many people who are marginalized, on the fringes, the 'outsiders'. But the crazy thing about the magic number is this: In one way or another, everybody on the planet belongs to a minority when you think about it: Train-spotters, Harry Potter fans, computer nerds, Science geeks, Classical musicians, Buddhists, homosexuals, old people...

Just looking around The Secret Seven, I am struck by the magic number recurring again and again.

How many people manage to maintain life-long relationships? And of those, how many spouses rapidly descend into dementia after their partner dies? (It's far more than we realize; another hidden statistic).

How many people discover their gender and their physical body do not match? And of those people, how many go and have a sex-change?

And what of all the gay people (or straight)? So many are longing for a deep, lasting relationship. But how many are lucky enough to find *one*?

Could it be that 10% is also the magic number for people who realize they were born to fulfill a 'special mission' in life? And 10% who actually go on to carry it out?

As for myself... I am part of the gay subset. So that's one 10% I belong to. But am I also part of another marginalized, counter-cultural group...? Those who are actively following an authentic spiritual path? And, of that group, what percentage persists to the end of their path?

Does 10% of the world's population belong to an ethnic group who are displaced, like Tibetans, wandering in exile?

When you look at any gathering of people in this way, you have to wonder: Isn't everyone part of a minority? Is that why we're so drawn to each other? Is there genuine unity in diversity?

Today at the hot springs is different to the last time. WE are different. On the cusp of moving on, after a long break, there is always an air of *inertia*. A kind of tension that lingers until something lights the spark that sets the wheels in motion. It's like a coiled spring. There is 'potential energy' that's ready to be unleashed once the initial hurdle of actually getting going is overcome. For now, we all continue to feel safe and lazy. But perhaps we'd soon grow tired of these beautiful pools anyway. Perhaps over dinner, something will light a fire under us all. Maybe after the second night in the same hotel, we'll be more than willing to hit the road and face whatever lies ahead.

But, for now, this place remains paradise to us. A safe haven from the pounding waves on the Infinite Ocean of Samsara.

We must be here a lot earlier than yesterday. Some women from the town are doing their laundry. It's fascinating to watch. Even though they're not compelled to by law, or by local custom, the effect their washing has on the environment is kept to a minimum. They briefly dunk each item of clothing into the hot pool nearest the river. Then they apply a drop of liquid detergent directly onto it and grind it between their strong hands to build up a good lather. Taking the individual item over to a large slab of rock by the riverside, they work and knead it like dough. Next, they rinse thoroughly in the cold river, and vigorously twist and mangle all the heavy wetness out. Finally, the garment is hung on a branch in the sun to dry while they repeat the process with the next one. Some women work alone. Others work in small teams, taking one step in the process each, to speed things up.

Meanwhile, we are up to our ears in the hottest water. All our worries are melting away. The Japanese have it right: Ritual daily bathing in a hot tub, whether alone or with family and friends, is an absolute must. Everybody on the planet should have this in their lives. Such carefree dignity and grace.

Even though we're chatting amongst ourselves, all around us there's a profound Peace that comes dropping slow.

Maria is checking that Gini is OK (not just in the *you-know-where* department, but on every level). She's concerned the heat might become too much for her. Tano is content sniffing around the trees. Old soul indeed, he is wise enough to accept that this time around he is just fine being a dog. Salvo and Pedro are trying not to test everyone's gag reflexes too much. Though their love is growing exponentially, they're trying not to let it run away from them or dominate the group dynamic.

I can tell Karl is anxious to begin in earnest the final phase of his 'coming out' process. He whispers to me he intends to break it to them gently after dinner. And that it's too late not to include Salvo at this stage. I whisper back: *You're the boss. It's all up to you now, Father. Maybe not everything in one go, though. But do SOMETHING at least. It's high time you got this ball rolling.*


Salvo's home is indeed as gorgeous as we could've imagined. An old property on the edge of town, which he's renovated into a wonderfully modern, Zen-like open space inside. The outside retains its white painted walls in keeping with tradition. There are many large windows looking out over his quaint terrace, which he has set up for tonight's dinner. The setting draws one's gaze as far as the eye can see, across the valley to the high *Alpujarras* and the *Sierra Nevada.*

The open-plan interior has all the feel of a New York loft apartment. It is L-shaped with a sleeping area and ensuite bathroom in one part, a beautiful sitting-dining room with a well-lit area for painting in the other, and a super-modern corner kitchen joining the two. It's like something out of a magazine: all very chic, very *Feng Shui*, very Now.

The boys have prepared a veritable feast intended to stimulate all the senses. Everything is laid out to share down the centre of the outdoor dining table. There are colourful salads and vegetables in an array of fine bowls, collected with loving attention. There are many tasty tapas to choose from and oodles of fresh, crispy bread torn into man-sized chunks. The centre-piece is the main dish, which is Salvo's mother's recipe for a slow-baked hybrid of *Paella*. He calls it *Mama-ella*. But tonight, Salvo declares he has prepared it with loving care in *Gini's* honour.

The magnificent spread, combined with the floribund setting on the Jasmine and Wisteria-festooned terrace, is an outrageously joyous riot of colour... It takes us two hours, five bottles of wine, seven litres of sparkling water, and one hell of a lot of fun to get through it all.

But consume every last scrap, we do.

As we sit in our rearranged chairs, we marvel at the spectacle the late evening sky is selflessly performing just for us. We're rendered speechless: bloated from our shameless over-indulgence, and aching from all the laughter.

Karl, sensing the arrival of his chance to come clean, begins to speak:

*I haven't been entirely honest with you all, I'm afraid. But I was only saying what I was instructed by British Intelligence to say if I had my back to the wall and needed an elaborate cover story... Salvo, you are now an integral part of our merry band of fugitives. So I cannot avoid saying what I have to say without you hearing it. Pedro will have to bring you up to speed later. But the fact of the matter is this...*

*He's like a spy! We've only just met him, Maria blurts out. And we're all on the run from his enemies until we can get him to Rome to complete his mission!*

# 45

Alright Maria, Gini cuts across her. *Let the man tell us the truth.*

... *Finally,* says Pedro (reaching for Salvo's hand). Karl continues, undistracted:

*Most of what I told you before is an elaborate but convenient lie, the main purpose of which was to explain why I'm in possession of certain, potentially damaging documents. I am bringing them to Rome to offer to the Vatican in exchange for the promise of radical reform in the Catholic Church.*

He pauses to catch his breath.

*... My name is Karl Neumann.*

*All the stuff I told you about being a married priest and living in the Andes is true: The women priests, the socio-political agenda, the Liberation Theology... That's all true.*

*But I am not the Pope's son.*

*However, all the background I told you about how the Vatican really works behind the scenes, how the succession of one Pope led to the other, and how Cardinal Ratzinger and the real powers-that-be have manipulated and controlled events... That, I believe, is all true too.*

*I am named after my Grandfather, the renowned Karl Neumann, who was director of the Nazi Department of Film and Propaganda during the Second World War... Or as his boss, Joseph Goebbels, called it: 'The Ministry of Public Enlightenment'. These films and documentaries were produced in their thousands and screened in every cinema and school across Germany. Hitler himself believed so strongly in the innate power of film rather than literature to convey his message to the ordinary citizens that he personally saw to it that sizeable amounts of the national budget were funneled into this department.*

*The most famous of these films were 'Triumph of the Will' and 'The Eternal Jew'. As you can imagine, the majority of the output of this evil propaganda factory was the vilest, Anti-Semitic, Aryan poison ever created. And the ordinary people came to believe in it, totally. Many of them even grew to love it and looked forward to the next one with great fervour. All the most famous stars of stage and screen in Germany were queuing up to be in them. Archive films of the Fuhrer ranting and raving at the mass Nazi rallies were a particular favourite of the young and old alike. Almost every boy was in the Hitler Youth. And every girl either wished she were a boy or settled for second best and resolved to do whatever she was called upon to do to assist in the war effort.*

*My mother was Karl's daughter, Lotti. She was still very young and naïve at the end of the war. When she was told they were moving to South America she considered it a great adventure, as would any child.*

*So many of the high-ranking Nazis – and a great number of inconsequential ones too – organized themselves to move abroad. This they achieved with a lot of help from foreign governments including, rather startlingly, the Italians, Spanish, British, Americans and the Argentinians.*

*Whether alone, or with the help of such governments and other agencies who must remain nameless a while longer, most Nazis who wanted to escape prosecution after the war simply disappeared to South America by means of these aptly-named 'Rat Lines'. The really useful ones – the scientists and the like – were siphoned off to Russia and the United States where they headed the nuclear programme and other such abominations.*

*Once in situ in countries like Argentina, the former leaders within the Nazi party just carried on as normal. Many of them didn't even change their names. They simply laid low, re-grouped and set up shop all over again.*

Salvo and the others can't believe their ears and dread where all this is going. I tell them to be patient. Not to worry. And to let Karl continue as far as he's prepared to go.

*... Before the war, in the 20s and 30s, the Russians had already developed methods for successfully freezing and later reusing sperm. They had their own sperm bank which contained donations from many of their leaders and prominent figures, and which they used with varying success.*

*They taught this to the Nazis who immediately perfected the techniques and set about putting them to good use. Later, in Argentina especially, there was a specific unit dedicated to the sole purpose of genetically engineering the basic building blocks from which the New Germany would arise like a phoenix.*

*All the most desirable candidates, according to the obvious Aryan parameters, were encouraged to donate. All the misguided clichés, really: Blond, blue-eyed, strong, disease-free, of 'sound mind' and 'good character', etc etc.*

*The sperm bank idea really came into its own in Argentina because so many key players from the Nazi movement were there. Their prime objective was nothing less than to create the Master Race and rule the world.*

*Once my mother Lotti was old enough, she was specially selected to participate in the programme. Can you imagine? She was barely pubescent, yet her own mother was overflowing with pride that her little Lotti had been personally hand-picked to give birth to the future super-race. She was brought by the hand to a clinic, along with hundreds of other suitable girls, where she suffered the indignity of having to undress, get up on that gynecologist's chair and have her legs spread and fixed to those awful, cold metal stirrups. Then she was impregnated with the semen of God only knows who.*

*The process was repeated for decades. Pregnancy after pregnancy, each girl produced a string of babies who were assessed and judged better or worse than the others. The desirable babies were taken away. The undesirable babies were also taken away, but to a different place. Lotti never knew which ones went where. Despite all this, she grew into a beautiful young woman. Eventually she asked to be excused from the programme but was not allowed.*

*A seed was sown in Lotti's mind: She had to get away.*

*By the second half of the 1960s, my mother had produced and handed over so many babies to the Nazis she got a medal for it. Right from the very first one they took away, she mourned and grieved each of them so deeply she vowed 'Never again'. She felt she was being continually raped.*

*My mother was never even allowed kiss a man her whole young life. She had to remain 'a pure vessel'.*

*She slowly became engulfed by her rage and longed for revenge.*

*The time she got pregnant with me was heralded by the party as THE momentous turning point in the struggle for supremacy. They announced to the chosen circle of potential mothers that the Fourth Reich had perfected its methods and, thanks to them, had already produced an entire army of the strongest young men possible. These men, in turn, would be used to produce the next generation of soldiers.*

*But the next glorious step, they said, had been to produce not mere soldiers but the actual men who would lead the new generation to historic victory. For this, they hand-picked the ideal women to carry the children, and they would be conceived using only the best semen... The frozen sperm of those considered the perfect Aryan leaders from the war years.*

*Lotti was chosen once again as the perfect receptacle, along with nine others. Although they daren't speak it aloud, they all must've been wondering whose sperm was being implanted in their wombs. None of the Nazi leaders they could recall seeing in pictures even vaguely resembled the ideal Aryan. So why was it suddenly good practice, after all the so-called 'perfecting' of the process, to produce dark-haired babies, babies who needed glasses, crazy babies with bad joints?*

*No questions were allowed, of course. Only 100% obedience to the cause. The faceless ones who were the real leaders of the Argentinian Reich didn't approve of thinking. Just obedience.*

*Nine months later, I was born.*

*My grandfather had always doubted the level of his importance in the new regime. He never really embraced his guilt either. Ultimately, he considered himself to have been more like a major Hollywood movie producer, with an almost unlimited budget. He imagined himself to have produced the world's largest film festival, nothing more.*

*But Grandfather Karl had hatched a plan from the very beginning in Germany. He secretly worked behind the scenes to gain possession of all the damning evidence he could get his hands on. Tangible proof, if proof were needed, of the Nazis' most horrific activities as the war unfolded. He made it his business to gather film and documented evidence of all the horror and all the hell that they routinely inflicted on the Jews, and others... He came to possess proof of what happened in the camps, who did it and most importantly who knew about it.*

*Whenever possible, he copied or stole whatever documents he could. He didn't do this to bear witness to their suffering or demise, but as an insurance policy just in case one day he himself would be deemed expendable and no longer worthy of the party's protection.*

*In the event, Karl didn't make it to Argentina. But his chest of secret files did, along with his wife and daughter. Grandfather Karl prematurely met his maker by accidentally walking under a bus in Rome, while trying to secure the family's papers for Argentina.*

*The secret treasure chest he indirectly bequeathed to Lotti, and so to me, contains the most horrendously shocking things imaginable. Everything from films demonstrating how to trick people into walking willingly into the gas chambers, to documents about which governments and agencies knew what the Nazis were up to but did nothing about it. There's also very clear proof that the same parties actually assisted the Nazis in using the 'rat lines'. In some cases, the Nazis were even permitted to travel under the guise of good Christian folk fleeing religious persecution in the post-war chaos that befell Germany. Hence, the involvement of Italy, Spain and Argentina. All upstanding Christian nations. Each one offering refuge to like-minded poor souls as they passed from Rome to Madrid to Buenos Aires... and all with legitimate Exit Documents and Entry Visas.*

*The evidence is damning indeed. These files are not with me here but in a secure place in Rome awaiting my safe arrival. Depending on what the documents say about them, major players on the world stage either very much don't want or really do want me to make them public. Some governments want to destroy me and the files. Others want to protect me and get this stuff out there. The Vatican fears the public knowing about their involvement in the Rat Lines. Afterall they were the 'honest brokers' who secured the necessary paperwork. They want me to trade them so they can be archived and forgotten forever.*

*Personally, I always believed my biological father must have been Goebbels or Goering. During my darkest times, I wondered if my father was Dr Mengele, or someone even worse.*

*In time, as a result of my religious faith, I came to the full realization that no man is his father's son. We all must make our own way in the world. And become the person we want to be.*

Addressing himself directly to Pedro, Karl concludes his *Confiteor*:

*That's why I was so keen the other day to make sure you weren't going to embark on the wrong path, believing who or what your father was is who you will become. DNA doesn't*

*count for very much at all, if you don't want it to. Otherwise I
and hundreds of other children who came from just those ten
hand-picked women would be monsters and psychopaths. And
I, for one, am certainly not.*

*But what happens in the end of Lotti's story?* Gini says,
with tears in her eyes. *What became of her, and how did you
turn out so well?*

*Mother,* Karl replies, *had an extremely profound
conversion on her personal road to Damascus. She simply
turned her back on all the insanity of the Nazis in Argentina.
The end of Lotti's story is that she took her baby boy – me –
and the 'insurance policy' chest, and ran for the hills. She wrote
her own mother a very forgiving goodbye note. Lotti literally
just disappeared into the Andes one day and they never could
find us. We never even knew if they tried.*

*When I was old enough, she told me some of her story. As
much as I could take on board anyway. When I asked which
senior Nazi had donated the sperm that made me, she told me
it was Goebbels. I never really believed her somehow. But she
stuck to her story all her life, so I had no choice.*

*Lotti lived and raised me in the same remote village where I
still live. Liberated from her own past, she forgave herself and
everyone else. She was a saint. Such an inspiration to all who
knew her.*

*On her deathbed, Mother pulled me down into the bed close
to her and whispered her last wishes to me. She told me the
name of my real father, where I could find the chest, and what
she wanted me to do with this knowledge.*

*That was two years ago.*

*And now here I am. Trying to get to the Vatican.*

As we lie awake in our beds, each of us has our very own torrent of Truth-overload cascading through our minds. The waves cause small ripples, then great tides. The effects are detected across the universe.

The only thing that truly unites us now is an overwhelming desire to get Karl to Rome, as soon as possible.

Salvo leads Pedro to his bed, holds him in his arms, and tells him to just name it – whatever he wants him to do for Karl – and it's done. Pedro feels so swamped by all this new information, despite having longed for it to finally come out. For some reason, he finds himself fixating on the fact that his own Dad, Benjamin, was Jewish. Salvo is a gypsy. They are both gay... Maria is a transsexual, I am a Buddhist, and Gini has a mental illness... If any of us had encountered Karl's biological father in Germany in the 40s, he would have exterminated us.

Gini is thinking about Benjamin too. His people were Spanish Jews, *Sephardim*. The Léons had lived and prospered in Spain for over a millennium. They had survived, and even thrived, despite centuries of Muslim and Christian rule and all the persecutions they unleashed. But if they'd lived in Germany, they would probably be dead.

Maria is wondering if the very surgery that helped her transform her life had actually been pioneered in Nazi Germany under Dr Mengele. The thought even crosses her mind that crude and barbaric sex-changes could've been performed first in the death camps on homosexual men, maybe even as a kind of degrading humiliation...

Karl himself is so relieved to have at least begun to tell the truth. As he lies in the single bed next to mine, I sense he is seeing his mother Lotti's face nodding her approval. His final act as he falls asleep is to imagine in the sky before him an enormous ball of glowing, multi-coloured light. For him, it represents the embodiment of all that is True and Just. It is the face of God. Karl imagines both he and the light move closer and closer to each other, until they finally merge and become one.

It is the spiritual practice of the 1st Century Church Fathers in the desert. It is the practice of Teresa of Avila, Meister Eckhart, John of the Cross and Francis of Assisi.

Fr Karl's spiritual practice is the same as the Buddha's too.

As I lay in my bed, just about to drop off to sleep, I practice Loving Compassion for all the victims of the Nazis. And for the Nazis themselves, and their followers.

As I let go and rest the mind after my practice, the name 'Karl Neumann' churns round and round in my brain.

What is it about that name which resonates with me so deeply? How do I know this name? I can't sleep till I work it out...

Suddenly, as if by some blessed miracle, I finally make the connection that'll allow me get some sleep tonight.

Another Karl Neumann had been my student in one of my previous lifetimes. It was during the nineteenth century and I was living in the *Dzogchen Valley* in Eastern Tibet, now irretrievably part of *Sechuan Province, China*.

Karl wrote me many times from Vienna, and even visited me twice in Tibet. I taught him everything he asked of me. And he became one of the first Western scholars of

Buddhism. His translations of the Texts into German are still read today: 'The Sayings of the Buddha' (*Dhammapada*), The *Sutras*, the entire *Pali Canon* in fact. Without him, the teachings may never have spread West at all.

So the name 'Karl Neumann' is not forever linked to the Nazis, their Nazi propaganda films, or syringes full of Nazi semen.

Just as we Buddhists must reclaim from the Nazis the beautiful symbol that is the *Swastika*, Fr Karl must purify the name 'Karl Neumann'.

We just have to make sure he gets to Rome.

Our young lovers are spending their second night of passion and tenderness together. They're locked in the strongest embrace on Salvo's huge bed with the windows wide open beside them. Wrestling and rolling, they are smiling deep into each other's eyes, as if to say: '*Now I've got you, I'm never going to let you go*'.

In the morning they'll awaken to a clear view of the high sierra, which can be seen without ever leaving Salvo's bed. Like so many couples before them, Salvo will ask Pedro about his dreams. And lying in the much longed-for, strong embrace of his lover's thick arms, Pedro will simply reply that *this* is what he's always dreamt of.

As for me... lying on my belly, I have one last glance around the room. A final stretch till my toes curl round the bottom edge of the mattress, and I am fast asleep.

46

It's another slow start to a typical day in Alhama. Salvo is keeping himself busy tidying up after the party.

Before leaving Alhama I skype my master. The conversation is scant as ever. But to the point.

He tells me it's time to get moving again. Stay in tourist places. Travel restrictions across Spain will be eased in a couple of days and Karl can make his escape to Rome then.

*The Sun's Rays* (or do we now call him *Lama Sunshine*) also informs me just how invaluable a part of our End Game Salvo will prove to be, and to make good use of all his skills.

Finally, Rinpoche says what I've been dreading for the past couple of days. He tells me once we reach Córdoba the *Secret Seven* must disband and go our separate ways. And that I'll not be there in person to witness how Karl's story ends. I'm told my main responsibility now lies with Gini.

Before hanging up, Nyima Özer reminds me to continue doing practice for all those who lost their lives in the region. Many people suffered and died during the era of the *Spanish Inquisition*, especially the Jews, Muslims and ordinary, liberal-minded Christians. Rinpoche says the word '*Holocaust*' shouldn't only refer to Nazi Germany. One

331

group has been wiping out another for millennia. It continues today. Just look at Tibet.

Soon, we're on the road again.

Another hire car, another sweeping highway that veers this way and that, and which stretches out ahead of us. Then rising up again for *Granada*.

It's been a difficult parting for Pedro.

Salvo tried his hardest to persuade him to stay. He only agreed to the temporary wrench asunder on condition that he could catch up with us in Córdoba a day later, once he has time to arrange holidays from work. Salvo is brave and determined to play his part in getting Karl to Rome.

The news on the car radio reminds us that – without actually calling it a State of Emergency – the Spanish Government has placed most of the country under lock down. The civil unrest has exploded into all-out revolution in the larger suburbs of many cities. Road-blocks and curfews have been in place for days. Some of Spain's major airports and train stations are closed till further notice. And the ones that remain open have extra levels of strict security to detect and control the inward and outward movement of what they've called 'The Undesirables'.

Even travelling by road has been made so much more problematic. The border crossings with Portugal and France – usually a straightforward, drive-through affair with no need for passports – have become nightmarish tedium. The officials can't prevent you from crossing, but they seem to be making a serious point nonetheless by disrupting the process and reducing it to a near standstill. They're showing the slaves who's boss.

My intuition tells me that all the clamp-downs – while directed at the rebel leaders and the key players – might also manage to catch Fr Karl in the net. The Spanish authorities placed his photo on the TV that night in Madrid not so much to entrap him but to flush him out and make sure he was safe and still prepared to make the perilous journey to Rome under his own steam. After all, it is still in the National Interest that Karl arrives unhindered and keeps their small part of this international scandal, this filthy little secret, hidden.

As we head for nearby Granada, I offer to let Pedro drive us in. He needs something to occupy his mind.

Once we're all settled again, I inform the group of how the next few days must play out:

*The situation we face is this: I really need you all to trust me, and follow my instructions to the letter.*

*Apart from the Hindus, I think all the major World Religions are involved in this drama of ours.*

*The three most powerful religious denominations on the planet are attempting to influence our course and dictate the outcome. They are the Christians, the Jews, and the Muslims... I'll explain this more fully later, once we get to our destination. But suffice it to say, all three have a vested interests in getting involved in what Karl's trying to do...*

*Well, obviously...* Maria jumps in: *The Vatican wants to bully Karl and make sure he goes through with handing over the documents without their contents becoming public knowledge. And the Israelis probably suspect who he is and want to assassinate him – No, better still, to KIDNAP Karl so THEY can expose the truth of who knew about the Holocaust and the Rat Lines themselves. Maybe they even want to put him on trial for the sins of his father?*

*Could be,* I say. *That could well be it.*

*But what about the Muslims?* Gini asks. *I don't see why the Muslims would be involved...*

*As I said... All in good time.* I reassure the group and try to allay their fears... *All will become crystal clear in due course.*

*For now,* I say, *I just want to ask for your maximum effort and support in getting through the next two days.*

*We will stay one night in Granada. Visit the Alhambra Palace, of course. Then change cars again and head to Córdoba. Pedro, you will arrange for Salvo to come meet us there. Something tells me he has already hatched a plan to help Karl.*

*Karl, you must not be alone for an instant. Even if you go to the bathroom, one of us must be outside the door, agreed?*

Karl puts himself completely in our care, perhaps for the very first time.

I ask him not to contact or get involved with British Intelligence. They're obviously still shadowing our every move.

We agree Karl should make contact with his people in Rome in preparation for his arrival.

Apart from those in the Vatican he's supposed to be meeting, Karl has friends and allies guarding his files there. They're also primed to make the whole lot go global, via *Wikileaks*, if anything should happen to him. Karl gives us their phone number to call, just in case our plans go terribly wrong, and he is indeed captured or worse. I tell them there's little point in disguising ourselves anymore. All the major players know what we look like now, and wouldn't be fooled by a sudden change in appearance.

All we have to do is be tourists for a while longer and keep our heads down till the travel restrictions are lifted in a few days, and Karl can get away.

Gini checks in with Pedro to see how he's doing. He says he has fallen for Salvo hook, line and sinker.

*I know Darling,* Gini says with all the wisdom of a mother who recalls vividly what it feels like to fall madly in love with 'The One'.

*But don't worry, Sweetheart* (Maria chips in). *Yours and Salvo's is a big old-fashioned love story. A great love like that cannot be denied. Soon, you'll be together and can begin making your new life. Isn't that right, Gini?*

*O Yes,* Gini reaches forward and places a comforting hand on Pedro's shoulder. *It most certainly is... Once we get this tiresome Karl fellow out of our hair, we can all get back to living our lives to the full again!*

This causes a much-needed laugh to ripple through the car. Even Karl sees the funny side and, raising his hand to his brow says: *Yes. Sorry about that. I swear, I'll be gone before you know it.*


In a matter of hours, we're checked in, showered and fed, and we've already walked around some of Granada's most ancient monuments and gardens. We're standing in the exquisite, Moorish courtyard of the *Generalife,* the very heart of the *Alhambra Palace.*

Although we're not very far from the Mediterranean's *Costa Tropical,* the city's elevated position belongs more to the foothills of the Sierra Nevada. All the windows and gardens of the *Alhambra* are oriented perfectly to maximize one's enjoyment of the mountain views. It is a large, yet simple construction dedicated to providing joy, peace of mind, and a pleasing, spacious home for the Sultan and his entourage.

As we stand in the main courtyard garden, so familiar from postcards and travel programmes on television, we silently marvel afresh at the splendour of it all. This gentle, open space was perhaps *the* technological miracle of the age. Without actually experiencing it for yourself, it's almost impossible to appreciate from a mere description of it... The *unadorned* majesty of it all. A rare jewel of the Late Middle Ages in Europe. And Oh! The sound of water flowing!

The impracticality of pumping water to such an elevation beggars belief. To fathom how they did it would take a far cleverer man than me. But they wanted courtyards and gardens with soothing water features, so that's what they did: The cooling energy of the many fountains that rise and cascade melodiously! Whose precious waters' sole purpose is to be gathered into ornamental pools! They flow into a single central channel, which runs across the middle of the huge square towards the seat of the noble ruler! ... It is breath-taking in its arresting simplicity.

Moving into the shade, we sit on some benches. We can chat together while still enjoying the view of the courtyard.

We all agree with Gini who exclaims how heavenly the place is. It's like the designer's intention was to create an earthly representation of what *Paradise* must feel like. So spacious and soothing.

Some nearby tourists move on, to complete the rest of their tour. And the bench they had been sitting on is soon occupied by what appears to be a Muslim family, probably on holidays from some distant Arab land.

Although we do our best not to be engaged in conversation by them, the father is particularly persistent. He has tears in his eyes as he shares with us his joy at being there. He tells us how proud he is of his Muslim brothers for creating such a living monument to Peace and Harmony.

*You see,* he proclaims quietly and with great humility, *We are not all bad...*

The short pronouncement is laden with meaning. In a modern age where Islam is commonly perceived as the 'Enemy of Freedom' – where September 11, *Jihad* and suicide bombers are all that so many of us know of their world – there still remain glimmers of light, for those prepared to open their eyes and look for them.

The man introduces himself as *Ibrahim.*

Like all his ancestors, going back hundreds of years, he is a *Sufi* (a branch of Islam dedicated to peace and enlightenment and which is largely only known in the West for its *Whirling Dervishes* and the sublime writings of the 13th Century mystic poet *Rumi*).

Ibrahim's companions drift away and wander round the square, like they are mindfully walking in the footsteps of the Great and the Good.

He takes the opportunity to move over to where we're sitting. Still speaking words of wisdom and reconciliation, Ibrahim squeezes in between me and Karl. Gini is fascinated by him. She strains to catch his every word. Pedro and Maria remain more distant, resolving to keep an eye on his every move...

*In many ways,* Ibrahim is busy saying, *this wonderful place represents the hay-day of Islam. A time when there was peaceful co-existence between the three 'Religions of The Book'. Muslims, Jews and Christians lived side by side and flourished here, in this Golden Age. Nowadays, we are living in a Dark Age. Nobody seems to be able to get along.*

*It all came to an end here too,* he continues. *The Fall from Grace happened right here in the 16th Century, and we all descended into darkness and misunderstanding.*

*At first, when the Catholic Monarchs took control of that which the Moors had always called 'al-Andalus', there was a treaty put in place: 'The Alhambra Decree'. It allowed Muslims and Jews to continue living and working in the region. It purported to guarantee them freedom of religion. But it didn't last long: Within just a few short decades, they grew intolerant of difference and an ultimatum was presented... Convert to Christianity or leave Spain. Although some did convert, the years that followed brought with them a wave of violence and terror that drove out the then-despised remnant of Muslims and Jews who had remained. They were forced to flee to North Africa and elsewhere in Europe.*

*But NONE of history makes sense, when you really examine it. The three religions behave like they're worlds apart from each other. But they all spring from the same root; Christianity is a reform of Judaism, and Islam is the new chapter. We are all sons and daughters of Abraham, our common ancestor. We all preach Fellowship and Love. So why all the problems? Nothing makes sense.*

Seeing that Gini is nodding her head in agreement, out of politeness Ibrahim enquires who she is.

*Oh me? My name is Virginia Scott-Thomas,* Gini replies in a flash like a pro. I'm a Greek scholar from Oxford.

Pointing to Pedro and Maria on either side of her, she continues in full flight: *And these are my Spanish friends Pablo and Elvira. Pablo is having a torrid love affair with another good friend of ours, a man no less, named Tito. And Elvira is not a real woman at all. She's a... now what-do-you-call-them? ... O Yes, that's it: Elvira is a Jungle Boy, I mean Tom Boy, I mean Lady Boy... My word! But young people make everything so complicated nowadays I find, don't you Ibrahim?*

*Yes. Quite complicated... But, what can I say? Each to their own. Everything is as God has intended, as long as nobody is harmed. That's the first tenet of my faith, anyway. Gay is cool with me... 'Trans-gender' is cool too.*

(Addressing himself directly to Maria) *I presume that's the word she was looking for?*

*Yes, quite the correct word. Thank you so much,* Maria makes a grand play of it... *'Le mot juste', as our dear old neighbours the Frenchies say.*

Ibrahim grins nervously not knowing how to follow that. He turns his gaze back to Karl and me. And pretending to scratch his nose, from behind his raised hand he whispers:

*If I might have a private word with you two, alone?*

I reply: *We have no secrets from each other here. Please speak freely, Brother.*

Ibrahim takes a moment before saying what he's obviously joined us to say. Checking he cannot be overheard by anyone passing nearby, Ibrahim clears his throat and begins to speak again:

Fr Karl of the Andes, Master Jalu of Tibet: I am your humble servant, Ibrahim Muhammad al-Molana, descendant of our esteemed poet Rumi. I am completely at your service...

Oh, for God's sake! Pedro exclaims. How much more of this are we expected to take?!

My sincerest apologies, Mister Pedro, Mrs Blake-Léon, Ms Maria... says Ibrahim, hand on heart.

I and my colleagues have been shadowing you for some time now. We are acting on behalf of M.I.A.T., Moderate Islam Against Terrorism ...

Oh, come ON?! Maria shrieks. Hijo de puta!!

Maria. Please! Gini snaps.

No, Gini. I'm sick of all this 'surprise' bullshit! Then turning back to Ibrahim: And who the hell were those people you first came over with? The woman with the veil, the children? Your bomb-disposal squad?!

Actually Maria, Ibrahim says with a tone of gentle correction, I have no idea who they were. We just made a bee-line for the bench at the same time. I was waiting for them to go before speaking with you... Now. If I may continue... for time is of the essence...

Karl and I guide Ibrahim's attention back to us, and invite him to go on.

We are a new organization on the world stage. I'm sure you've never heard of us. Nobody has, really. But Al Qaeda and the Israelis know very well who we are. We are dedicated to preventing terrorism whenever possible. When we are successful, nothing happens. That's why nobody realizes we're even here. We gather information of impending terrorist attacks about to be carried out by Jihadists and the like, or by the State of Israel. We gather the information and – for all the *good it does – we send it to the United Nations, the Americans, and the British.*

*From time to time, we get more involved in the field, especially when we detect that Israeli agents such as Mossad, and others, are about to inflict another injustice on the world... They have no right. And we won't let them secretly get away with it anymore.*

*That's why we're following you, Fr Karl. Since that ETA explosion in Madrid accidentally threw your mission into jeopardy, you ended up on the run down here. Your intention to get to the Vatican and use those Nazi files as a bargaining chip with the Pope? Well, that is indeed a master stroke. But just let's say this: Your mission has to be the worst-kept secret in the history of espionage.*

*That was us who chased off those Vatican thugs on the bridge the night in Ronda. We couldn't understand why the Brits were watching but did nothing, so we just weighed in.*

*Actually, we thought it was Mossad. They've been stalking you off and on since the airport.*

*The Israelis want to kidnap you. They want to make a very public example of you on account of your father's war crimes and crimes against humanity. Even though you yourself are an exemplary good man, and personally did nothing against the Jews, they want blood. A show trial. Big media circus. 'The whole nine yards', as they say in America. Of course, Israel thinks that by capturing you they'll also get the files. They'd like to study them at length and then drip-feed the goriest bits to the foreign press for years! ... I hope you've set things up to go the Wikileaks route, if this mission of yours ends in tears?*

*Yes I have, as a matter of fact,* Karl says with a suppressed gasp.

*Apart from ourselves and the British, Ibrahim races on, all the others lost track of you when you went up to Alhama. It was quite amusing to watch. At one point in Málaga, the Vatican guys got too close to the Mossad guys. They each thought the other had discovered who they were. That an international incident was about to be caused outside your hotel. So they flashed certain hand gestures at one another, brandished their weapons, and both parties retreated – no, fled – in opposite directions, temporarily losing sight of you as you came out to your car... Hysterical, isn't it?*

*But WE are very serious about our mission. In your case, we are here to protect you from kidnap, attack or assassination, if we can.*

*We don't hate the Jews. Far from it. As I've already told you, we are moderate Muslims. We want a peaceful, harmonious world. But we will not allow the State of Israel to simply do whatever it likes. Not just against Muslims, but against anyone they choose. You have no idea... Umbrellas with razor-sharp tips dipped in lethal, untraceable poison so secret it doesn't even have a name. Gas attacks that are over in an instant, in which only the intended victim is affected. Precision sniper fire from a distant rooftop takes out one person travelling in a fast car, yet the person sitting right beside them has no idea anything's occurred.*

*The cell following you, Fr Karl, is just like all the others Mossad's dispatched in recent times: three or four people, usually men, equipped for every possibility. Often they're what they call 'sleepers', already living in the country for many years. They get the call individually. Meet up. Do the 'job'. Disperse. And just get back to normal life as before. The public never finds out who was responsible for whatever atrocity they've perpetrated. You just discover the result. We thought the Madrid bomb was them, until ETA claimed it.*

*Sometimes, what they've done doesn't even get into the news. Of course, it remains on the radar of the International Intelligence Community, for a while. But then it gets filed away, and is largely forgotten.*

Ibrahim remains with us, chatting  a bit longer. He pledges the allegiance of his group to help Karl avoid capture or death at the hands of Mossad. But he reminds us, that none of us is truly safe as long as we're with Karl.

He says the whole situation is very volatile and unpredictable. And, depending on what's happening elsewhere in the world, the Israelis could either call off their hounds to send them somewhere else or suddenly order them to kill us all.

He tells us not to be unduly scared, however. To remain alert, yet relaxed. His group is heavily armed and more than prepared to stop Mossad in their tracks.

He says, to use violence to prevent an atrocity from occurring is an act of great wisdom and compassion. And that's what they'll try to do.

As we watch Ibrahim, descendant of the poet Rumi, walk past the fountains and out of the Royal courtyard garden, we just sit there with our mouths open.

*At least we have friends,* I say to myself.

None of us ever met anyone like him. We don't know how to react.


Words fail us... So we don't speak a single one.

Part Four

END GAME

47

Despite selecting an extremely comfortable and very expensive suite of inter-connecting rooms in a fine hotel, the night we spend in Granada is very tense and uncomfortable.

Regardless of all the instructions we've been given to continue acting like tourists and gravitate towards large crowds, our hearts are no longer in it. We're worn out by it all. The only thing any of us can think about is the danger we're in. Our bizarre encounter with Ibrahim is foremost on the surface of our minds. However, that primeval part of the human brain, which still belongs to the reptile world is screaming at us to take flight or be prepared to fight.

We're stir-crazy. The suite fast becomes a prison. We pass the long evening watching TV, surfing the net on the computer they've provided in a corner of the biggest room, and ordering food and drinks from downstairs. But Room Service is more trouble than it's worth, our nerves are gone; every knock at the door – even though it's accompanied by a polite young lady's voice saying '*Room Service*' – makes us freeze in sudden terror. The fear drops downwards and makes our stomachs churn with a sickening paralysis. Each time a new order arrives, we have to take turns to steel ourselves and go open the door to her.

The food's not so great either, so we just pick at it. We have no appetite. We're probably just eating out of nervousness and boredom.

The movie version of Umberto Eco's *The Name of the Rose* is on TV. Sean Connery is smouldering. But we can do without the plot: Church Secrets, poisonings, fear, the Inquisition.

Gini feels unwell and rests on a chaise longue close to me while Pedro speaks in hushed tones on the phone with Salvo from the next room. Maria's on the net, researching her future, and Karl is watching the movie with me. We keep all the curtains pulled and the inter-connecting doors between rooms firmly open. All the external doors are locked tight. We resist the temptation to jam heavy furniture against them, like you see in films. We try not to create an air of panic.

I sense Pedro and Salvo have indeed prepared a strategy for helping Karl when they're reunited in Córdoba.

The evening draws glacially towards midnight and into the small hours. You can hear a pin drop in the corridor outside our fortress. Some of us have retired to bed while others shift restlessly from here to there.

Pedro researches *Rumi* online and transcribes one of his most famous love poems into his notebook. He translates it into Spanish and emails it to Salvo:

A moment of happiness,
you and I sitting on the verandah,
apparently two, but one in soul, you and I.

We sense the flowing water of life here,
you and I, with the garden's beauty
and the birds' singing.
The stars will be watching us,
and we will show them
what it is to be a thin crescent moon.
You and I, *un-selfed*, will be together,
indifferent to idle speculation, you and I.
The parrots of heaven will crunch sugar-cane
as we laugh together, you and I.
In one form upon this earth,
yet in another form in a timeless sweet land.


Deep in our hearts, we all know – or at least hope – that Love conquers all. But we also know that Love never stopped a bullet. We're fully cognizant our hotel is surrounded by forces who've all declared and demonstrated dark intent towards us. For all we know, they're inside the hotel too.

I sit in meditation on my bed for a couple of hours, aware of every breath and each turn of the others as they try to sleep. I finally allow myself to lie down and nap at about five o'clock.


The new day brings with it a surprisingly light, airy feeling. We order breakfast in the suite and prepare to go.

When we leave our sanctuary and make for the lift we find ourselves surrounded by Spanish police, and what appear to be private security guards. They are also waiting for the lift to arrive. The lift comes up from the lobby. The polished steel doors open to reveal the Hotel Manager, accompanied by a portly man who looks like the city's Mayor in all his finery, and some visiting foreign dignitaries.

At a glance, Maria instantly recognizes the Asian lady they're escorting to her suite. She's wearing a black trouser-suit by Chanel and has her hair tied back in a black satin bow.

*Ms Shinawatra... Sa-wat-dee Kaaah! Welcome to Spain,* Maria calls to her through the layers of burly guards. It's the most recent Ex-Prime Minister of Thailand, Shinluck Shinawatra, sister of the now-disgraced former Premier, Thaksin.

Shinluck is so amazed to have been addressed in Thai. She's flattered to be so instantly recognized such a long way from home. She says she's on what's supposed to be a very low-key, no media, 'trade visit'. She parts her security wall with a single smile. She and Maria *wai* to one another. The traditional Thai greeting. Feels very nice too, pressing ones palms together near the chin and gracefully bowing the head till the tip of the nose touches the fingertips.

Shinluck steps to one side and introduces Maria to the older man beside her. It's none other than Thaksin himself, the exiled 'despot', or 'hero', depending on which newspapers you read. We are doubly shocked. It's all so unexpected and so incongruous that Maria should be just yapping away with them.

*Maria, this is my brother. He's spending a lot of time in Paris these days and popped down to see me while I'm here. Isn't he sweet?*

*Yes. Very,* replies Maria lost for words. Thaksin has very little to say, but oozes charm and menace all the same. We can just about overhear Shinluck covering an awkward gap saying, *My brother represents the will of 90 percent of the ordinary Thai people. We're all working day and night for his speedy return to power.*

*In reality,* Karl whispers in my ear, *the Thai elites will never allow that. It took one military coup to oust Thaksin. And another to oust Shinluck.*

*Anyway,* I say, *most countries are run by gangsters and business tycoons. Thailand's not unusual. Democracy and human rights are the lie of our age!*

The Shinawatras and Maria behave like old friends. They briefly chat in English about generalities.

To the absolute astonishment of Pedro and Gini, Maria announces her plans to move back to Thailand very soon. Shinluck declares Maria simply *must* contact her office as soon as she settles and is free. She says her people can still arrange a visit to the Parliament Buildings and they can have a private lunch together somewhere nearby, if she's not 'in Paris' with her brother. None of their brief encounter makes sense. They don't know each other. And they'll never meet again. I amuse myself with visions of *Cosmopolitans* and raucous laughter. A veritable girly-fest of make-up tips and plans for a beach holiday together in the Bahamas. Naughty emails from Thaksin inviting Maria to the *Côte d'Azur.*

Maria tells Ms Shinawatra we're just about to leave the hotel but – without going into the finer details, as she's sure the ex-Prime Ministers can appreciate – we're slightly apprehensive and find ourselves in need of some security to see us on our way. If she wouldn't mind lending us a few of her men?

Minutes later, our silver Four Wheel Drive has been brought round to the front by the valet. And, thanks to a generous flank of magnificent Thai muscle, we're safely on our way.

## 48

There are several routes from Granada to Córdoba, all of which involve crossing the mountains and an indirect, three-hour twisting ascent. It's a bright sunny day but we have no more illusions. Darkness is ever-present.

We've discussed at length the merits of opting for a quieter, country route which would entail winding our way up back roads and less-travelled passes. However, all the advice has been to avoid the inherent risks of isolation. So we take the main highway.

This more or less leads us back the way we came a few days before: West towards Málaga and a sharp turn Northwards once we've reached the outskirts of Antequera. We resist the temptation to stop along the way, although we're exhausted and in need of lunch. For a moment, we feel close to Alhama again. Maria, who's driving today, playfully taunts Pedro and says the steering wheel seems to be pulling us in Salvo's direction. Pedro says he wonders what Salvo is doing at this very moment, and what time he'll set out for Córdoba.

Gini is still quite weak and *appears* to drift in and out of clarity, perhaps now more than ever. She insists that Pedro calls Salvo to check.

Ten mushy minutes later, and Pedro is reassured and confident again. All is under control and Salvo will meet us there in the late afternoon.

Although Gini seems, on the surface at least, to be fairly scatty and confused, for the most part she's open and content enough, taking everything in. I can see she has reached a point in her general awareness where she's calm but doesn't miss a trick. A good balance, if you ask me.

It must be all that talk about mindfulness and awareness, which has finally taken root in Gini and is beginning to bear fruit. That kind of quality is infectious. The whole group becomes far more centred and observant. We know this is the final push and, if we play our cards right and stay focused, Fr Karl will soon be on his way.

Maria's tuned the radio to a station that plays the most uplifting Spanish pop and traditional music: *Miguel Poveda, Ginesa Ortega* and, of course, the incomparable *Rosario Flores*... We're even treated to a surprise appearance by *Arianna Savall* whose voice on the classic *L'Amor*, so reminiscent of her mother's, soars and floats above her own accompaniment on the harp...

Black clouds are spotted rolling in. Our worst fears. Suddenly, we're being over-taken by two cars – one black, one silver – speeding past in what appears to be reckless pursuit. Maria can see in the rear-view mirror a third car, a red BMW, is tearing up behind us too. Narrowly avoiding a major pile-up, and serious loss of life, the black car turns in abruptly and skids to a sideways halt in front of us. We're forced off the road. We've stopped partly in a ditch. The red Beamer that appeared out of nowhere has done the very same at the rear of our car. We're trapped.

The silver car's gone from being alongside us to a full stop, a small distance further along on the left-hand side of the busy road. Cars are honking and swerving to avoid collision. But mostly they just don't wish to be delayed. They must think it has something to do with the police or riot suspects on the run.

I'm pretty sure we've been sandwiched in by agents of Mossad. One from each vehicle is out of their cars, moving cautiously towards us and obviously armed. The other two remain behind the steering wheels of their respective vehicles, ready for a hasty getaway. It appears our time is up, and something extremely nasty is about to happen.

Karl says: *It must be Mossad! They're going to take me! Whatever happens, don't lift a finger. I'm certain it's only me they want.*

Gini is amazingly calm. I always worried this kind of sudden drama could kill her outright. But she's OK; the only thing she utters is an exasperated: '*What the fuck is going on NOW?!*'

Maria and Pedro are a revelation! They are fearless and perfectly focused on every angle and nuance of the moment.

Pedro says: *Don't worry, Mother. This is not how it ends.*

*Try to remain calm everyone,* Maria says, as if it's just a threat or a taunt from a school-yard bully we are facing. *Don't move a muscle. It'll all be over in two minutes.*

One of the Mossad guys opens the passenger door of our car, pointing his gun at each of us as he scans from face to face. His buddy is covering his back, his weapon primed and trained on us from a short distance away.

In Spanish, the first man orders Karl to get out of the vehicle and go quietly with them... This is it: Karl is about to be snatched right before our eyes, while we stand by helpless to do a thing. After all our efforts to keep this from happening. Here it is...

Like an earth-shattering thunderbolt from the heavens, an ear-splitting gunshot rings out. Its shock wave parts the air that hovers shimmering between us.

Ibrahim has fired an expertly-placed warning shot at the ground beneath our assailant's feet. It is he and his Moderate comrades who occupy the third car on the opposite side of the road. The two windows with perfect views of the action are open. And Ibrahim and a markswoman have their high-velocity riffles poised to prevent what is already in progress from escalating.

Before a ludicrous situation arises where we become stuck in the middle of total stalemate, and deadly standoff is their only option, without losing another millisecond Karl seizes the miniscule gap created by the volley and high-kicks his would-be kidnapper's gun clear into the air. He leaps back fully into the safety of our chariot and slams the door shouting: *Go!*

Ibrahim and his female colleague-in-arms instantly shoot the two Mossad agents in the leg and hand. Turning their weapons on both cars, they shatter the windscreens and explode the tyres.

Cool as the proverbial cucumber, Maria slams our car into reverse, hits the floor on the accelerator, ramming the vehicle behind us back a full metre, and screeches forward onto the busy road. We're away.

49

As we drive the last thirty minutes into Córdoba, we're still reeling from the ordeal.

Nobody's said very much at all apart from Karl apologizing profusely for all the danger he brought us into, and the rest of us congratulating Karl and Maria for their extreme courage and quick thinking.

The outside temperatures are climbing, something quite unexpected for such an elevation at this time of day.

Before matters took such a dramatic turn, we'd all looked forward to enjoying what's left of Moorish Córdoba. Its unique historical importance cannot be overestimated. Under Moorish rule, generations of Muslims, Jews and Christians lived there peacefully, side by side. Near the original *Mesquita*, there was even a Jewish quarter with a magnificent Temple.

But the jewel in Cordoba's crown was undoubtedly the Ancient Library, referred to locally as *The House of Wisdom*.

As well as a vast collection of works on Islam, the Arts and Sciences, and Philosophy, the Library also contained a greatly-treasured archive of practically *everything* that remained from the ancient world. Whatever texts from Antiquity they could source were gathered and brought together in the shining haven that was Córdoba in the 8th Century; all the accumulated knowledge of humankind including that of the Persians, the Egyptians, the Greeks, and the Romans. Before it was destroyed, the Ancient Library of Córdoba housed a reputed 600,000 books, all of which were available for anyone to consult (And all this at a time during the so-called 'Dark Ages', when an equivalent library elsewhere in Europe could merely boast a few dozen folios). The catalogue alone in Córdoba – which listed the names and authors of all they had collected – stretched to 44 volumes!

In 1013, Moorish rule in *al-Andalus* was brought to an unexpected end by a sudden upheaval that arose amongst the Arab peoples themselves. The new Muslim rulers in the region abhorred any materials relating to the *Infedel* and his misguided *secular* world. So they saw to it that the magnificent collection of books was drastically reduced. The remainder was divided up and either destroyed or dispersed to the four winds. Soon afterwards, all of Spain would fall under Christian rule once more. And so it was that Córdoba's renowned miscellany of wisdom – which had rivaled and probably surpassed that of Alexandria or Baghdad – simply disappeared. Apart from a few priceless volumes, known to have come from the collection at Córdoba, and which are kept today in vaults belonging to private collections, it appears the rest has been lost forever.

Since our roadside trauma, we have understandably become pre-occupied with making haste. But if the others could read my mind they might be aghast to discover that I'm actually contemplating peace, and books, and wisdom. So I say nothing.

All our good intentions and best-laid plans for Córdoba will have to be shelved... Further proof of the cosmic maxim: *Things change. Get used to it.*

While I've had my bookish head stuck in some dusty volume or other at Córdoba's legendary *House of Wisdom*, Karl's contacted his people in Rome about recent events on the highway, and Pedro has fully briefed Salvo.

When he gets off the phone, Pedro informs us Salvo's insisting we cancel our hotel reservation. He'll book us into a much safer, family-run *Hostal*, belonging to a distant relative of his. It's ideally located between Córdoba's main police station and the most famous tourist attraction, the *Mesquita*.

Salvo will phone again shortly with the address, once the reservation has been confirmed. He says we must go directly there and stay in our rooms until he gives us further instructions.

Finally Pedro, with a totally mystified look, imparts Salvo's final instruction regarding very *specific* items of clothing. More drag. Salvo's prepared individual outfits for each of us to be wearing by the time he phones. Then we'll go outside our hostal to meet him. This special request comes not so much as an 'instruction' but as an order, from a military general. Because we now trust Salvo completely and utterly, we comply without question.

Karl is stumped for something to say. The thing about wearing special clothes at this late stage has thrown him. He doesn't want to bring up Mossad or the Nazis, so he asks me a most unexpected and *unrelated* question:

*Jalu, I know you're called Jalu 'Yogi'. But, if you don't mind me asking, what exactly does 'Yogi' mean? I've only ever heard*

*that word in the context of the children's cartoon character
'Yogi Bear'.*

*Oh that,* I respond. *As far as Buddhist masters go, there
are usually two kinds, both with Sanskrit names. The 'Pandita'
is a great scholar, especially learned in matters to do with the
actual texts containing the Buddha's teachings, and many of
the later commentaries on them.*

*The other category is that of the 'Yogi'. He or she is
someone who is dedicated to and expert in all things to do with
Meditation Practice and the Mind. Sometimes yogis are
ascetics and often live solitary, nomadic lives. Sometimes they
simply hide in plain sight living unremarkable, undiscovered,
ordinary lives among the people as shepherds, gardeners,
insane alcoholics and the like.*

Seeing this last remark generates a much-needed giggle, I
shamelessly venture forth:

*Now as far as 'Yogi Bear' is concerned,* I enunciate with
great clarity, and looking particularly to Pedro and Maria,
*Well I think 'Yogi Bear' would be the perfect name for a stocky
gay man who just loves to meditate all day...*

My corny joke doesn't get the huge belly-laugh I was
anticipating, and seems to go completely over Karl's head:

*Ah yes. I see...* he says rather blankly. His
uncharacteristic expression leaves us suspended in mid-
air... *So which kind of Yogi are you, then?*

*My dear Fr Karl, haven't you worked that one out yet?* I
reply with the grin of a master leg-puller... *I am the 'Jalu'
kind of Yogi. Jalu by name, Jalu by nature. I'm a 'Rainbow'.... A
multi-coloured, multi-denominational, multi-faceted Rainbow.*

*When conditions are such that a rainbow's what's required, I appear. When they change, and the moment for a rainbow has passed, I'm gone again.*

Gini's laughing under her breath as if she's the only one to get what I'm really saying. Karl's continued blank stare surprises me, and seems to say it all.

Pedro's phone rings. It's Salvo again, as expected. The reservation at the *Hostal Alonso* has been confirmed and he'll text the street address momentarily. He double-checks Pedro is totally clear who's to wear what exactly, from the shoes right up to the headscarves and caps. Beyond that, Salvo doesn't give us the smallest hint.

Soon, we've arrived at the *Alonso* and are already waiting together in another terrified room, dressed in Salvo's very curious choice of drag. The only thing we can deduce is we're wearing something he must've liked on us when we first met, or something he feels makes us look sufficiently invisible and non-descript.

To fill time, Karl remarks on the woeful state of the rear end of the hire car. He insists I send him the bill. I ignore his kind offer, choosing to pass the time in silence.

When Salvo's phone call comes, it is precisely 4.30. Some of us are so sick from the rising tension we nearly jump out of our skin.

He says we should go downstairs, get ourselves round the corner to the *Mesquita* – Córdoba's ancient Mosque – and go all the way inside to the very centre of it, where he will meet us.

I wonder if Gini is up to the strain. I suggest she and I stay behind. She goes into a wild rant that ends: *'I wouldn't miss this for the world!'*

As we leave our lodgings and go out into the street below, we are immediately struck by how odd everything now appears.

The whole scene looks completely wrong, somehow. Where there'd previously been a quiet side street with precious few people, now there are endless streams of people walking up and down. There are children playing on the road with bicycles and antique spinning tops. Men standing with their friends on every corner, chatting, smoking and spitting on the ground. There's even an old lady selling vegetables from the back of a horse and cart. The whole energy of the situation is so surreal and put on. The only way I have of interpreting what I'm perceiving is that we've stumbled straight into a film set.

The Buddha says: '*With our thoughts, we make the world*'.

No sooner have I formed the thought than we spot the camera crew further along the street, loaded onto the back of a truck that's running and ready to move.

The director shouts '*Action!*' And a group of policemen from next door approach us. One of them says to Maria: '*Thank you so much for your visit, Mrs Picasso. Please allow us to accompany you to the Mesquita, where your husband's waiting for you*'.

Realising that we're indeed at the heart of a movie in the making, we play along for all it's worth and walk to the Mosque with our very own escort from the *Guardia Civil*.

Pedro whispers in my ear: *Salvo is a fucking genius! I just love that man of mine!*

*What sleepy neighbourhood*, I reply, *wouldn't jump at the chance at a moment's notice, for a thousand Euro between them, to be in a motion picture albeit a fake one about the great man himself. And it's being filmed right down your own street!*

*Precisely,* Pedro nods with amateur over-enthusiasm. *Pure genius! I can barely imagine what else he has up his sleeve...*

We walk down the road and pass the camera crew whose truck is now slowly shadowing us. All without looking into the camera, of course, we're not amateurs. We turn the corner into the beautiful square that forms the entrance to the noble *Mesquita*.

The intoxicating scent of the orange trees hangs on the early evening air.

The 'director' – who is really Salvo's film student second cousin from Málaga – shouts *'Cut! That's magnificent! It's a wrap! Thank you everybody...'*

As he continues thanking the good people for all their patience and superb acting ability, we simply keep on walking towards the enormous doors. I thank the police guard for their kindness, and we walk right inside to the reception area where we pay the required entrance fee and pass through the metal turn-style.

50

S alvo's most excellent plot has unfolded at such a pace we're at least twenty feet inside the astonishing *Mesquita* before we even pause for breath. Our heads are reeling.

We are slowly moving deeper and deeper into a vast Muslim prayer hall that appears to be bigger than a soccer pitch. It stretches to infinity in every direction.

Built on the site of a Roman Temple, and an early Christian church, construction on the *Mesquita de Córdoba* began in the 8th Century. The enormous roof that floats far above us is supported by countless ornate double-arches. The lower ones are in the shape of horse-shoes. The upper arches are semi-circular. It's the union of the commonplace with sacred geometry. The whole edifice rests on a forest of what must be  one thousand ancient columns of jasper, onyx, marble and granite – gathered from all over the former empires of the Romans and the Greeks.

The original creators of the *Mesquita* famously declared they'd used "countless pillars like rows of palm trees in the oases of Syria."

To the ordinary people of *al-Andalus*, "the beauty of the mosque was so dazzling that it defied any description."

The mesmeric lure of the spectacle invites us to enter its cool shade further still. We wander as one, in and out, around and beyond, until we approach what feels like it must certainly be near the centre.

Then, still in the distance, through the marble forest appear the first glimpses of the strangest thing you ever saw:

Slap bang in the centre of the Mosque – right in the very heart of it – is a Renaissance Christian Cathedral interior, built in honour of the Spanish King, Charles V... In all honesty, although it's very nice and everything, the alien superimposition is so obviously a deliberate two fingers in the face of Islam, you'd have to call it a misguided abomination... Even when Charles V himself eventually saw it with his own eyes, he is reported to have said: "They have taken something unique in all the world and destroyed it to build something you can find in any city."

*This day just seems to trip from one shock to another,* Gini says.

We simply stand and stare, agog. Aghast.

From stunned silence, Karl's exasperation overflows:

*This illustrates precisely why it's so easy to judge the Vatican. They think they can get away with ANYTHING!*

Then he has nothing more to say.

I hold my tongue till the moment for agreement has passed.

Pedro receives a text. It's Salvo. The message simply reads:

*Look to your right, my Love. Tell the others to stay where they are. Then, just you and Karl walk casually over to me.*

We stay put, as requested, and watch in complete amazement as Salvo's *Piece de Resistance* plays out under the noses of whoever's around to witness it.

Salvo is shrouded in half-light next to a majestic Corinthian column. As they approach him, Karl (who is dressed, as instructed, in jeans, white tee-shirt and black cap) and Pedro (wearing black trousers, pale blue shirt and a red cap) disappear from view, behind the pillar, for an instant.

Then, with seamless continuity of the flow, reappear round the other side and turn to walk back towards the group.

When they get close enough for us to check what their expressions reveal from under the peaks of their caps, we try not to gasp aloud. Maria, Gini and I instantly tumble to the simple perfection of Salvo's master plan.

All five of us leave the magnificent *Mesquita* and move unhindered back across the square, round the corner and through the buoyant street party that is in full swing, thanks to the day's fortuitous earnings.

As dusk creeps into our basic, now happy residence for the night, we sit on Karl's and Pedro's twin beds: Maria, Gini and I ... plus two perfect strangers.

Salvo is indeed a fucking genius!

*'The Old Switch-a-roo'*, Maria says.

*I just can't believe it,* sobs Gini with tears of relief running down her cheeks.

*Ah yes girls,* I intone. *The oldest trick in the book... Classic!*

*Elvis has left the building,* says Stranger Number 1.

*And that's all she wrote,* says Number 2.

51

S alvo has whisked Karl and Pedro away.

We sit in the bedroom that was supposed to be theirs. Three cherished members of *The Secret Seven* are busy vanishing into thin air. Salvo's ingenious end game of cloaks and daggers created the essential smokescreen.

Fr Karl is gone.

Because we don't really know them from Adam, it's suddenly awkward speaking with Salvo's two friends who volunteered to swap places with Karl and Pedro.

We don't even know how much they know about us. I don't suppose it matters a jot at this stage anyway. They'll remain with us for the night and presumably we'll all go on the AVE to Madrid tomorrow after a leisurely breakfast and facing the clerk at Hertz with our damaged bumper.

Slowly, the true nature of the situation we now find ourselves in dawns upon us: Pedro and Salvo are continuing to put their lives at risk for Karl. But he is gone. And we'll probably never see him again. We are suddenly set free.

Nobody can touch us now. Gini, Maria and I have not done anything wrong. We're not in the process of doing anything wrong either. And we certainly have no plans to do wrong in the future. We have broken no laws. The worst thing you can say about us is we have two strange men in our rooms after dark, and we have out-foxed some of the main players on the World Stage at their own game.

We feel liberated, beyond fear, and can once again respond to life with all the carefree dignity of the innocent.

The only information we can get out of Salvo's two friends is this:

Number 1 tells us they both owe their lives to Salvo, from their army days. And he'll be in touch as soon as they're a good distance away, safely along the road North.

Number 2 says the two of them can leave any time we choose. But if they go too soon, their cover will be blown and the others won't get the head start they wanted. The success of their getaway depends greatly on our 'shadowy stalkers' not realizing anything has changed.

At that point, we three look at each other scanning for an opinion as to *when exactly* would be a good time to have these two lovely *looky-likeys* go their own way.

Maria suggests: *How about tomorrow, as we board the train?*

I'm thinking we take them all the way to Madrid with us. It's only two hours by AVE.

Gini's had enough of everything. She is becoming bewildered again and says: *Call Pedro. I want to speak with my son. You can ask Salvo's opinion then too?*

I call Pedro but it goes directly to voicemail. I say nothing and hang up.

Just as we're thinking the worst, my phone rings. It's Pedro.

*We're all safe and sound,* he says. *I'll put Salvo and Karl on in a while. Hand me to Gini, would you?*

I pass the phone to Gini who receives it into her two hands like she's being handed her new-born baby boy for the first time.

*Pedro, Darling. Is it really you, Son?* Gini asks, choking back the tears.

*Hola Mama. It's me, Pedro,* he replies.

*O Sweetheart, I was worried about you. I thought I'd never hear from you again. I can't help thinking of all the things I forgot to tell you...*

*Like what, Mum?*

*Like "I love you." Things like "You're nothing at all like what's-his-name Cavendish." I meant to tell you "You're every inch the fine, upstanding man your father Benjamin was"... I adore you, Pedro. I always have and I always will. Right from the very first time the nurse placed you in my arms and our eyes met. It was love at first sight, Darling...*

*I know, Mama. There was never a moment's doubt about that. I adore you too, Gini. You'll never cease to amaze me. You'll never cease...* (Pedro's voice suddenly falters and cracks. He can't say any more)

*Now the other things I wanted to tell you, Pedro...* Gini races ahead, as if nothing intimate has just been exchanged and Pedro is not weeping on the other end of the line. Gini's eccentricity is quite nuts, and I mean that lovingly. Her Britishness. Not wanting to get bogged down by gushing emotions. Perhaps she's the last Miss-Marplesque figure of our time.

*Yes, Mother. I'm listening. Do go on...*

*Well, Dear. I'm going to let these two nice fellows sleep in your beds tonight. It'd be a shame to waste the money. Anyway, I don't think they've anywhere else to go. They seem to be just hanging around here, making the place look untidy... And another thing. We're going to Rome tomorrow on the AVE.*

*You mean Madrid, Mummy?*

*Yes. That's what I said. Now, when I get into the apartment, I'll leave something nice in the fridge for you and Salvo to eat when you get there. It might be late and I'll be in bed. Jalu's staying too for a while. He's teaching me some Tibetan chants. They really are sublime. You know, after all this disappointing bullshit with 'London Calling', I'm seriously considering changing my nationality on my passport to Tibetan.*

*That's lovely, Mama. You do that... Listen, it's getting late and we still have such a long way to drive tonight. I'll have to go. Tell Jalu here's Karl and Salvo on the line for him. I love you, Mum.*

*OK Dear. I love you too, Son. With all my heart. Talk soon. Ciao Baby.*

Gini hangs up and hands the phone back to me:

*Pedro didn't seem to want to talk to you, Jelly Yoghurt. Sorry about that, Rinpoche.*

*No problem. Don't worry about it,* I say trying to smile beatifically. I call Pedro straight back. Voicemail again. As soon as I hang up, he is calling me.

*Sorry about that, Pedro.*

*Don't worry. She's a dote, isn't she?*

*Yeah. Great gas altogether.*

*Here's Karl for you now,* Pedro says handing over the phone.

Karl is a man transformed by his escape. He's like a caged animal released. Full of energy and heading for the hills as fast as his legs will carry him.

We speak only briefly. The main thing he wants to impress upon me is his deep gratitude for all we've done. He can't face saying goodbye to Gini over the phone, and perhaps forever. Or to me or Maria, for that matter. He's storing all his courage for what lies ahead. He tells me to convey his deepest feelings to the others, and to reassure them that Pedro and Salvo will be back home very soon. There is practically no risk involved now. So, not to worry or think too much.

Next Salvo comes on the line...

*Rinpoche!*

*Please call me Jalu, I insist. Well-well! What can I say, man? You played a blinder today. I take my hat off to you, Salvo. Congratulations, Darling! If I ever get married, I want you to be my wedding planner. I'm thinking Bollywood meets Kung Fu Panda meets The Sound of Music?*

*Hilarious! I'm in! You know you can count on me, right? But you'll have to find a good man of your own first. I'm taken.*

*You're a scream.*

*So I've been told.*

*Oh, You're BOLD! Listen, I just wanted to say Thank...*

*Not another word about it. Let's just get this priest bloke over to Rome and we'll see you all for something nice to eat in Gini's real soon.*

*Perfect, I say. So what's the plan now?*

*You lot go back to Madrid on the train tomorrow whenever suits. Bring the two imposters with you. They haven't been in the capital for years. Just leave them at Atocha station. They can look after themselves from there.*

*I heard on the car radio,* he continues, *travel restrictions are set to ease considerably from today on. I also caught a news flash that two Israeli nationals, with dual Spanish citizenship, were shot and injured. They suspect Al Qaeda sleepers were responsible...*

*You can't be too careful nowadays,* I say.

*I know, right?* Salvo laughs. *So, we're going to drive to Rome in a van I borrowed from friends. We all have I.D. with us, so we should be OK. We're planning on sharing the driving between us. We should cross the border into France sometime during the night. And we'll just keep going till we get Karl to his friends in Rome. Pedro and I intend taking trains back to Madrid in a couple of days, all going well. The van's owners will fly to Italy sometime soon for a holiday anyway. So they can drive it back to Spain themselves.*

*Well, you seem to have thought of everything,* I say... *A real pro.*

*That's the training,* he says. *Mindfulness and awareness is everything.*

*Don't I know it,* I chuckle at the thoughts of the Universe continually mirroring the teachings back to us.

*Say Hi to Maria for us. And please take good care of Gini for Pedro. He's very upset at just leaving her like that.*

*I will. And tell Pedro not to worry about Gini. I've already promised her I'll do my best for her... Thanks for everything, Dear Friend,* I say from the heart. *Good luck to Fr Karl, and all our love to you and Pedro. See you both in a few days. Have a nice Insalata Caprese and a glass of the finest Barolo on us!*

*Thanks, Jalu. See you in a few days. You're a star.*

*... A rainbow, actually.*

I hang up and report everything. Then I go for a wander downstairs to chat with Salvo's relatives at reception and ask for a tray of strong coffee.

## 5 2

My conversation with Salvo's relations yields not only coffee and the promise of a good meal for later on, it fills in some of the blanks about Salvo's past.

But first, there's news about our smashed up rear end; Salvo *has* been a busy boy...

It seems, although nobody in Córdoba really knows him at all, Salvo's reputation alone is capable of unlocking many doors. He is so well respected in the region because over ten years ago he and a couple of friends managed to oust a mafia drug-lord from Madrid who had his sights set on opening up a new operation based in Málaga. Apparently, Salvo – the man we now consider so gentle and cuddly – led a tight, crack team of local thugs and ex-military colleagues who used their Special Ops training and leftover weaponry to maximum effect. Salvo is a dark horse indeed. Like an Andalucían *Zorro*, the people have lionized him and reverently remember him as the masked hero of the working class... Think *Rambo* meets *Francis of Assisi*, and you're half-way there.

The owner of our Hostal is Salvo's second cousin, many times removed. She's only spoken to him a handful of times herself, but she'd do anything for him. This is plainly evident: The film set, the police escort, the street party… It was all organized at a moment's notice stemming from a five-minute phone conversation with Salvo.

The final miracle to emanate from their brief chat concerns our hire car.

The local big boss in Hertz has already agreed to use his friend's panel-beating shop to fix the damage we caused. The bill has already been agreed and paid by Salvo, in cash.

Now I have no doubt whatsoever about his ability to achieve something as ordinary as driving a friend to Italy.

After sharing supper in the largest of our rooms, we play cards till well after midnight. Even then, we continue to sit up talking and watching TV. It's still hard to unwind.

Shortly after 3 am we get the call we've all been so eagerly awaiting. Salvo, Pedro and Karl are just about to cross into France. The border check-point is open, as anticipated, and lies just ahead of them.

Gini's not doing well at all. She is sleeping when the call comes so we don't wake her. Maria and I put Pedro on *speaker-phone* so we can both listen in to what he has to say.

They shared the driving all the way between the three of them, only stopping in *Valencia* for a quick sandwich with old friends of Salvo. Ramon and his husband Marciá know Salvo from a previous life. He calls them *Los Lobos* (The Wolves).

They thought about staying the night further up the coast with other angels, Tony and Jesús in *Sitges,* and make the border crossing the next morning. But there'd be Happy

Hour in *El Horno,* an invitation to Tony's delicious Beef in Guinness stew, a knicker-wetting rummage through Jesús' dressing up box... So, reluctantly, they decide to press on. The prospect of darkness and sleepy check-point guards proved an irresistible draw.

Pedro is making the call from the van, which Karl has parked on an elevated roadside to swap over with Salvo. He will deal with the guards and drive them over. There's a dramatic drop to the right of the road. Pedro says you can clearly see the border crossing for the train far below. It's well lit up and looks for all the world like a scene from an old *James Bond* movie. There's a long, floodlit concrete platform for the train to stop at so passengers' documents can be checked by teams of uniformed guards. The platform was hewn out from a natural gap between two great hills. There's a tunnel at either end; the train comes out of one, stops for passport control on the platform, and disappears into the second tunnel. The setting is so well lit that it can be seen from a great distance by anyone viewing it from a height.

The check-point for those crossing by road is an entirely different affair. Far less complicated.

We wish them the best of luck, and ask them to call again when they're across safely. We hang up leaving them to it.

The road rises to the top of the hill that straddles both countries. At the summit, there are a few small kiosks with barriers stretching between them. Guards do spot-checks on passports and quick searches on 'vehicles of interest'.

As they near the crossing, it's plain to see that only one kiosk is operational tonight. The guard is awake, but the barrier is raised. Salvo slows down as they approach. The official waves them through with a sullen yawn, and they simply drive on.

They're in France.

Nobody is looking for them. Nobody even knows they've left Córdoba.

When Salvo calls to announce the good news, he tells us they'll continue to drive across Southern France and into Italy. They intend to maintain their formidable head-start on any would-be pursuers.

Salvo has checked the distance and time online with his smart phone: If they're lucky with traffic, and don't exceed any speed limits, they could reach Rome in as little as eleven and a half hours.

So that is their intention.

While we sleep, shower, breakfast... and finally board the late-morning AVE with baseball-capped 1 and 2 in tow, Karl is traversing *Provence* and the *Cote d'Azur* with Love's Young Dream in a powder-blue VW Kombi-Van.

As they finally cross the border and head South into Italy, Salvo remarks how relieved he is. He didn't even have to call on his old friend *Tito* for assistance.

Pedro and Karl are so used to imagining by now that Salvo has a million sub-strategies up his sleeve that they almost let the comment slide past them.

Unwilling to allow an opportunity for melodrama pass unnoticed, Salvo reaches under the passenger seat and pulls out his old service revolver...

*Have you met Tito?*

53

All things arise like a rainbow.

It is the nature of everything that manifests. It assembles, comes into being, remains for a while, and then dissolves once more into *Open Space* (Sanskrit: *Shunyata*).

That's just the way of things: You, me... all phenomena.

The trick – if there is one – is to perceive oneself and all manifestations with this extraordinarily liberating view... It is *The View of Spaciousness*.

'The View' provides the key to transcending suffering and fear, for once and for all.

Even though I truly do realize this, from the very core of my being, the rate of Gini's sudden decline takes even me by surprise.

When we get into Gini's apartment on *Gran Via*, things seem to dis-improve at an alarming rate. I'm struck by how beautiful her home is. So many memories of her life there with Benji come flooding back. All the furnishings and every last object they lovingly collected and placed around it.

Though there are still glimmers of lucidity, Gini behaves more and more like a dying patient. Neither Maria nor I want to take full responsibility for how to proceed. So I call Pedro to let him know the situation. Although I try my best not to panic him, he's understandably distressed.

They've just arrived at the outskirts of *Rome*, and were planning on staying with Karl for two days before going by train back to Madrid.

He tells me Karl is so well organized: he has almost everything in place for his big *finale*.

Between Salvo and Karl, Pedro quips, it's like being trapped in a tin can on wheels with two control freaks. Of course Pedro is only joking, but I get the point.

I come right out with it and request Pedro to stay only one day then *fly* back to Madrid rather than take the train. He instantly agrees and, with his consent, I arrange for Gini's doctor to make a house call in the evening. Pedro jumps at the chance of having a real project of his own to occupy his mind. As soon as they check into their hotel, he books flights.

I instruct Maria to go get whatever she deposited in her friend's bar for safe keeping before they left Madrid. Then to go to her own place, and begin putting into motion her exit strategy. I know she wants to start wrapping up her life in Spain and go to Thailand very soon, now that our road trip has finally finished. So I encourage her to keep moving and make her dream come true.

After Maria has left, Gini displays many of the characteristics relatives find so distressing. She's confused and becomes obsessed with finding things in the apartment she hasn't seen for years but now fears have been stolen by intruders while she was out of town. She wants to gather whatever money she can lay her hands on, and keep it on her person at all times. The erratic mis-firings of poor Gini's brain are causing a great storm on the surface of her mind. It has all the appearance of blind panic and madness. But I choose to see it for what it is... surface... appearance. However long she is stuck in this particular groove, Gini's *True Nature* remains untouched and undamaged by it. And, like all things, it too will pass.

When the doctor arrives, he's an old family friend of the Léons. But there's not much he can do. He recommends further tests in hospital as soon as possible. He prescribes more medication, and leaves us with a bottle of medium-strength, anti-anxiety pills. He warns that from now on all medication must be kept well out of Gini's reach. It should only be administered as instructed, or when required. Before he goes, he gives Gini two of the tablets 'to get her started'. They slowly have a calming effect and I suspect she'll soon need to sleep, so I put her to bed.

Just as I've settled Gini in, she surprisingly springs back to life and is more herself again, momentarily. Her clarity is shocking, considering the state she was in only 30 minutes before.

She asks me to tell her again why Buddhists meditate.

I tell her we want to train the mind and open the heart.

We dedicate our time in meditation to going deep into our *Buddha Mind*, beyond all the chaos and upset on the surface. We go *far* beyond all that and see the world from a much broader, purer perspective. When we rest in the *Buddha Nature* like this, we're in the mind's Natural State: open and content, overflowing with loving compassion.

She remarks how lovely it all sounds, and how she wants to live out the rest of her life like that. But she's not convinced she has trained enough, having come to the practice so late in life. She doubts if she has it in her.

I seize the moment and remind her she houses limitless possibilities within her still. She should have no fear of failure on that count.

I tell Gini my master wonders if she realizes she is a direct descendant of the English poet and artist *William Blake.*

Gini replies in a flash she's well aware of that. She wonders if I'm actually trying to say she's mentally ill like him. Or she's experiencing some kind of divinely-inspired madness or spiritual ecstacy, rather than a disease of the brain. I assure her I'm not. She settles down again. Says she rejoices in her connection to Blake.

For a minute or two Gini rambles through her memory banks and dredges up favourite phrases from Blake's mystic poetry...

*Tiger tiger burning bright, in the forest of the night... ... O Rose, thou art sick. The invisible worm that flies in the night, in the howling storm... ... To see a world in a grain of sand and heaven in a wild flower. Hold infinity in the palm of your hand and eternity in an hour... He who binds to himself a joy doth the winged life destroy. But he who kisses the joy as it flies lives in Eternity's Sunrise...*

Allowing some time to pass, for Gini's mind to become more grounded again, I simply sit in silence with her till she settles.

Then I share with her one of my own favourite lines from Blake, telling her this is the answer to her question; *This* is why we meditate:

*If the doors of Perception were cleansed, EVERYTHING would appear as it is... Infinite.*

Gini is centred again, and Blake's words of wisdom are penetrating to her core. The answer was there all along.

In a relatively short time, she's coming out of her temporary spin. And, although she's still very tired, she suggests going down to *Chicote* for cocktails. I laugh out loud and tell her she must rest, 'Doctor's orders'. She doesn't recall the doctor being there so I distract her with an unexpected question:

*If we do go out, tomorrow, for cocktails at Chicote, what would you like to drink?*

*Oh, Alexanders or Cosmos, most probably,* she replies with a cheeky grin.

*Did you know there's actually a cocktail named 'London Calling'?* I enquire, with an equally mischievous smirk.

*Is there really?* Gini asks, pretending to be interested, a dark cloud descending over her face. *What's in it?*

*Oh yes,* I reply. *Maria and I tried them once at the Oriental Hotel in Bangkok. Very posh... It's Bombay Dry Gin, Italian Vermouth (Rosso) and something called Orange Bitters. Mixed by the right hand, it's scrummy!*

*Oh really, Darling? They have hotels in Bangkok now?* Gini keeps up her façade of total disinterest in anything called 'London Calling'... *Sounds to me like it's just a 'Gin and It.' –* the Queen Mother's favourite drink. *It's all the rage in London, you know. She still has outrageous, nightly drinks parties in*

*Clarence House, where she force-feeds the stuff to all her homosexual friends.*

I haven't the heart to tell her the Queen Mother's been dead for years, so I let the matter drop.

Appearing more content to stay home tonight, Gini looks like she's preparing to sleep for a while. Adjusting her pillows, she asks me to sing to her... *One of those gorgeous Tibetan chants. A soothing mantra, perhaps?*

*Perfect choice,* I say, almost with tears in my eyes; Tibetan Buddhists consider mantra to be very powerful indeed. Sacred syllables, uttered in perfect awareness, from the heart to the heart. Mantra is that which protects and awakens the Buddha Mind itself.

I sing a primordial, slow air. A sumptuous melisma I learned from my own mother. It renders the mind Natural, Open and Awake:

*Om... Ah... Hung... ... Ben-za... Gu-ru... Pé-ma... Sid-dhi... ... Hung... ...*

Gini slumbers softly like a baby, her mind finally at peace.

54

Next morning, Gini asks me to take her for a drive and a picnic.

I'm concerned she may not be up to an excursion. So I call Pedro again for advice. He says he'd prefer we didn't, but if she persists – and it's not just a passing whim – to go ahead and take the car from the garage. He and Salvo will be on the late afternoon flight.

By the time Maria calls round, Gini has asked me several times more to take her. She wants to go to *Segóbriga*, an hour outside Madrid.

Maria's opinion is to take the chance and go anyway. It's not so far away from home if Gini feels unwell, and going to another place she and Benjamin adored might actually do her some good.

Gini's excited and enthusiastic, but doesn't want Maria to go with us. She says it's nothing personal, but she wants me all to herself today.

So we gather a few necessary bits and pieces for a small picnic. Before Maria leaves, she checks Gini's incontinence pad is fresh and dry and there are spares in the bag.

Just as Gini and I leave the apartment, the phone rings. She tells me to go on ahead while she goes back inside to answer it.

*London Calling,* the voice on the other end of the phone says.

*Oh FUCK Off!!* Gini replies, and hangs up.

When I ask her who it was, Gini says it was no one of any importance... Nobody at all.

We go down to the Léon family's lock-up garage around the corner. When we get inside and switch on the lights, Gini instructs me to remove the dust cover from the car. A rare beauty is revealed, in all its pristine splendour. I stand in total awe, admiring the Classic silver *Aston Martin DB5.* It crouches before me like a panther clutched from the jaws of extinction.

*Gini,* I exclaim. *That's James Bond's original car! Where on earth did you get it?*

*It's Benjamin's pride and joy,* she replies with a swell of nostalgia. *Pedro's been caring for it all these years, since Benji passed away. He lovingly maintains it. We used to take it for a run together at least once a month.*

I'm flabbergasted. And, if the truth be told, can't wait to get behind the wheel on the open road. In less than twenty minutes, we're out of town and heading for the *Cuenca* region where we will find *Segóbriga.*

Maria's keeping herself busy at home. She's set in motion some wheels of her own. Wheels, which will tidy up and leave behind her life in Spain indefinitely and carry her once more to her beloved Siam.

Karl has meticulously begun to execute his strategy in Rome.

He spent much of his spare time since his mother Lotti died, scanning, copying and cataloguing the contents of the sordid treasure chest. He's sent selected documents to his media connections in Rome to tantalize and prepare them for action, should he need to resort to 'Plan B'. He's also sent some to the *Vatican,* which relate specifically to their shameful role during and after World War II.

As bargaining chips, they've really rattled some cages. Karl was promised a meeting with senior Vatican officials as soon as he arrived in Rome.

But, when Karl makes the call to say he *has* arrived, there's obviously quite a lot going on behind the scenes at the Vatican. The senior Cardinal from the *Curia's* Head Office seems extremely tense and unprepared. Fr Karl smells a rat. He repeats his intention to take the information elsewhere if Rome doesn't show sufficient interest. They need to enter into urgent, detailed dialogue towards Church Reform with him right away. Rightly or wrongly, Karl throws down the gauntlet one last time and insists that the promised meeting go ahead this afternoon, at the latest... And that Ratzinger, *His Holiness Pope Benedict* himself, must be in attendance. Otherwise the deal is off.

Of course this raises a torrent of haughty derision. Barely-suppressed laughter from the Cardinal warns Karl about getting in over his head. He reminds him of his *'place'* in the grand scheme of things. Karl retorts that he knows his place only too well. That he is a *nobody,* with no say at all. But, he insists, his motivation is to give a voice to all the 1.2 Billion *nobodies* in the Roman Church. And the Pope had better sit up and listen to what they've got to say. The Cardinal says an audience with the Pope is out of the question. So Karl hangs up.

He is practically alone in Rome. Vulnerable and apprehensive, with no one he can really trust to talk things over with.

Pedro and Salvo are at the airport waiting in the departure lounge when Karl calls. Pedro's already very anxious to get on board but the flight won't be called for another while yet, which makes him even worse. So, Salvo is charged with taking the call. He wanders away a little bit so he can hear Karl more clearly. They chat for a good few minutes and Salvo seems to have put Karl's mind more at ease. As he walks back over, Pedro catches Salvo's last words to Karl: *Go for it, Father. God bless you.*

I'm parking the *Aston* dream-maker in the parking lot at the Visitor's Centre beside *Segóbriga*. Gini couldn't be in better form. I am amazed. We chatted and sang songs the whole way there. Gini brought the subject round, a few times, to what happens the mind at the moment of death.

We are walking on a path across the fields to what remains of the Roman city of *Segóbriga*. Long before Madrid existed, it was there. The vast citadel, with its gladiatorial Amphi-theatre, ornate Bath Houses, and of course the incredible open-air Theatre we've come to see... it is almost completely intact. Segóbriga was built by the Emperor Augustus Caesar (nephew of Julius) a century before Jesus, the son of a carpenter, walked the shores of Galilee. The atmosphere is scintillating. And the afternoon is the perfect time to get there.

The boys are on board their flight to Madrid and have their phones switched off. Maria's in her apartment enjoying a long soak in her bath, with the telly on in the other room. Karl is walking from the *Green Room* at the BBC World studios in Rome towards the Press Conference, his heart in his mouth. The world's media have gathered at short notice. Karl has given up on the Vatican... Time for 'Plan B'.

As Gini and I get to the Theatre, we are greeted by an almost empty space. We have the whole place practically to ourselves. We climb as high as Gini is able and set out our picnic between us on the granite. The seats, more like giant steps really, can sit in excess of 2000 people. They wrap around the stage, which lies in the middle-distance down below us. The setting is magnificent! Behind the stage platform, there are some classical statues, which gently lead the eye out towards the open countryside beyond, and way off to the far horizon. The sun is slowly approaching dusk. In just an hour or two, another day will come to a close as the fiery orb disappears all crimson and saffron beneath the fields. Gini jokes that the sun is 'a blessing in dis-guise', a blessing in 'the skies'. I hold her hand softly and tell her she's indeed a poet worthy of the *Blake* family name. We sit there watching the changing skies, eating the last of our sandwiches and allowing our consciousness to merge in silence. Eventually, Gini asks me again how to meditate while in the moment of death. I tell her it's like what we're doing now. Release and relax, let go with every outbreath... *Aahhh.* Just as our minds are merging now, in comfort and ease, I tell her to merge her mind with the mind of her master, or the universal Buddha Mind, or with the *Mind of*

*God.* I say she should feel like a child running into her mother's arms, simply allowing her mind to merge effortlessly and completely with the bigger mind, the source of all.

Karl has prefaced his press conference with a concise summary of his background. He's centred mainly on Lotti's story, including all the details of the Nazi sperm banks and the countless children they brought into the world. Now people are really sitting up in anticipation. The world's Press is hanging on every syllable as it is translated to them. Without warning, Karl announces that the entire contents of the chest are gradually being made available, right now, via the *Wikileaks* website. The originals are being sent to *The Hague* where they will be verified and archived, ready for the entire world to freely investigate on demand.

The whole assembly is shocked by Karl's courage, which borders on headstrong naivety. He explains that his original intention was to force the issue of Church Reform on the Vatican. In return, he would have allowed them to bury the damning evidence. But their arrogance has led them to self-sabotage. They denied Karl the appropriate forum to discuss with the Pope and his advisers the importance of *Liberation Theology* in the lives of ordinary people – all the 'nobodies' who constitute the main body of the Roman Catholic Church. He says Rome left him with no other option.

Karl opens up the floor for questions. He insists he will not be dragged into an undignified session of mud-slinging about the Pope. He has no interest in addressing any of the rumours about the Pope's past or present: his membership of *Hitler Youth* as a boy in Germany, or the like. Again Karl stresses that rumours about Cardinal Ratzinger's sexuality or his alleged personal involvement in covering up child sex abuse by clerics remain in the realm of idle speculation. They should be a matter for the courts. Such rumours and allegations don't even *begin* to compare with the darkness of his Truth Archive.

Pedro and Salvo are holding hands on their anxious journey home, unaware of what is about to unfold. Maria is watching Karl's drama escalate on the TV news as she sits on the sofa in her wet towel, gob-smacked.

Gini and I are just about to leave the Theatre at Segóbriga. We descend the steps cautiously, hand in hand. But she stumbles on the second last step, her hand slips out of mine, and poor Gini falls to the ground flat on her back. I drop the picnic basket and rush to her side.

She's a bit stunned but says she is OK. She wants help to get up. She is standing almost upright now, in my arms, and bang – like a flash of lightening across the twilight – she has a massive stroke and collapses like a ton of bricks, back down onto the ground clutching her chest. Karl is elucidating the evidence for the *Rat Lines* and how the Vatican actually helped Nazi leaders and officials posing as oppressed German Catholics to get the necessary papers for safe passage via Rome, through Spain, to South America. He speaks of files which clearly show that the Vatican during the 1940s – and even Pope Pius XII himself – knew of the Nazi death camps, but didn't dare speak out. The British, the Americans, the Russians – so many governments – they all had intelligence reports that pointed to the extermination of Jews and others, and failed to act or even raise the alarm. Gini is in a very bad state. I'm sitting behind her craddling her body, which I've propped up against mine. She is rigid and her breathing is very distressed. Maria continues to watch the TV, her mouth open. Pedro senses something may be happening at home and needs reassurance from Salvo. I do all I can to help Gini let go. Little by little, with every outbreath. Together we do it, calmly and quietly: *Aah... Aaahh... ... Aaaahhh... ...* Karl is finally asked the question on everybody's mind: *Which Nazi leader was your biological father? Whose son ARE you?* ... Karl announces that his father was thought to have died in Germany but escaped to Argentina and lived there undercover until his death, aged seventy-eight. Shortly afterwards, in 1967 – to ensure the revered donor's immortality – Karl and almost a hundred other children were born by means of artificial insemination using the last of the same sample.

As Karl enunciates the true name of his famous Nazi father, Maria's wine glass drops to the floor and drains into the white rug like a vast bloodstain that threatens to engulf the world...

Karl's biological father is Adolf Hitler...

# 55

Pedro's chest is tight with stress. He can't stop massaging it... Gini is less contorted now. She is slowly going limp in my arms. I prop her against the upright of the bottom step and sit before her inviting her to open her eyes and allow her gaze to unite with mine. The lids of her baby-blue eyes slowly open and meet mine, in profound recognition *the moment* has indeed come. Our minds merge, we are one with God and Nature. The all-pervasive Buddha Mind is awakened and everything glows with rainbow-light, perfect in being just as it is. Three last, long outbreaths and Gini's wide eyes gaze lovingly with deep compassion right through me and out into the vast infinity of the sun's rays as it sets. She has passed on...

A middle-aged man, with all the appearance of someone on the edge of sanity rushes to the podium where Karl is still speaking. Taking out an aerosol, he sprays some of its contents right into Karl's face. He is blinded and gasping for air. Nobody else around him is affected. The nerve gas has an immediate effect on Karl. He loses consciousness. Enormous blisters rise on the backs of his hands where he's raised them to protect himself... Amid panicked screams and all the chaos, the BBC switches back live to the main news studio: *The following report is just coming in ... Citing poor-health, and advanced age, Pope Benedict XVI has just issued a statement to tender his resignation. The statement was given in Latin to a private gathering of select reporters and Vatican hierarchy. The statement reads as follows...*

Gini's brain has ceased to live. Her consciousness transcends it. It always has. She completely lets the body drop away like a garment no longer needed, a dressing robe which falls from the shoulders to the bathroom floor just as you walk into the soothing waters of the shower... Tears flow inexplicably down Pedro's face. He is so frustrated with the seemingly endless flight that separates him from Gini... Maria is beside herself about the attack on Karl. The 'rolling news' runs across the bottom of the TV screen. It says he's been rushed to hospital, where his condition is extremely critical... Gini's essential energies are in the process of gathering into the central channel of her 'subtle body'. It's so important not to disturb or distress her mind as it begins to exit. I remain open and calm in her presence. She is fast-becoming so liberated from all the confines and restrictions of the body that she has a heightened sense of everything within and around her. She's quite raw at the same time, from the newness of the experience. She has awakened a high degree of clairvoyance, which is capable of picking up on everything in the vicinity. She could so easily become distracted and hindered by whatever thoughts of intense loss or suffering her passing is causing to others. Luckily I am the only one around and can manage to remain calm and spacious. I use my presence as a support for Gini's transition... Maria tries to call me to say what's happened to

Karl. But I've switched off my phone... Pedro's flight is far from landing, and Salvo is doing his best to comfort and calm him ... Gini's essence gathers at her heart centre. Suddenly, it moves swiftly upwards through the central channel to make its exit at the crown of her head. I am doing the practice for the actual moment of death, known as *Pho'wa*, which I learned from my first master, *Dzogpa Chenpo Rinpoche*. With that, Gini's consciousness shoots right out through the *fontanelle* – the small aperture at the top of the skull – and is liberated into the open spacious luminosity that awaits it. Gini is resting in natural great peace, and is already well en route to her next incarnation.

She is free.

## 5 6

Gini's cremation service is extremely beautiful. A very simple affair. There are poems and prayers from all religious traditions, uplifting music, tributes and eulogies from old friends and new. Pedro can't bring himself to speak at it. His only words are whispered to Maria: *At least she's with Benjamin now.*

The weeks that follow are a different matter, however. Pedro becomes inconsolable with grief and needs to talk more and more about Gini. He says he'll never forgive himself for not being with her when she needed him most. His only comfort is Salvo, who holds his wounded heart in the palm of his hand. His love and kindness is ever-present, and he always seems to know just what to say.

Whatever they say about it, Time may not be the greatest healer but it passes anyway whether you want it to or not.

Over a month and a half pass after Gini's sudden death. Forty-nine days, to be exact. But it has not been easy.

Each one of us misses her terribly in our own way. Some days time appears to slow down and come to a complete stop. But we're determined not to fall into a rut. I do my best to keep things moving forward for each of them. However, I'm mindful not to move on too fast, or appear to have all the answers. The best I can offer Pedro, in particular, is another shoulder to lean on and some fresh ears to listen to his deep loss as it comes over him in waves. It'll take a lot of love and patience to carry him forward into his new life with Salvo.

Fr Karl has been transferred by private plane to the hospital nearest his beloved village in the Andes. However, it is still a huge journey from there to his parish. He can't wait to improve just enough to get back to his family and flock. The skin on Karl's face and hands has been burnt beyond recognition. Even his beautiful, kind eyes are so damaged they have to remain covered by dark, protective goggles for the time being. His assailant was identified immediately but still cannot be linked to any particular agency. He claims he was overwhelmed by Fr Karl being Hitler's son. He just happened to have the toxic aerosol with him and can't remember how he got it. The gas will probably never be identified. They say it's completely unknown to those you'd imagine should know all about such things. The world of international affairs, of course, would never admit it anyway. When analysed, it bears no relation to any known nerve gas. The long-term effects on Karl's health are devastating. He will never breathe or see properly again. And the damage to his brain has yet to be fully assessed. It'll take years to even begin to understand it. For now, his lungs and vocal cords are shot. His powers of communication are so greatly reduced, he appears for all the world like someone who's suffered a massive stroke.

But Karl feels at peace with himself. He has fulfilled his mission. And he is alive.

Pope Benedict has now resigned and is once again referred to in some quarters as Cardinal Ratzinger. Nobody quite knows how to address a *Former Pope.* It hasn't happened since 1415.

The man selected to succeed Benedict is as far from a *Vatican Insider* as you can get, or so it appears. Of course he'll probably be ultra-conservative. That's his job after all. And he's unashamedly evangelical with it. But he hails from none other than *Buenos Aires, Argentina!*

Pope Francis, as he's named himself, is the son of a migrant railway worker. His upbringing was that of any ordinary working-class boy. He's always worked tirelessly on behalf of the poor and disenfranchised. Once he was made Cardinal, he refused to move into the lavish Palace that went with the job, preferring instead to live frugally in the small rented flat in which he lived before. He continued to cook for himself, ride the buses like everyone else, and even walk to work every day... A Vatican P.R. spin-doctor's dream come true. But, behind all the freshness, and the spin, this new pope is anything but liberal. In time he'll refuse to meet the Dalai Lama, deny the equality of gay people, and oppose all manner of other human rights initiatives.

Beneath his bandages, behind his black goggles, Fr Karl giggles uncontrollably at the very thought of an Argentinian pope. He laughs till his tears sting his eyes.

In another few weeks, the rest of us meet over Brandy Alexanders and Cosmos in *Chicote.* It's the last occasion we all see each other together.

Soon, Pedro will be living the life he always dreamt of with Salvo and his faithful terrier Tano, in Alhama de Granada. He'll wake up every morning in his lover's strong arms and look out the window at the view of the valley and the high mountains beyond. He will write. Salvo will paint. And together they'll own and run the bar that already bears Pedro's name.

Before long, Maria will fly to Bangkok. But she won't stay there for long. She'll go island-hopping in search of a nice beach bar café. Something in her price range with a sweet room above it to call home.


Everything that manifests eventually disperses. This is true of matter, energy, memories, and rainbows.

In the fullness of time I too will be gone, on a flight to Dublin.

The next *Dharma Noir* novel in The Jalu Series will be


MONSTER MONSTER

Jalu Wakes A Tiger